THE CHRONICLES OF
ARTHUR

SWORD OF
FIRE AND ICE

BY JOHN MATTHEWS
ILLUSTRATED BY MIKE COLLINS

ALA

NEW YORK   LONDON   TORONTO   SYDNEY

To Mark Ryan, Mike Grell, and Rachel Pollack, who first showed me the power of graphic fiction—J. M.

To my wife, Karen, and our daughters, Bethan, Becky, and Rhainnon. Arthur had his not-of-this-world Nine, but I'm content with my fabulous four.—M. C.

ALADDIN
An imprint of Simon & Schuster Children's Publishing Division
1230 Avenue of the Americas, New York, NY 10020
First Aladdin paperback edition September 2009
Text copyright © 2009 by John Matthews
Illustrations copyright © 2009 by Mike Collins
All rights reserved, including the right of reproduction in whole or in part in any form.
ALADDIN is a trademark of Simon & Schuster, Inc., and related logo is a registered trademark of Simon & Schuster, Inc.
Also available in an Aladdin hardcover edition.
For information about special discounts for bulk purchases, please contact Simon & Schuster Special Sales at 1-866-506-1949 or business@simonandschuster.com.
The Simon & Schuster Speakers Bureau can bring authors to your live event. For more information or to book an event contact the Simon & Schuster Speakers Bureau at 1-866-248-3049 or visit our website at www.simonspeakers.com.
Designed by Lisa Vega
The text of this book was set in WildAndCrazy.
The illustrations for this book were digitally rendered.
Manufactured in the United States of America
10 9 8 7 6 5 4 3 2 1
Library of Congress Control Number 2009926149
ISBN 978-1-4169-5908-3
ISBN 978-1-4169-8683-6 (hc)

This story is about King Arthur. It's not about the mythical King Arthur most people know; the one who lived in the Middle Ages, rescued beautiful ladies, fought the occasional giant, searched for the Holy Grail, and sat at a great round table with a hundred and fifty of his bravest knights before setting out on adventures.

The Arthur of our story is different. This Arthur lived nearly seven hundred years before the medieval king. In fact, he wasn't called a king at all. . . .

So who was he?

Our Arthur may not have been a king, but he *was* a hero—a warrior who led a ragtag army against a cruel invader.

The time: 537 AD.

The enemy: the Saxons—wild fighters from the Northlands who had set out to conquer the land of Britain.

You might be surprised to hear that this Arthur *really existed*! And although we don't know much about him, we do know that he was alive sometime at the beginning of the sixth century and that he was known as the most powerful leader of his time. Thanks to a few scraps of information written down by poets and monks who still remembered Arthur, we can say that he was a real person—one who's still written about to this day . . . more than fifteen hundred years after he lived!

To understand how all these events came about, we have to go back even farther in time, to when the Romans invaded Britain in the first century AD. At that time, the Romans established the farthest outpost of their empire in the cold lands of Britain. They stayed there for four hundred years, but in the end, when barbarians from the east threatened them, the Eternal City itself, the Romans left, leaving Britain unprotected and without a true leader.

After the Romans withdrew at around 410 AD, the tribes who had been their enemies turned on one another. Arthur was one of several native British leaders who emerged at this time. He was a mystery from the start. No one knows for certain where he came from. We do know, however, that Arthur managed to organize the feuding Celtic tribes into an army that was able to defend the land against a new threat: Saxons from Germany, Fresia, and Jutland.

With Arthur's command and leadership, the British forces drove the Saxons back to the coastline of the country and pinned them there for nearly forty years. During that time, the invaders became settlers, farming the land around the shoreline and marrying into British families. Eventually they founded a new race of people: the Anglo-Saxons, from whom most of the population of England is descended.

Although we know a bit about who Arthur was, we still don't know how or when he died. Stories suggest that he may have fought a final war against some of his own people. Arthur vanished from history around 545 AD, leaving a tale so powerful that it has gone on being told right up to the present time.

At first, the stories told about Arthur were simple accounts of his battles against the Saxons. But they gradually began to change. Elements of magic and fantastical new characters were added to the stories, and the myths and legends of Arthur were born.

Instead of a simple soldier's blade, Arthur now wielded Excalibur, a magical weapon linked with his destiny—the Sword of Fire and Ice in our story. When at one time he would have lived in a simple wooden building, Arthur now had the great castle of Camelot, where he and his knights met at a mighty round table large enough to seat a hundred and fifty.

Old tales of battle and bravery turned into powerful retellings, filled with strange and wonderful creatures and otherworldly characters, like the Lady of the Lake and Merlin, the wise and powerful magician who was often in the background helping Arthur obtain his wondrous sword and protecting him from the evil plots of his bitterest foe—his own half sister, Morgana le Fay.

The truth is there is not just one Arthur; there are several. There's the Arthur of medieval romance and legend; the noble leader of a band of knights who came together at the great round table in Camelot. There are earlier Arthurs: a second-century Roman cavalry officer named Lucius Artorius Castus, and the Arthur of the sixth century, who bore the Roman title "Dux" (Duke) rather than "king" but who led a company of warriors into battle against overwhelming odds.

Arthur has remained a timeless and fascinating hero. As many as two hundred new books, movies, plays, and poems about him are published every year! There have been operas, musicals, TV series, radio adaptations, plays, and video games that draw inspiration from the Arthurian tales.

Despite all the wonderful and magical stories of the medieval Arthur, the older tales have always fascinated us. What was that earlier Arthur like? What adventures did he have? And, especially, what happened to him before he became king, when he was just a boy growing up in a dangerous time?

When we were asked to tell the story of a young Arthur, we decided to go back to these first tales, some of which have survived in odd, out-of-the-way corners, and to see if we could fill in some of the gaps in the later tales.

So began *The Chronicles of Arthur*.

Merlin had to be there, of course, and if, as all the stories later told, he was Arthur's teacher, what kind of things might he have taught? What mysteries would he share with his pupil? We also wanted to show how the old magic (the kind that another writer, C. S. Lewis, called "the deep magic from before the dawn of time") was still around in Arthur's day.

The setting is the land of Albion, one of the ancient names for Great Britain, as seen from the heart of the mysterious Golden Wood, and from the otherworldly island of Avalon, ruled over by a group of otherworldly women known as the Nine. As well as these mysterious, dreamlike places, many other real ones may still be visited today.

In our story there is no specified time period, although you may hear echoes of the sixth and thirteenth centuries as we follow the young Arthur and his companions through the wild and tangled woods of the Arthurian world.

So, here is a first adventure for the boy who would, one day, be king. We hope you enjoy reading it as much as we enjoyed telling it.

Join us now at the beginning of Arthur's adventures. Turn the pages and prepare to be lost, for a time, in a magical world where all things are possible and only the unexpected is sure to be encountered!

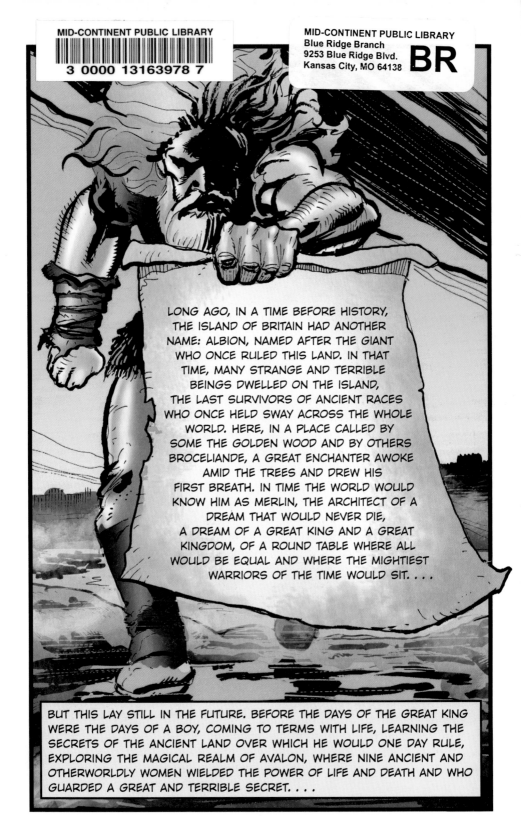

LONG AGO, IN A TIME BEFORE HISTORY, THE ISLAND OF BRITAIN HAD ANOTHER NAME: ALBION, NAMED AFTER THE GIANT WHO ONCE RULED THIS LAND. IN THAT TIME, MANY STRANGE AND TERRIBLE BEINGS DWELLED ON THE ISLAND, THE LAST SURVIVORS OF ANCIENT RACES WHO ONCE HELD SWAY ACROSS THE WHOLE WORLD. HERE, IN A PLACE CALLED BY SOME THE GOLDEN WOOD AND BY OTHERS BROCELIANDE, A GREAT ENCHANTER AWOKE AMID THE TREES AND DREW HIS FIRST BREATH. IN TIME THE WORLD WOULD KNOW HIM AS MERLIN, THE ARCHITECT OF A DREAM THAT WOULD NEVER DIE, A DREAM OF A GREAT KING AND A GREAT KINGDOM, OF A ROUND TABLE WHERE ALL WOULD BE EQUAL AND WHERE THE MIGHTIEST WARRIORS OF THE TIME WOULD SIT. . . .

BUT THIS LAY STILL IN THE FUTURE. BEFORE THE DAYS OF THE GREAT KING WERE THE DAYS OF A BOY, COMING TO TERMS WITH LIFE, LEARNING THE SECRETS OF THE ANCIENT LAND OVER WHICH HE WOULD ONE DAY RULE, EXPLORING THE MAGICAL REALM OF AVALON, WHERE NINE ANCIENT AND OTHERWORLDLY WOMEN WIELDED THE POWER OF LIFE AND DEATH AND WHO GUARDED A GREAT AND TERRIBLE SECRET. . . .

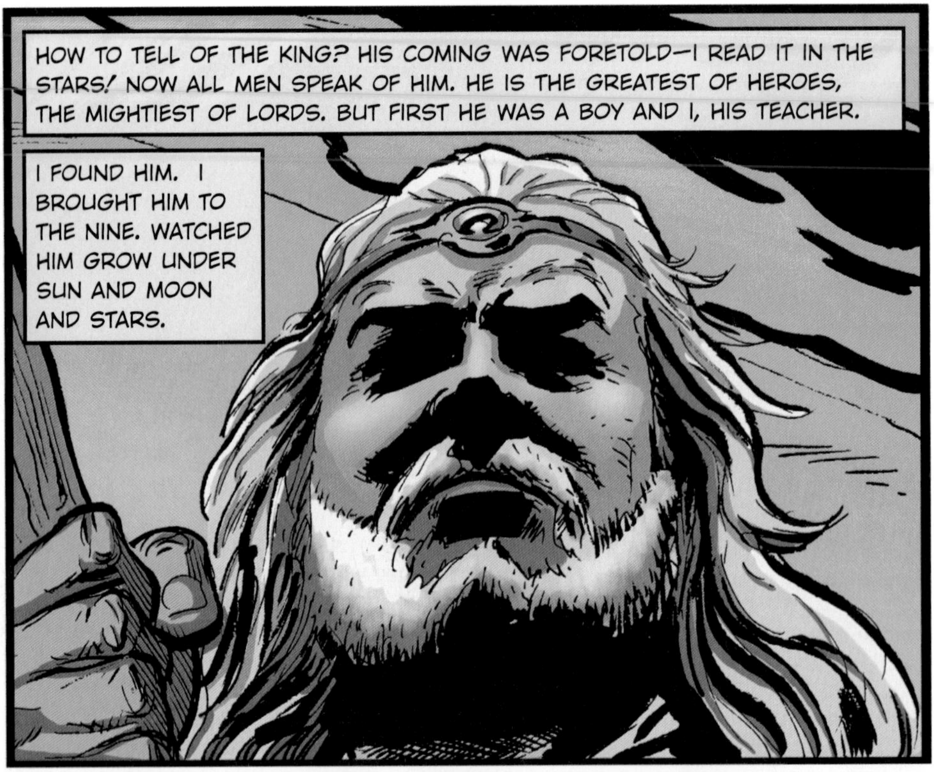
HOW TO TELL OF THE KING? HIS COMING WAS FORETOLD—I READ IT IN THE STARS! NOW ALL MEN SPEAK OF HIM. HE IS THE GREATEST OF HEROES, THE MIGHTIEST OF LORDS. BUT FIRST HE WAS A BOY AND I, HIS TEACHER.
I FOUND HIM. I BROUGHT HIM TO THE NINE. WATCHED HIM GROW UNDER SUN AND MOON AND STARS.

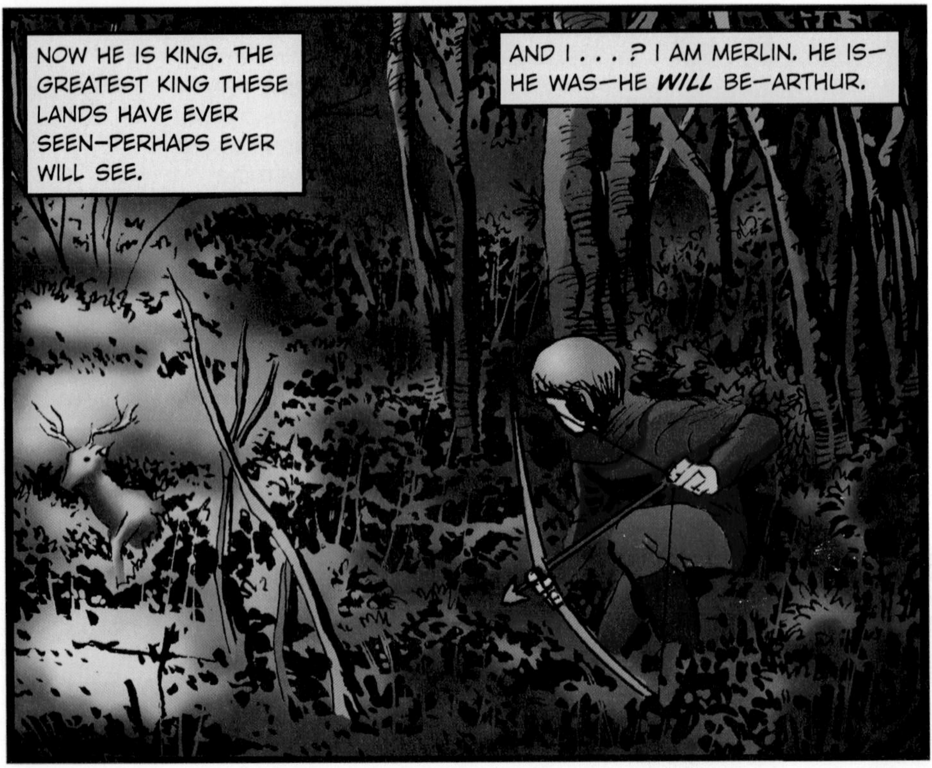
NOW HE IS KING. THE GREATEST KING THESE LANDS HAVE EVER SEEN—PERHAPS EVER WILL SEE.
AND I . . . ? I AM MERLIN. HE IS—HE WAS—HE ***WILL*** BE—ARTHUR.

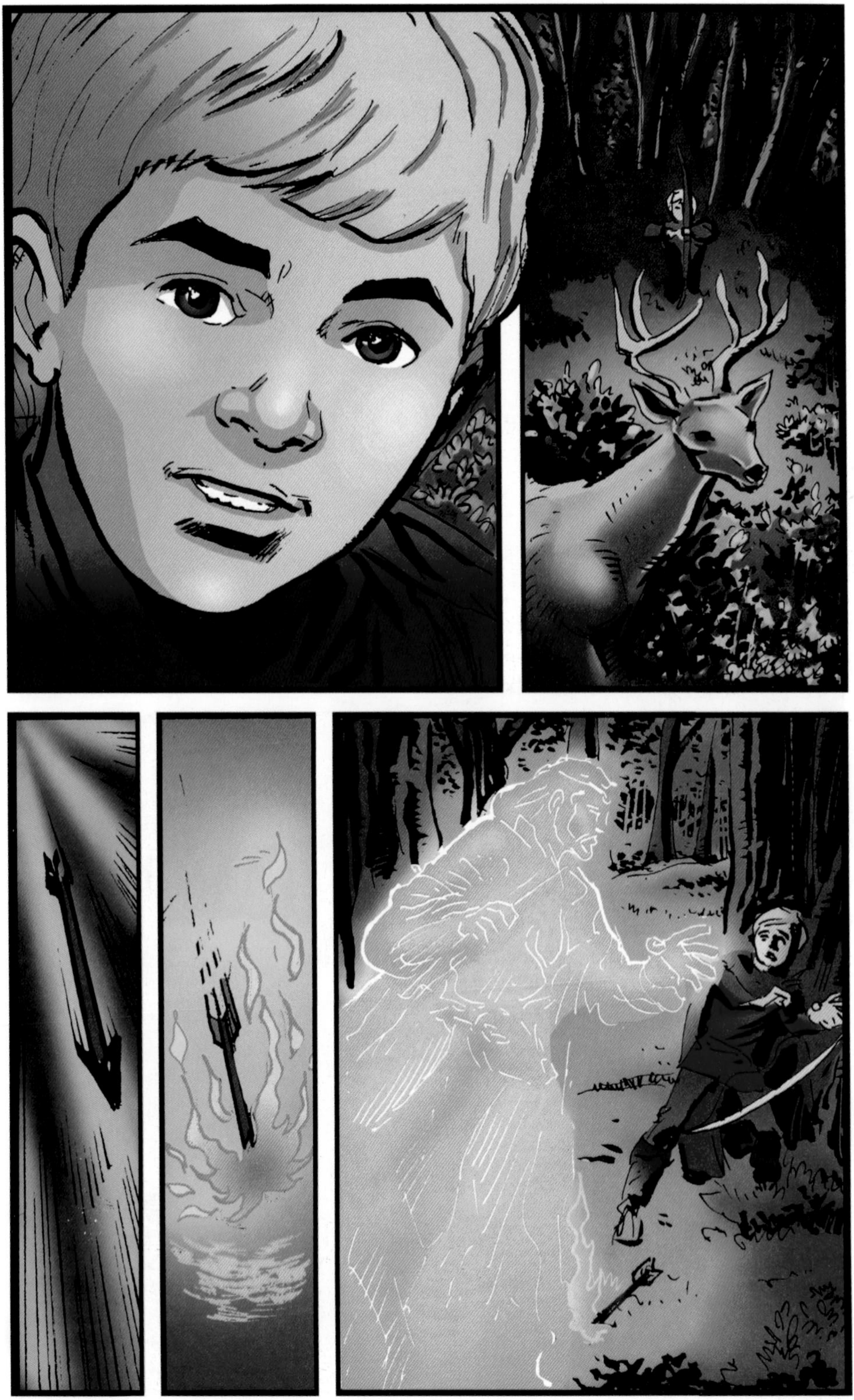

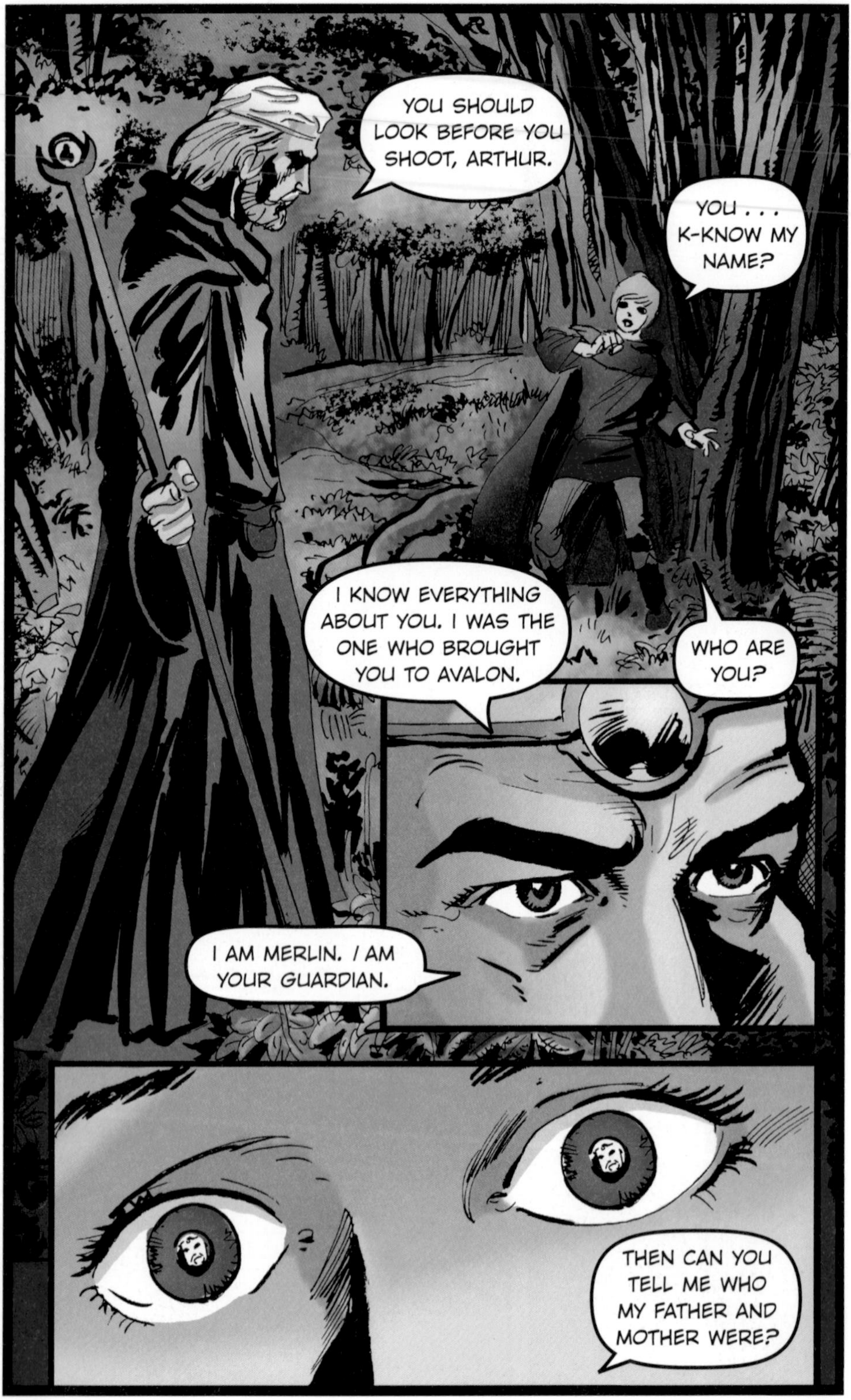
YOU SHOULD LOOK BEFORE YOU SHOOT, ARTHUR.
YOU . . . K-KNOW MY NAME?
I KNOW EVERYTHING ABOUT YOU. I WAS THE ONE WHO BROUGHT YOU TO AVALON.
WHO ARE YOU?
I AM MERLIN. I AM YOUR GUARDIAN.
THEN CAN YOU TELL ME WHO MY FATHER AND MOTHER WERE?

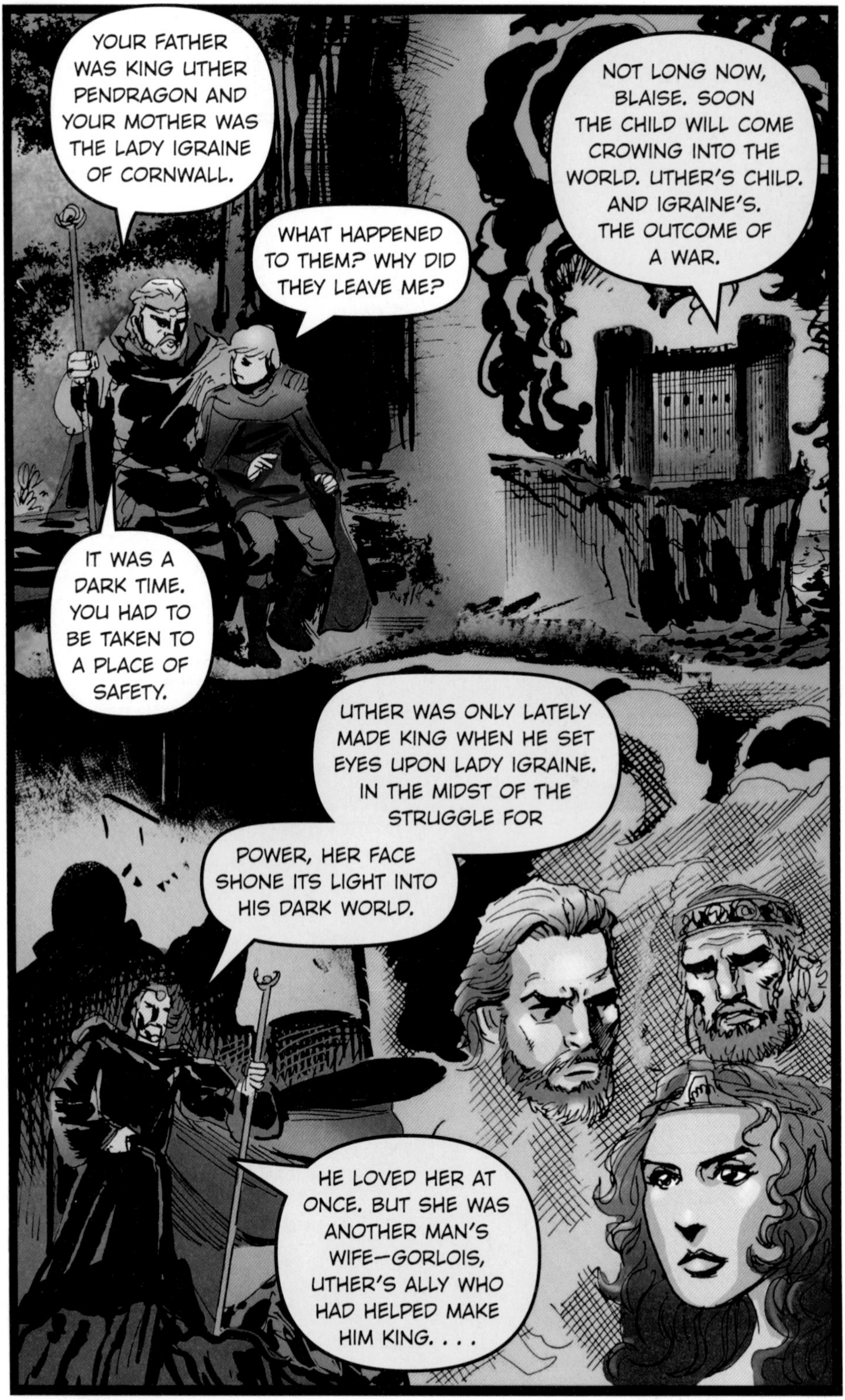
YOUR FATHER WAS KING UTHER PENDRAGON AND YOUR MOTHER WAS THE LADY IGRAINE OF CORNWALL.
WHAT HAPPENED TO THEM? WHY DID THEY LEAVE ME?
IT WAS A DARK TIME. YOU HAD TO BE TAKEN TO A PLACE OF SAFETY.
NOT LONG NOW, BLAISE. SOON THE CHILD WILL COME CROWING INTO THE WORLD. UTHER'S CHILD. AND IGRAINE'S. THE OUTCOME OF A WAR.
UTHER WAS ONLY LATELY MADE KING WHEN HE SET EYES UPON LADY IGRAINE. IN THE MIDST OF THE STRUGGLE FOR
POWER, HER FACE SHONE ITS LIGHT INTO HIS DARK WORLD.
HE LOVED HER AT ONCE. BUT SHE WAS ANOTHER MAN'S WIFE—GORLOIS, UTHER'S ALLY WHO HAD HELPED MAKE HIM KING. . . .

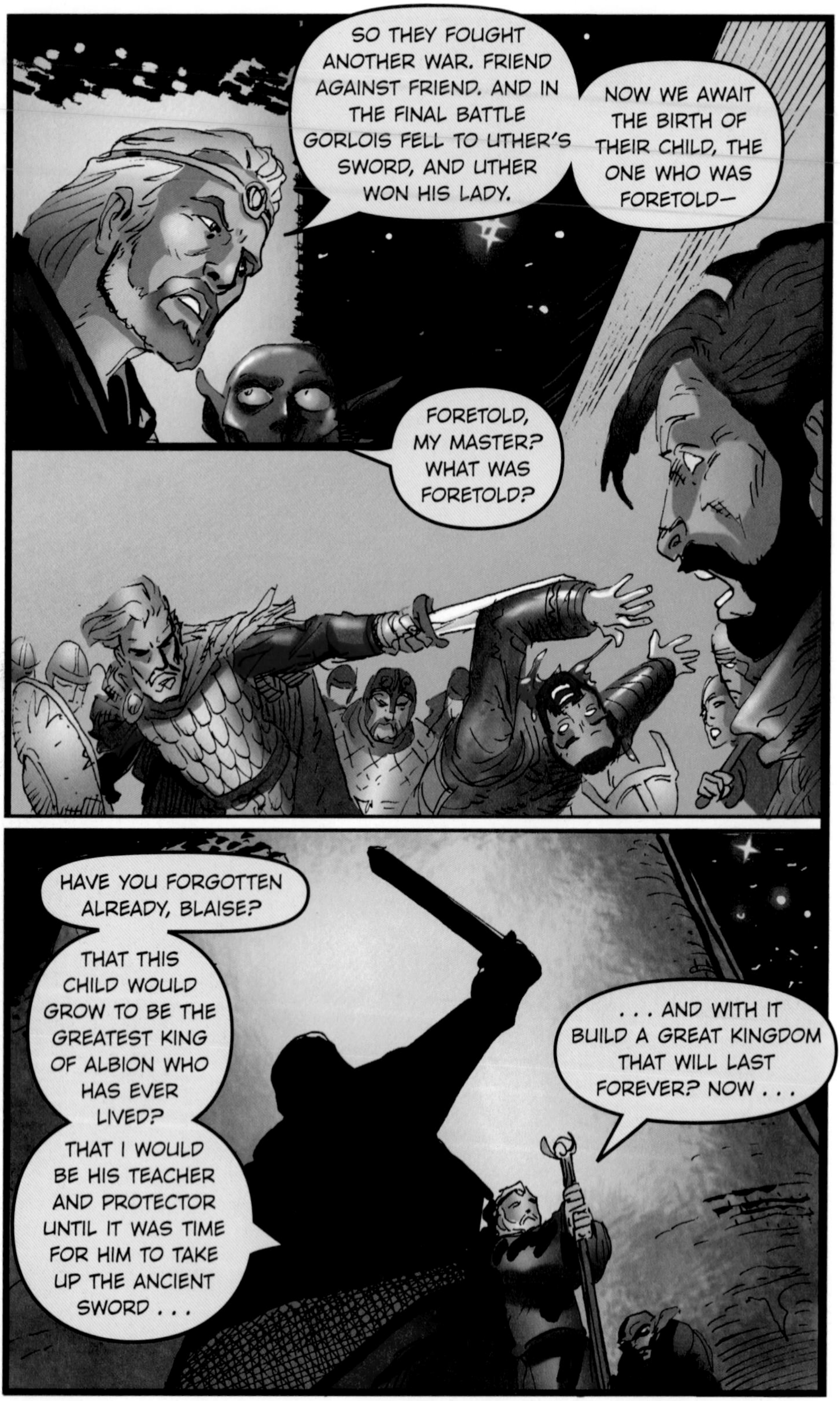
SO THEY FOUGHT ANOTHER WAR. FRIEND AGAINST FRIEND. AND IN THE FINAL BATTLE GORLOIS FELL TO UTHER'S SWORD, AND UTHER WON HIS LADY.
NOW WE AWAIT THE BIRTH OF THEIR CHILD, THE ONE WHO WAS FORETOLD—
FORETOLD, MY MASTER? WHAT WAS FORETOLD?
HAVE YOU FORGOTTEN ALREADY, BLAISE?
THAT THIS CHILD WOULD GROW TO BE THE GREATEST KING OF ALBION WHO HAS EVER LIVED?
THAT I WOULD BE HIS TEACHER AND PROTECTOR UNTIL IT WAS TIME FOR HIM TO TAKE UP THE ANCIENT SWORD . . .
. . . AND WITH IT BUILD A GREAT KINGDOM THAT WILL LAST FOREVER? NOW . . .

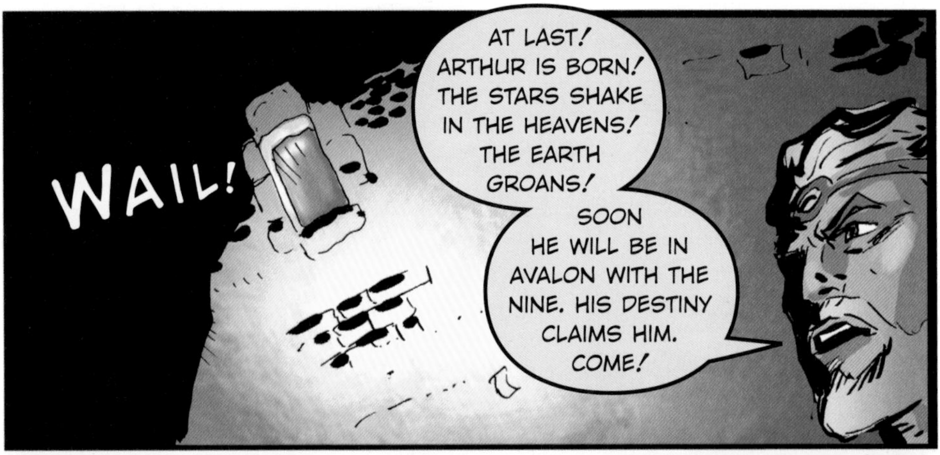
WAIL!
AT LAST! ARTHUR IS BORN! THE STARS SHAKE IN THE HEAVENS! THE EARTH GROANS!
SOON HE WILL BE IN AVALON WITH THE NINE. HIS DESTINY CLAIMS HIM. COME!

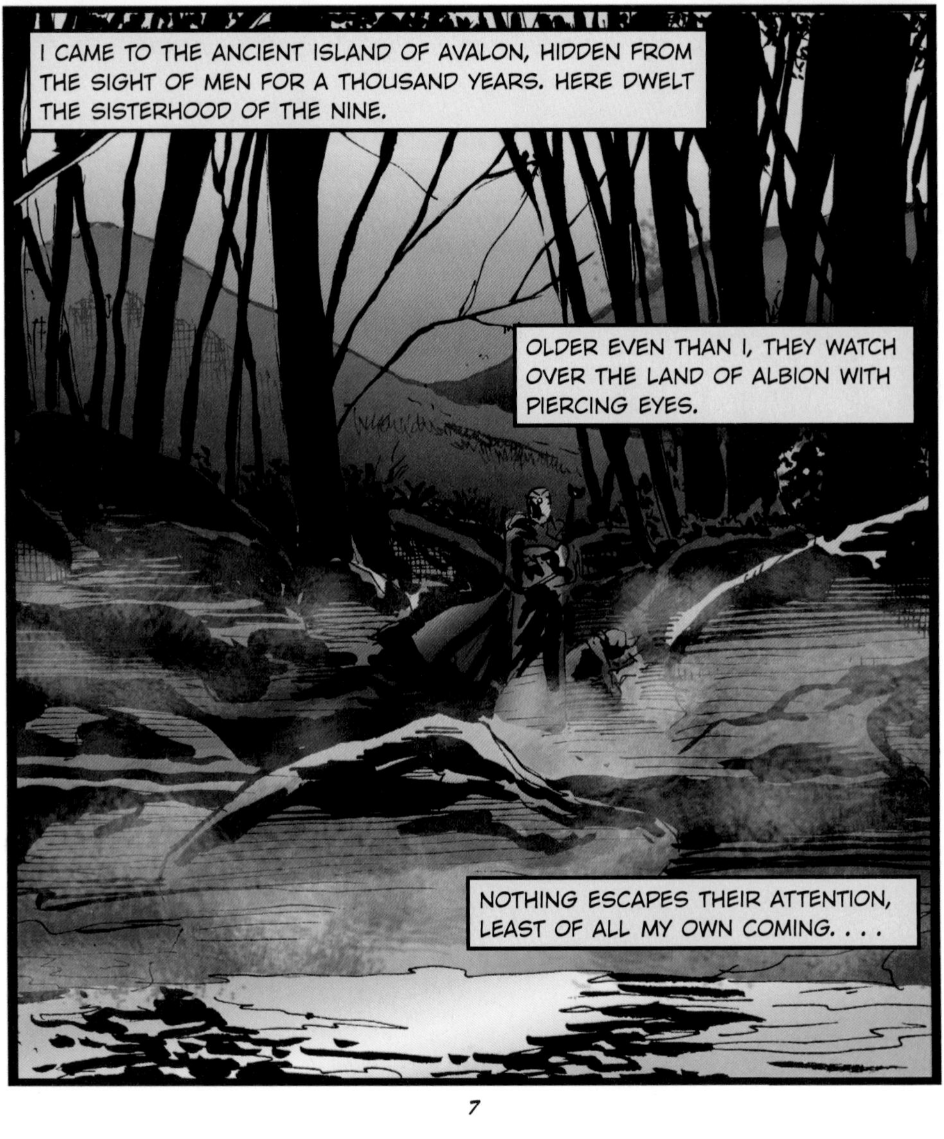
I CAME TO THE ANCIENT ISLAND OF AVALON, HIDDEN FROM THE SIGHT OF MEN FOR A THOUSAND YEARS. HERE DWELT THE SISTERHOOD OF THE NINE.
OLDER EVEN THAN I, THEY WATCH OVER THE LAND OF ALBION WITH PIERCING EYES.
NOTHING ESCAPES THEIR ATTENTION, LEAST OF ALL MY OWN COMING. . . .

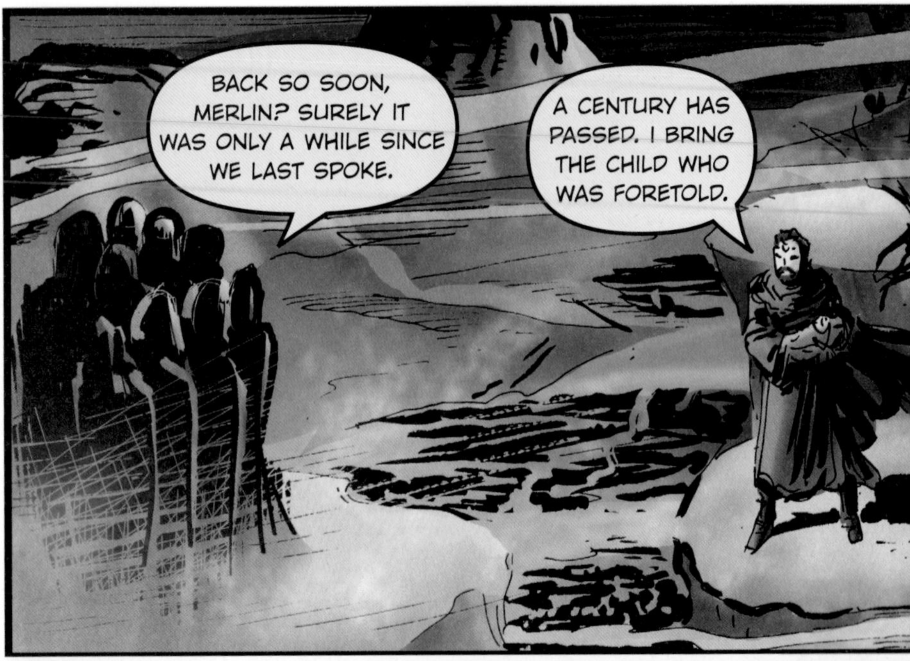
BACK SO SOON, MERLIN? SURELY IT WAS ONLY A WHILE SINCE WE LAST SPOKE.
A CENTURY HAS PASSED. I BRING THE CHILD WHO WAS FORETOLD.

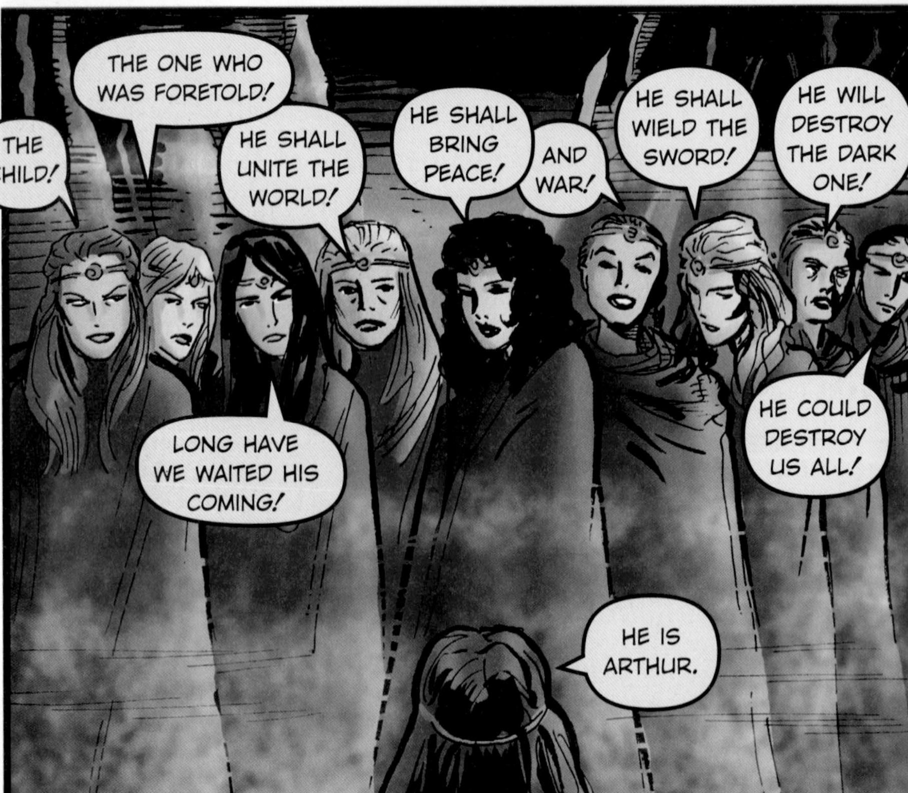
THE CHILD!
THE ONE WHO WAS FORETOLD!
HE SHALL UNITE THE WORLD!
HE SHALL BRING PEACE!
AND WAR!
HE SHALL WIELD THE SWORD!
HE WILL DESTROY THE DARK ONE!
LONG HAVE WE WAITED HIS COMING!
HE COULD DESTROY US ALL!
HE IS ARTHUR.

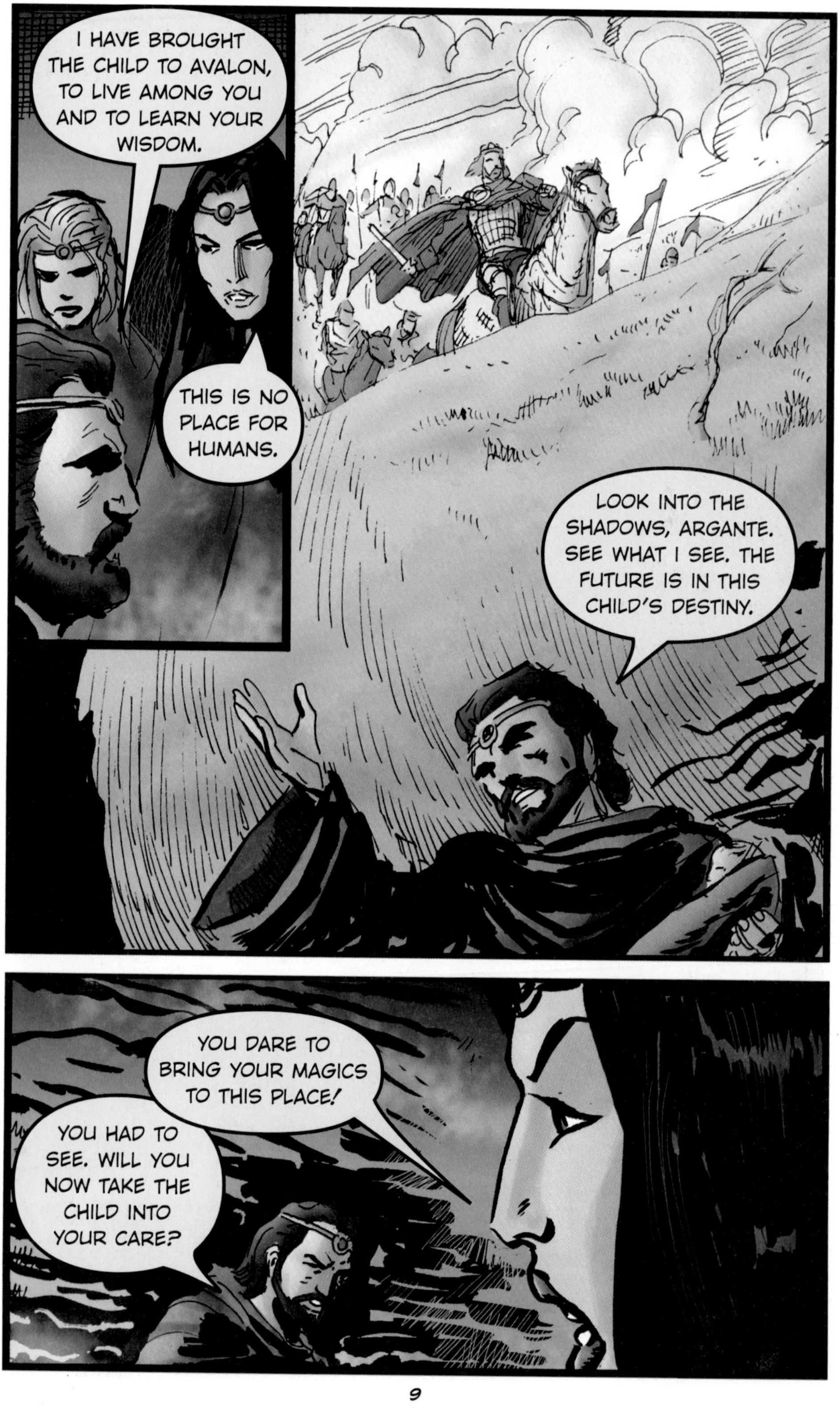
I HAVE BROUGHT THE CHILD TO AVALON, TO LIVE AMONG YOU AND TO LEARN YOUR WISDOM.
THIS IS NO PLACE FOR HUMANS.
LOOK INTO THE SHADOWS, ARGANTE. SEE WHAT I SEE. THE FUTURE IS IN THIS CHILD'S DESTINY.
YOU DARE TO BRING YOUR MAGICS TO THIS PLACE!
YOU HAD TO SEE. WILL YOU NOW TAKE THE CHILD INTO YOUR CARE?

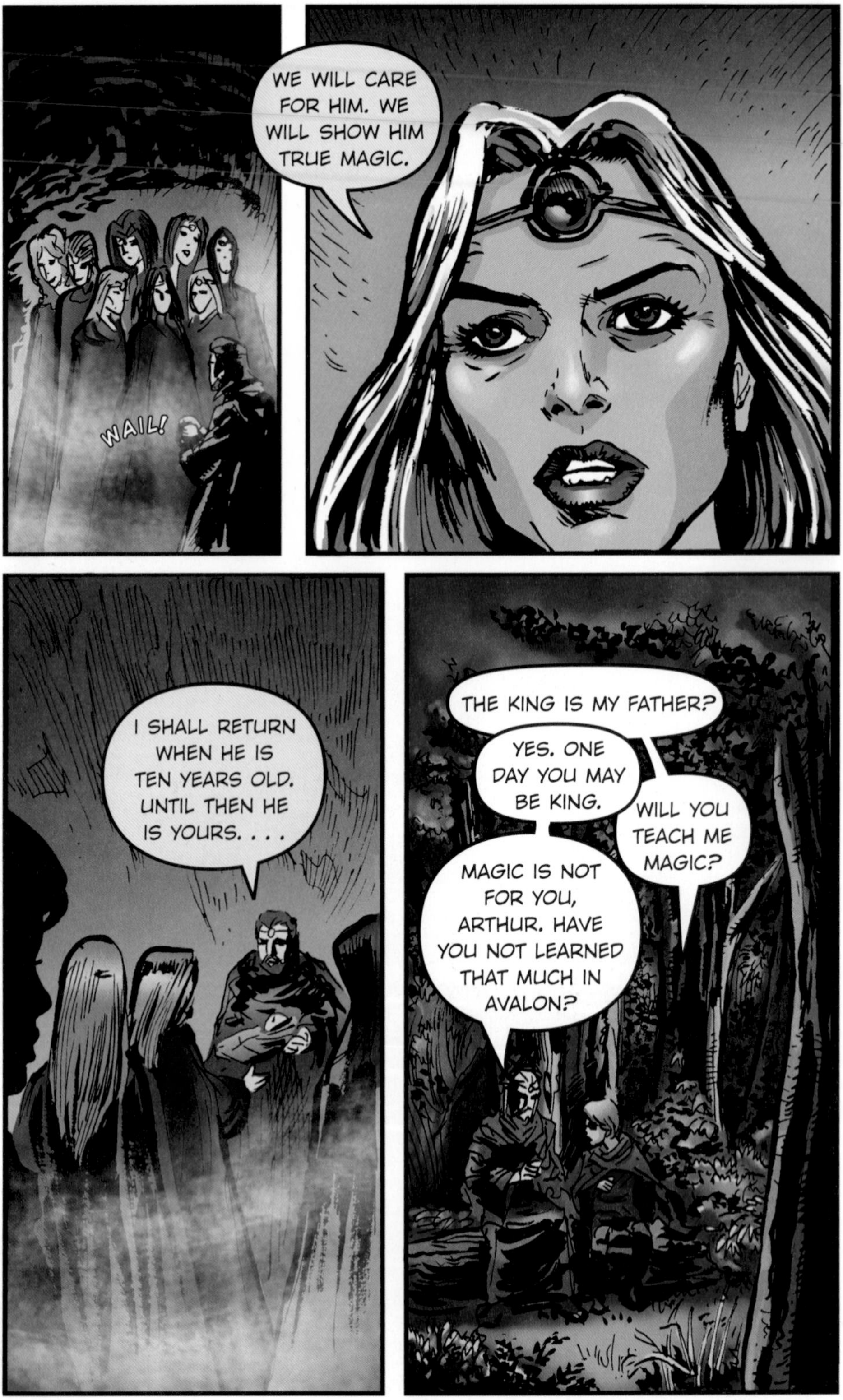
WAIL!
WE WILL CARE FOR HIM. WE WILL SHOW HIM TRUE MAGIC.
I SHALL RETURN WHEN HE IS TEN YEARS OLD. UNTIL THEN HE IS YOURS. . . .
THE KING IS MY FATHER?
YES. ONE DAY YOU MAY BE KING.
WILL YOU TEACH ME MAGIC?
MAGIC IS NOT FOR YOU, ARTHUR. HAVE YOU NOT LEARNED THAT MUCH IN AVALON?

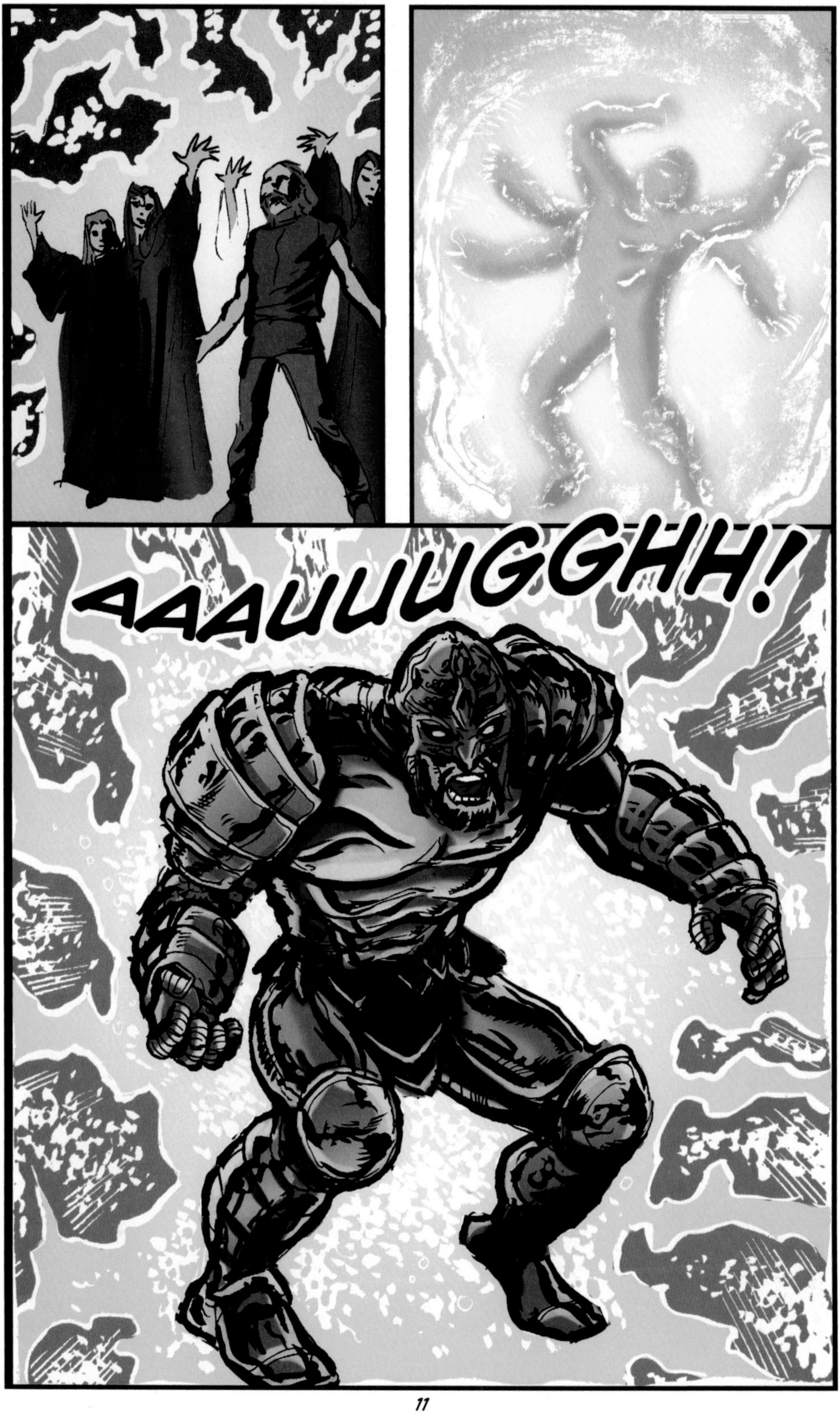
AAAUUUUGGHH!

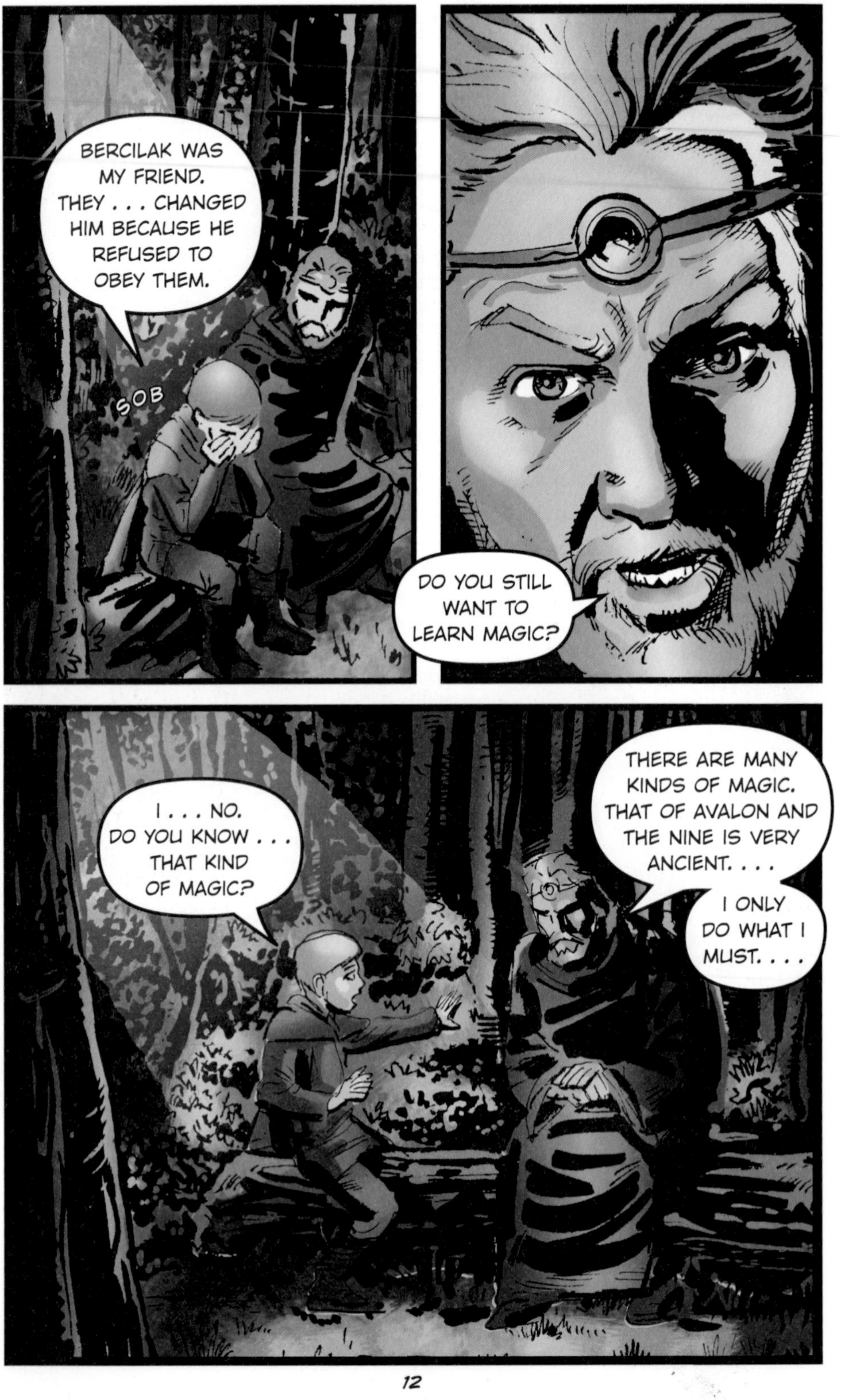
BERCILAK WAS MY FRIEND. THEY . . . CHANGED HIM BECAUSE HE REFUSED TO OBEY THEM.
SOB
DO YOU STILL WANT TO LEARN MAGIC?
I . . . NO. DO YOU KNOW . . . THAT KIND OF MAGIC?
THERE ARE MANY KINDS OF MAGIC. THAT OF AVALON AND THE NINE IS VERY ANCIENT. . . .
I ONLY DO WHAT I MUST. . . .

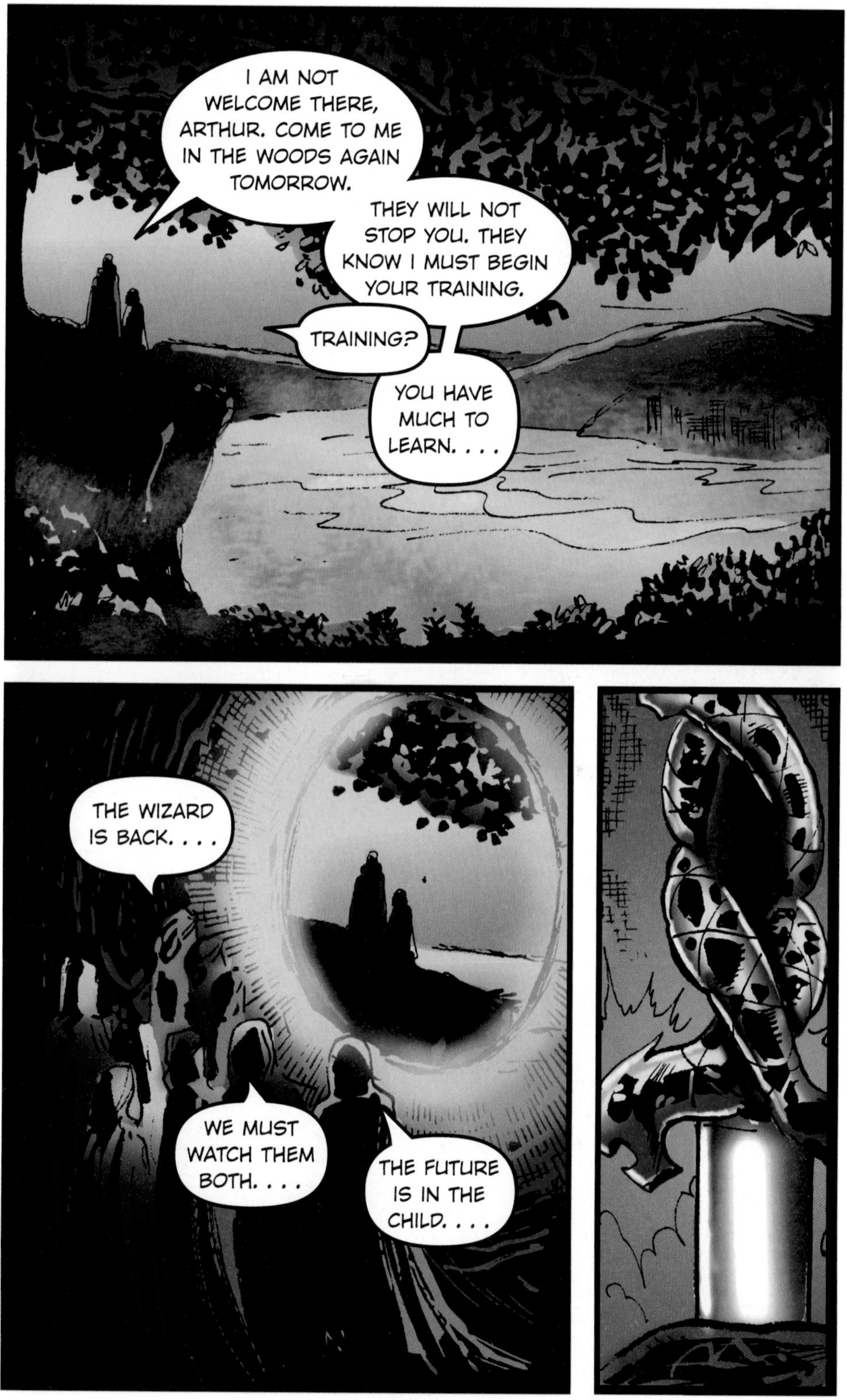
I AM NOT WELCOME THERE, ARTHUR. COME TO ME IN THE WOODS AGAIN TOMORROW.
THEY WILL NOT STOP YOU. THEY KNOW I MUST BEGIN YOUR TRAINING.
TRAINING?
YOU HAVE MUCH TO LEARN. . . .
THE WIZARD IS BACK. . . .
WE MUST WATCH THEM BOTH. . . .
THE FUTURE IS IN THE CHILD. . . .

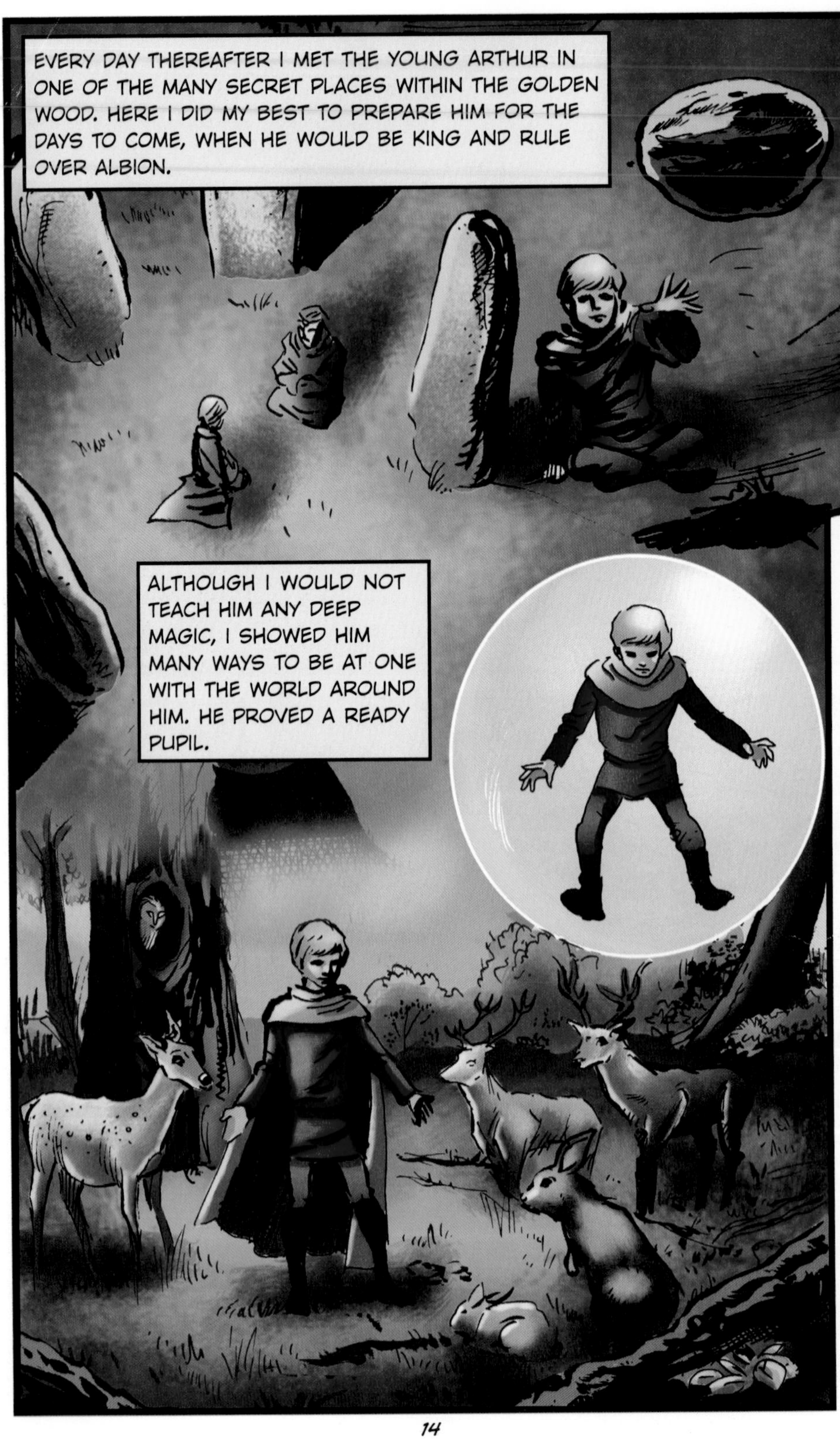
EVERY DAY THEREAFTER I MET THE YOUNG ARTHUR IN ONE OF THE MANY SECRET PLACES WITHIN THE GOLDEN WOOD. HERE I DID MY BEST TO PREPARE HIM FOR THE DAYS TO COME, WHEN HE WOULD BE KING AND RULE OVER ALBION.
ALTHOUGH I WOULD NOT TEACH HIM ANY DEEP MAGIC, I SHOWED HIM MANY WAYS TO BE AT ONE WITH THE WORLD AROUND HIM. HE PROVED A READY PUPIL.

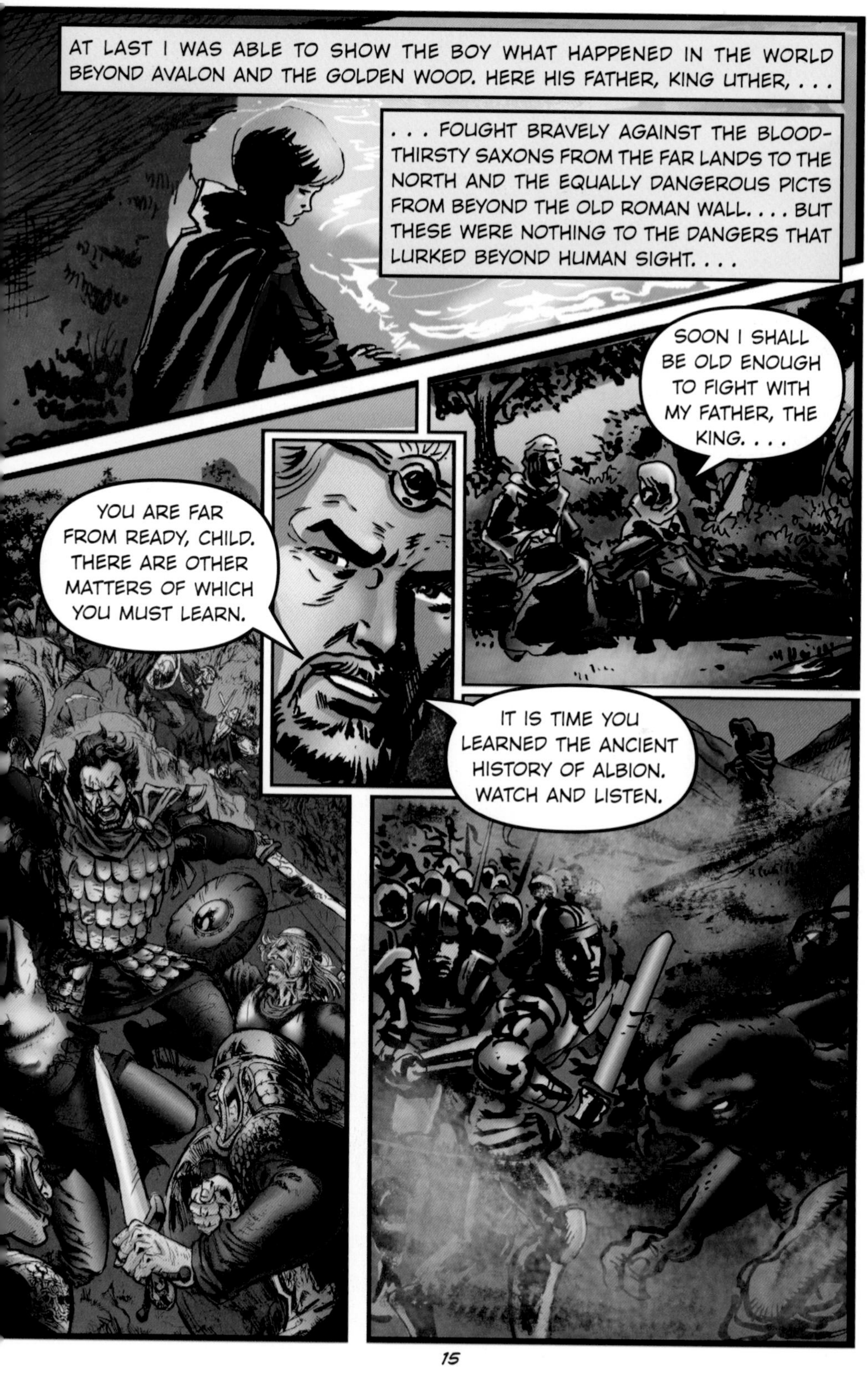
AT LAST I WAS ABLE TO SHOW THE BOY WHAT HAPPENED IN THE WORLD BEYOND AVALON AND THE GOLDEN WOOD. HERE HIS FATHER, KING UTHER, . . .
. . . FOUGHT BRAVELY AGAINST THE BLOOD-THIRSTY SAXONS FROM THE FAR LANDS TO THE NORTH AND THE EQUALLY DANGEROUS PICTS FROM BEYOND THE OLD ROMAN WALL. . . . BUT THESE WERE NOTHING TO THE DANGERS THAT LURKED BEYOND HUMAN SIGHT. . . .
SOON I SHALL BE OLD ENOUGH TO FIGHT WITH MY FATHER, THE KING. . . .
YOU ARE FAR FROM READY, CHILD. THERE ARE OTHER MATTERS OF WHICH YOU MUST LEARN.
IT IS TIME YOU LEARNED THE ANCIENT HISTORY OF ALBION. WATCH AND LISTEN.

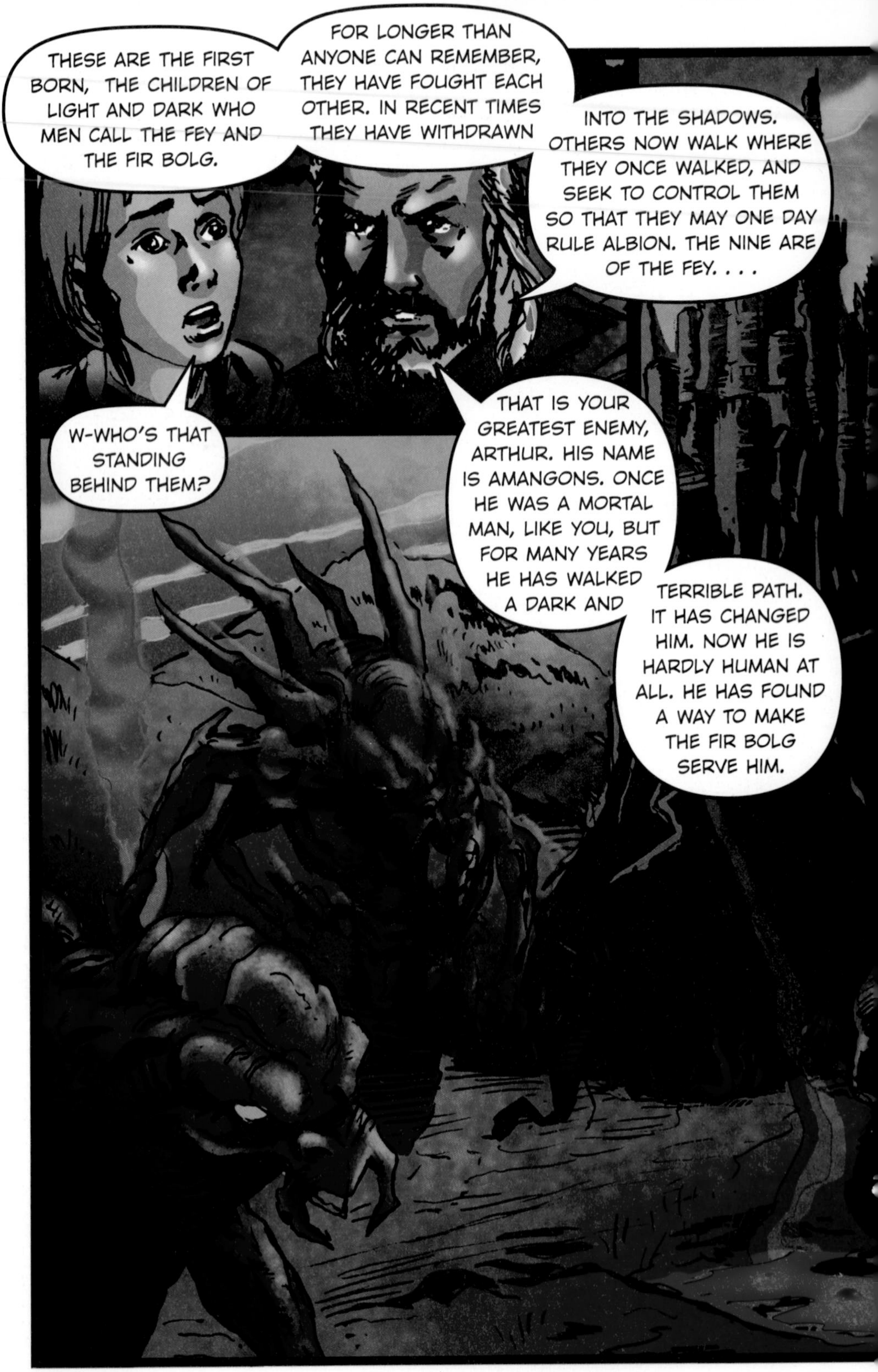
THESE ARE THE FIRST BORN, THE CHILDREN OF LIGHT AND DARK WHO MEN CALL THE FEY AND THE FIR BOLG.
FOR LONGER THAN ANYONE CAN REMEMBER, THEY HAVE FOUGHT EACH OTHER. IN RECENT TIMES THEY HAVE WITHDRAWN
INTO THE SHADOWS. OTHERS NOW WALK WHERE THEY ONCE WALKED, AND SEEK TO CONTROL THEM SO THAT THEY MAY ONE DAY RULE ALBION. THE NINE ARE OF THE FEY. . . .
W-WHO'S THAT STANDING BEHIND THEM?
THAT IS YOUR GREATEST ENEMY, ARTHUR. HIS NAME IS AMANGONS. ONCE HE WAS A MORTAL MAN, LIKE YOU, BUT FOR MANY YEARS HE HAS WALKED A DARK AND
TERRIBLE PATH. IT HAS CHANGED HIM. NOW HE IS HARDLY HUMAN AT ALL. HE HAS FOUND A WAY TO MAKE THE FIR BOLG SERVE HIM.

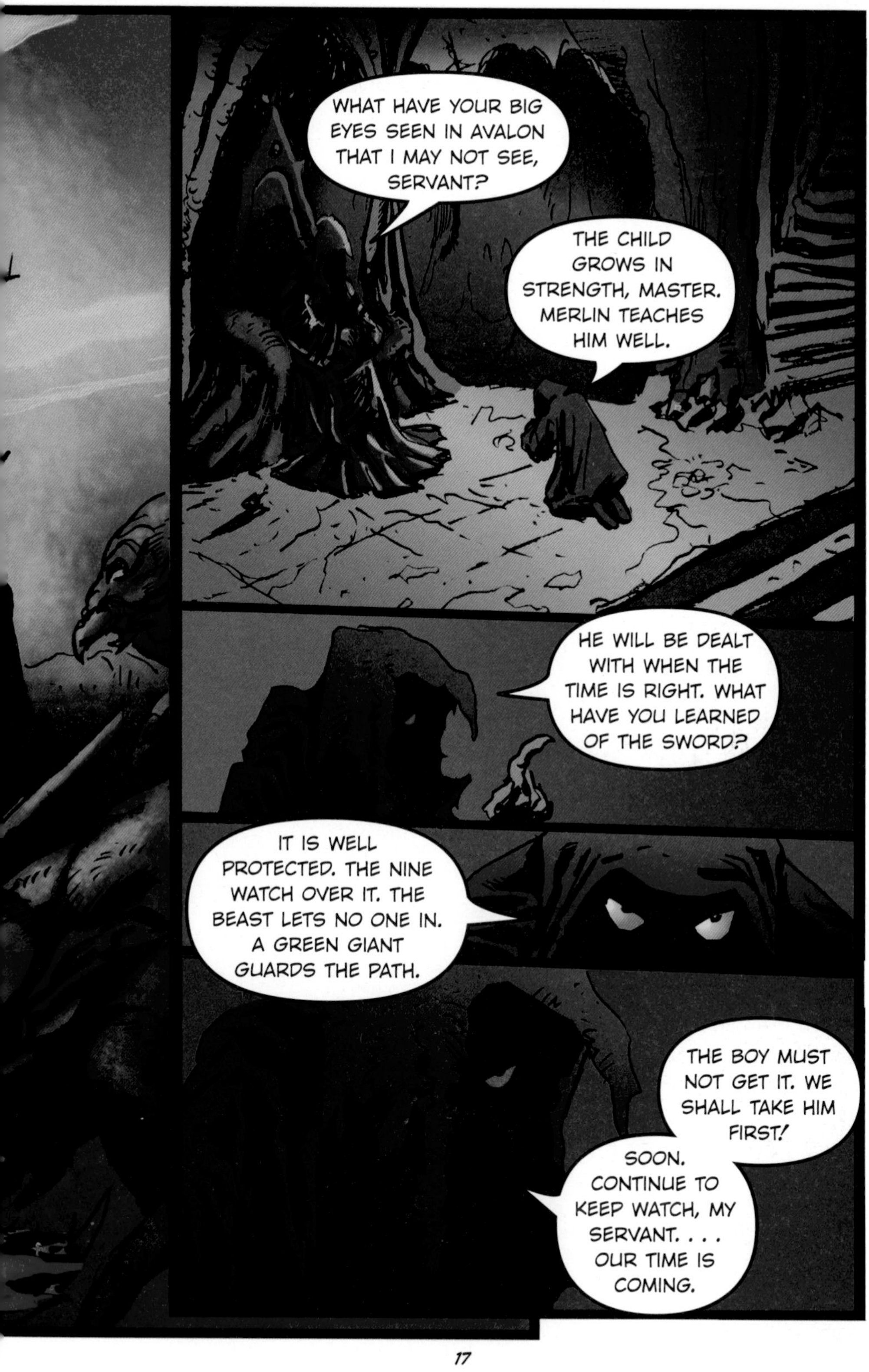

WHAT HAVE YOUR BIG EYES SEEN IN AVALON THAT I MAY NOT SEE, SERVANT?
THE CHILD GROWS IN STRENGTH, MASTER. MERLIN TEACHES HIM WELL.
HE WILL BE DEALT WITH WHEN THE TIME IS RIGHT. WHAT HAVE YOU LEARNED OF THE SWORD?
IT IS WELL PROTECTED. THE NINE WATCH OVER IT. THE BEAST LETS NO ONE IN. A GREEN GIANT GUARDS THE PATH.
THE BOY MUST NOT GET IT. WE SHALL TAKE HIM FIRST!
SOON. CONTINUE TO KEEP WATCH, MY SERVANT. . . . OUR TIME IS COMING.

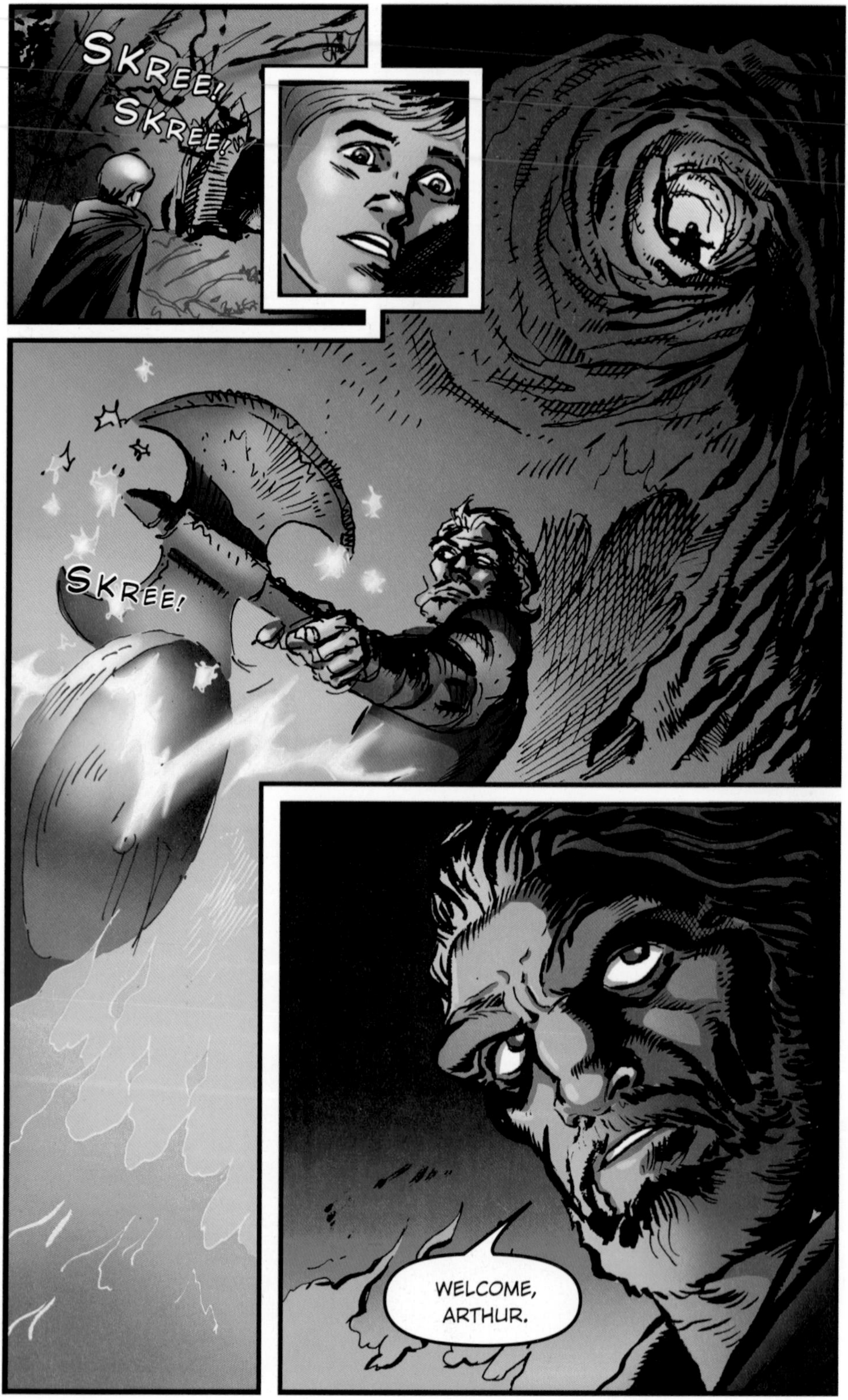
SKREE!
SKREE!
SKREE!
WELCOME, ARTHUR.

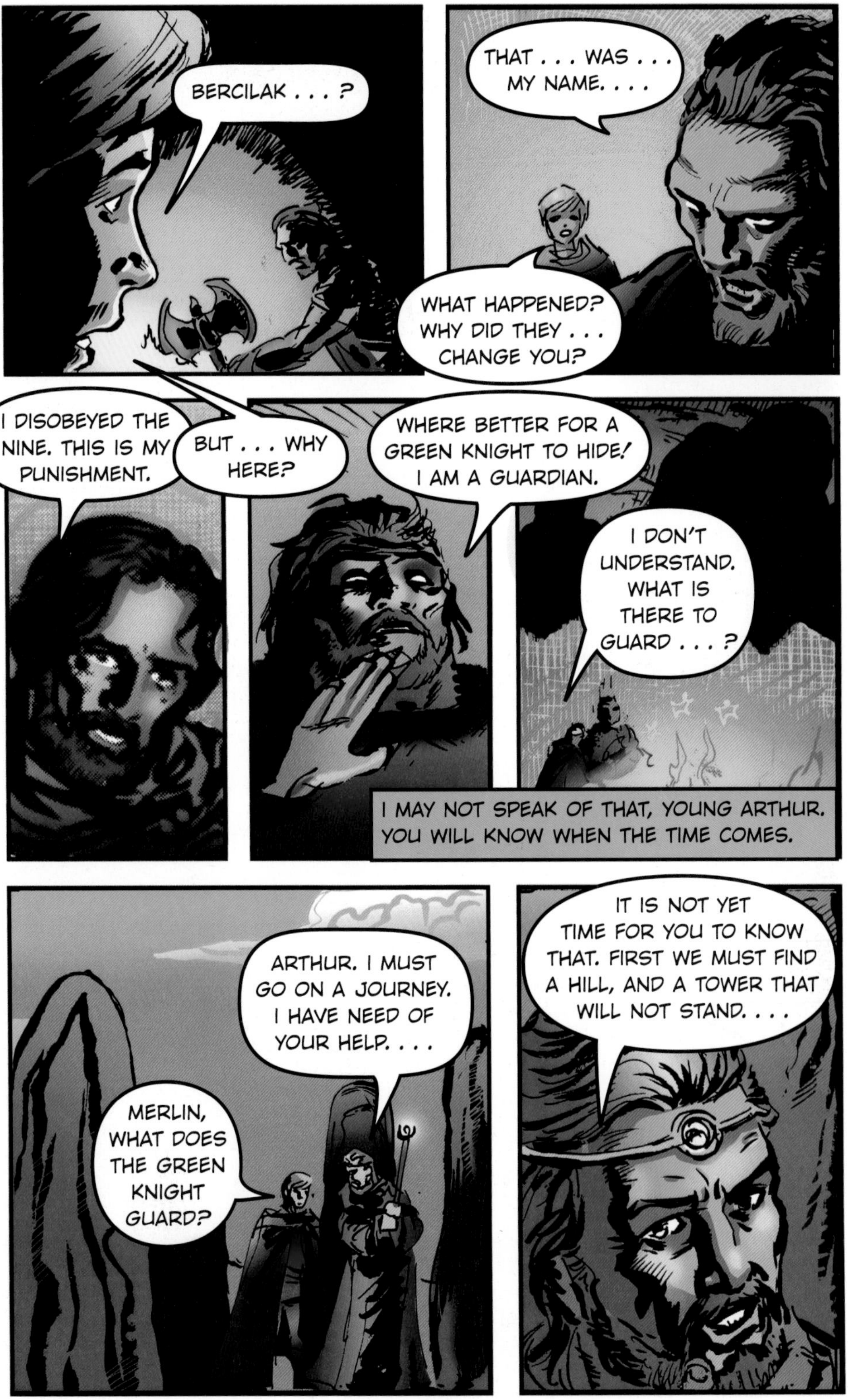
BERCILAK . . . ?
THAT . . . WAS . . . MY NAME. . . .
WHAT HAPPENED? WHY DID THEY . . . CHANGE YOU?
I DISOBEYED THE NINE. THIS IS MY PUNISHMENT.
BUT . . . WHY HERE?
WHERE BETTER FOR A GREEN KNIGHT TO HIDE! I AM A GUARDIAN.
I DON'T UNDERSTAND. WHAT IS THERE TO GUARD . . . ?
I MAY NOT SPEAK OF THAT, YOUNG ARTHUR. YOU WILL KNOW WHEN THE TIME COMES.
ARTHUR. I MUST GO ON A JOURNEY. I HAVE NEED OF YOUR HELP. . . .
MERLIN, WHAT DOES THE GREEN KNIGHT GUARD?
IT IS NOT YET TIME FOR YOU TO KNOW THAT. FIRST WE MUST FIND A HILL, AND A TOWER THAT WILL NOT STAND. . . .

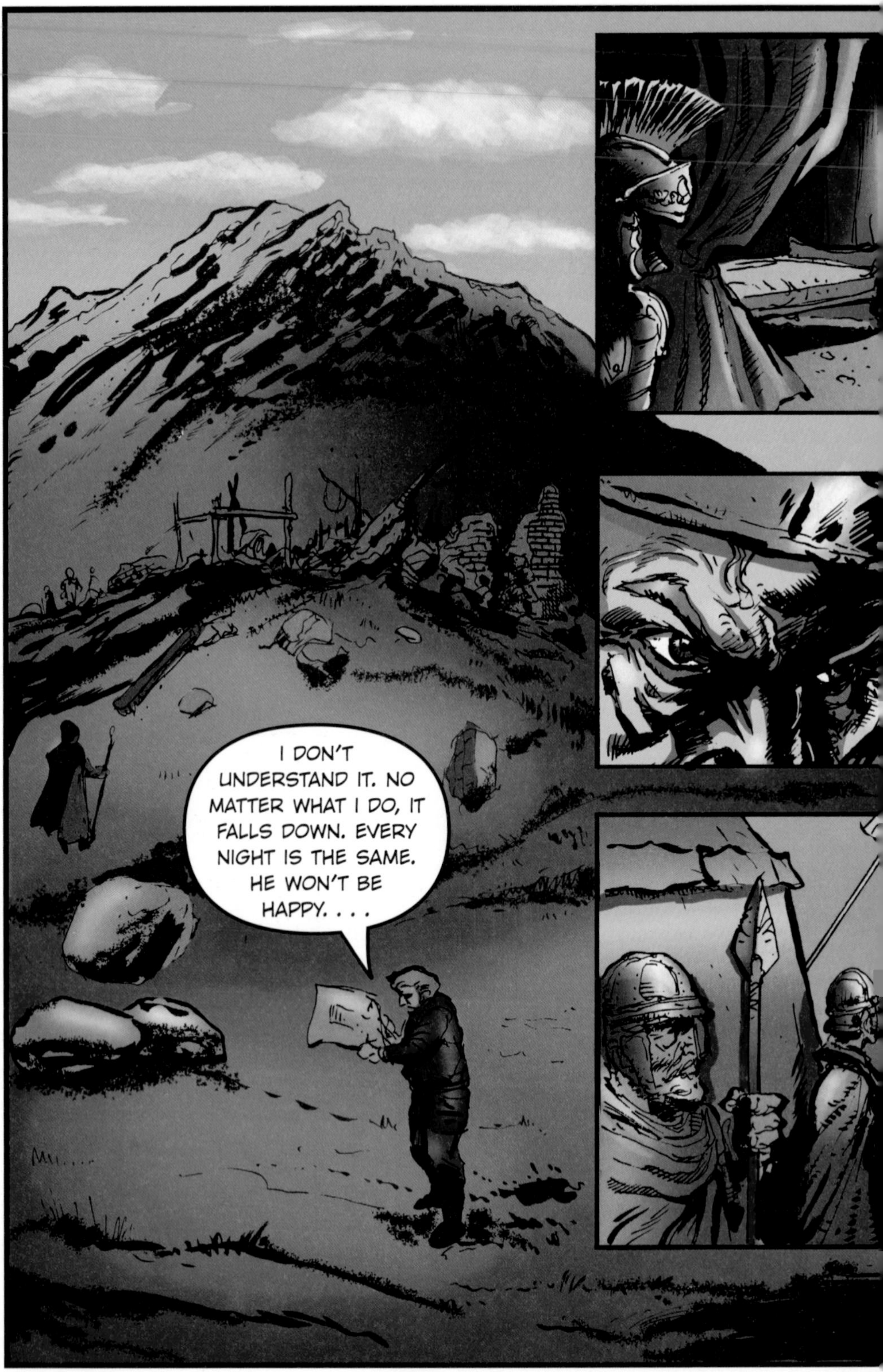
I DON'T UNDERSTAND IT. NO MATTER WHAT I DO, IT FALLS DOWN. EVERY NIGHT IS THE SAME. HE WON'T BE HAPPY. . . .

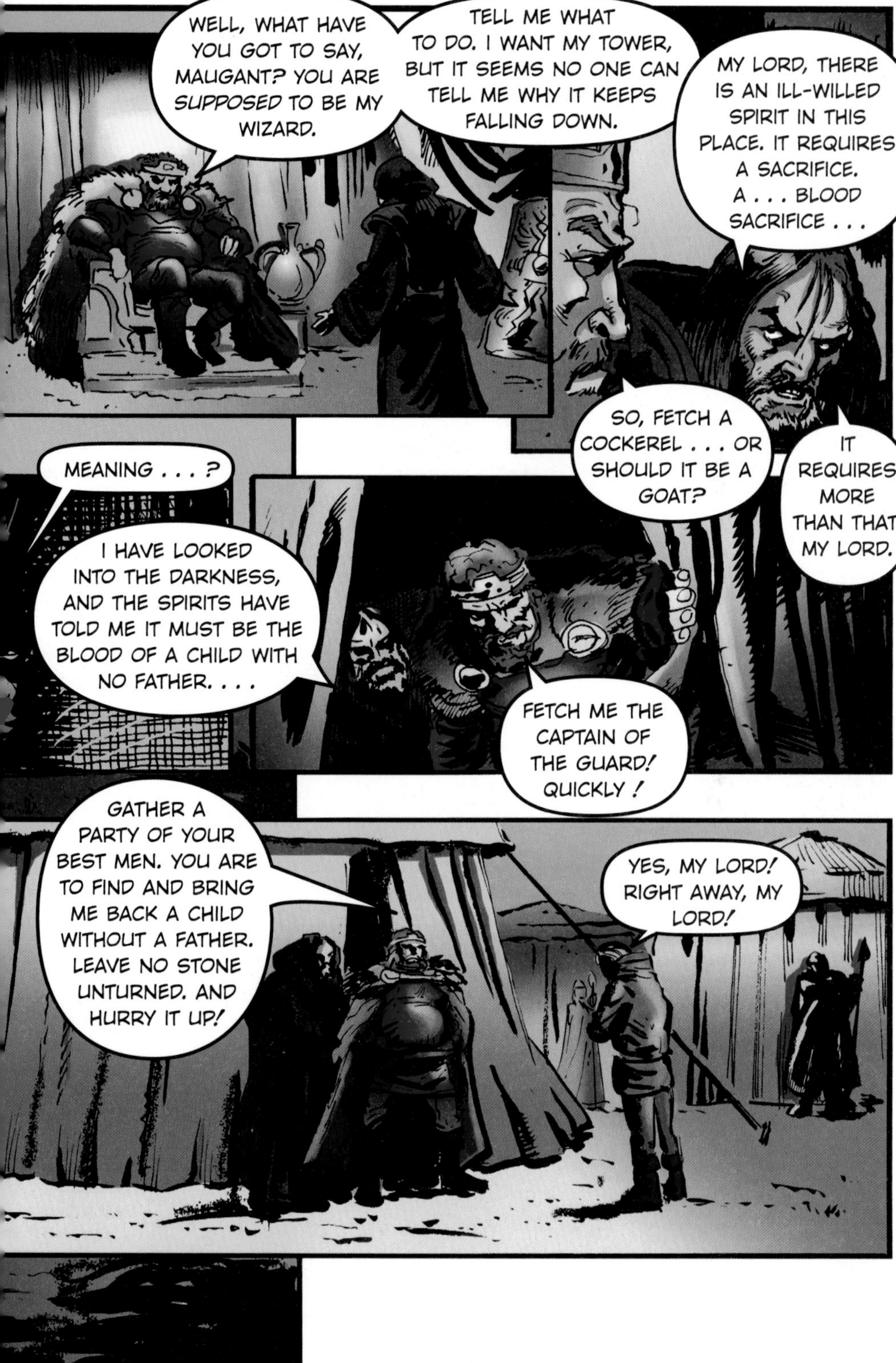
WELL, WHAT HAVE YOU GOT TO SAY, MAUGANT? YOU ARE SUPPOSED TO BE MY WIZARD.
TELL ME WHAT TO DO. I WANT MY TOWER, BUT IT SEEMS NO ONE CAN TELL ME WHY IT KEEPS FALLING DOWN.
MY LORD, THERE IS AN ILL-WILLED SPIRIT IN THIS PLACE. IT REQUIRES A SACRIFICE. A . . . BLOOD SACRIFICE . . .
SO, FETCH A COCKEREL . . . OR SHOULD IT BE A GOAT?
IT REQUIRES MORE THAN THAT, MY LORD.
MEANING . . . ?
I HAVE LOOKED INTO THE DARKNESS, AND THE SPIRITS HAVE TOLD ME IT MUST BE THE BLOOD OF A CHILD WITH NO FATHER. . . .
FETCH ME THE CAPTAIN OF THE GUARD! QUICKLY!
GATHER A PARTY OF YOUR BEST MEN. YOU ARE TO FIND AND BRING ME BACK A CHILD WITHOUT A FATHER. LEAVE NO STONE UNTURNED. AND HURRY IT UP!
YES, MY LORD! RIGHT AWAY, MY LORD!

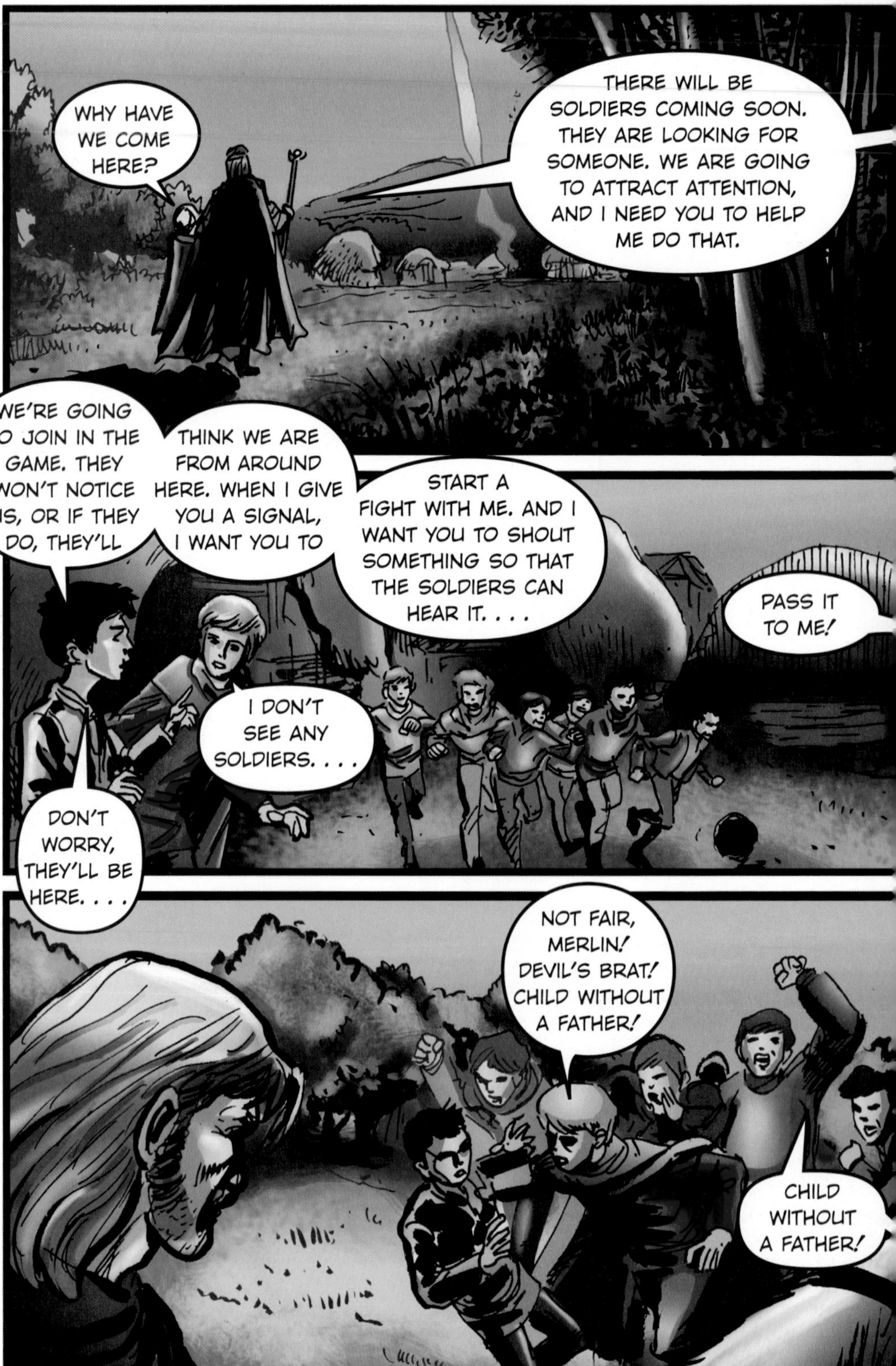
WHY HAVE WE COME HERE?
THERE WILL BE SOLDIERS COMING SOON. THEY ARE LOOKING FOR SOMEONE. WE ARE GOING TO ATTRACT ATTENTION, AND I NEED YOU TO HELP ME DO THAT.
WE'RE GOING TO JOIN IN THE GAME. THEY WON'T NOTICE US, OR IF THEY DO, THEY'LL
THINK WE ARE FROM AROUND HERE. WHEN I GIVE YOU A SIGNAL, I WANT YOU TO
START A FIGHT WITH ME. AND I WANT YOU TO SHOUT SOMETHING SO THAT THE SOLDIERS CAN HEAR IT. . . .
PASS IT TO ME!
I DON'T SEE ANY SOLDIERS. . . .
DON'T WORRY, THEY'LL BE HERE. . . .
NOT FAIR, MERLIN! DEVIL'S BRAT! CHILD WITHOUT A FATHER!
CHILD WITHOUT A FATHER!

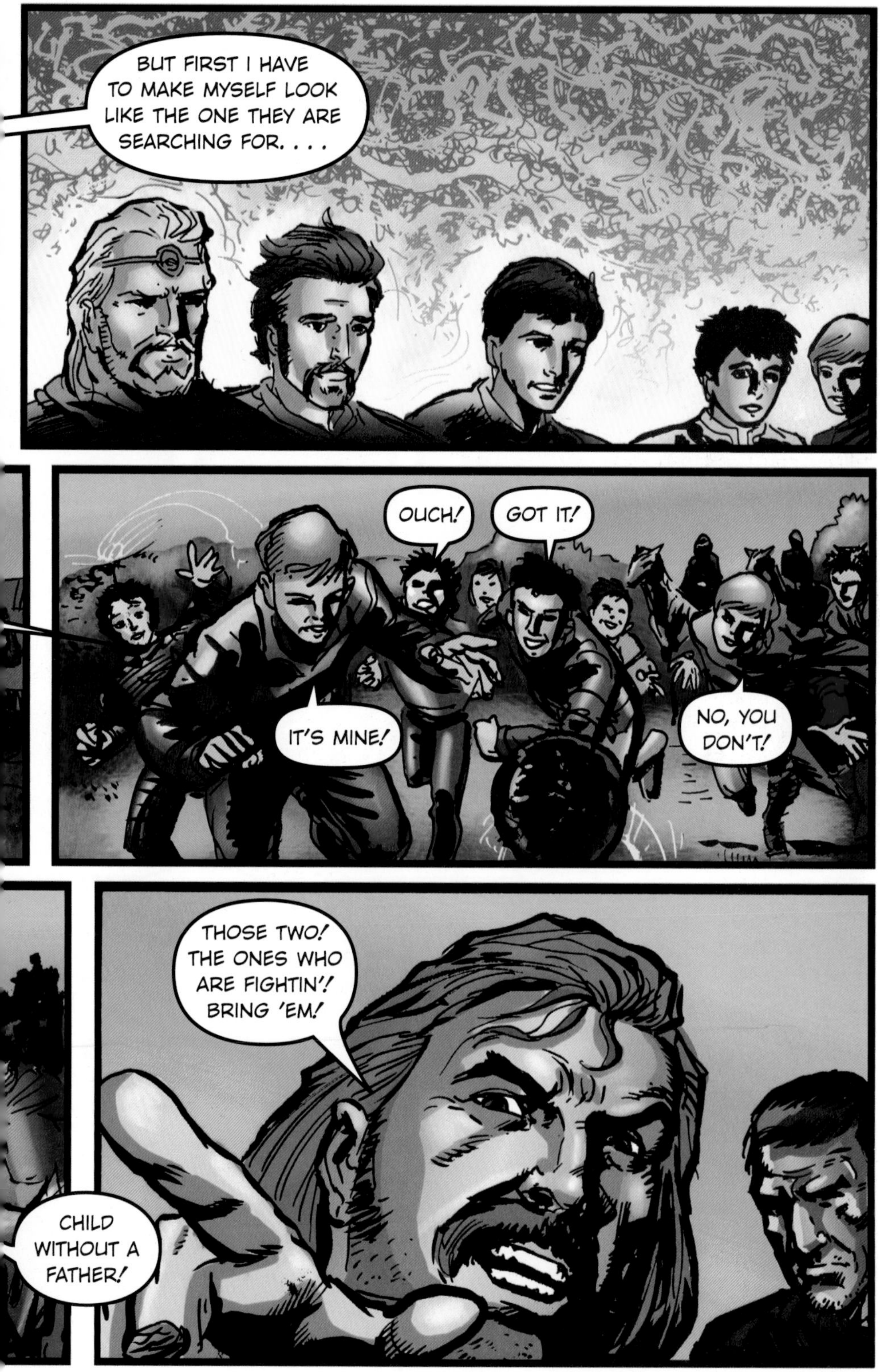
BUT FIRST I HAVE TO MAKE MYSELF LOOK LIKE THE ONE THEY ARE SEARCHING FOR. . . .
OUCH!
GOT IT!
IT'S MINE!
NO, YOU DON'T!
THOSE TWO! THE ONES WHO ARE FIGHTIN'! BRING 'EM!
CHILD WITHOUT A FATHER!

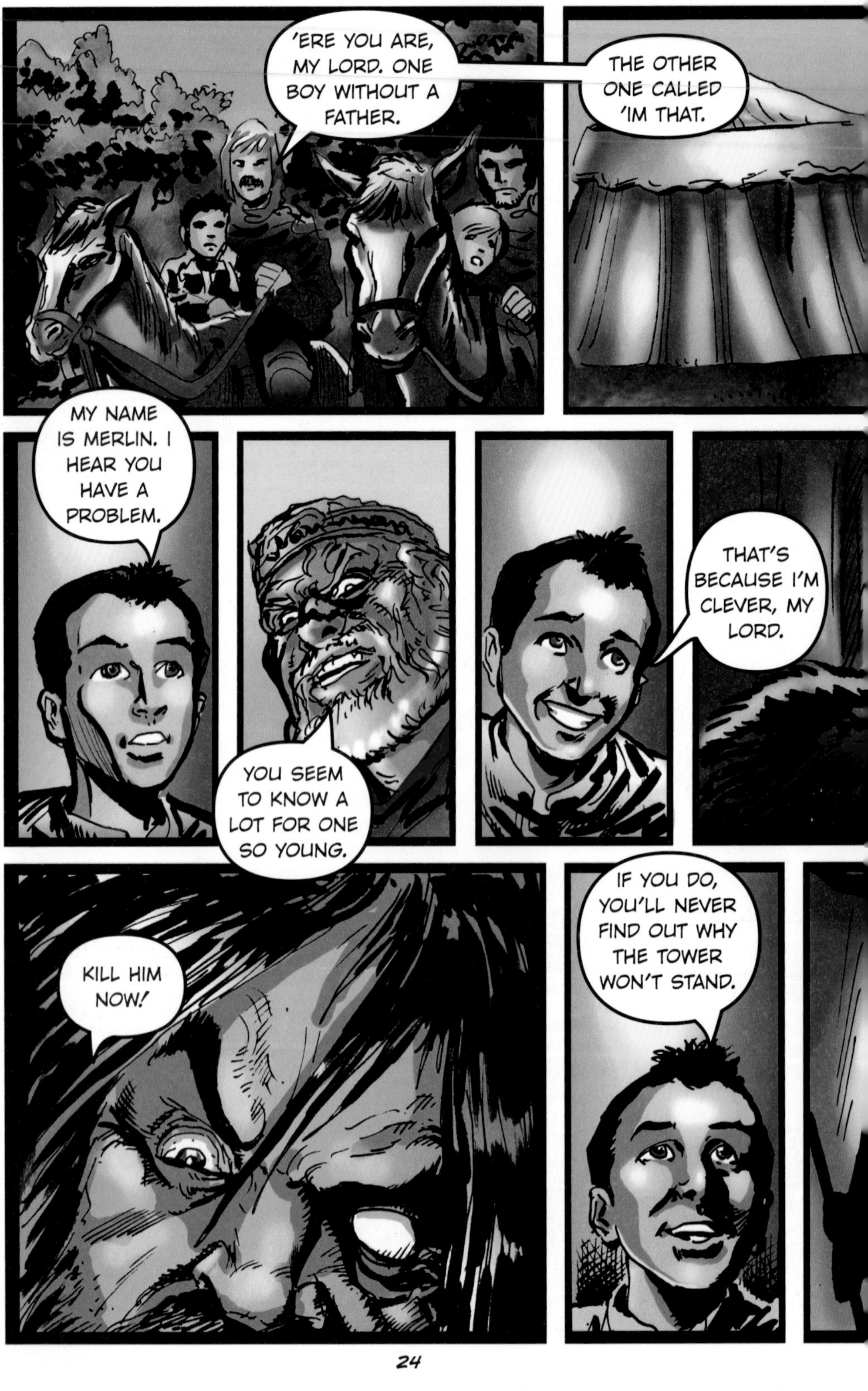
'ERE YOU ARE, MY LORD. ONE BOY WITHOUT A FATHER.
THE OTHER ONE CALLED 'IM THAT.
MY NAME IS MERLIN. I HEAR YOU HAVE A PROBLEM.
YOU SEEM TO KNOW A LOT FOR ONE SO YOUNG.
THAT'S BECAUSE I'M CLEVER, MY LORD.
KILL HIM NOW!
IF YOU DO, YOU'LL NEVER FIND OUT WHY THE TOWER WON'T STAND.

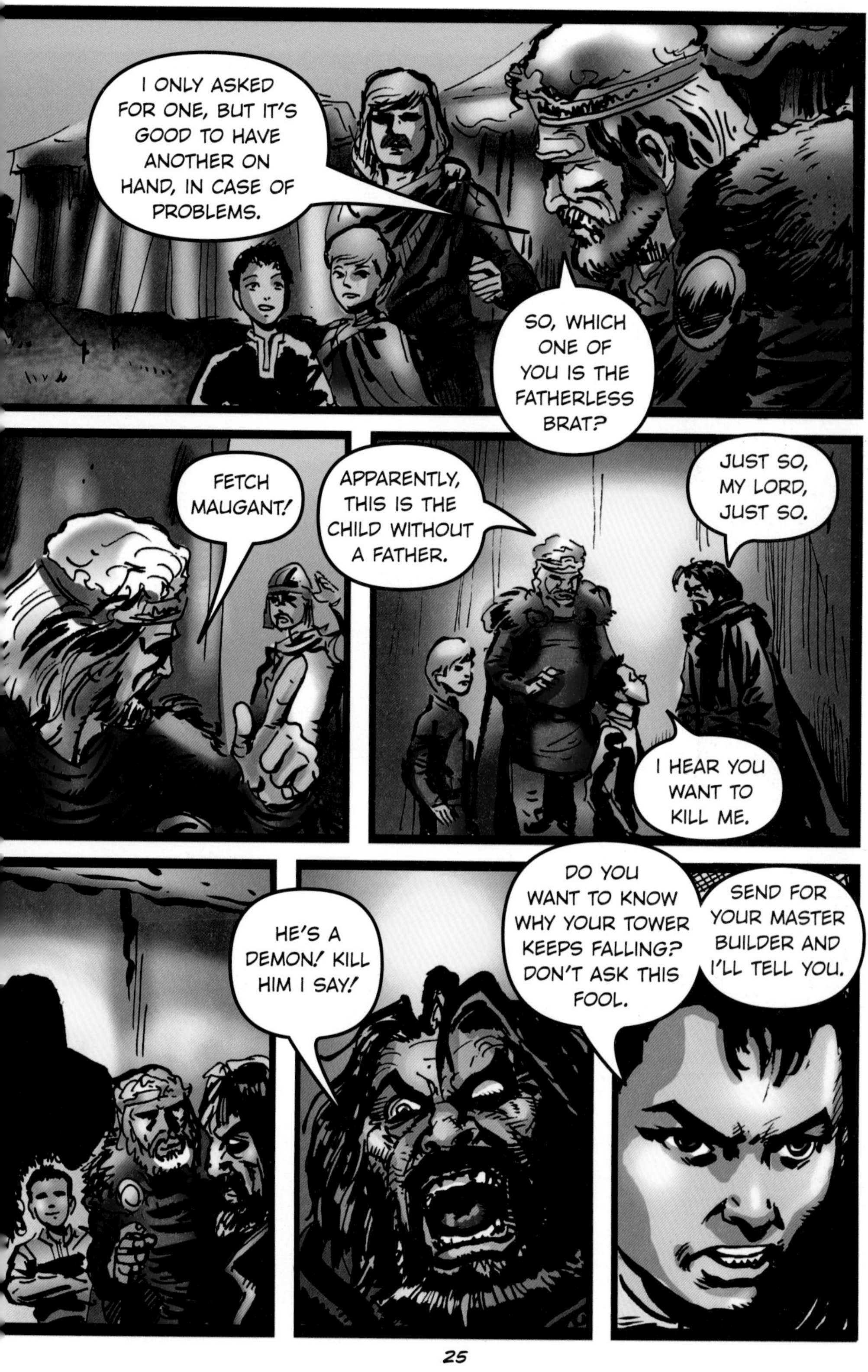
I ONLY ASKED FOR ONE, BUT IT'S GOOD TO HAVE ANOTHER ON HAND, IN CASE OF PROBLEMS.
SO, WHICH ONE OF YOU IS THE FATHERLESS BRAT?
FETCH MAUGANT!
APPARENTLY, THIS IS THE CHILD WITHOUT A FATHER.
JUST SO, MY LORD, JUST SO.
I HEAR YOU WANT TO KILL ME.
HE'S A DEMON! KILL HIM I SAY!
DO YOU WANT TO KNOW WHY YOUR TOWER KEEPS FALLING? DON'T ASK THIS FOOL.
SEND FOR YOUR MASTER BUILDER AND I'LL TELL YOU.

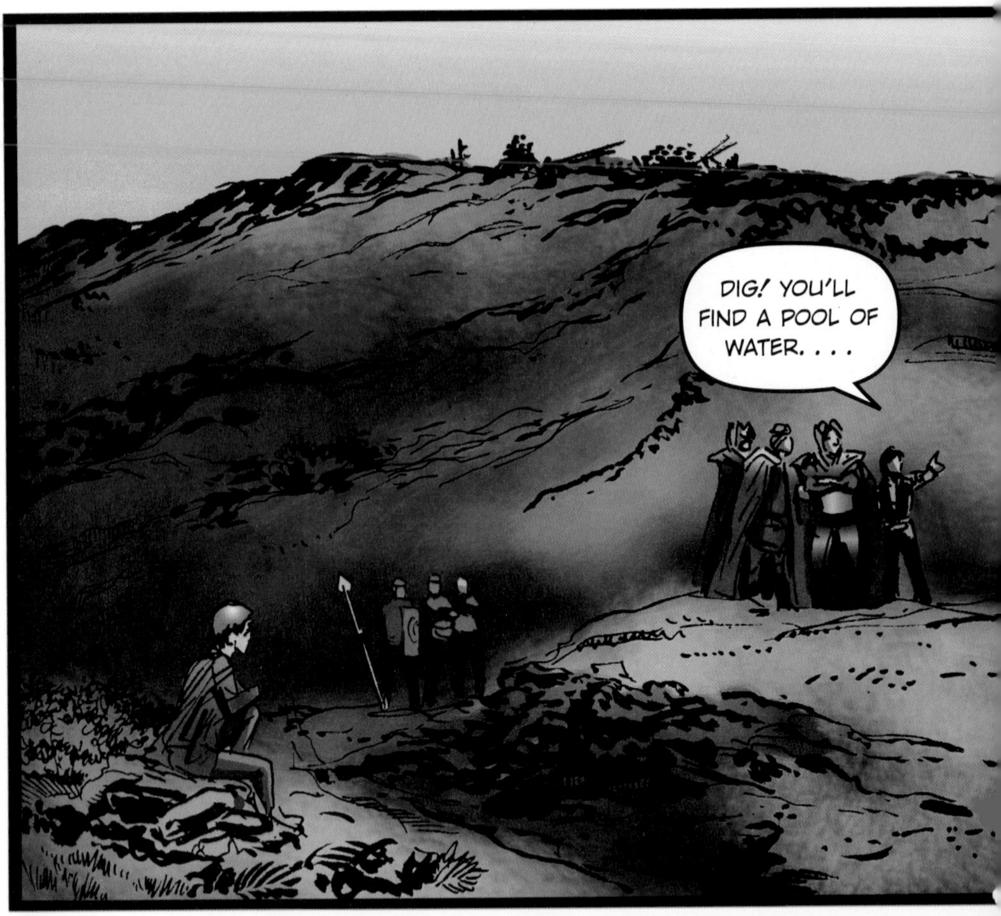
DIG! YOU'LL FIND A POOL OF WATER. . . .

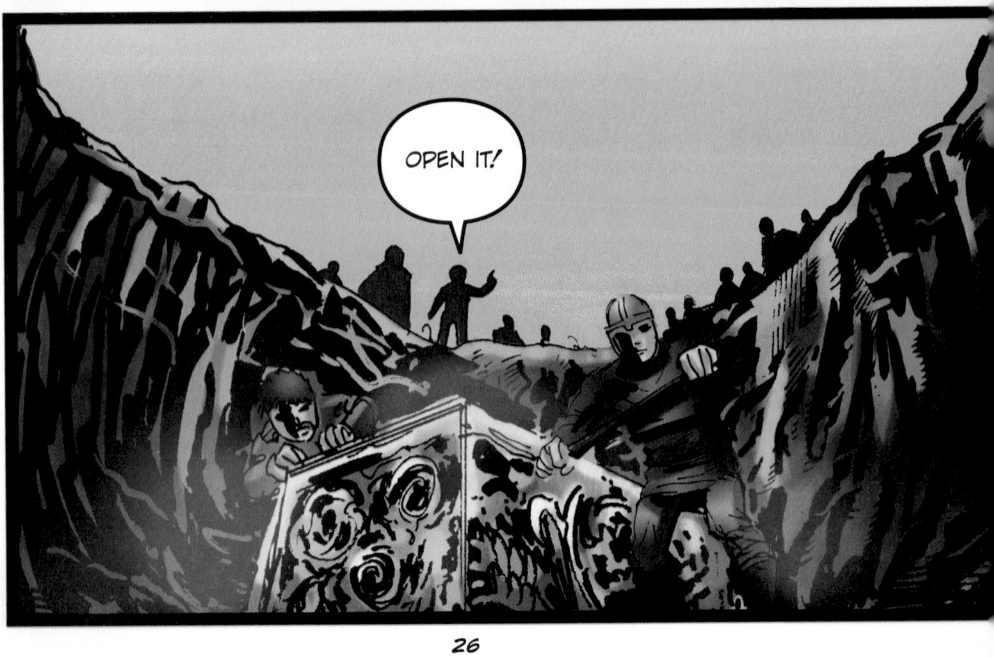
OPEN IT!

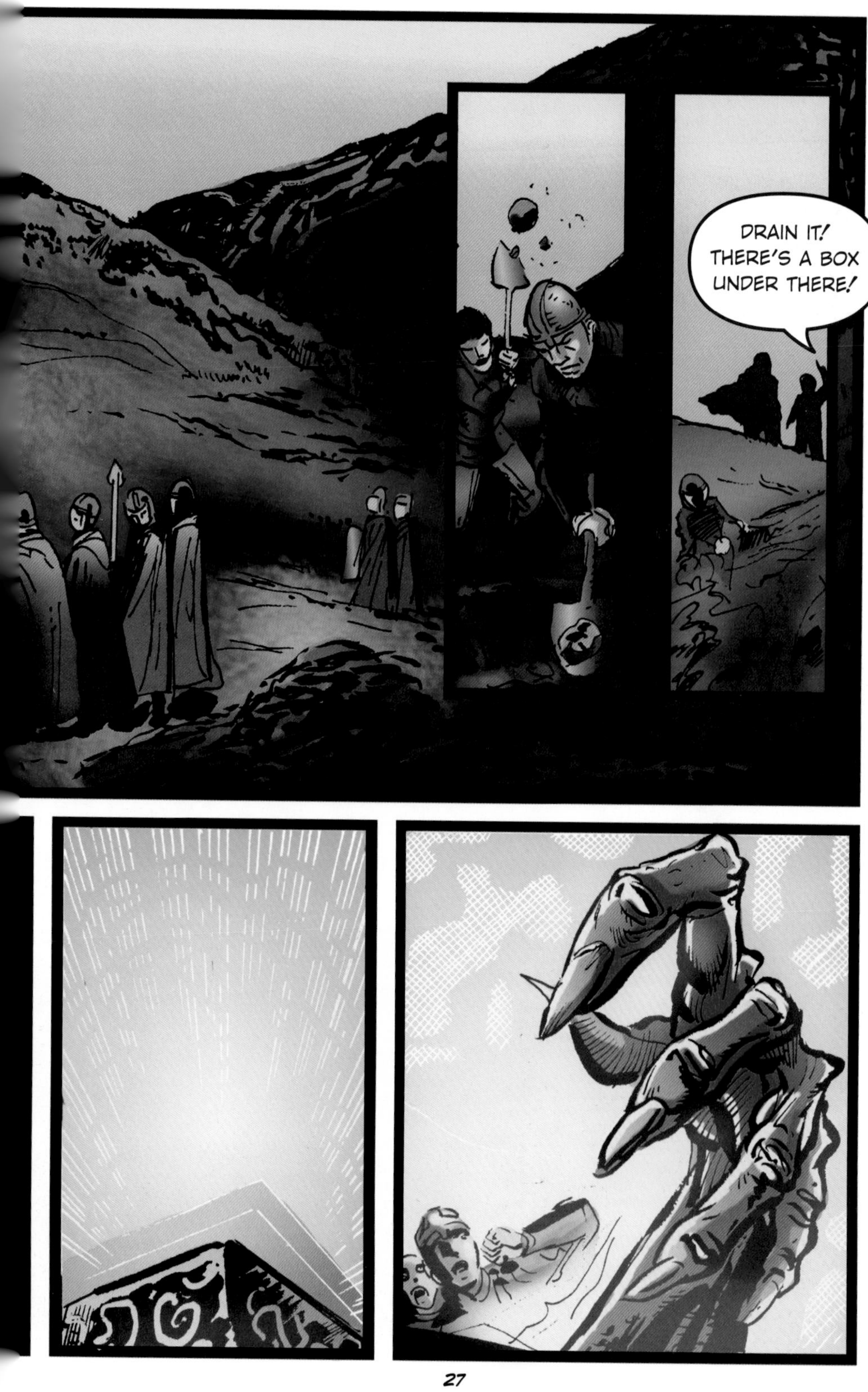
DRAIN IT! THERE'S A BOX UNDER THERE!

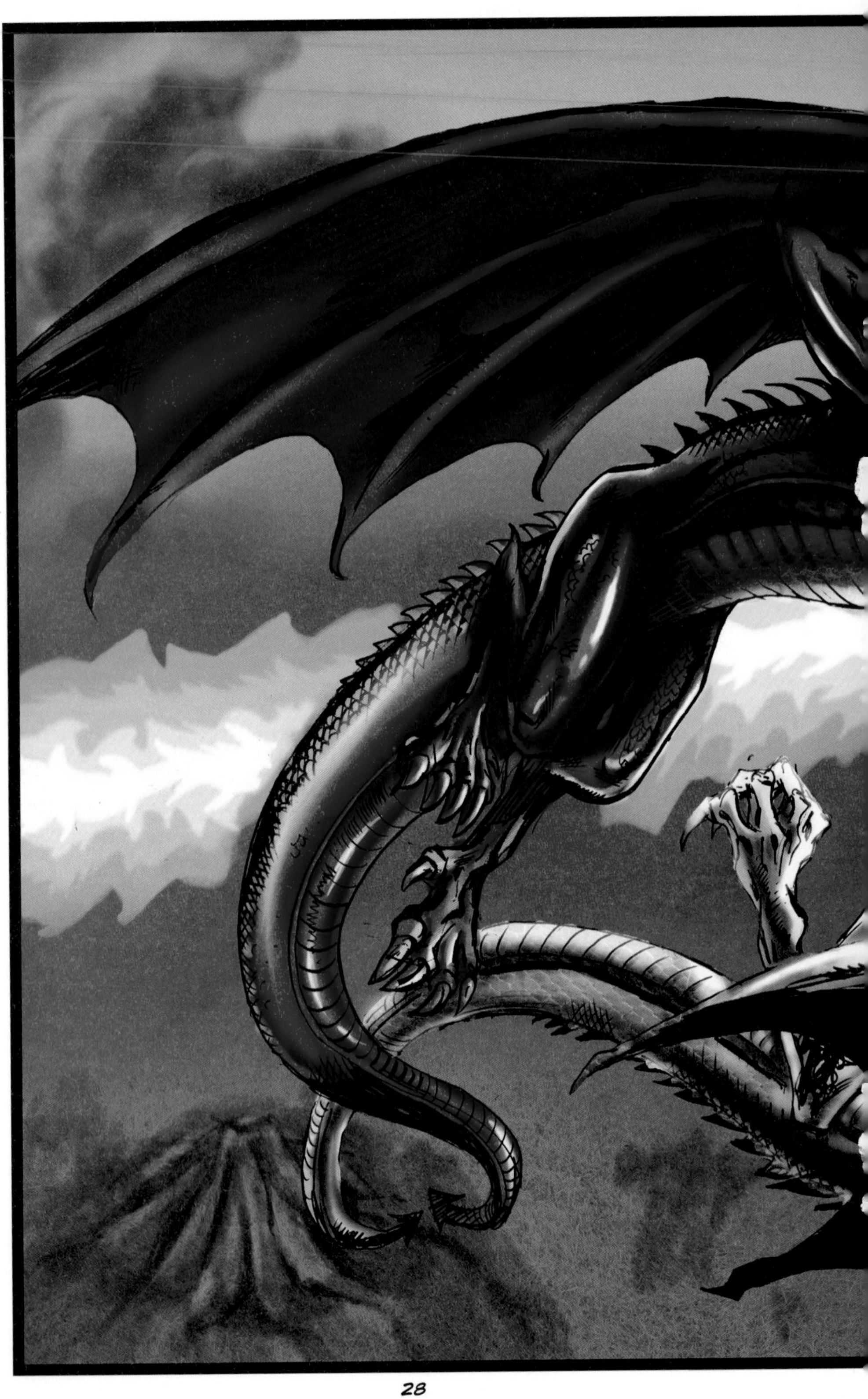

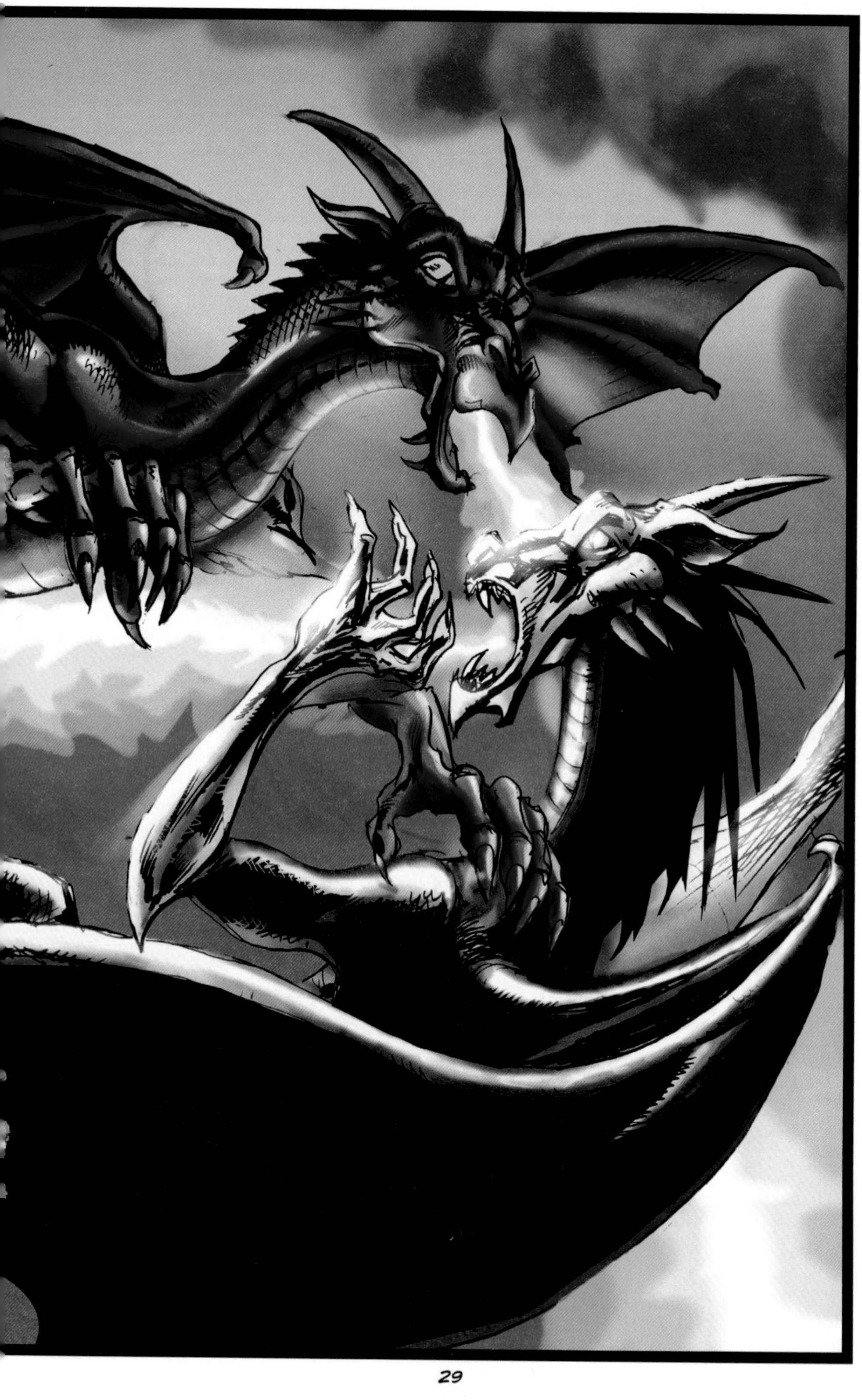

HE NEVER WAS MUCH OF A WIZARD. . . . WHAT DOES THIS MEAN?

IT MEANS YOUR TOWER WILL STAND, BUT THAT YOU WON'T ENJOY ITS PROTECTION FOR LONG.

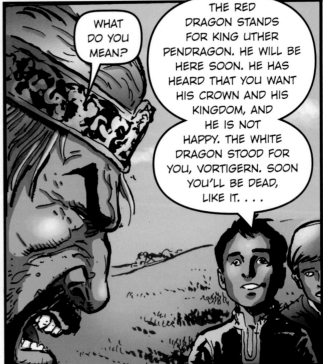

WHAT DO YOU MEAN?

THE RED DRAGON STANDS FOR KING UTHER PENDRAGON. HE WILL BE HERE SOON. HE HAS HEARD THAT YOU WANT HIS CROWN AND HIS KINGDOM, AND HE IS NOT HAPPY. THE WHITE DRAGON STOOD FOR YOU, VORTIGERN. SOON YOU'LL BE DEAD, LIKE IT. . . .

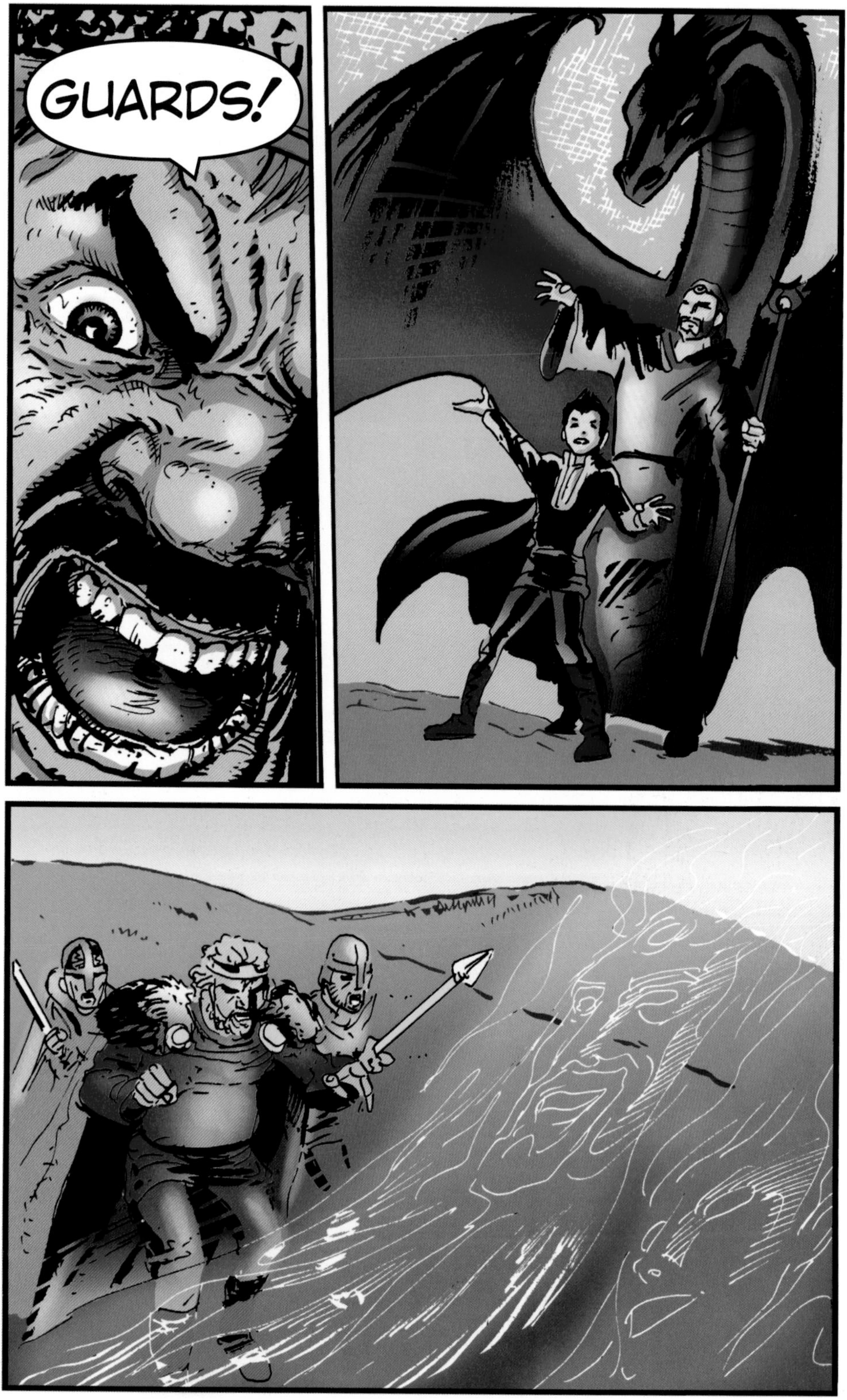
GUARDS!

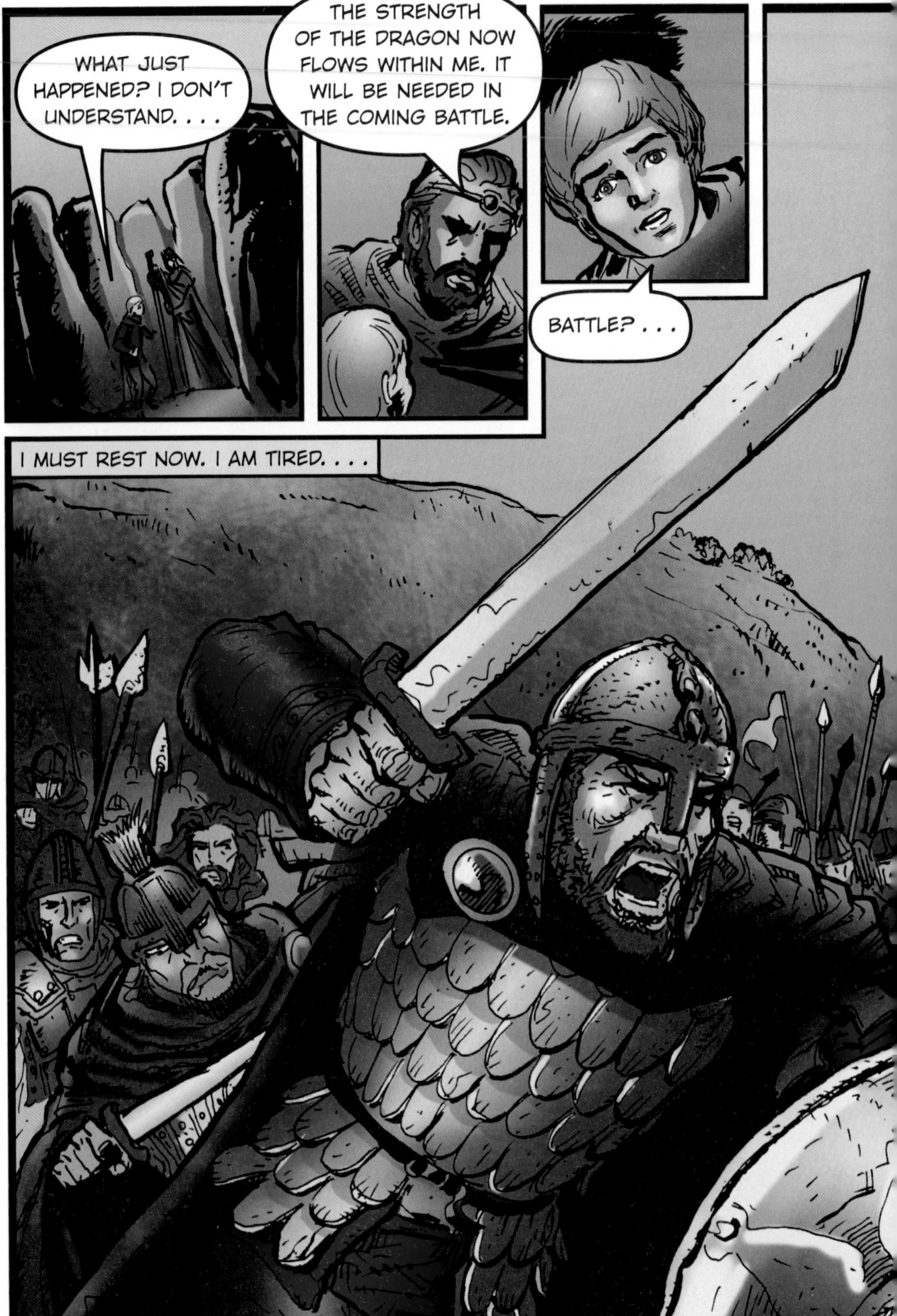
WHAT JUST HAPPENED? I DON'T UNDERSTAND. . . .
THE STRENGTH OF THE DRAGON NOW FLOWS WITHIN ME. IT WILL BE NEEDED IN THE COMING BATTLE.
BATTLE? . . .
I MUST REST NOW. I AM TIRED. . . .

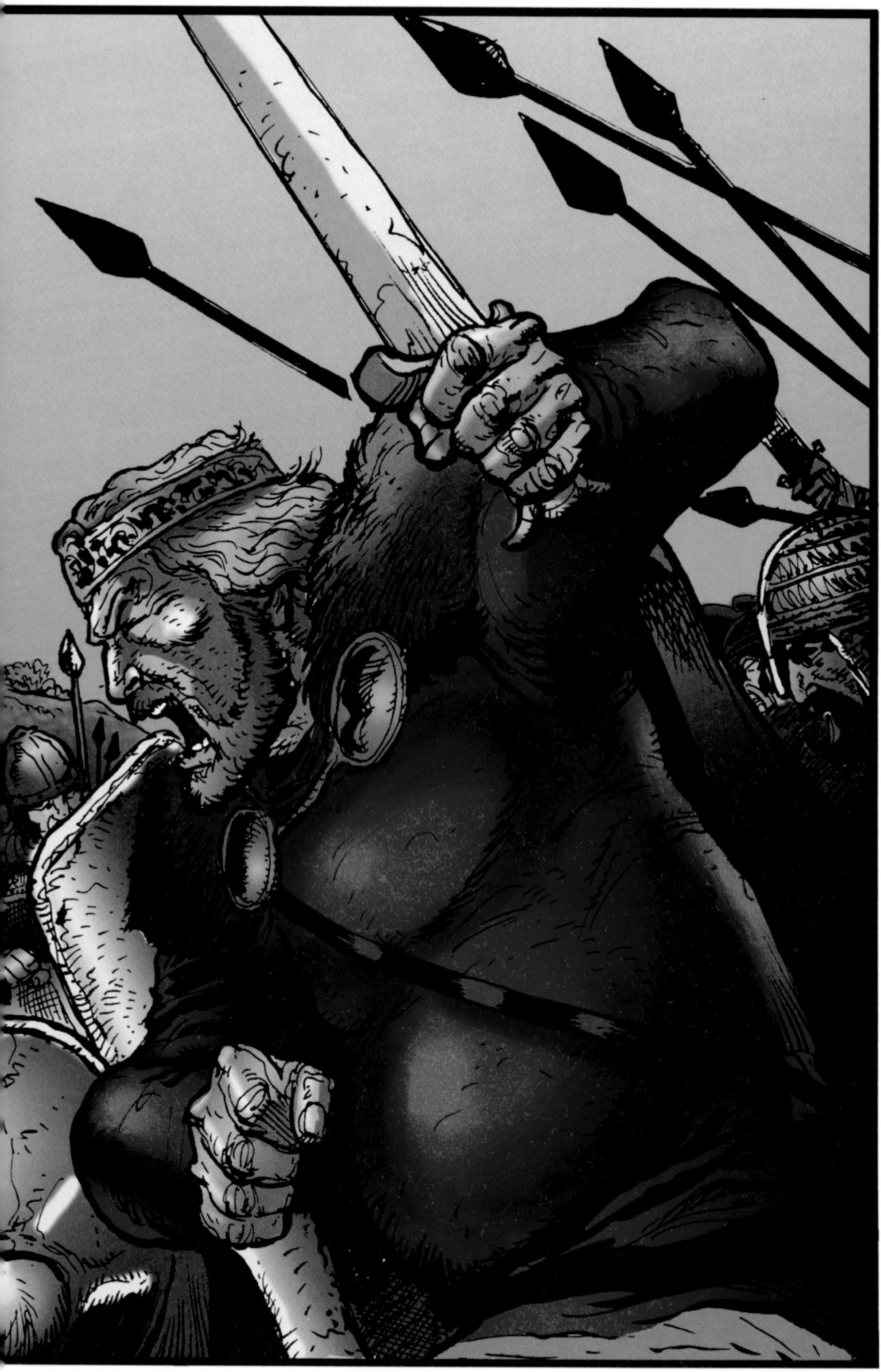

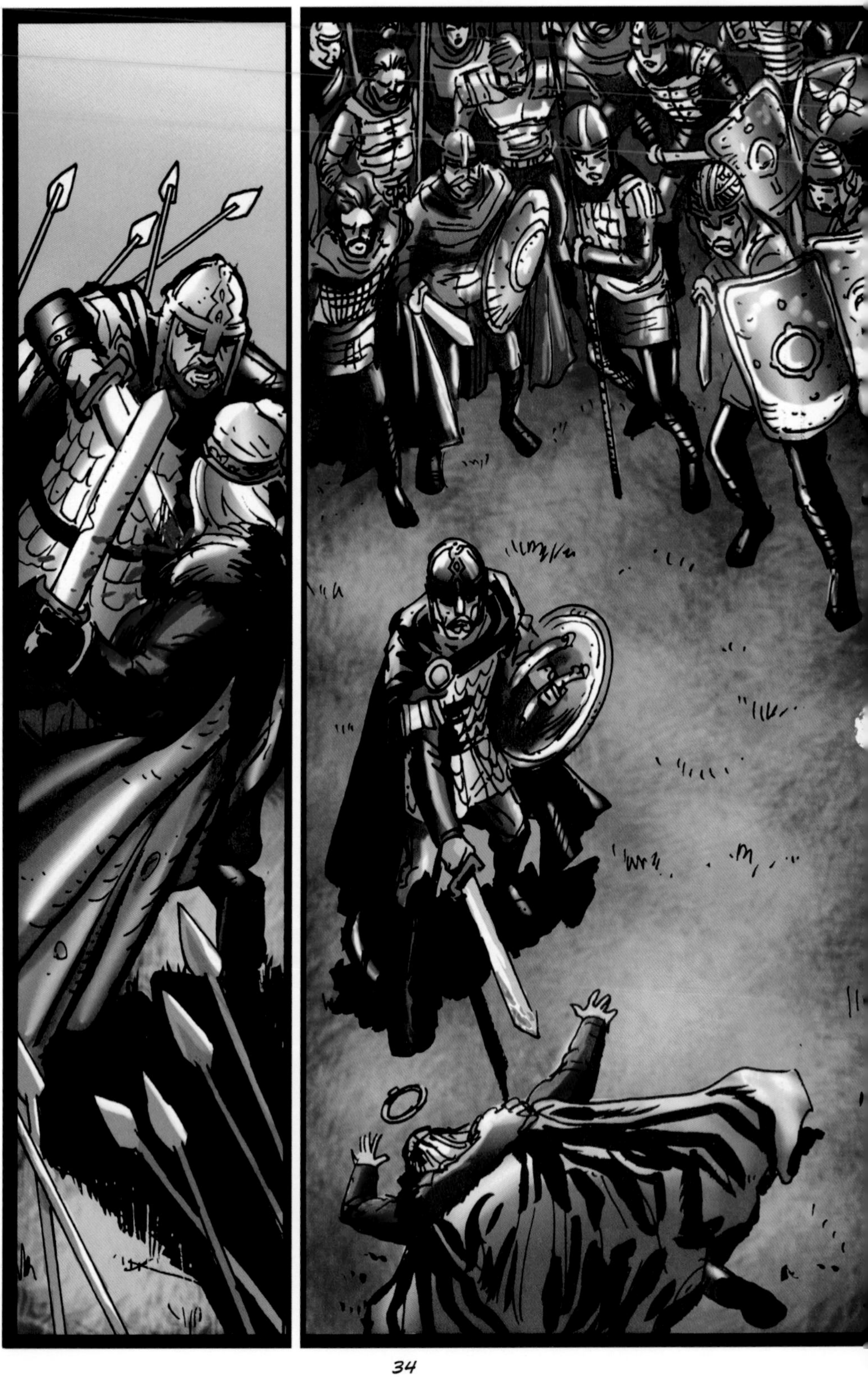

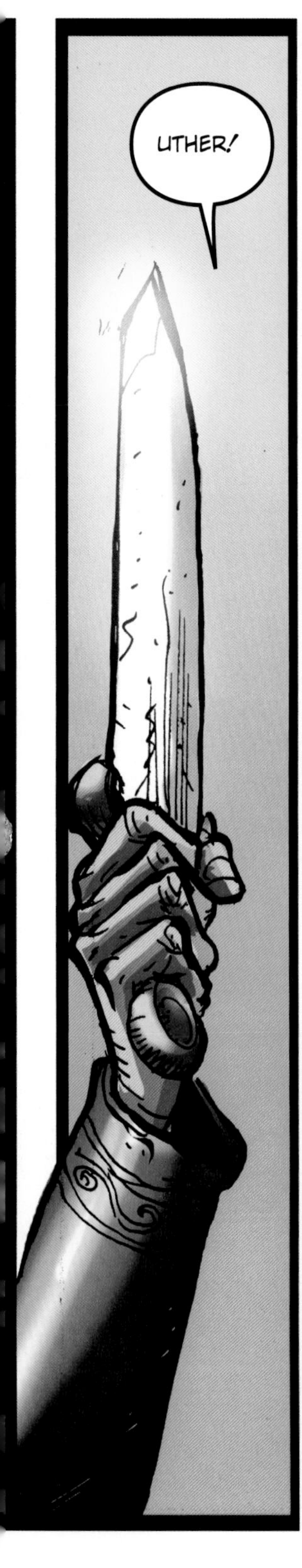
UTHER!

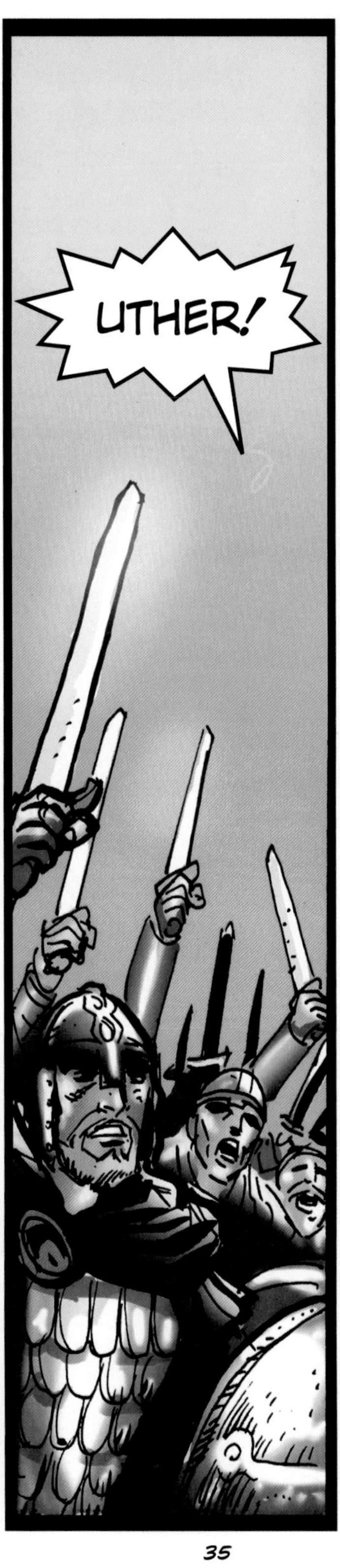
UTHER!

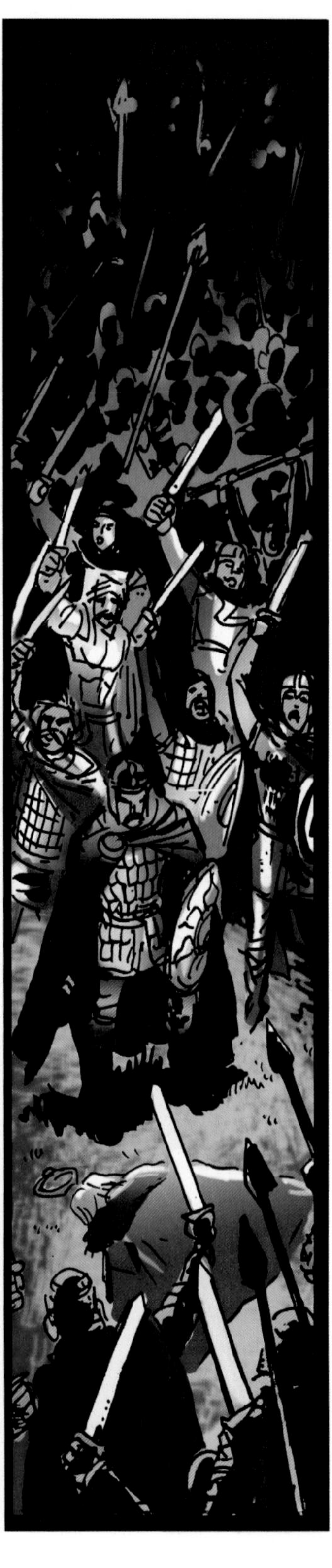

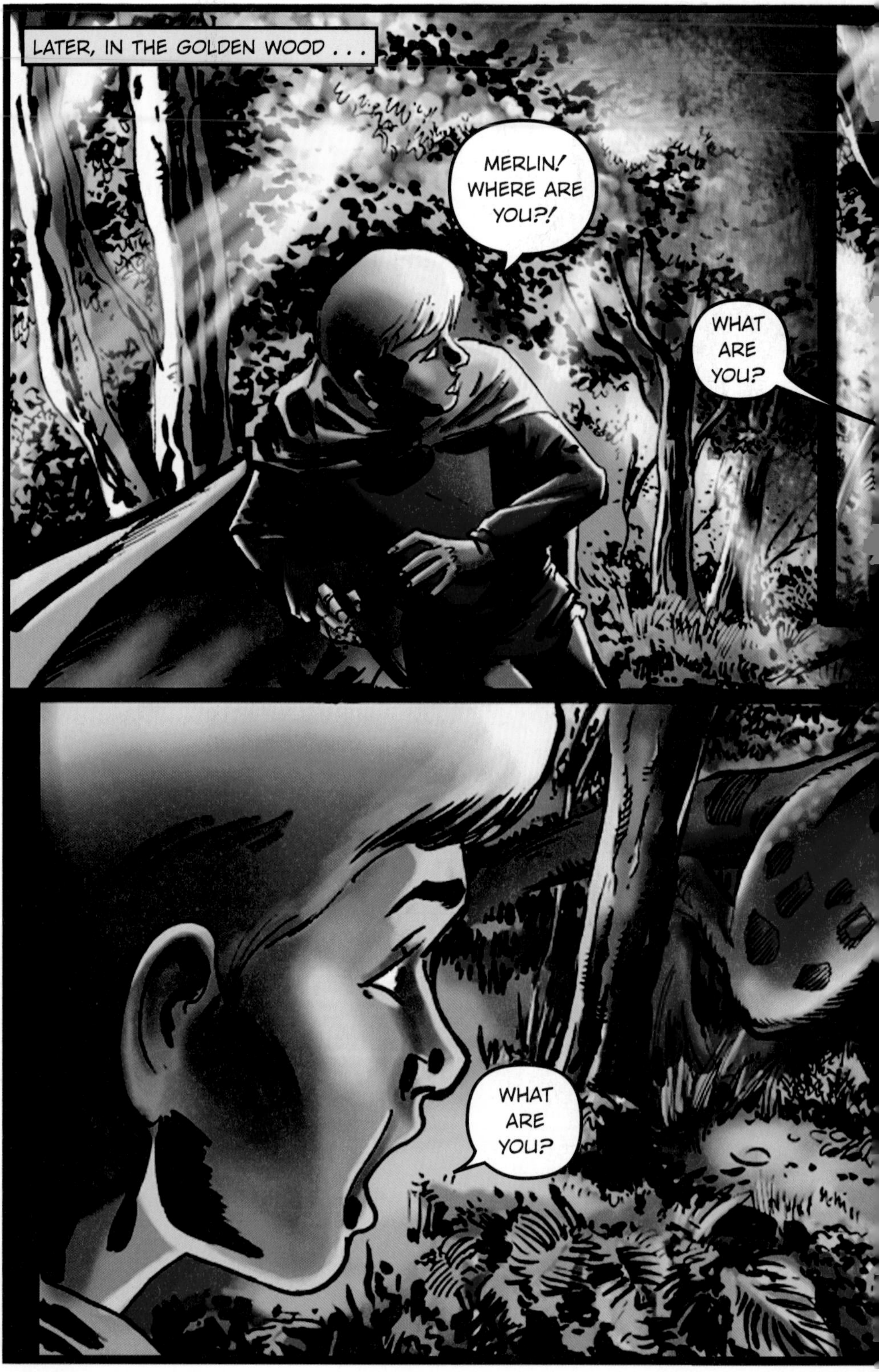
LATER, IN THE GOLDEN WOOD . . .
MERLIN! WHERE ARE YOU?!
WHAT ARE YOU?
WHAT ARE YOU?

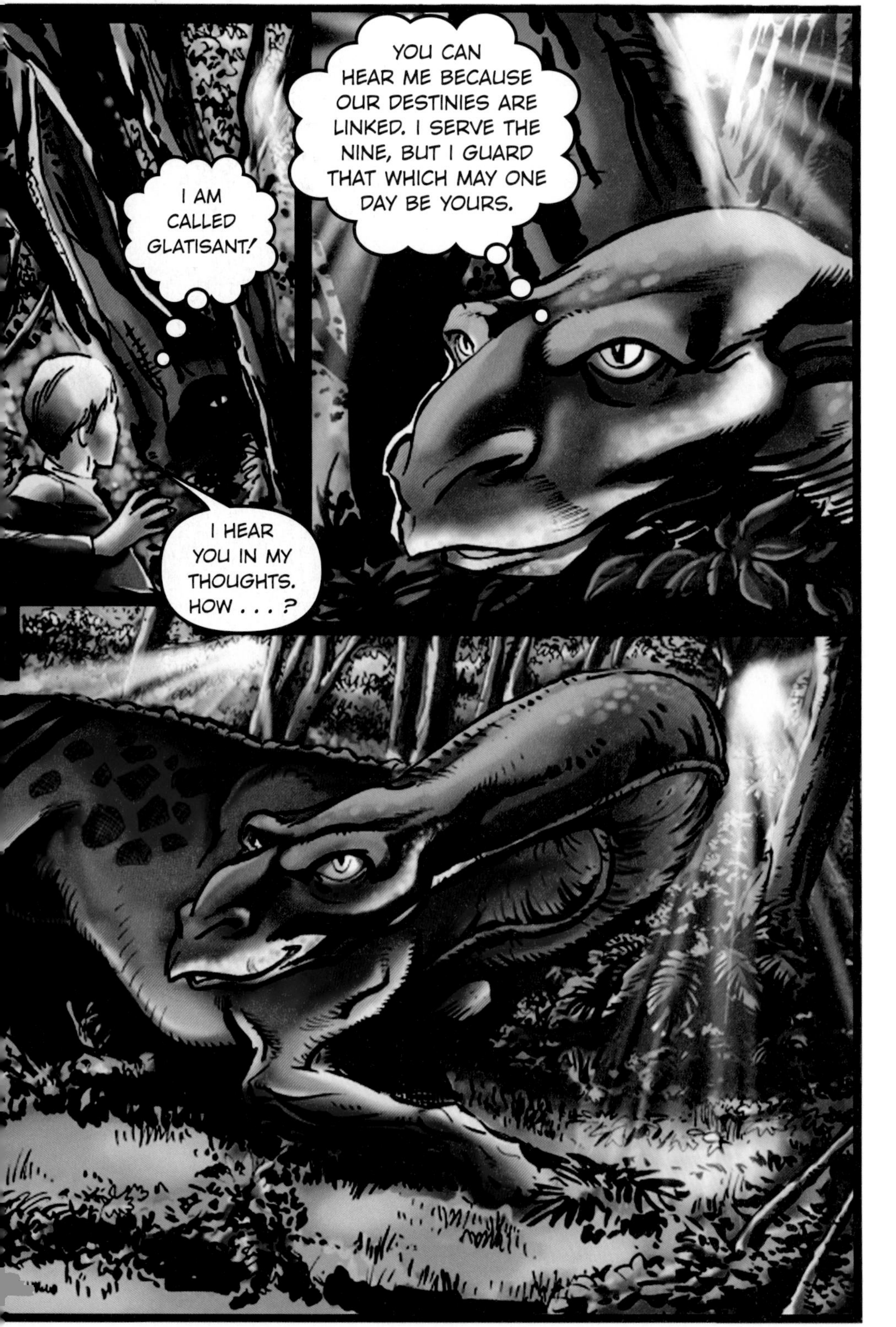
I AM CALLED GLATISANT!
I HEAR YOU IN MY THOUGHTS. HOW . . . ?
YOU CAN HEAR ME BECAUSE OUR DESTINIES ARE LINKED. I SERVE THE NINE, BUT I GUARD THAT WHICH MAY ONE DAY BE YOURS.

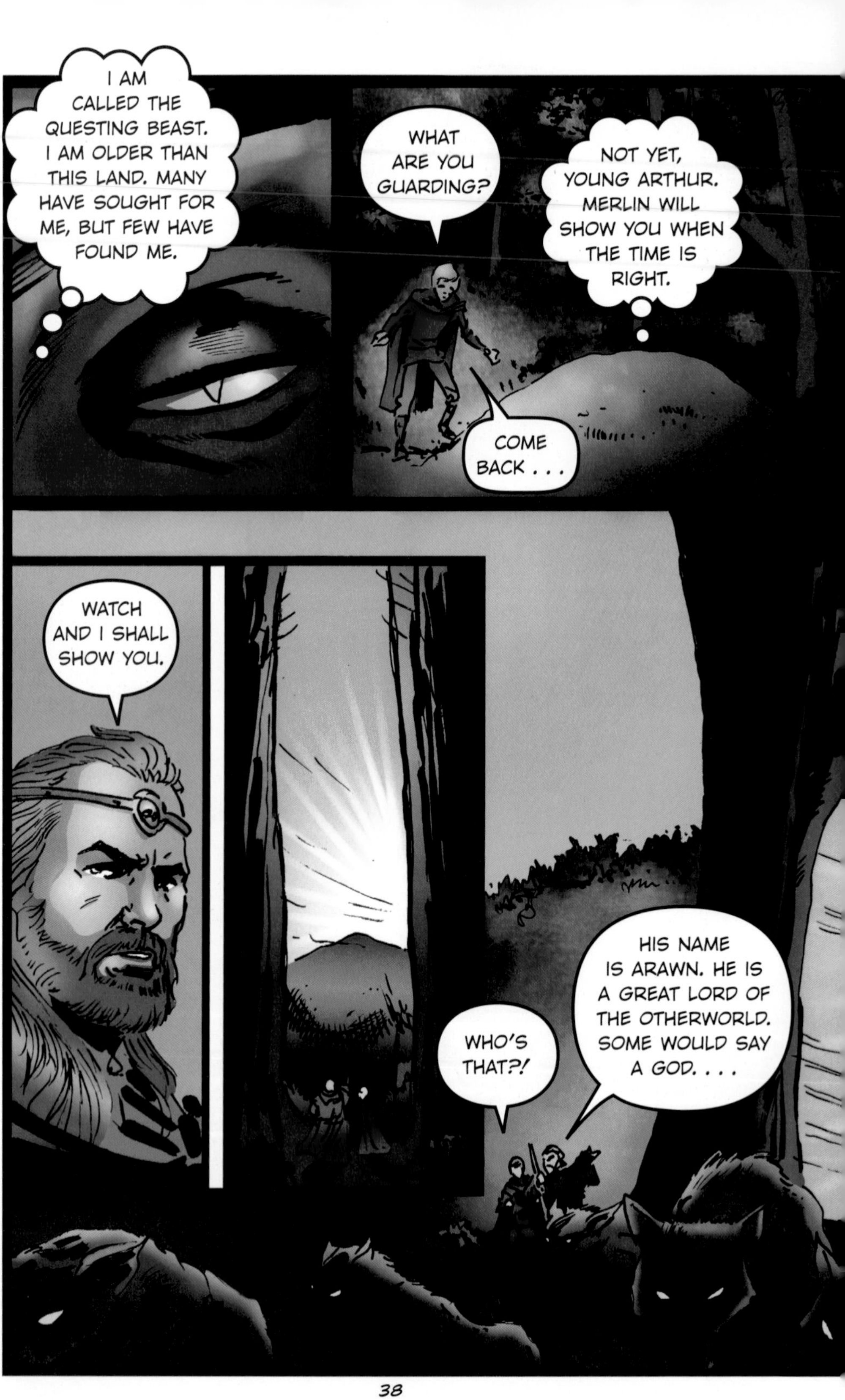
I AM CALLED THE QUESTING BEAST. I AM OLDER THAN THIS LAND. MANY HAVE SOUGHT FOR ME, BUT FEW HAVE FOUND ME.
WHAT ARE YOU GUARDING?
NOT YET, YOUNG ARTHUR. MERLIN WILL SHOW YOU WHEN THE TIME IS RIGHT.
COME BACK . . .
WATCH AND I SHALL SHOW YOU.
WHO'S THAT?!
HIS NAME IS ARAWN. HE IS A GREAT LORD OF THE OTHERWORLD. SOME WOULD SAY A GOD. . . .

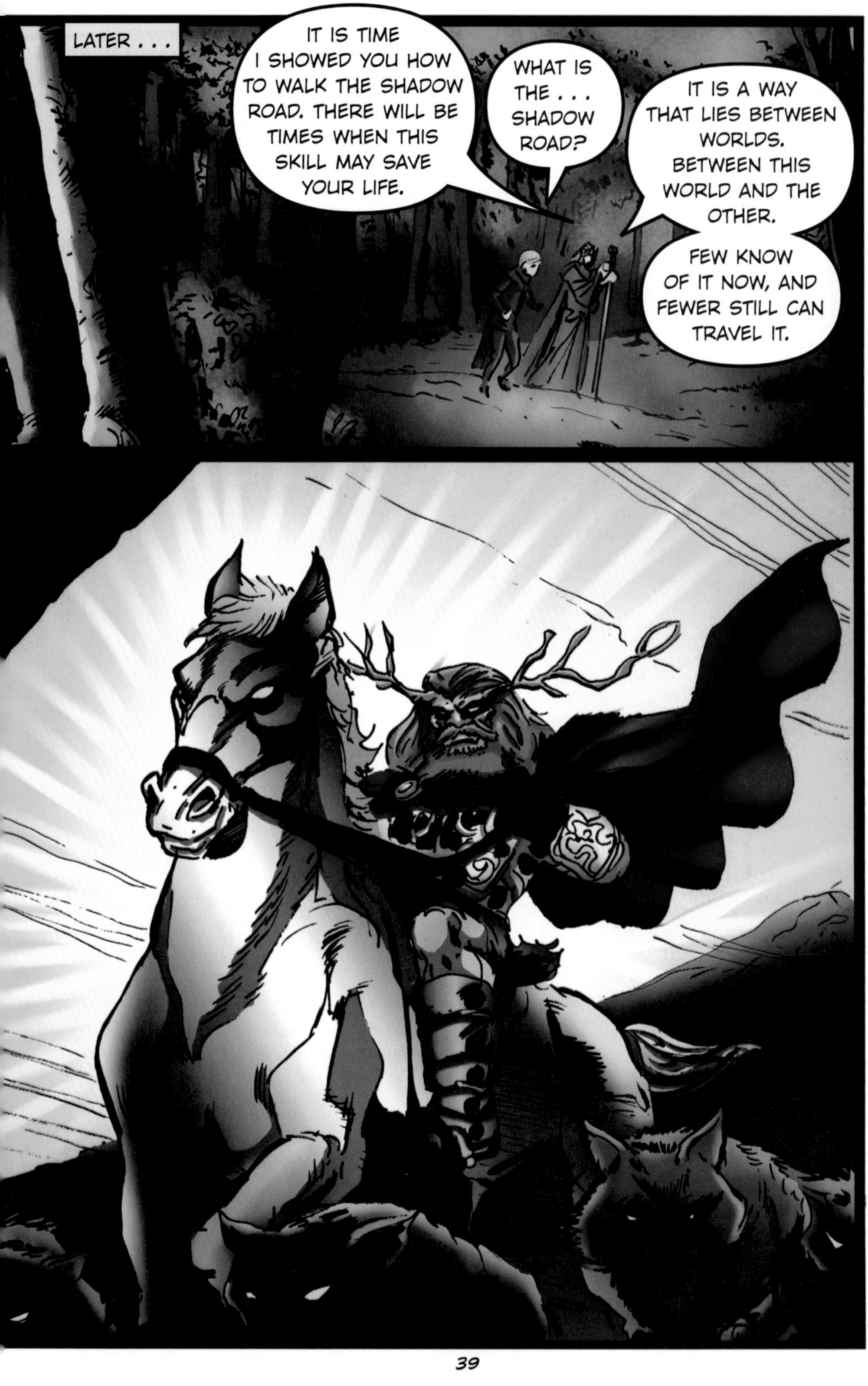
LATER . . .
IT IS TIME I SHOWED YOU HOW TO WALK THE SHADOW ROAD. THERE WILL BE TIMES WHEN THIS SKILL MAY SAVE YOUR LIFE.
WHAT IS THE . . . SHADOW ROAD?
IT IS A WAY THAT LIES BETWEEN WORLDS. BETWEEN THIS WORLD AND THE OTHER.
FEW KNOW OF IT NOW, AND FEWER STILL CAN TRAVEL IT.

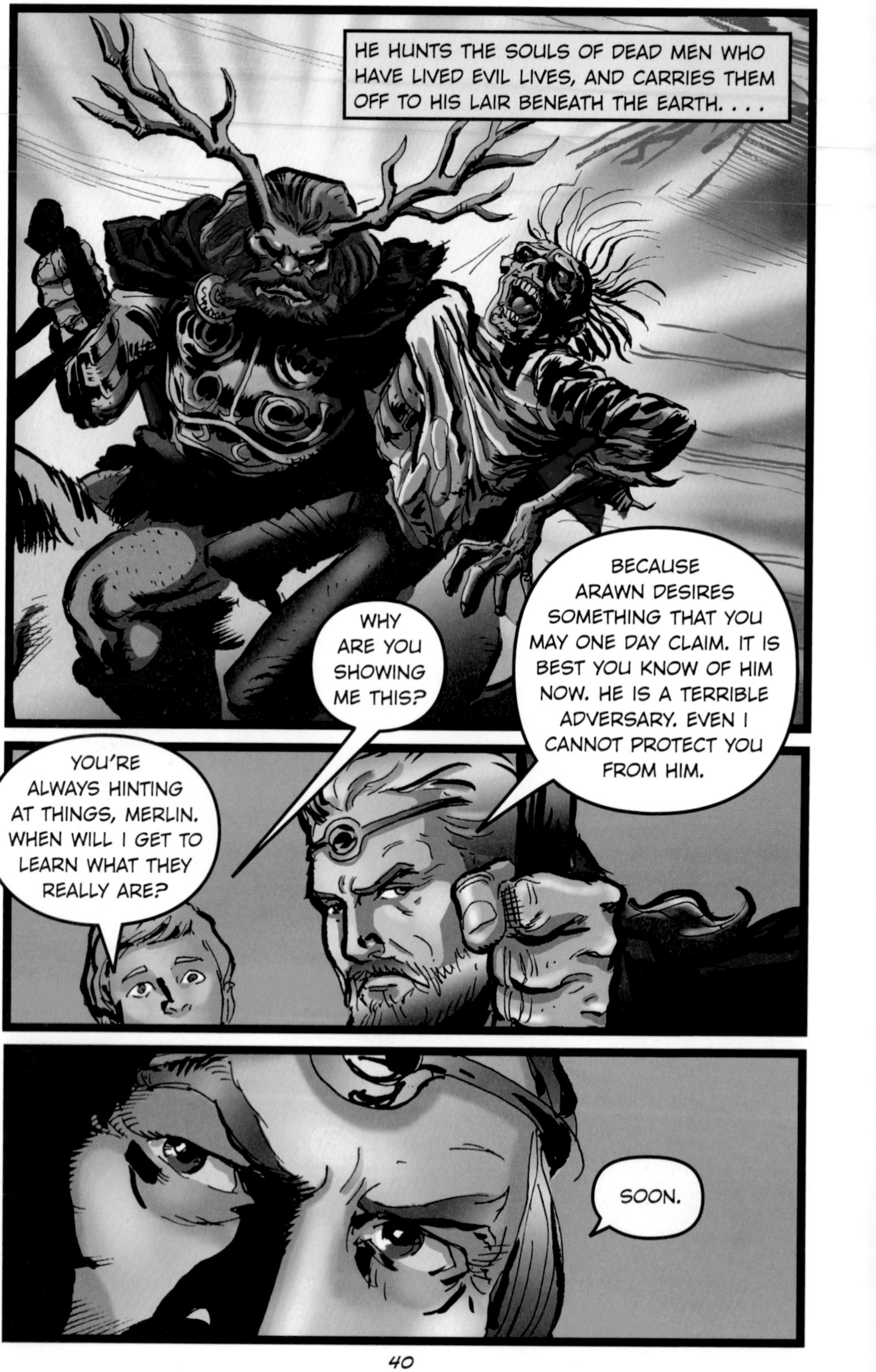
HE HUNTS THE SOULS OF DEAD MEN WHO HAVE LIVED EVIL LIVES, AND CARRIES THEM OFF TO HIS LAIR BENEATH THE EARTH. . . .
WHY ARE YOU SHOWING ME THIS?
BECAUSE ARAWN DESIRES SOMETHING THAT YOU MAY ONE DAY CLAIM. IT IS BEST YOU KNOW OF HIM NOW. HE IS A TERRIBLE ADVERSARY. EVEN I CANNOT PROTECT YOU FROM HIM.
YOU'RE ALWAYS HINTING AT THINGS, MERLIN. WHEN WILL I GET TO LEARN WHAT THEY REALLY ARE?
SOON.

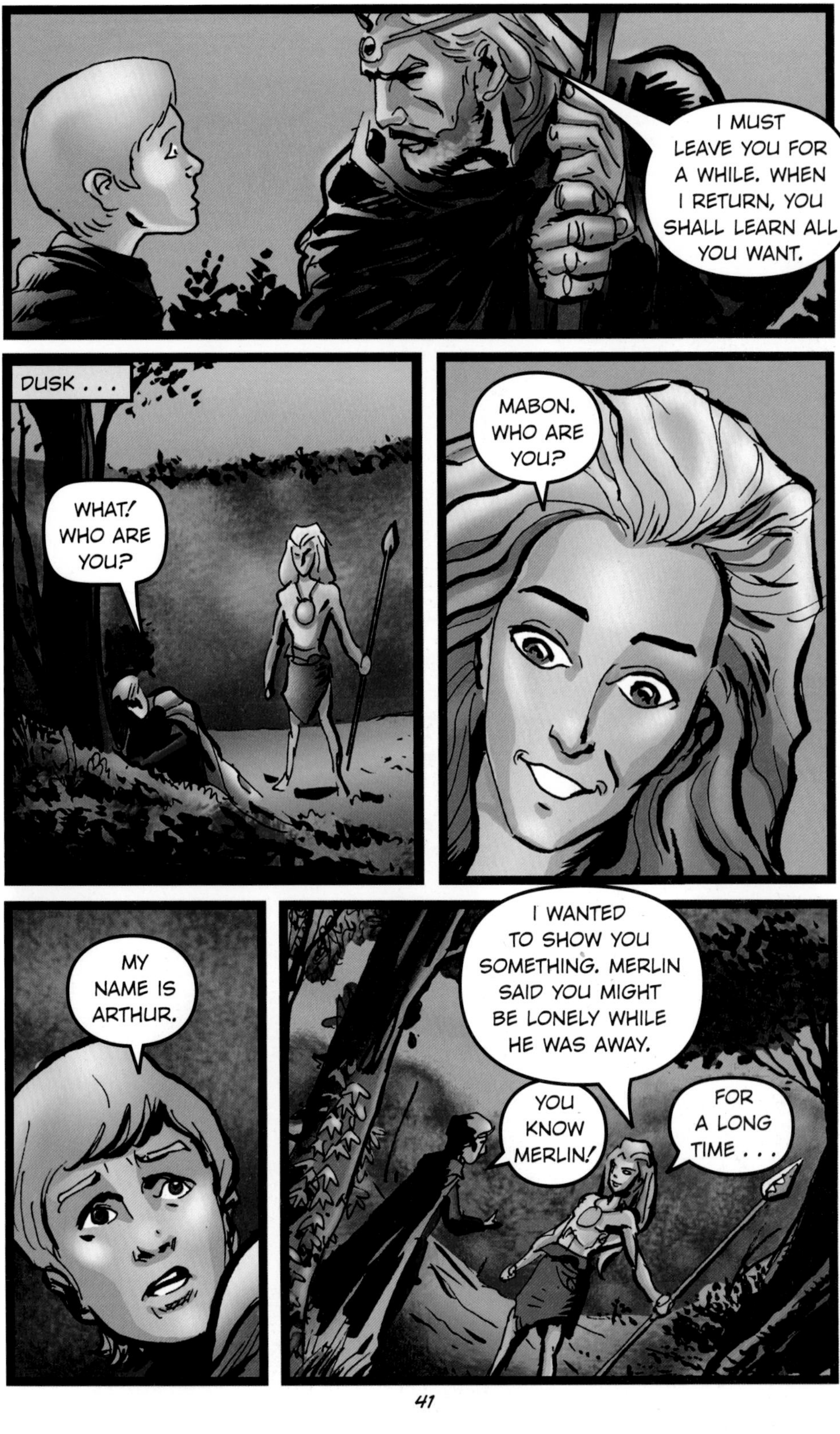
I MUST LEAVE YOU FOR A WHILE. WHEN I RETURN, YOU SHALL LEARN ALL YOU WANT.
DUSK . . .
WHAT! WHO ARE YOU?
MABON. WHO ARE YOU?
MY NAME IS ARTHUR.
I WANTED TO SHOW YOU SOMETHING. MERLIN SAID YOU MIGHT BE LONELY WHILE HE WAS AWAY.
YOU KNOW MERLIN!
FOR A LONG TIME . . .

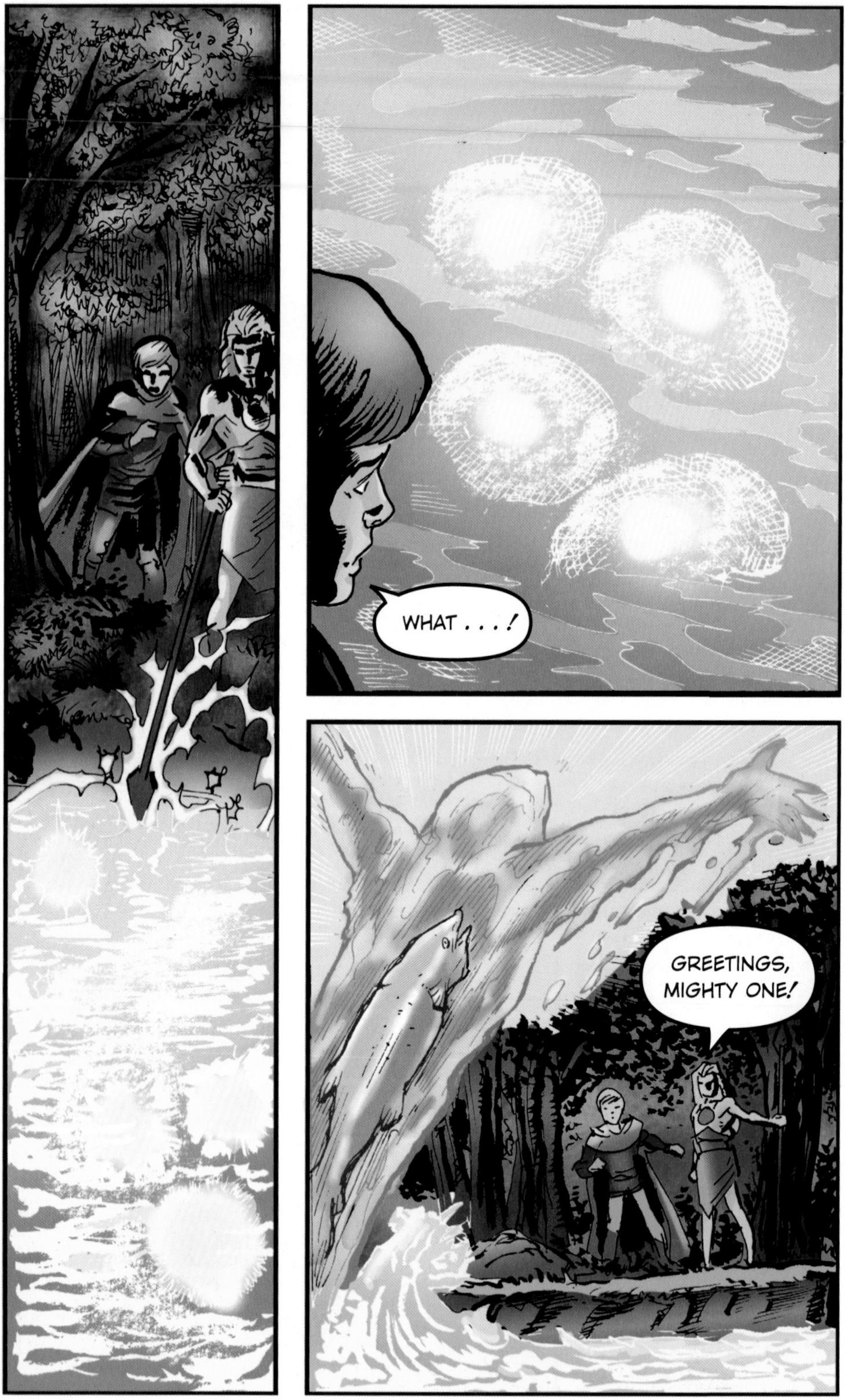
WHAT . . . !
GREETINGS, MIGHTY ONE!

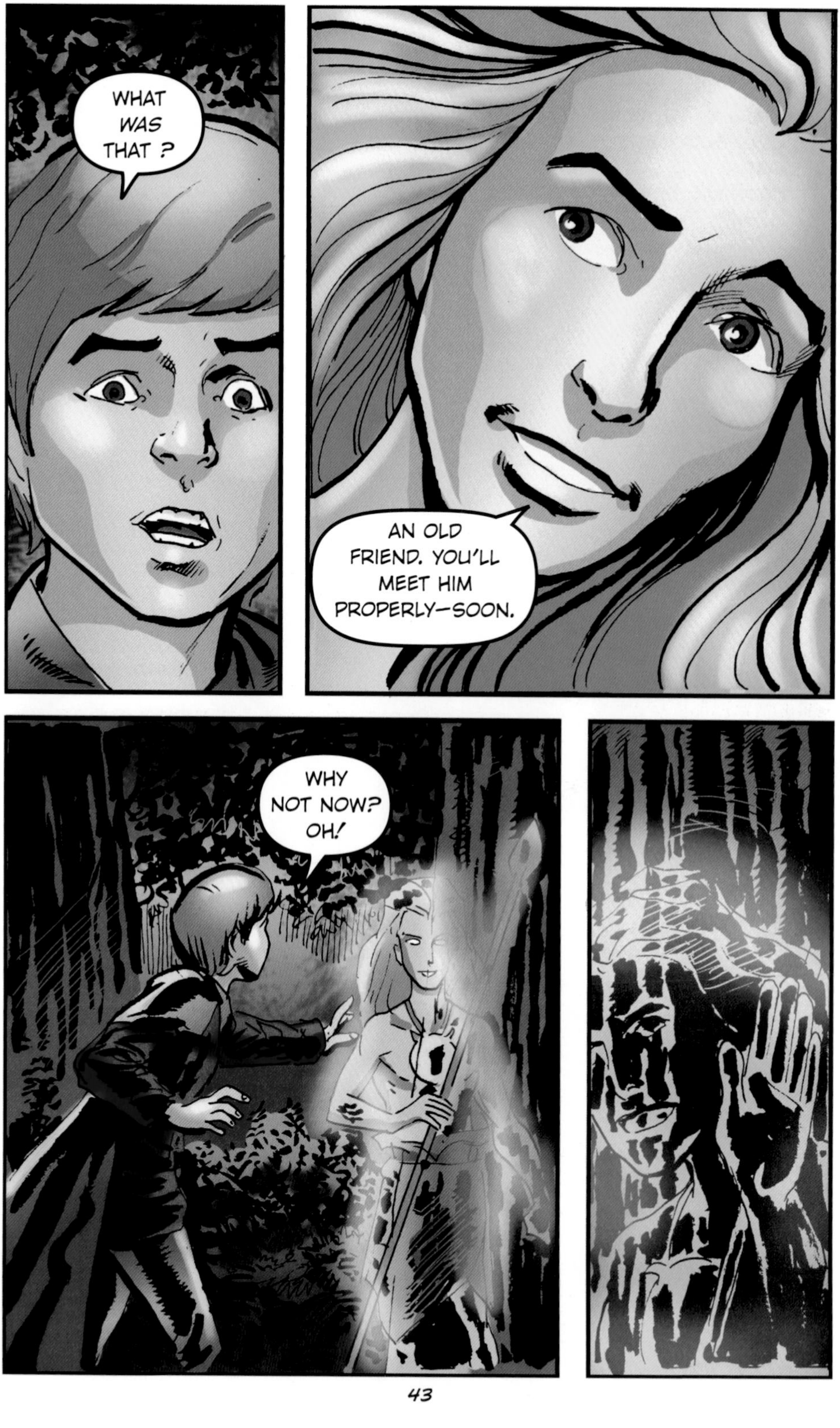
WHAT *WAS* THAT ?
AN OLD FRIEND. YOU'LL MEET HIM PROPERLY—SOON.
WHY NOT NOW? OH!

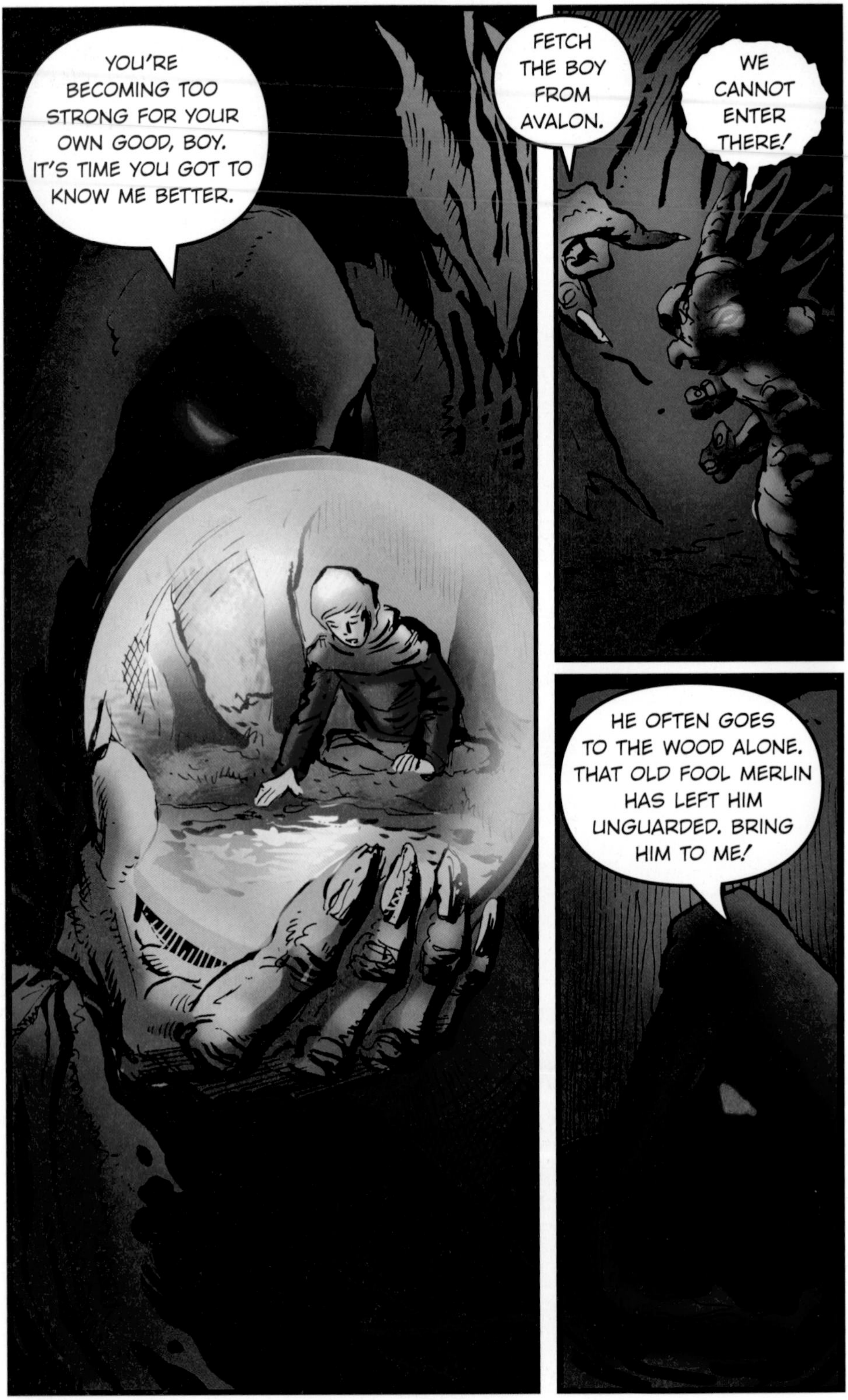
YOU'RE BECOMING TOO STRONG FOR YOUR OWN GOOD, BOY. IT'S TIME YOU GOT TO KNOW ME BETTER.
FETCH THE BOY FROM AVALON.
WE CANNOT ENTER THERE!
HE OFTEN GOES TO THE WOOD ALONE. THAT OLD FOOL MERLIN HAS LEFT HIM UNGUARDED. BRING HIM TO ME!

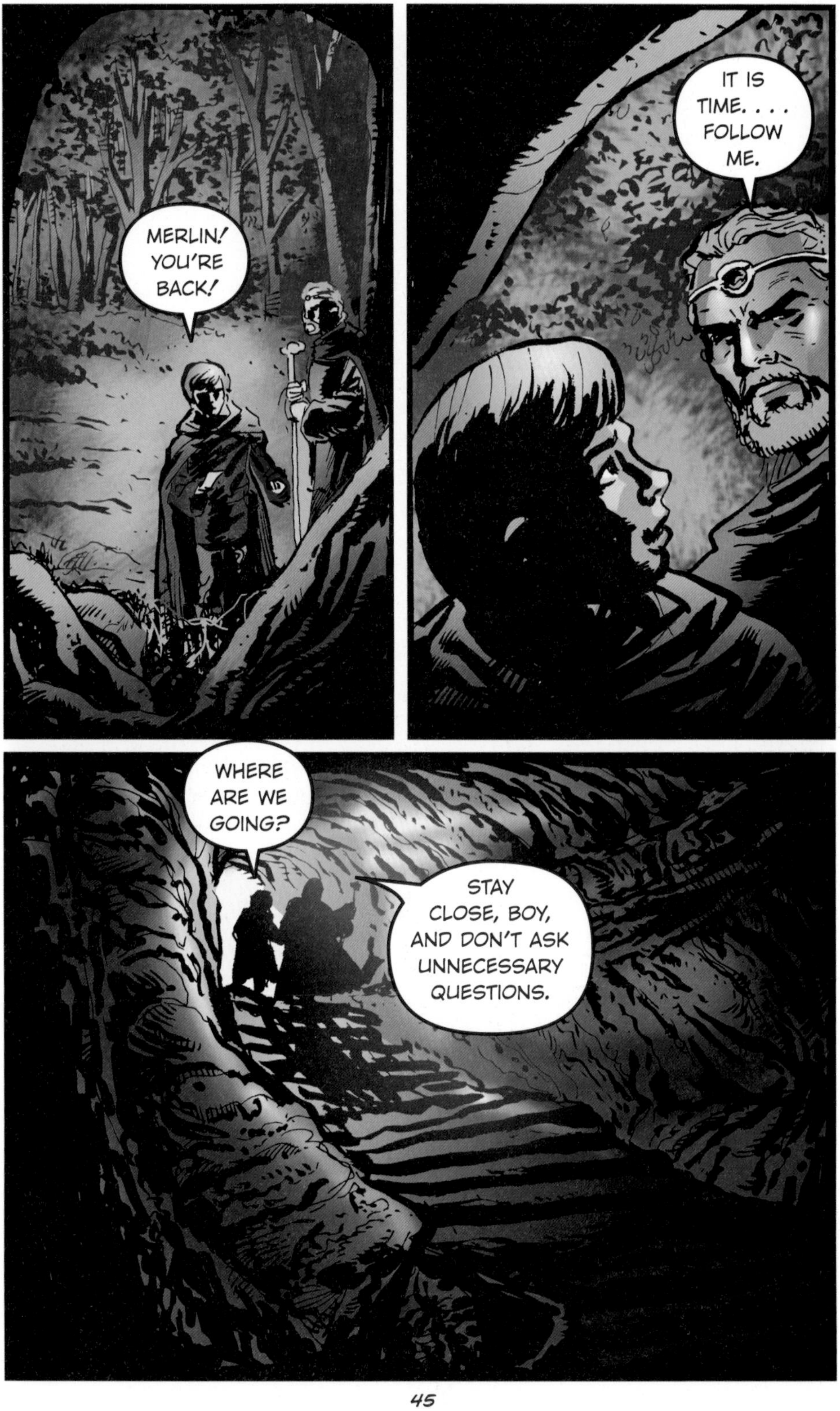
MERLIN! YOU'RE BACK!
IT IS TIME. . . . FOLLOW ME.
WHERE ARE WE GOING?
STAY CLOSE, BOY, AND DON'T ASK UNNECESSARY QUESTIONS.

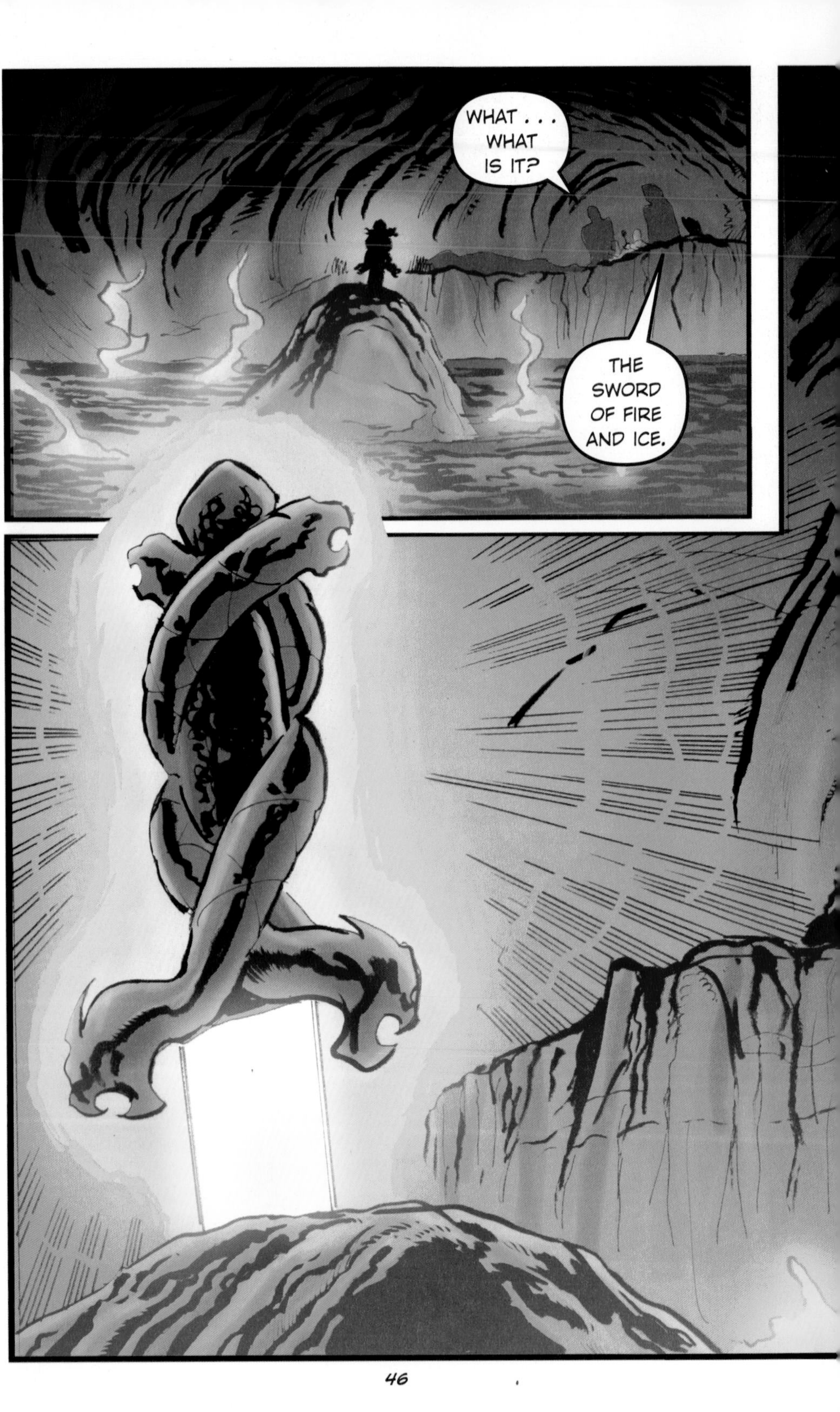
WHAT . . . WHAT IS IT?
THE SWORD OF FIRE AND ICE.

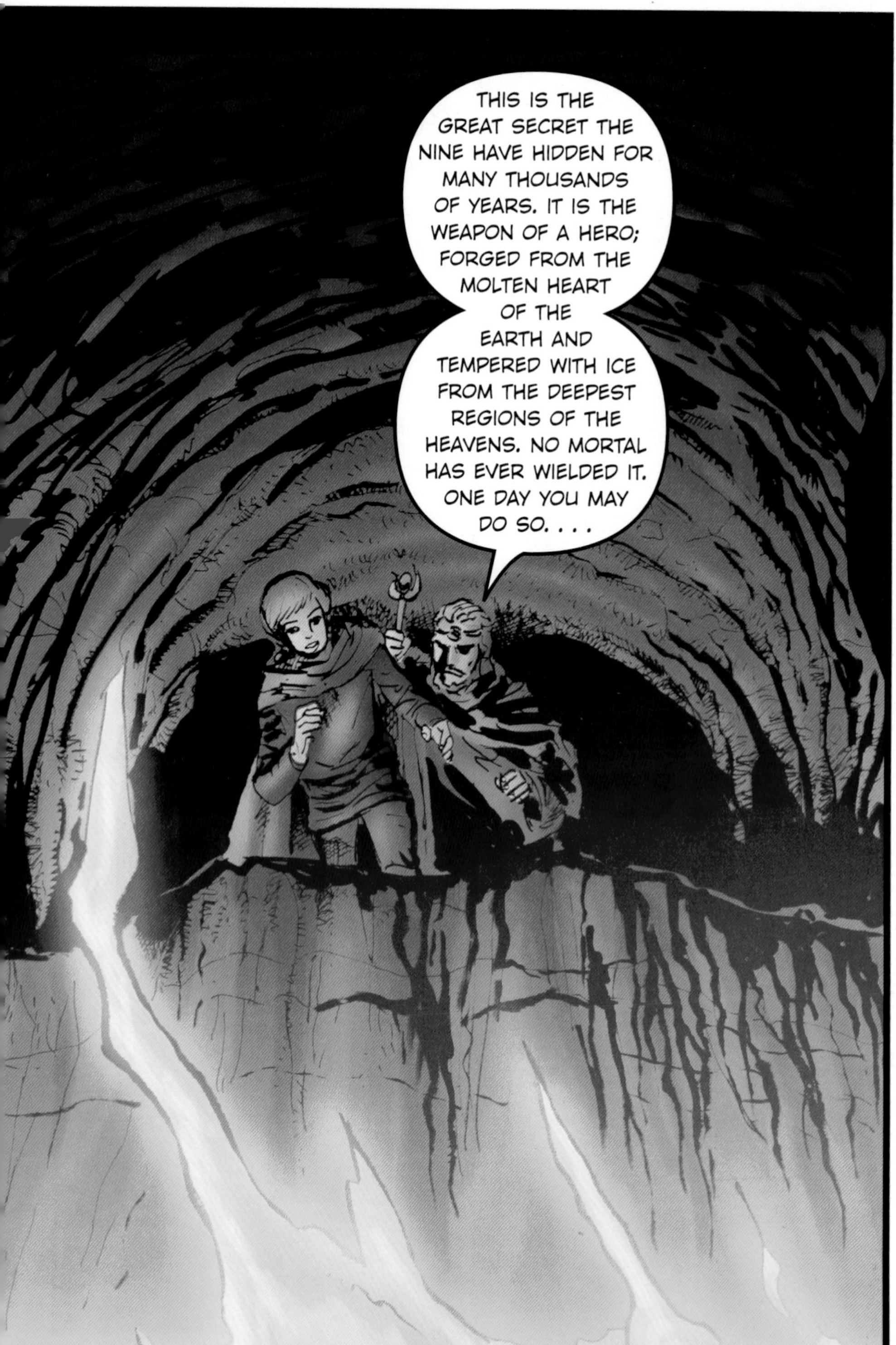
THIS IS THE GREAT SECRET THE NINE HAVE HIDDEN FOR MANY THOUSANDS OF YEARS. IT IS THE WEAPON OF A HERO; FORGED FROM THE MOLTEN HEART OF THE
EARTH AND TEMPERED WITH ICE FROM THE DEEPEST REGIONS OF THE HEAVENS. NO MORTAL HAS EVER WIELDED IT. ONE DAY YOU MAY DO SO. . . .

THIS IS NOT YOUR PLACE, MERLIN. NOR IS IT TIME.

ARGANTE. I JUDGED IT TIME FOR THE BOY TO SEE HIS HERITAGE.

POSSIBLE HERITAGE. THE OUTCOME IS NOT YET KNOWN.

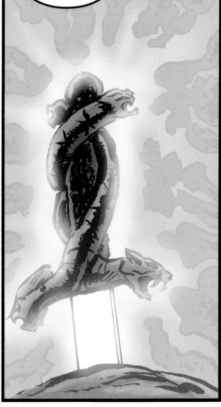

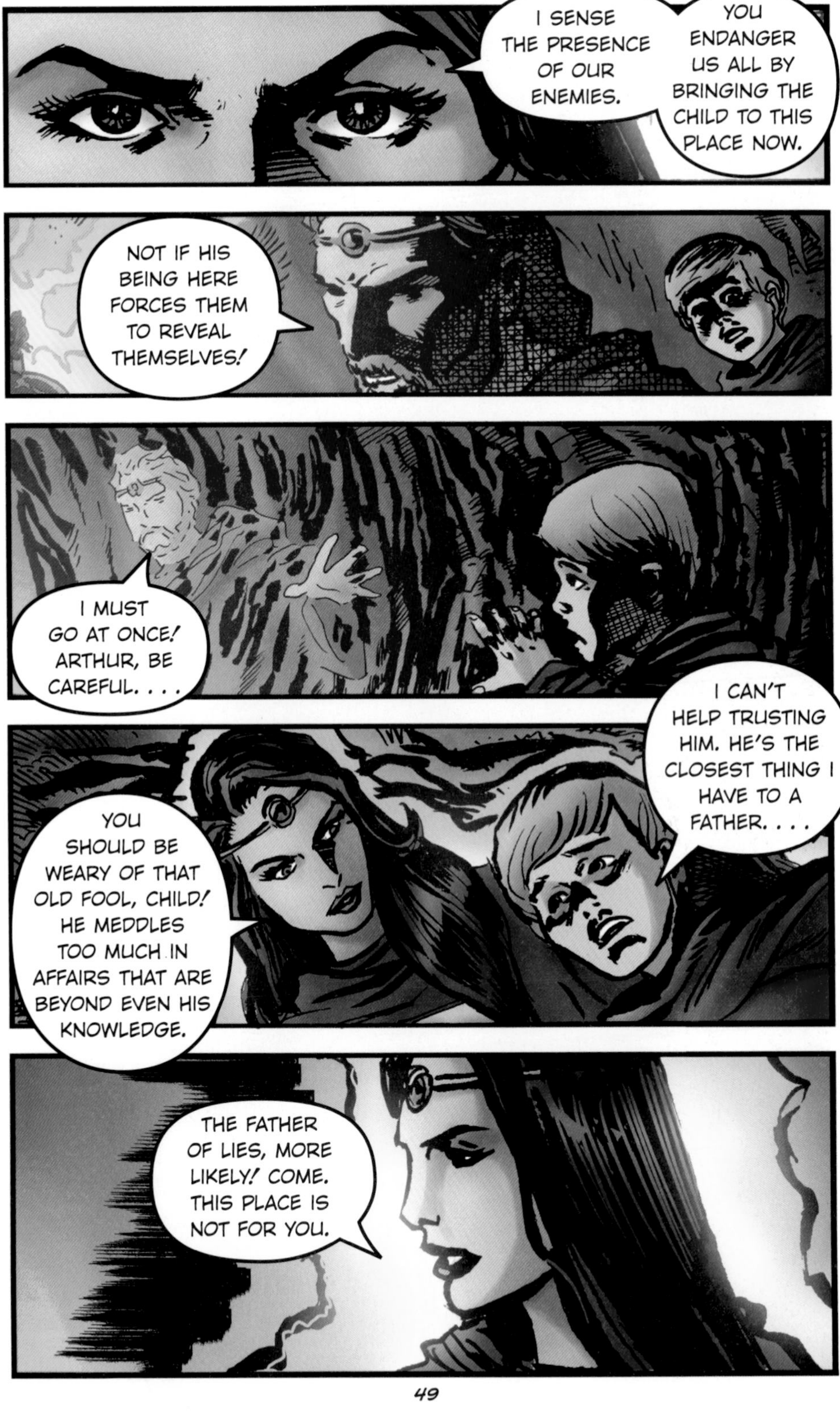
I SENSE THE PRESENCE OF OUR ENEMIES.
YOU ENDANGER US ALL BY BRINGING THE CHILD TO THIS PLACE NOW.
NOT IF HIS BEING HERE FORCES THEM TO REVEAL THEMSELVES!
I MUST GO AT ONCE! ARTHUR, BE CAREFUL. . . .
YOU SHOULD BE WEARY OF THAT OLD FOOL, CHILD! HE MEDDLES TOO MUCH IN AFFAIRS THAT ARE BEYOND EVEN HIS KNOWLEDGE.
I CAN'T HELP TRUSTING HIM. HE'S THE CLOSEST THING I HAVE TO A FATHER. . . .
THE FATHER OF LIES, MORE LIKELY! COME. THIS PLACE IS NOT FOR YOU.

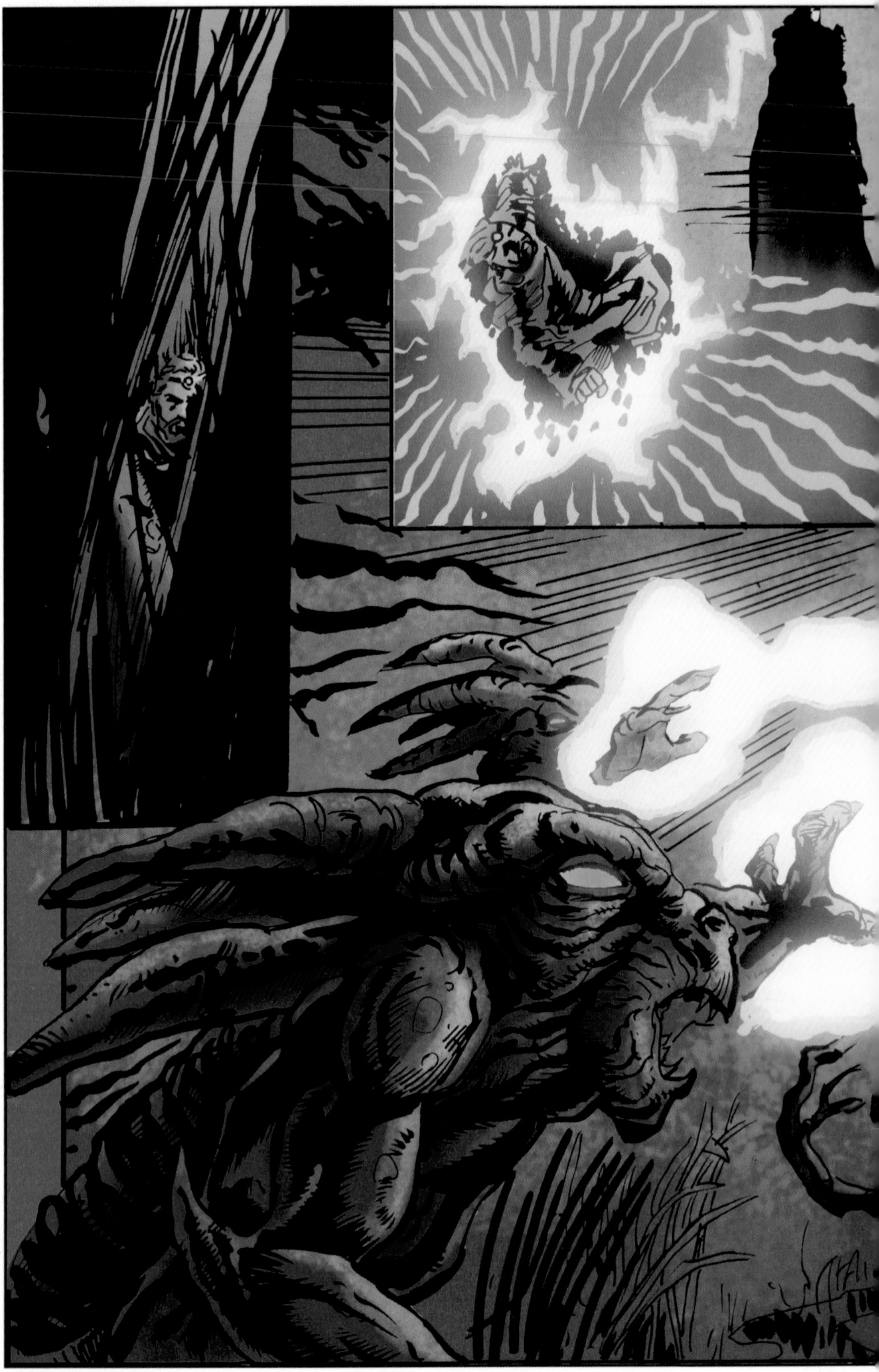

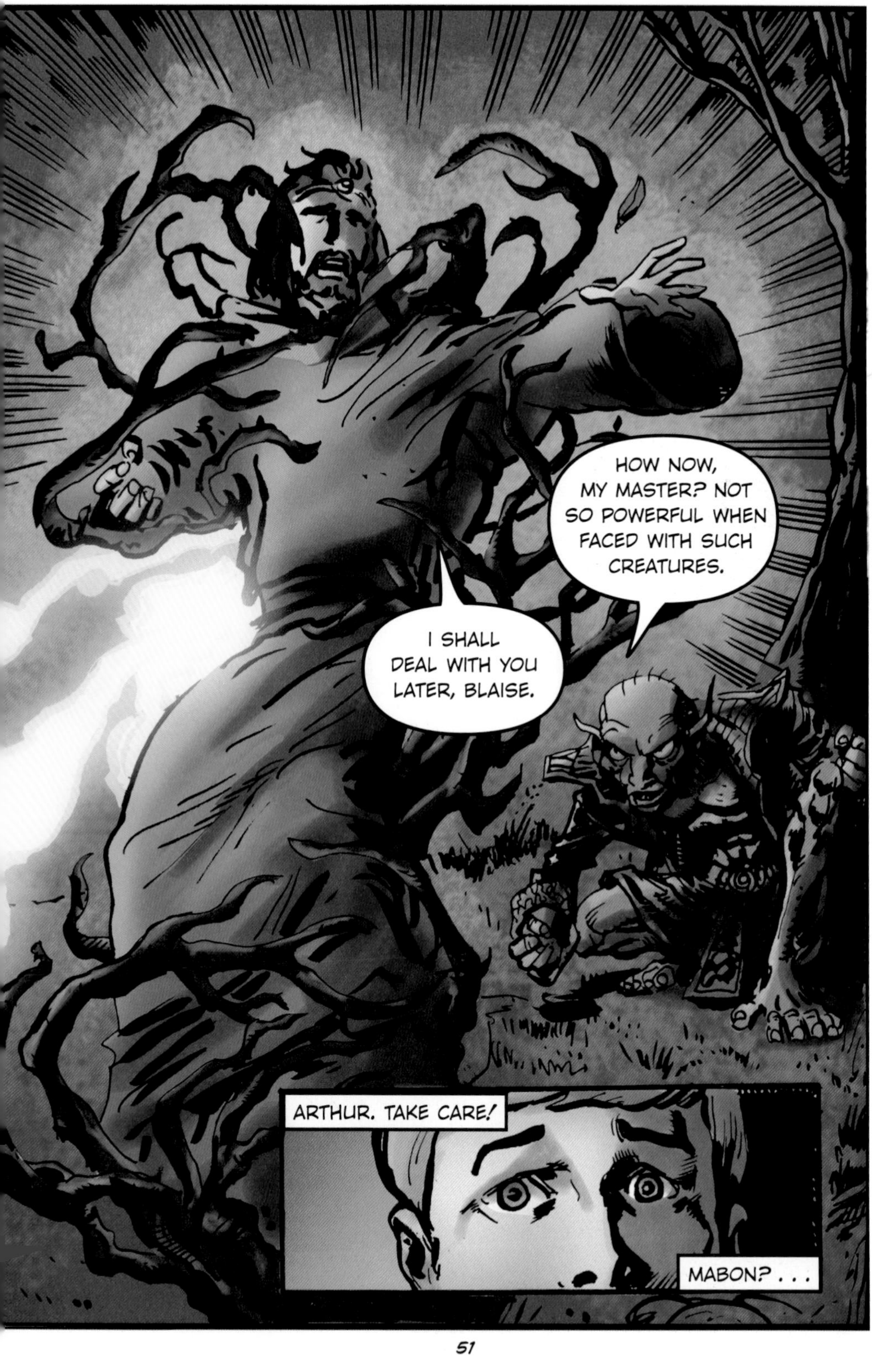
HOW NOW, MY MASTER? NOT SO POWERFUL WHEN FACED WITH SUCH CREATURES.
I SHALL DEAL WITH YOU LATER, BLAISE.
ARTHUR. TAKE CARE!
MABON? . . .

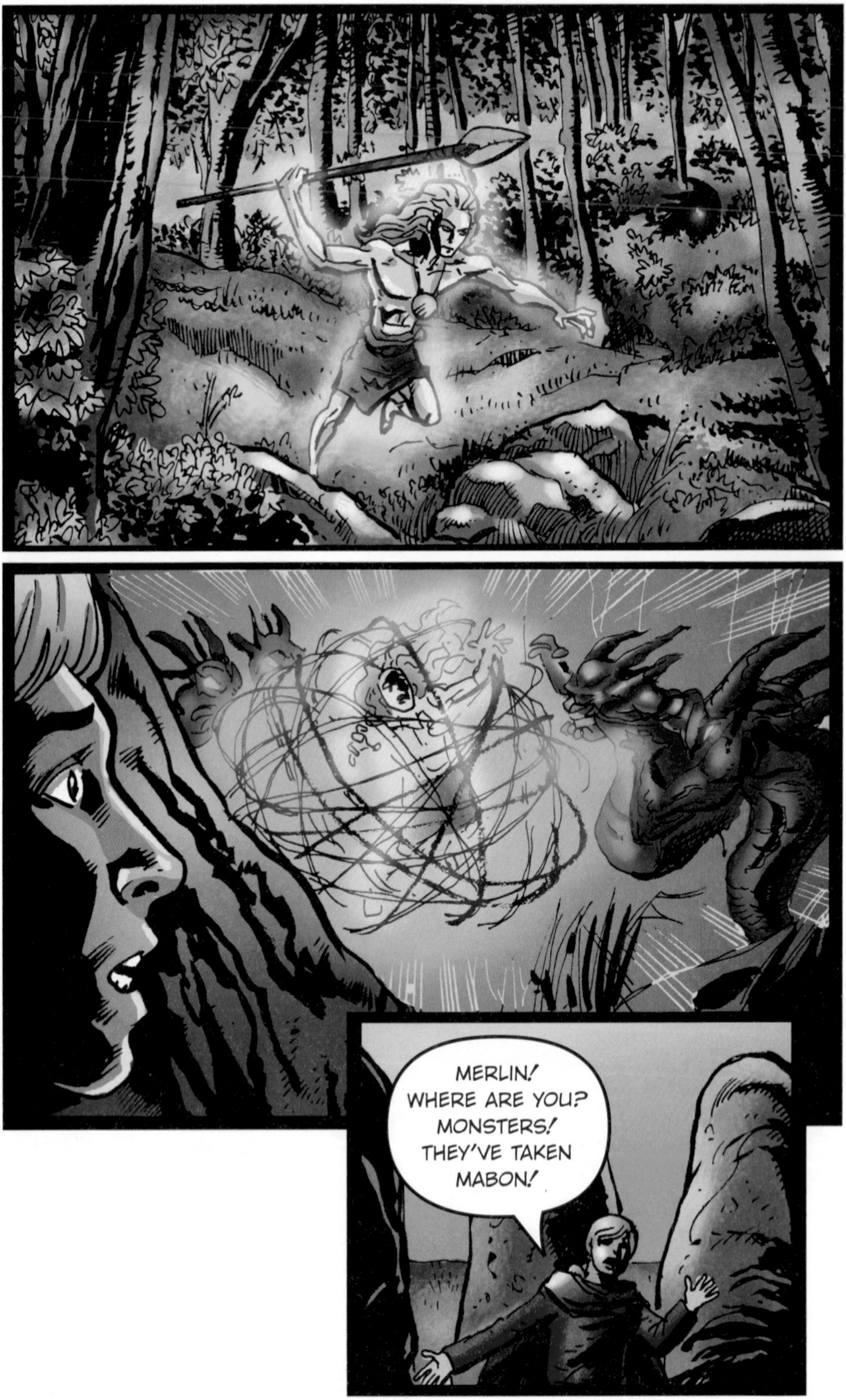
MERLIN! WHERE ARE YOU? MONSTERS! THEY'VE TAKEN MABON!

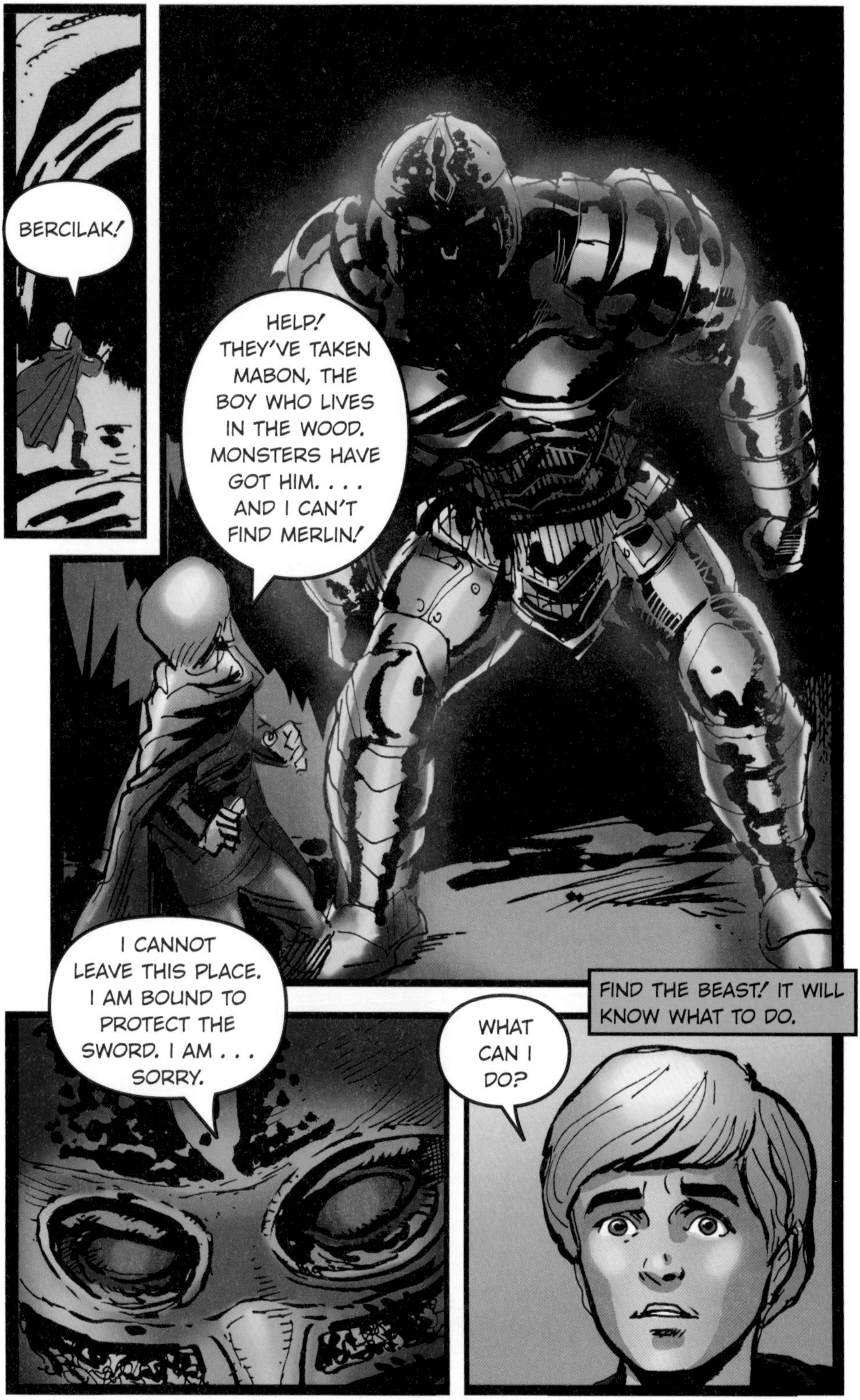
BERCILAK!
HELP! THEY'VE TAKEN MABON, THE BOY WHO LIVES IN THE WOOD. MONSTERS HAVE GOT HIM. . . . AND I CAN'T FIND MERLIN!
I CANNOT LEAVE THIS PLACE. I AM BOUND TO PROTECT THE SWORD. I AM . . . SORRY.
WHAT CAN I DO?
FIND THE BEAST! IT WILL KNOW WHAT TO DO.

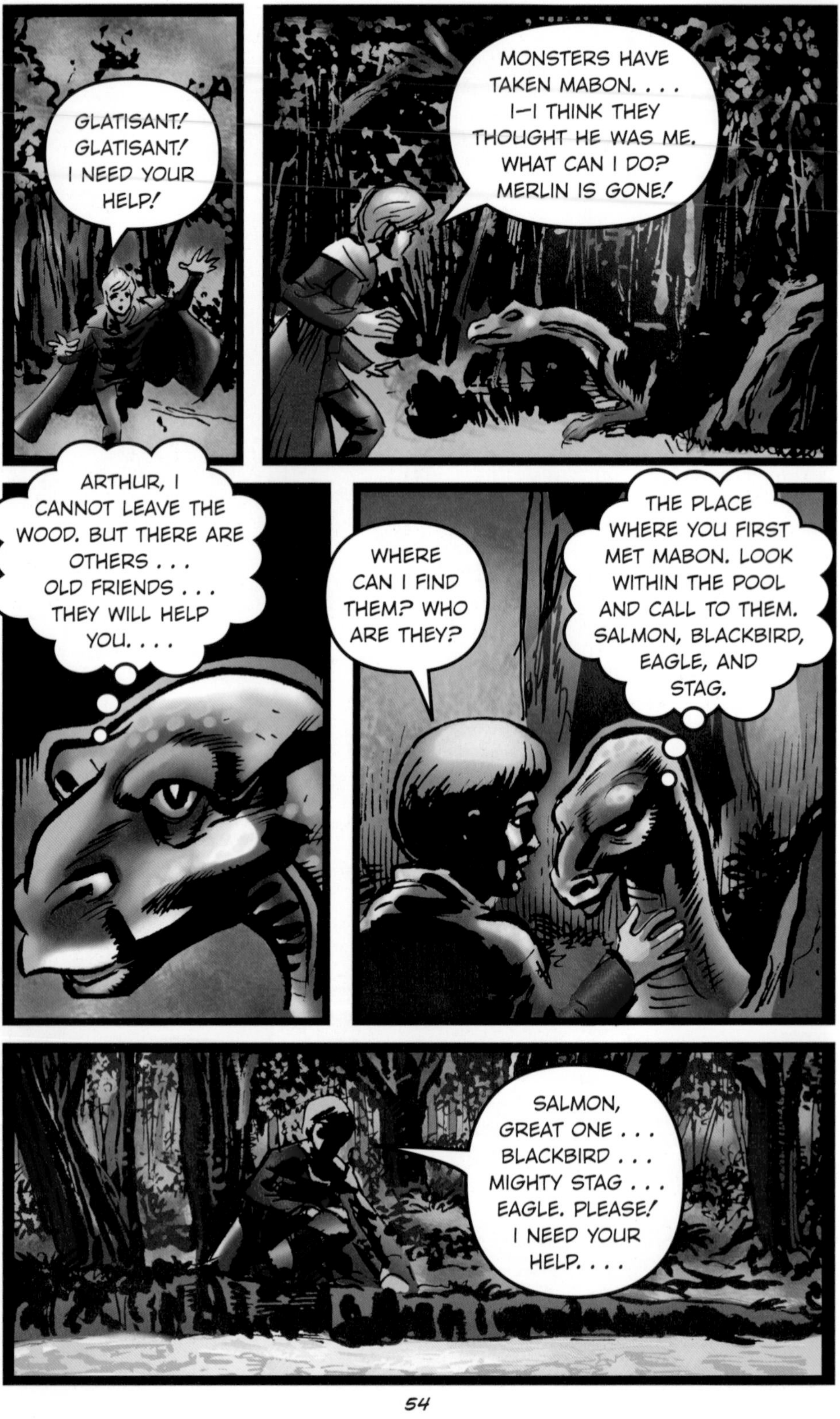
GLATISANT! GLATISANT! I NEED YOUR HELP!
MONSTERS HAVE TAKEN MABON. . . . I—I THINK THEY THOUGHT HE WAS ME. WHAT CAN I DO? MERLIN IS GONE!
ARTHUR, I CANNOT LEAVE THE WOOD. BUT THERE ARE OTHERS . . . OLD FRIENDS . . . THEY WILL HELP YOU. . . .
WHERE CAN I FIND THEM? WHO ARE THEY?
THE PLACE WHERE YOU FIRST MET MABON. LOOK WITHIN THE POOL AND CALL TO THEM. SALMON, BLACKBIRD, EAGLE, AND STAG.
SALMON, GREAT ONE . . . BLACKBIRD . . . MIGHTY STAG . . . EAGLE. PLEASE! I NEED YOUR HELP. . . .

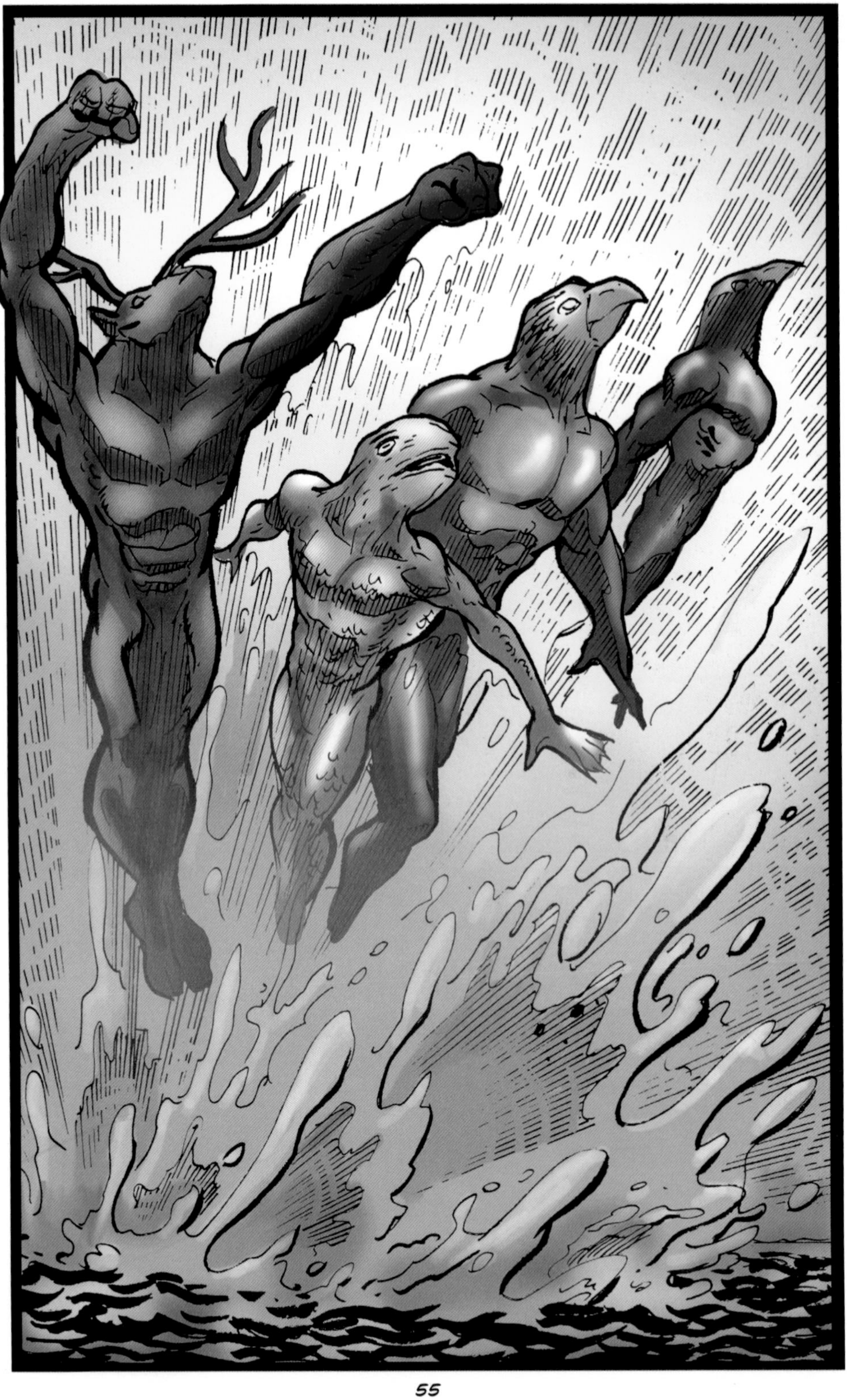

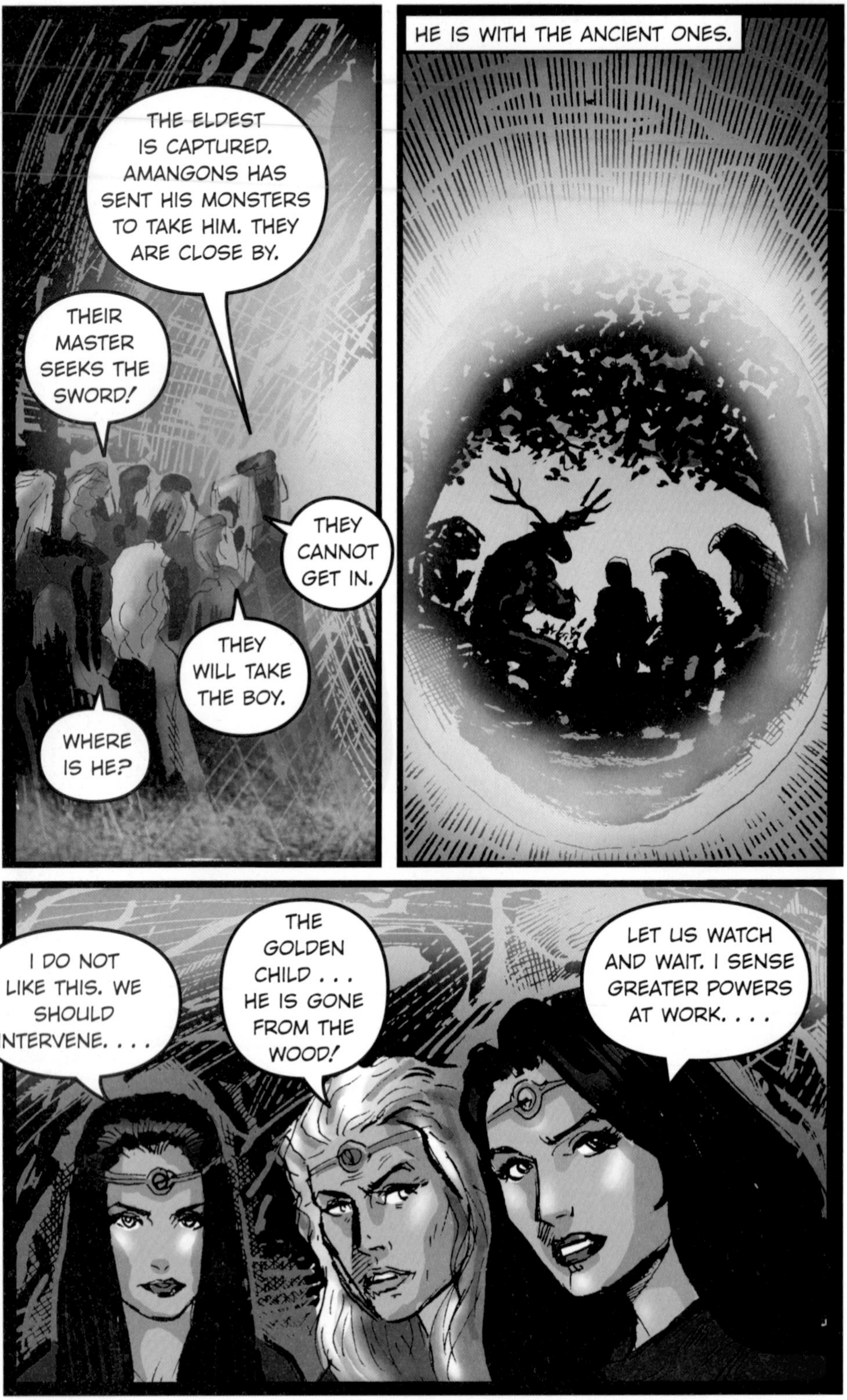
THE ELDEST IS CAPTURED. AMANGONS HAS SENT HIS MONSTERS TO TAKE HIM. THEY ARE CLOSE BY.
THEIR MASTER SEEKS THE SWORD!
THEY CANNOT GET IN.
THEY WILL TAKE THE BOY.
WHERE IS HE?
HE IS WITH THE ANCIENT ONES.
I DO NOT LIKE THIS. WE SHOULD INTERVENE. . . .
THE GOLDEN CHILD . . . HE IS GONE FROM THE WOOD!
LET US WATCH AND WAIT. I SENSE GREATER POWERS AT WORK. . . .

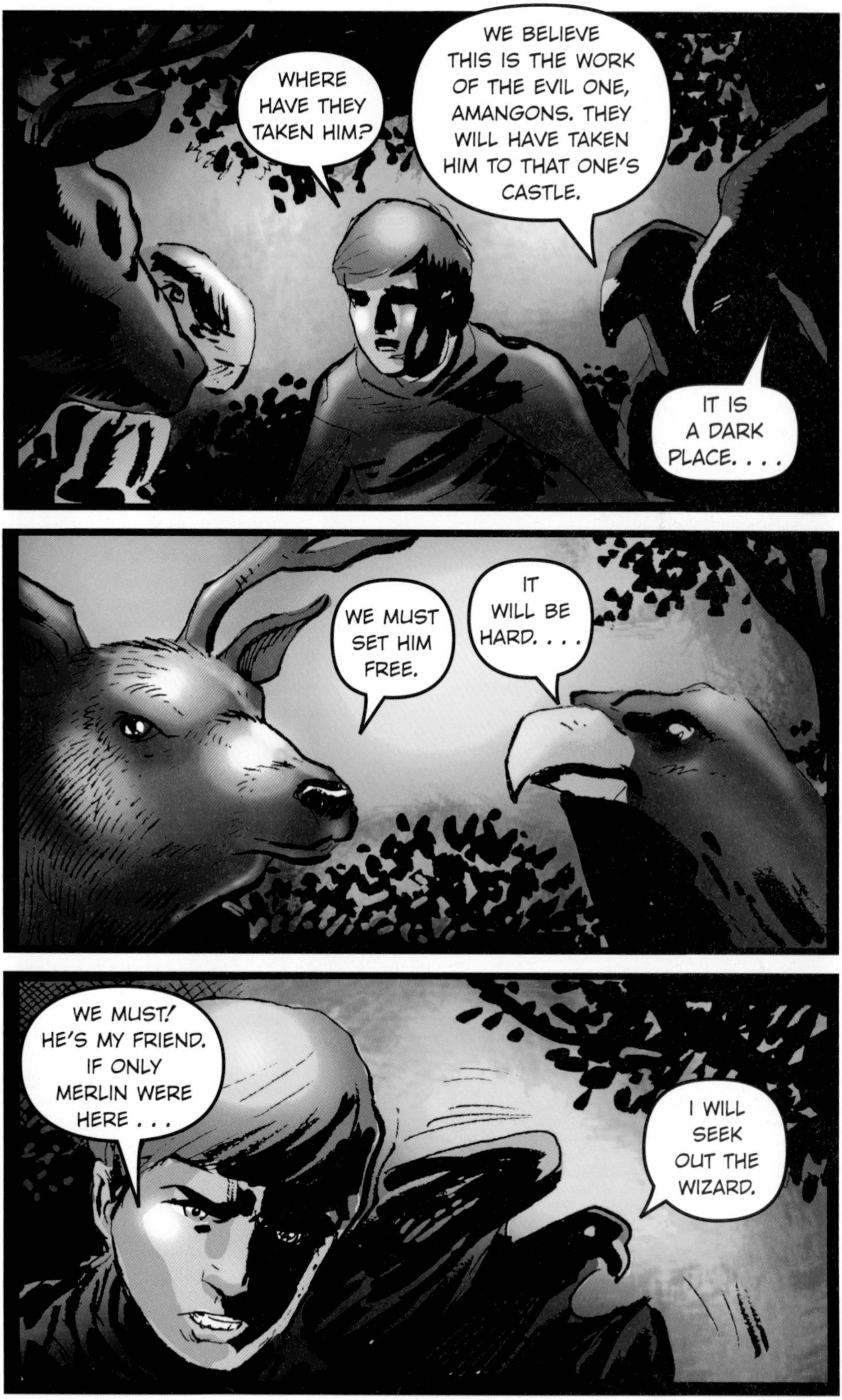
WHERE HAVE THEY TAKEN HIM?
WE BELIEVE THIS IS THE WORK OF THE EVIL ONE, AMANGONS. THEY WILL HAVE TAKEN HIM TO THAT ONE'S CASTLE.
IT IS A DARK PLACE. . . .
WE MUST SET HIM FREE.
IT WILL BE HARD. . . .
WE MUST! HE'S MY FRIEND. IF ONLY MERLIN WERE HERE . . .
I WILL SEEK OUT THE WIZARD.

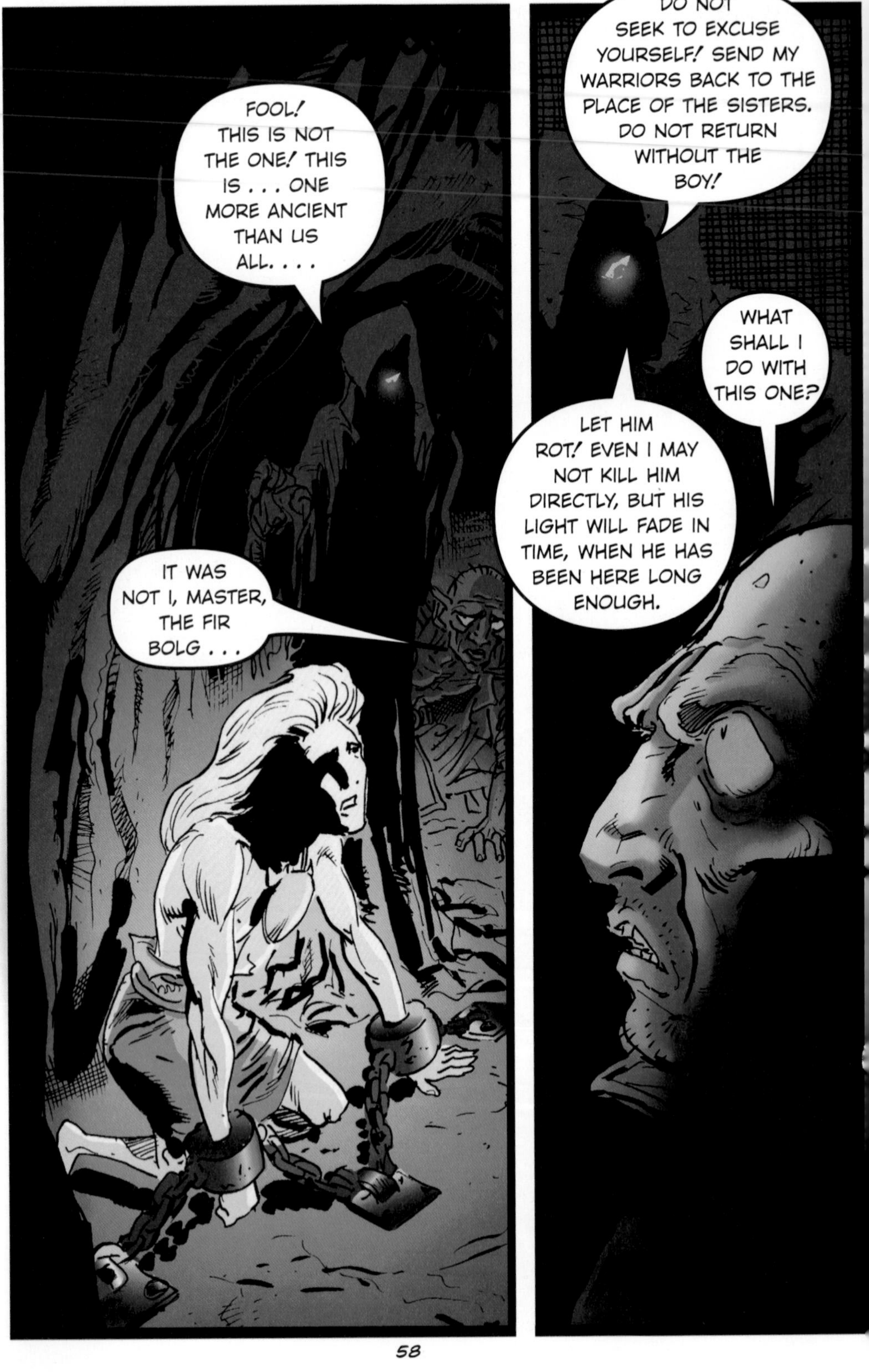
FOOL! THIS IS NOT THE ONE! THIS IS . . . ONE MORE ANCIENT THAN US ALL. . . .
IT WAS NOT I, MASTER, THE FIR BOLG . . .
DO NOT SEEK TO EXCUSE YOURSELF! SEND MY WARRIORS BACK TO THE PLACE OF THE SISTERS. DO NOT RETURN WITHOUT THE BOY!
WHAT SHALL I DO WITH THIS ONE?
LET HIM ROT! EVEN I MAY NOT KILL HIM DIRECTLY, BUT HIS LIGHT WILL FADE IN TIME, WHEN HE HAS BEEN HERE LONG ENOUGH.

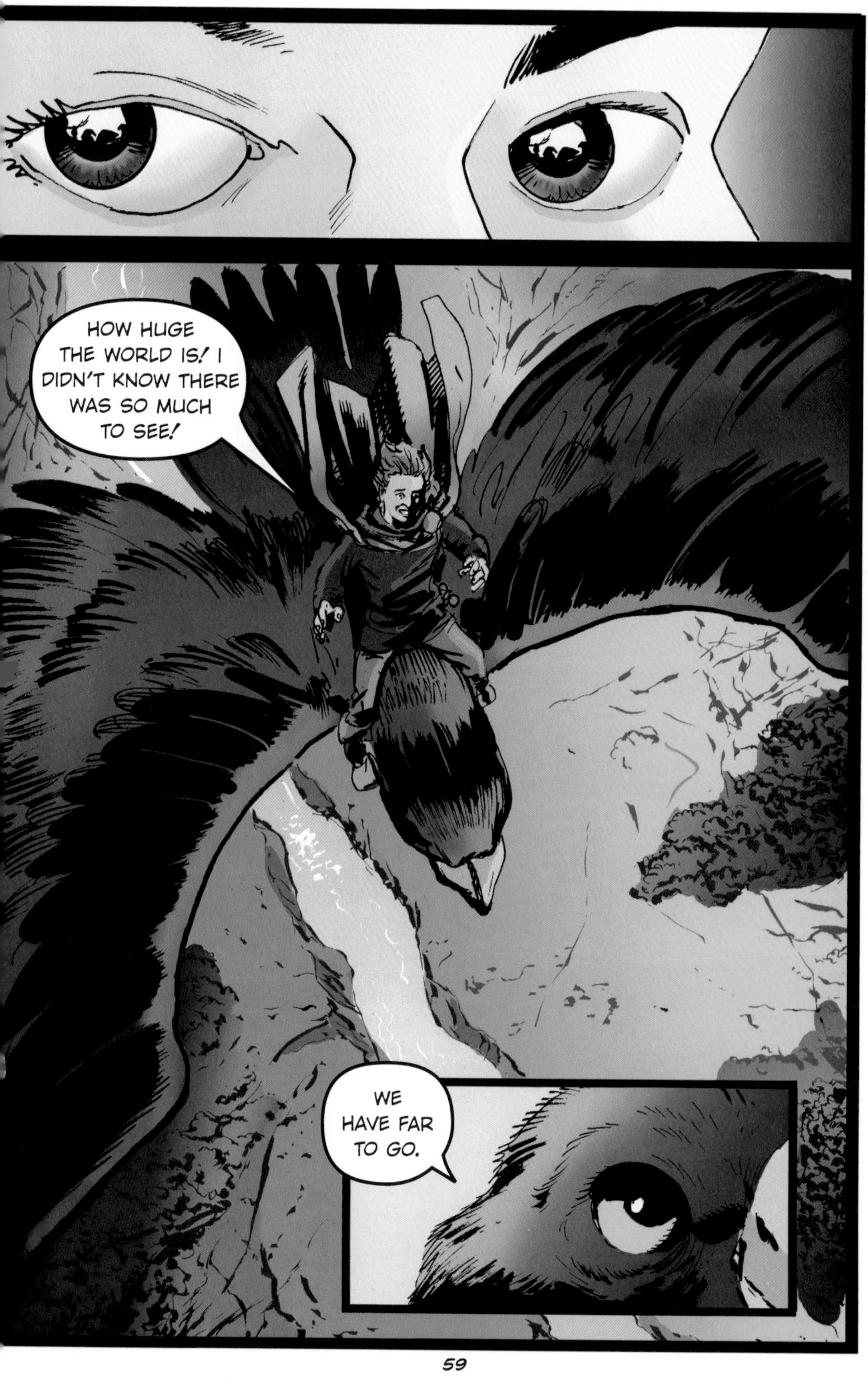
HOW HUGE THE WORLD IS! I DIDN'T KNOW THERE WAS SO MUCH TO SEE!
WE HAVE FAR TO GO.

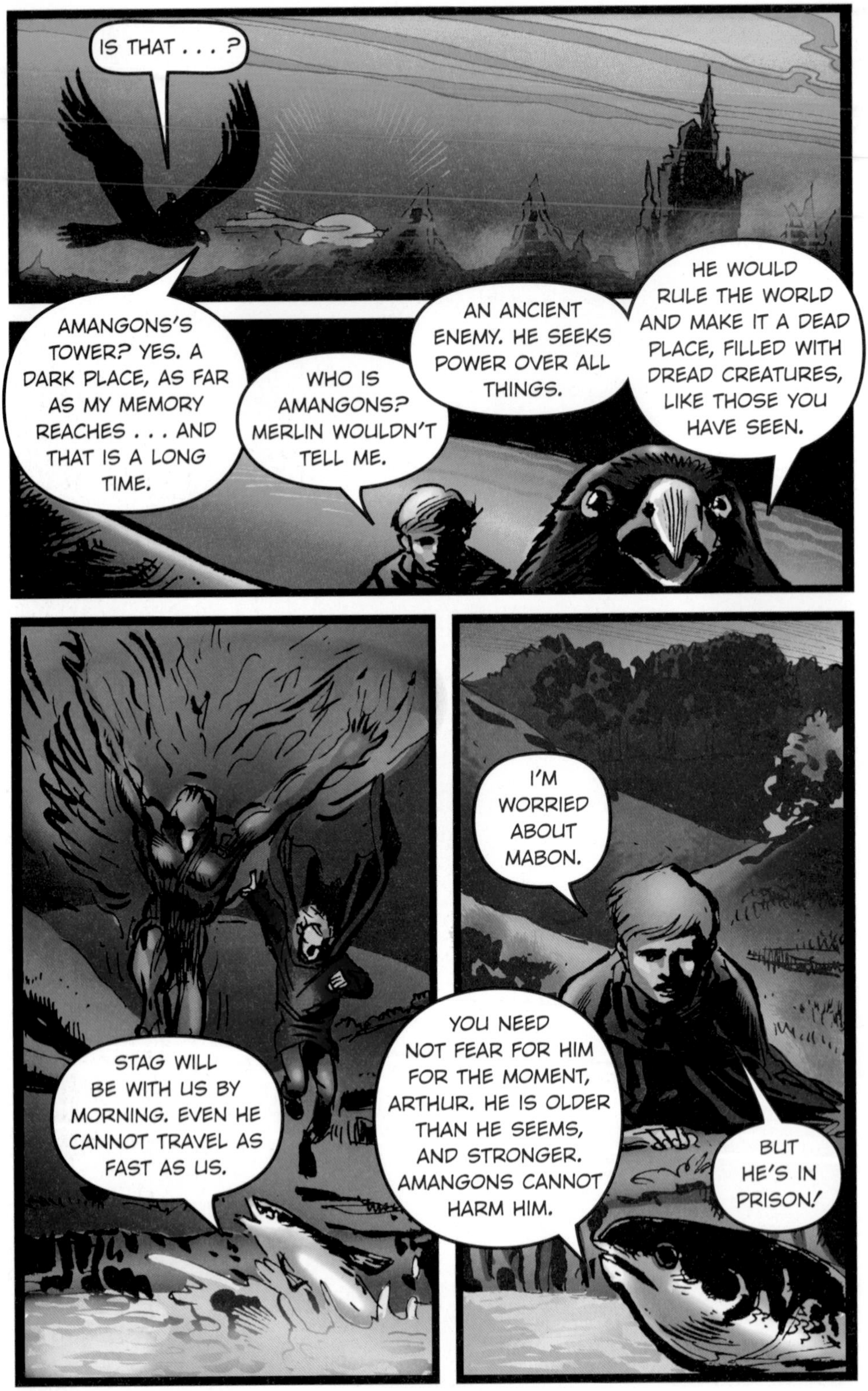
IS THAT . . . ?
AMANGONS'S TOWER? YES. A DARK PLACE, AS FAR AS MY MEMORY REACHES . . . AND THAT IS A LONG TIME.
WHO IS AMANGONS? MERLIN WOULDN'T TELL ME.
AN ANCIENT ENEMY. HE SEEKS POWER OVER ALL THINGS.
HE WOULD RULE THE WORLD AND MAKE IT A DEAD PLACE, FILLED WITH DREAD CREATURES, LIKE THOSE YOU HAVE SEEN.
STAG WILL BE WITH US BY MORNING. EVEN HE CANNOT TRAVEL AS FAST AS US.
I'M WORRIED ABOUT MABON.
YOU NEED NOT FEAR FOR HIM FOR THE MOMENT, ARTHUR. HE IS OLDER THAN HE SEEMS, AND STRONGER. AMANGONS CANNOT HARM HIM.
BUT HE'S IN PRISON!

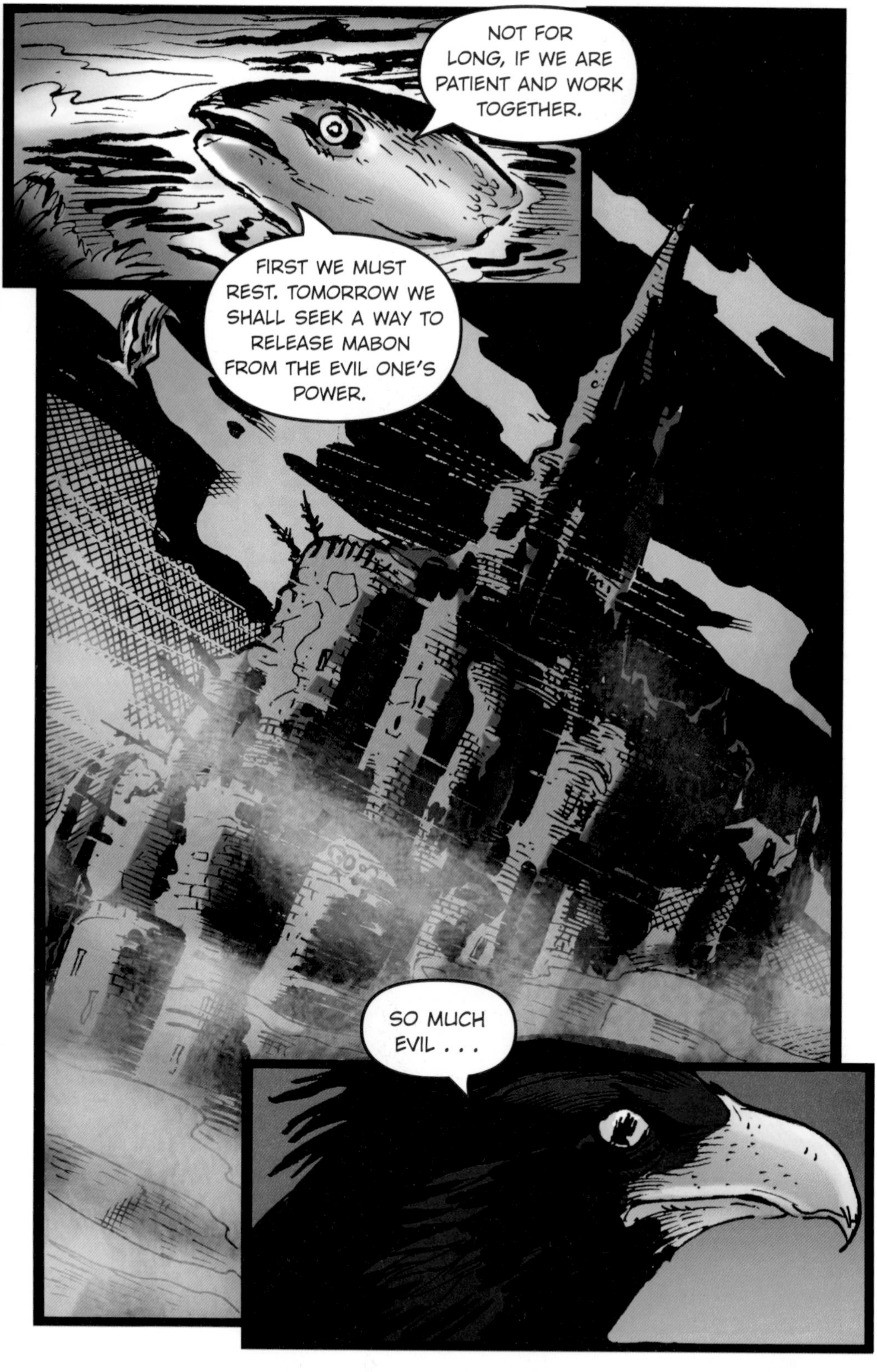
NOT FOR LONG, IF WE ARE PATIENT AND WORK TOGETHER.
FIRST WE MUST REST. TOMORROW WE SHALL SEEK A WAY TO RELEASE MABON FROM THE EVIL ONE'S POWER.
SO MUCH EVIL . . .

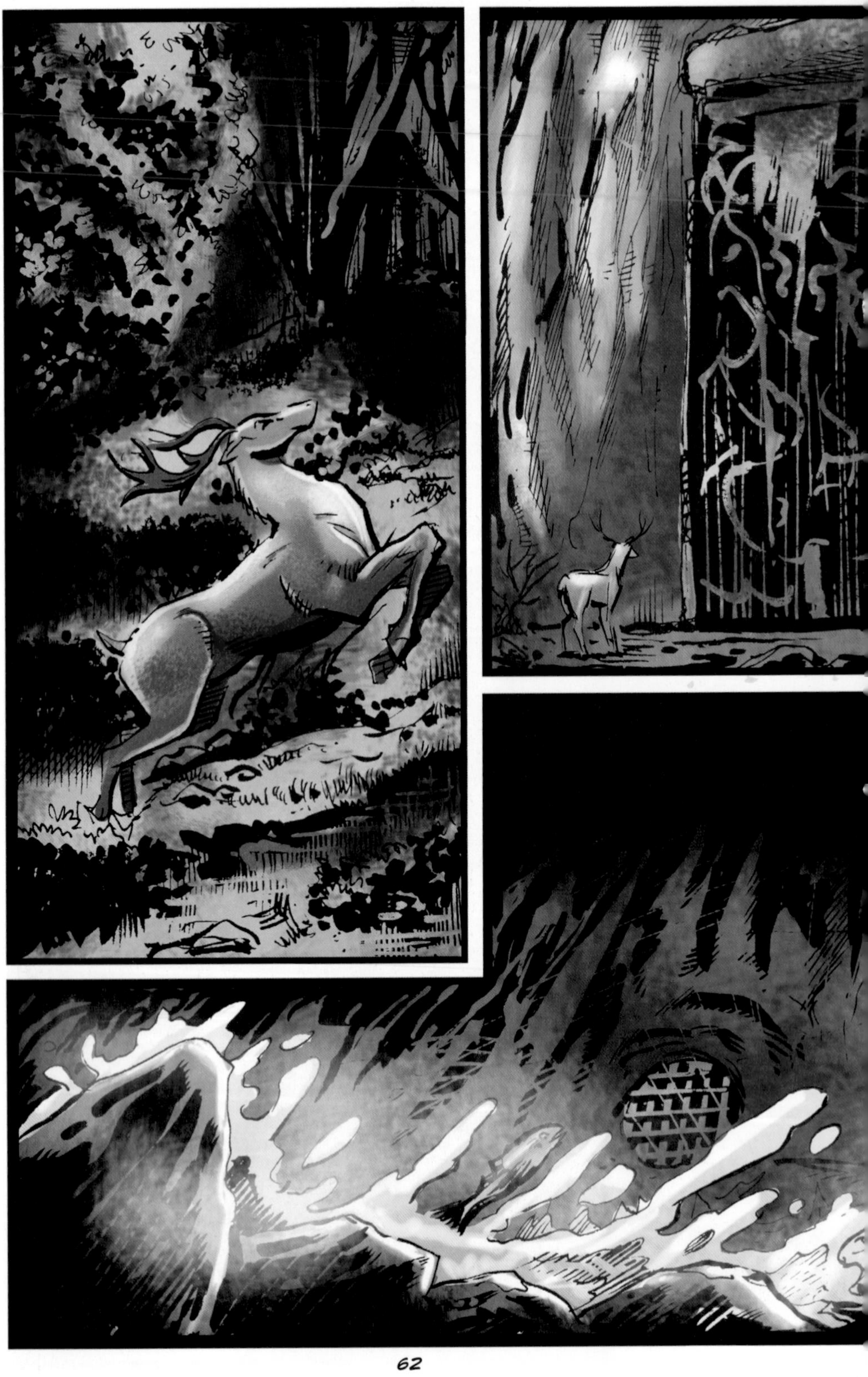

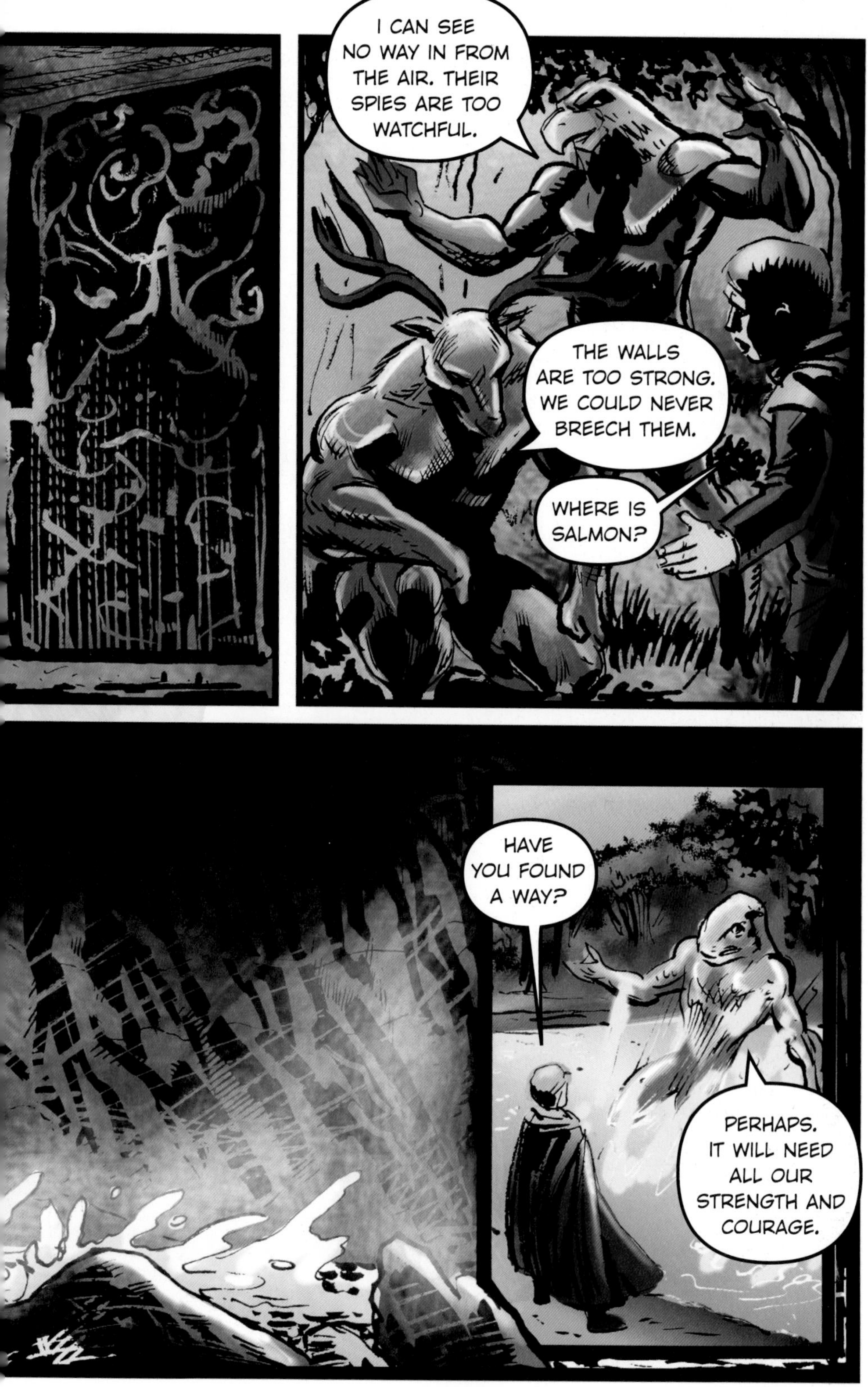
I CAN SEE NO WAY IN FROM THE AIR. THEIR SPIES ARE TOO WATCHFUL.
THE WALLS ARE TOO STRONG. WE COULD NEVER BREECH THEM.
WHERE IS SALMON?
HAVE YOU FOUND A WAY?
PERHAPS. IT WILL NEED ALL OUR STRENGTH AND COURAGE.

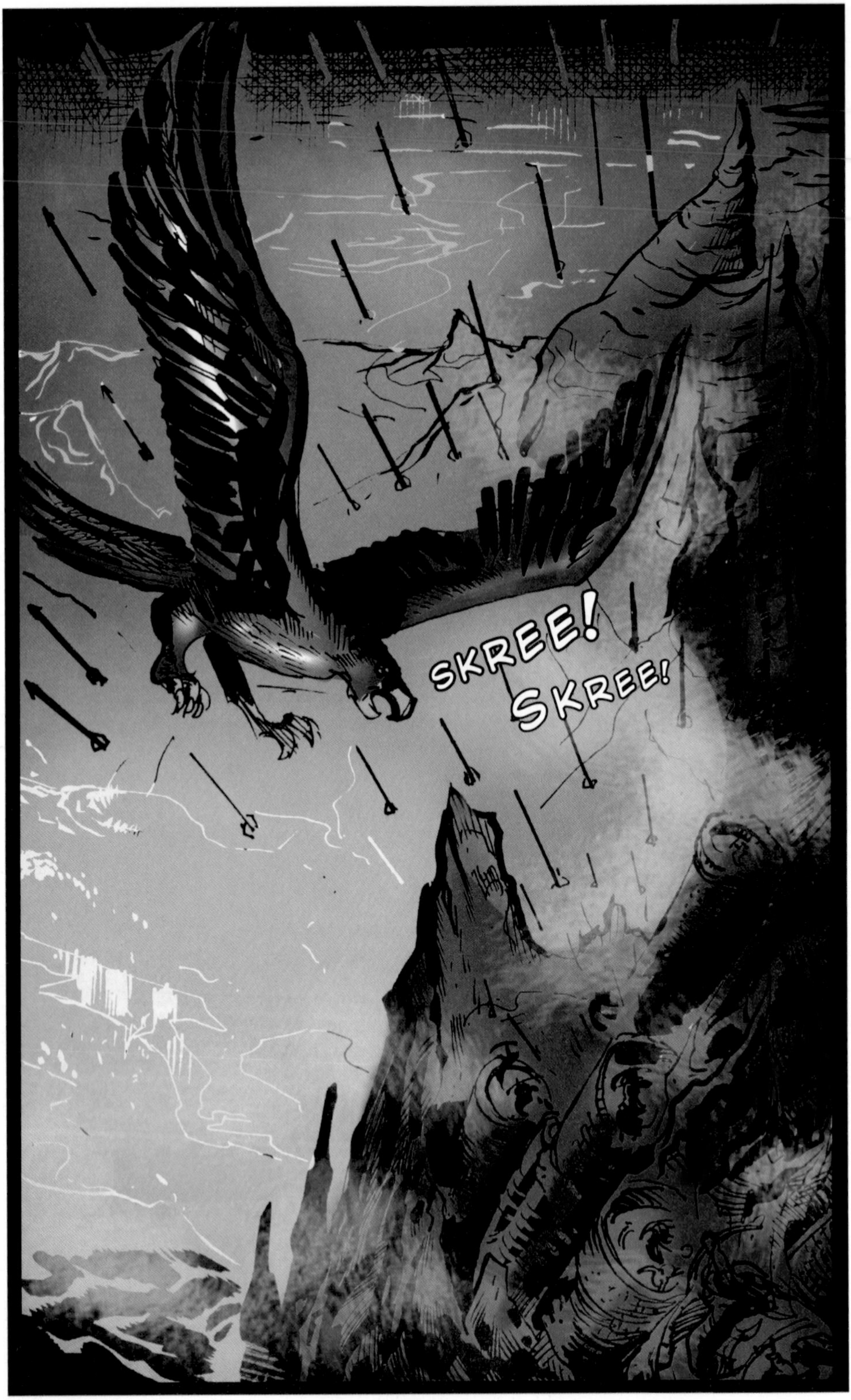
SKREE!
SKREE!

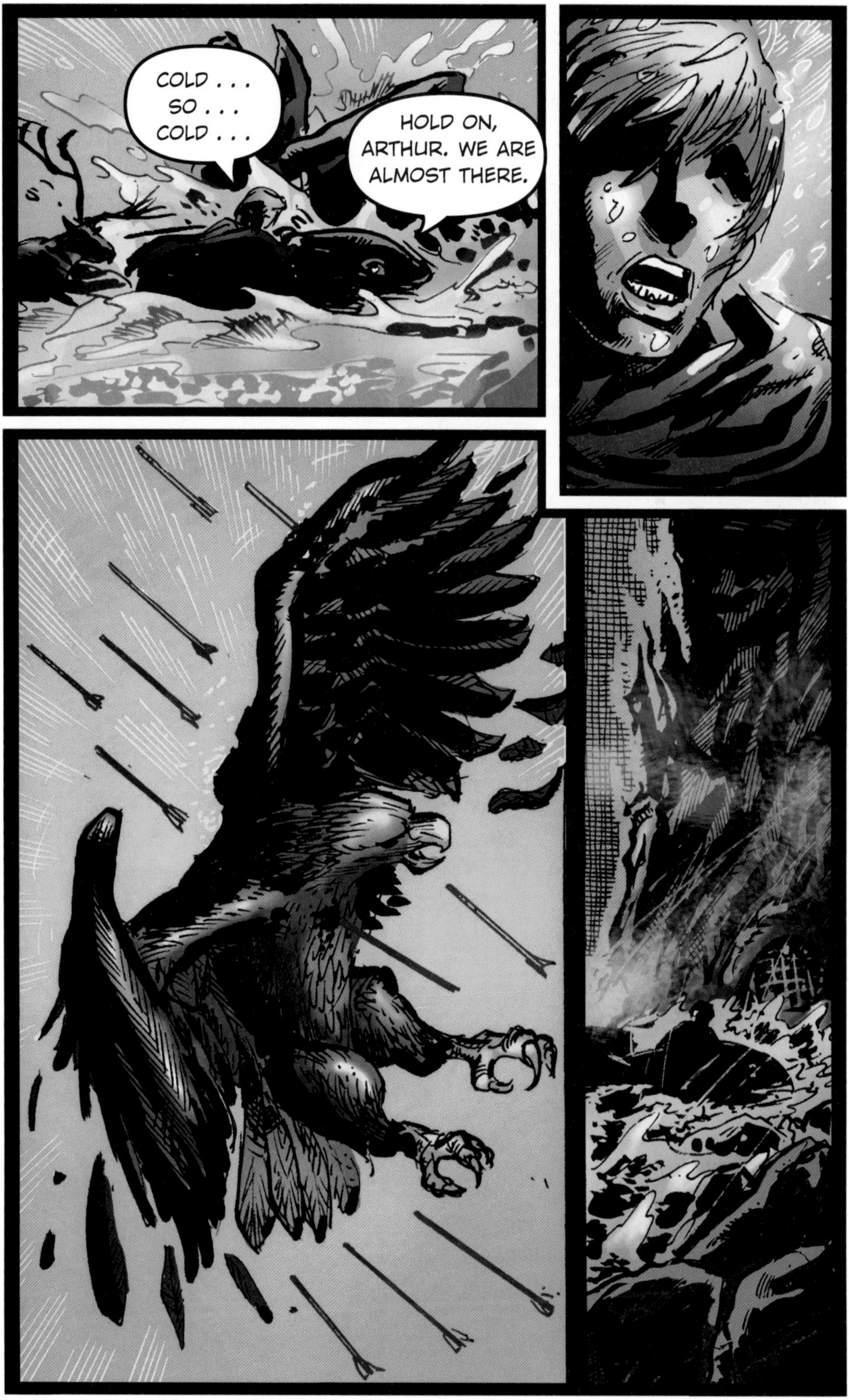
COLD . . .
SO . . .
COLD . . .
HOLD ON, ARTHUR. WE ARE ALMOST THERE.

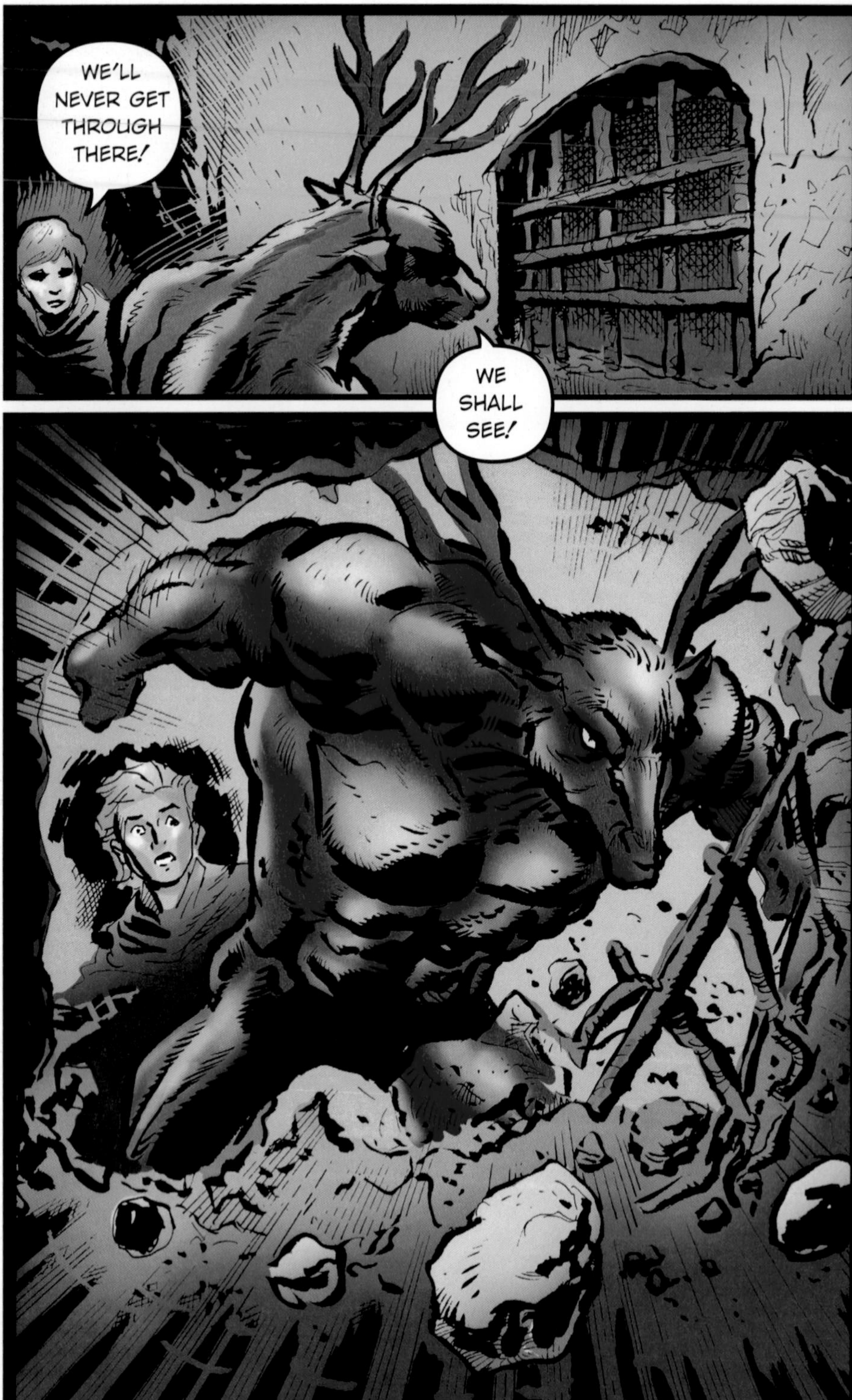
WE'LL NEVER GET THROUGH THERE!
WE SHALL SEE!

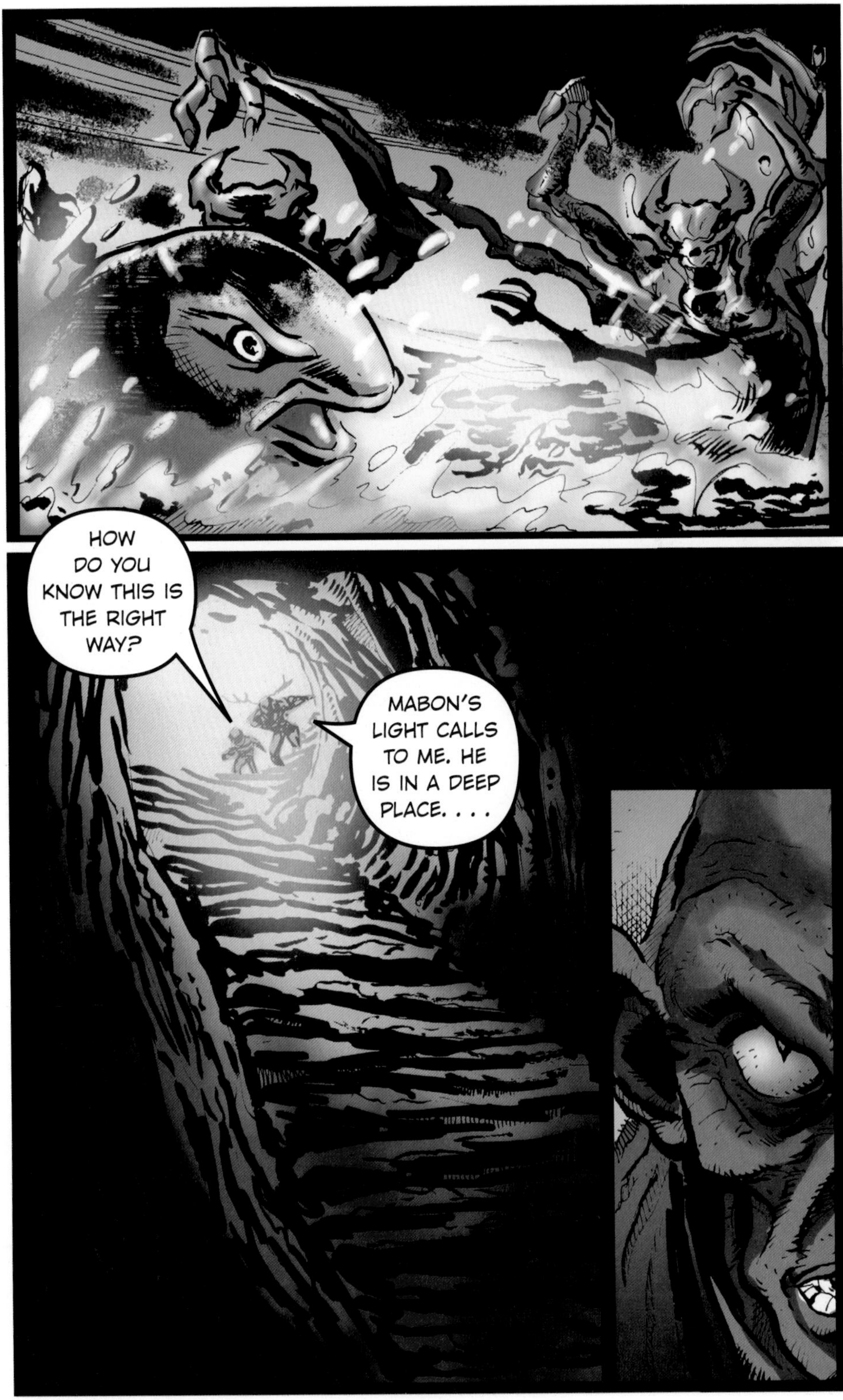
HOW DO YOU KNOW THIS IS THE RIGHT WAY?
MABON'S LIGHT CALLS TO ME. HE IS IN A DEEP PLACE. . . .

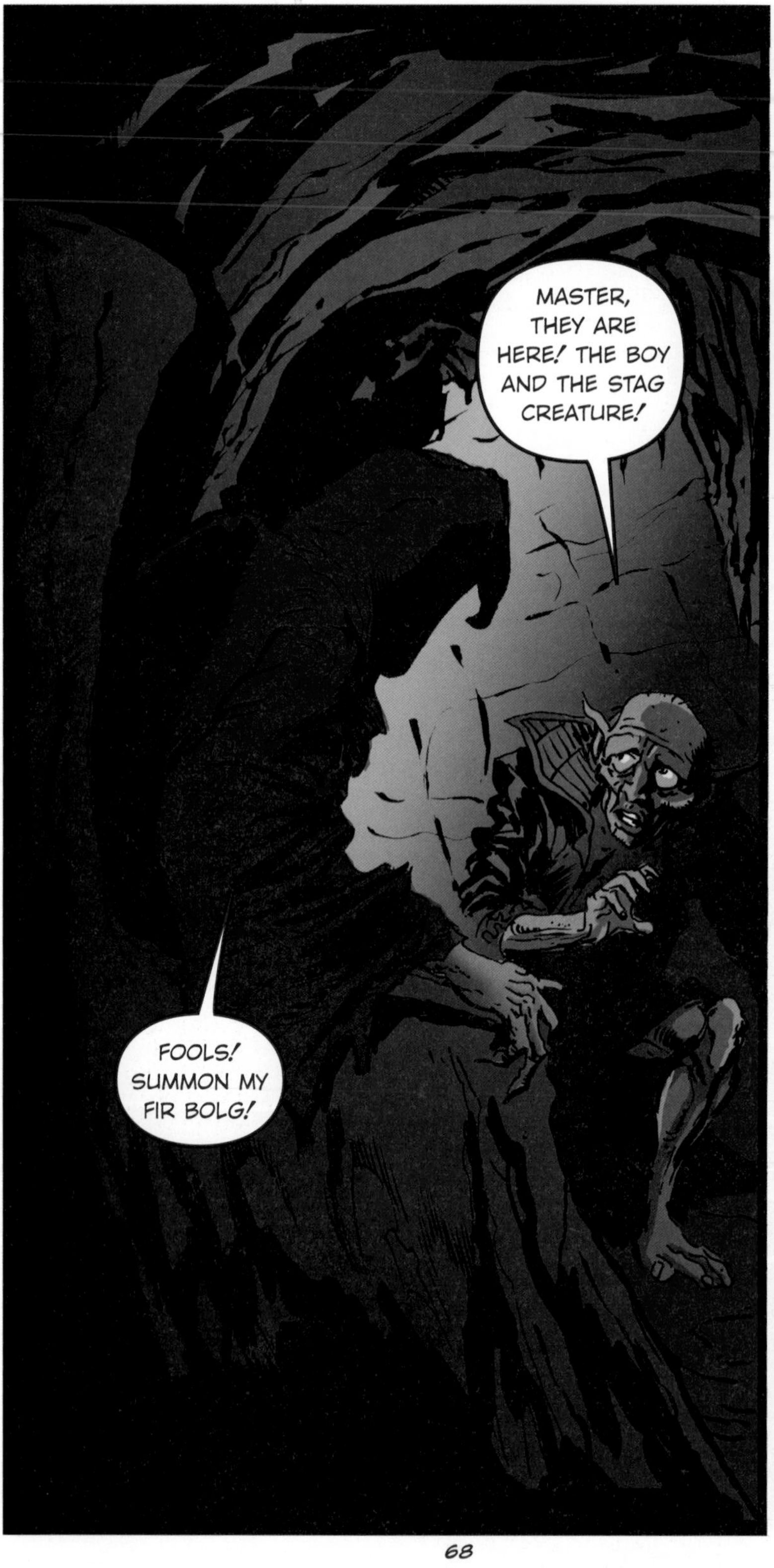
MASTER, THEY ARE HERE! THE BOY AND THE STAG CREATURE!
FOOLS! SUMMON MY FIR BOLG!

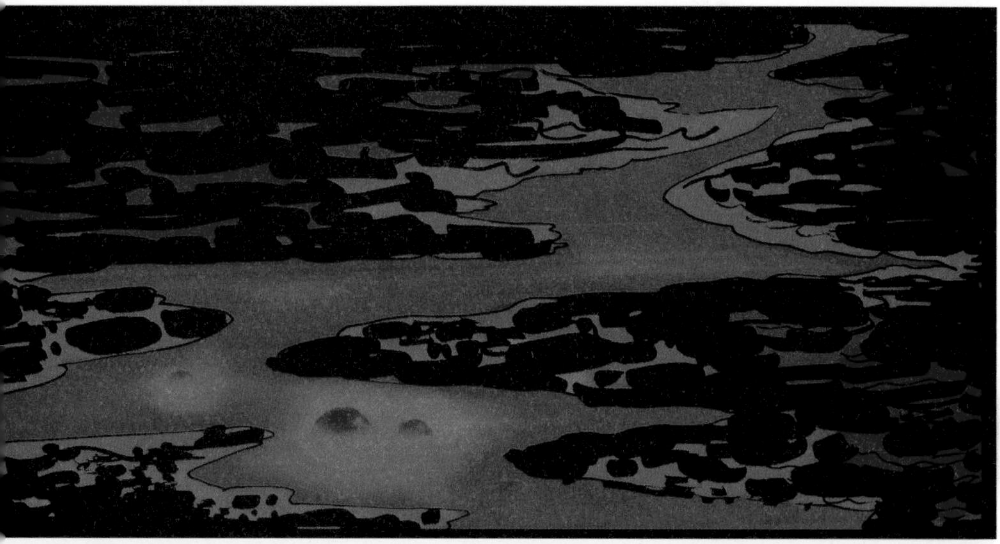

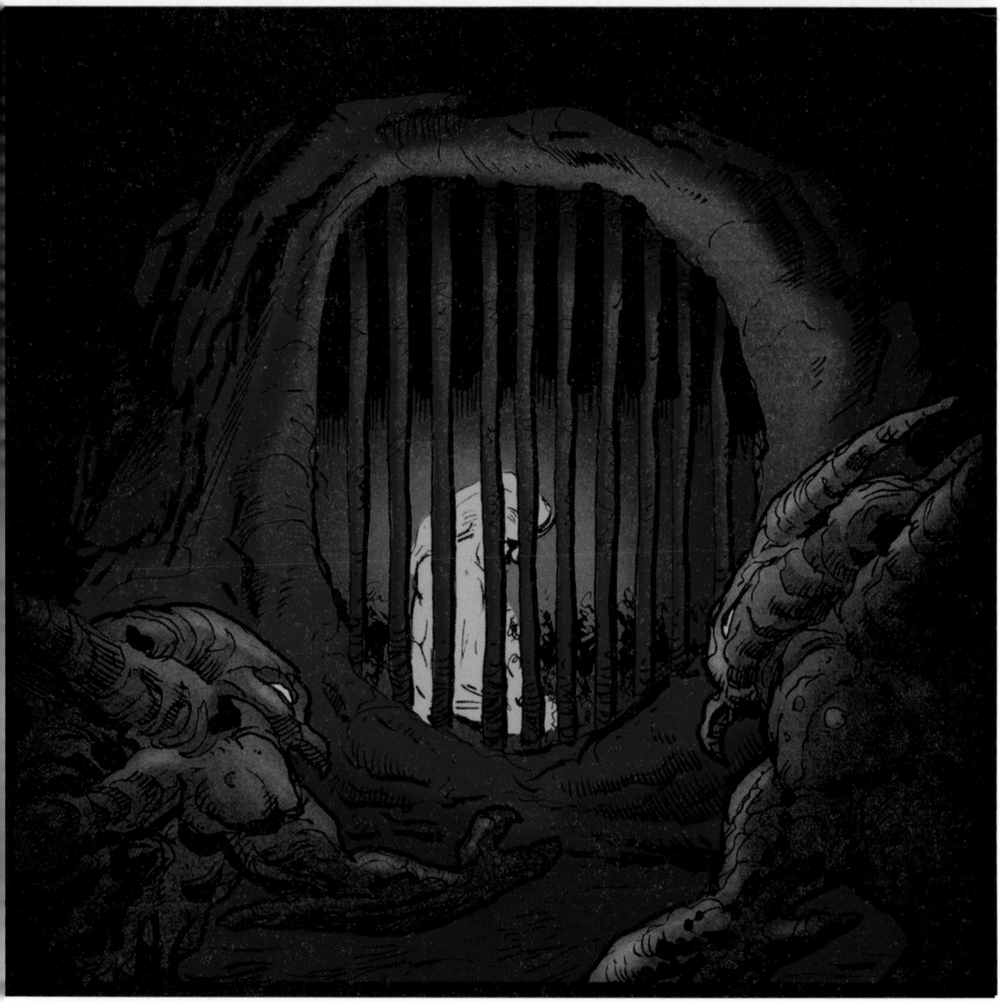

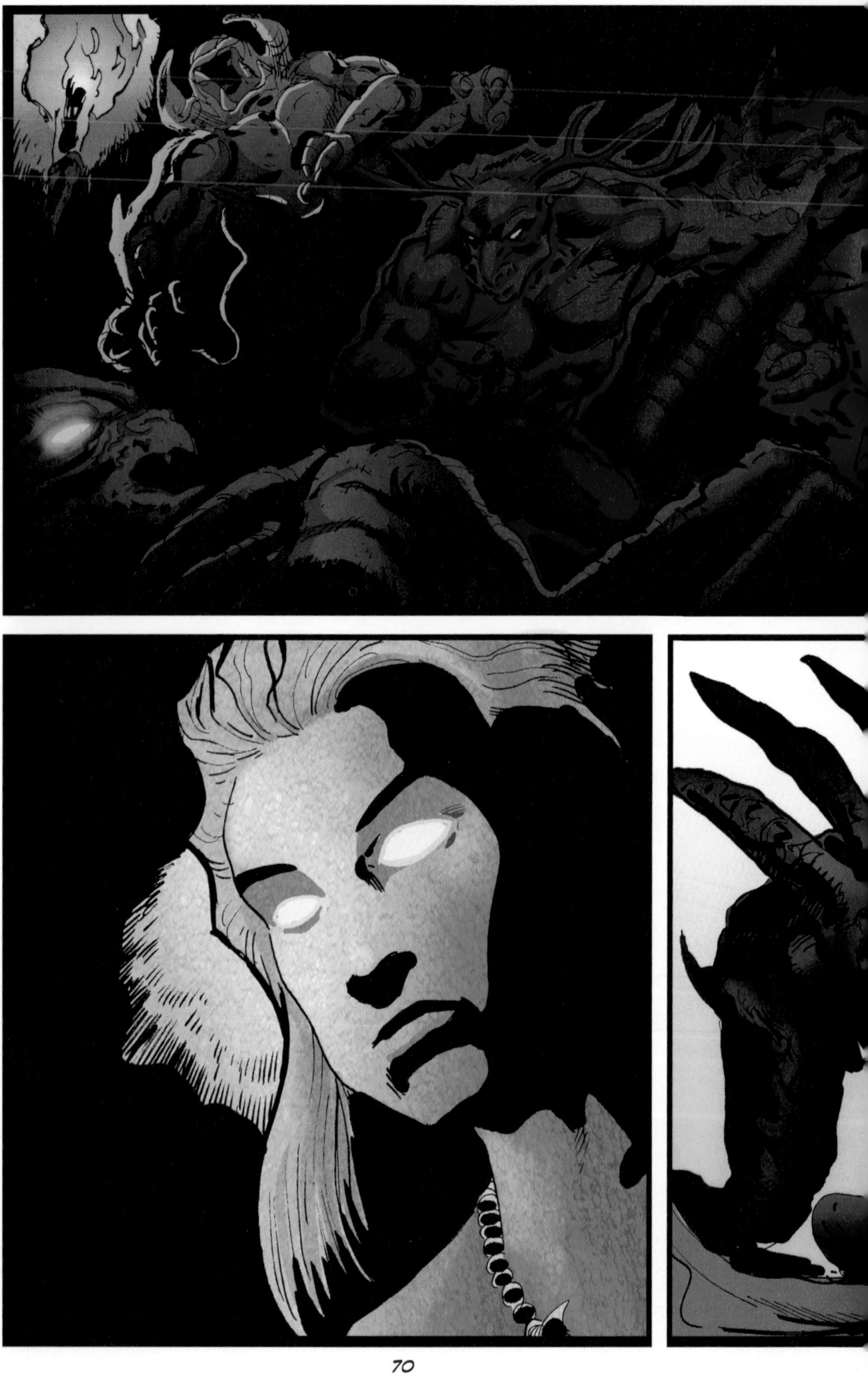

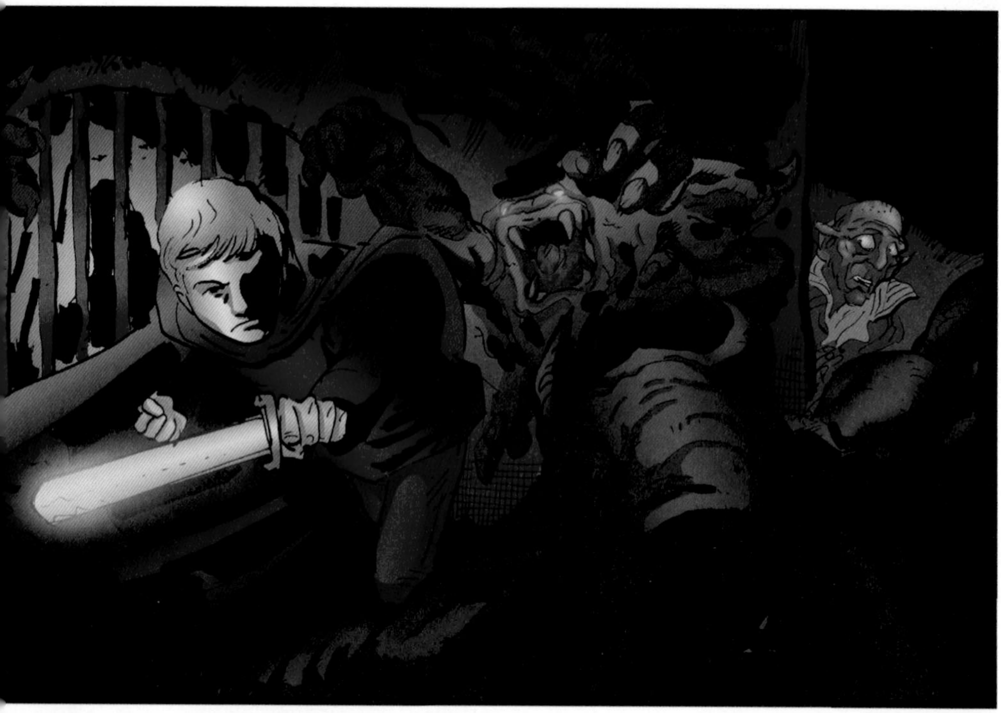

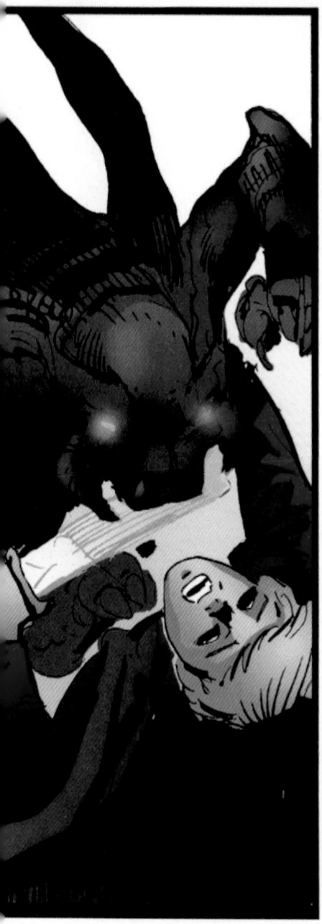

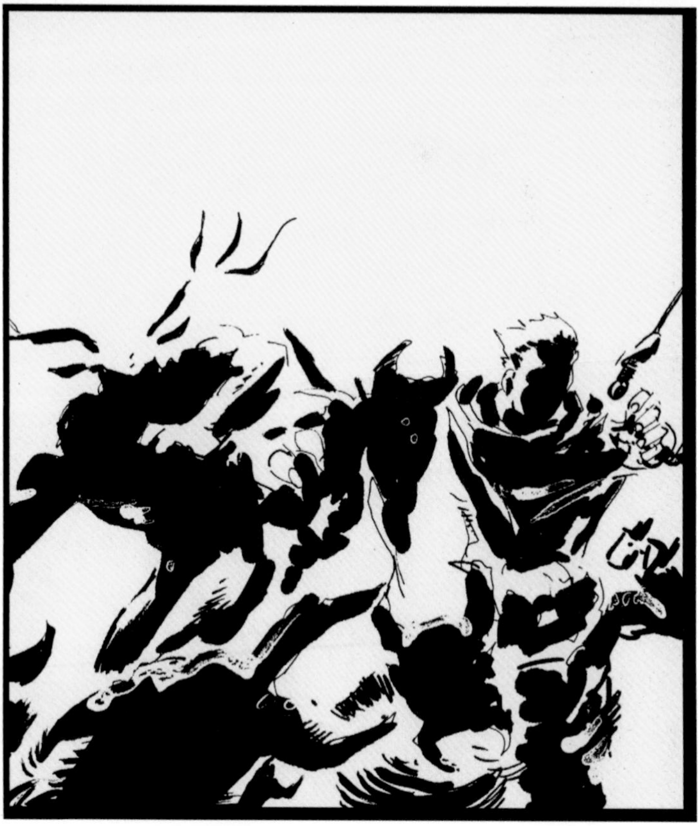

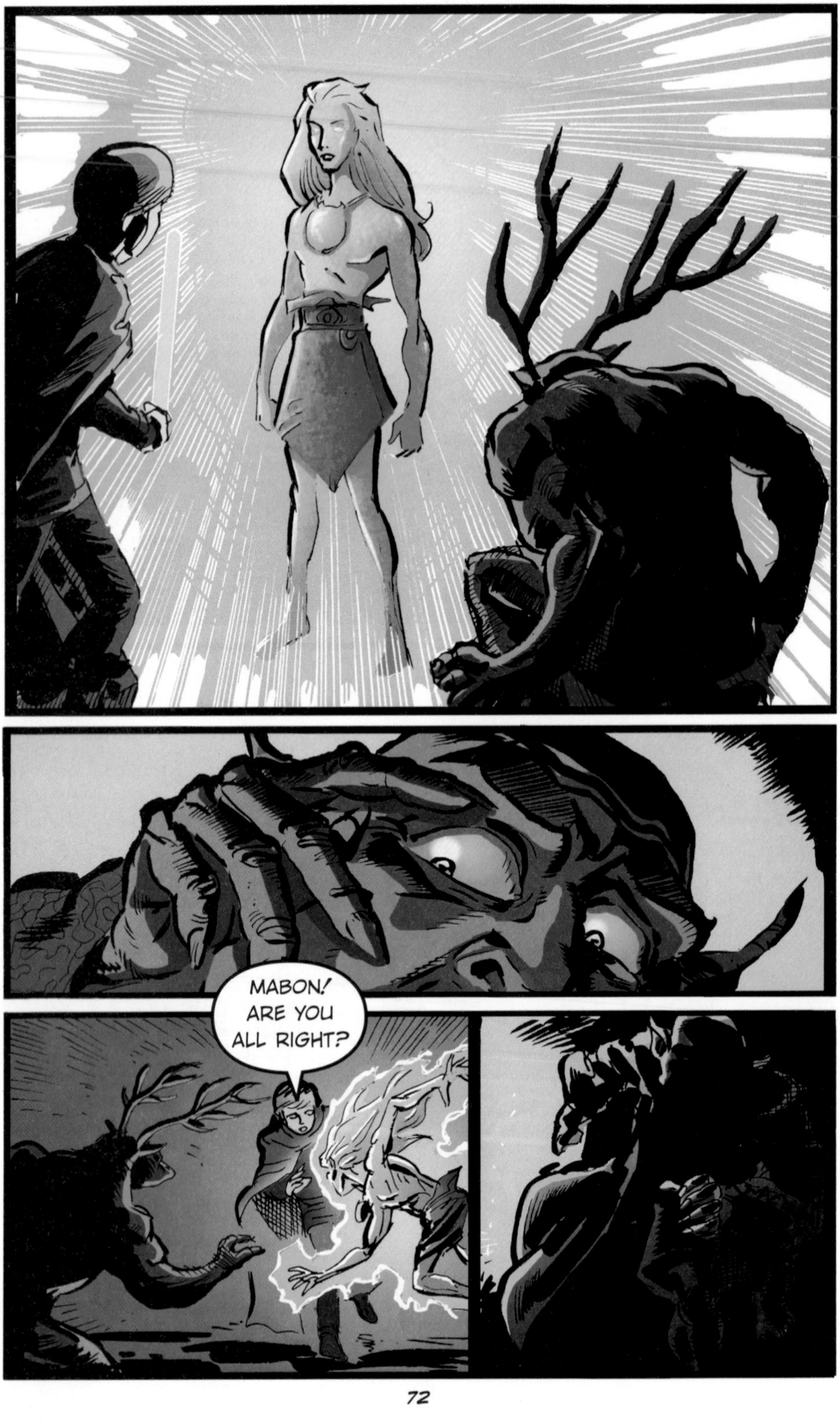
MABON!
ARE YOU
ALL RIGHT?

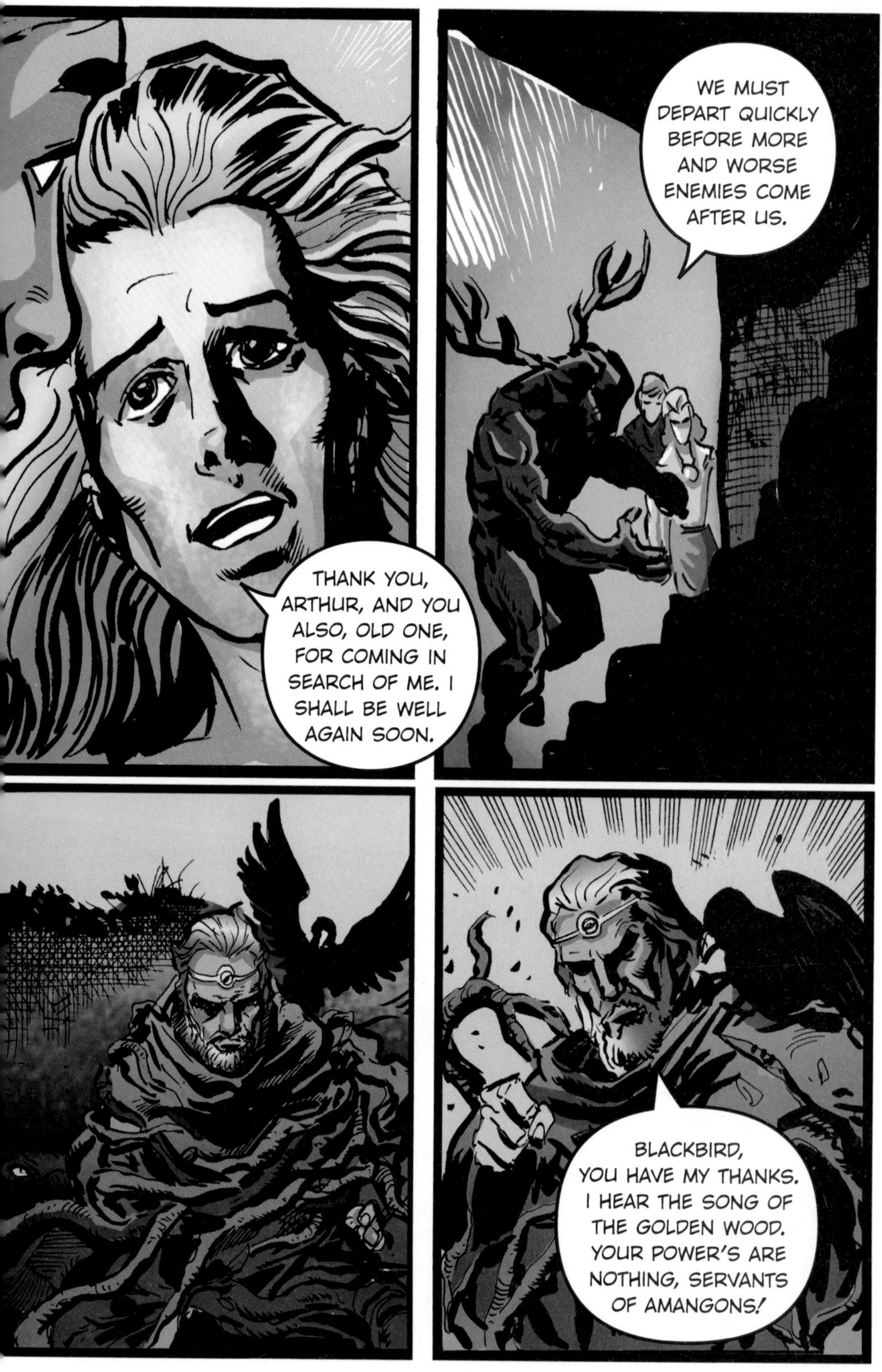
THANK YOU, ARTHUR, AND YOU ALSO, OLD ONE, FOR COMING IN SEARCH OF ME. I SHALL BE WELL AGAIN SOON.
WE MUST DEPART QUICKLY BEFORE MORE AND WORSE ENEMIES COME AFTER US.
BLACKBIRD, YOU HAVE MY THANKS. I HEAR THE SONG OF THE GOLDEN WOOD. YOUR POWER'S ARE NOTHING, SERVANTS OF AMANGONS!

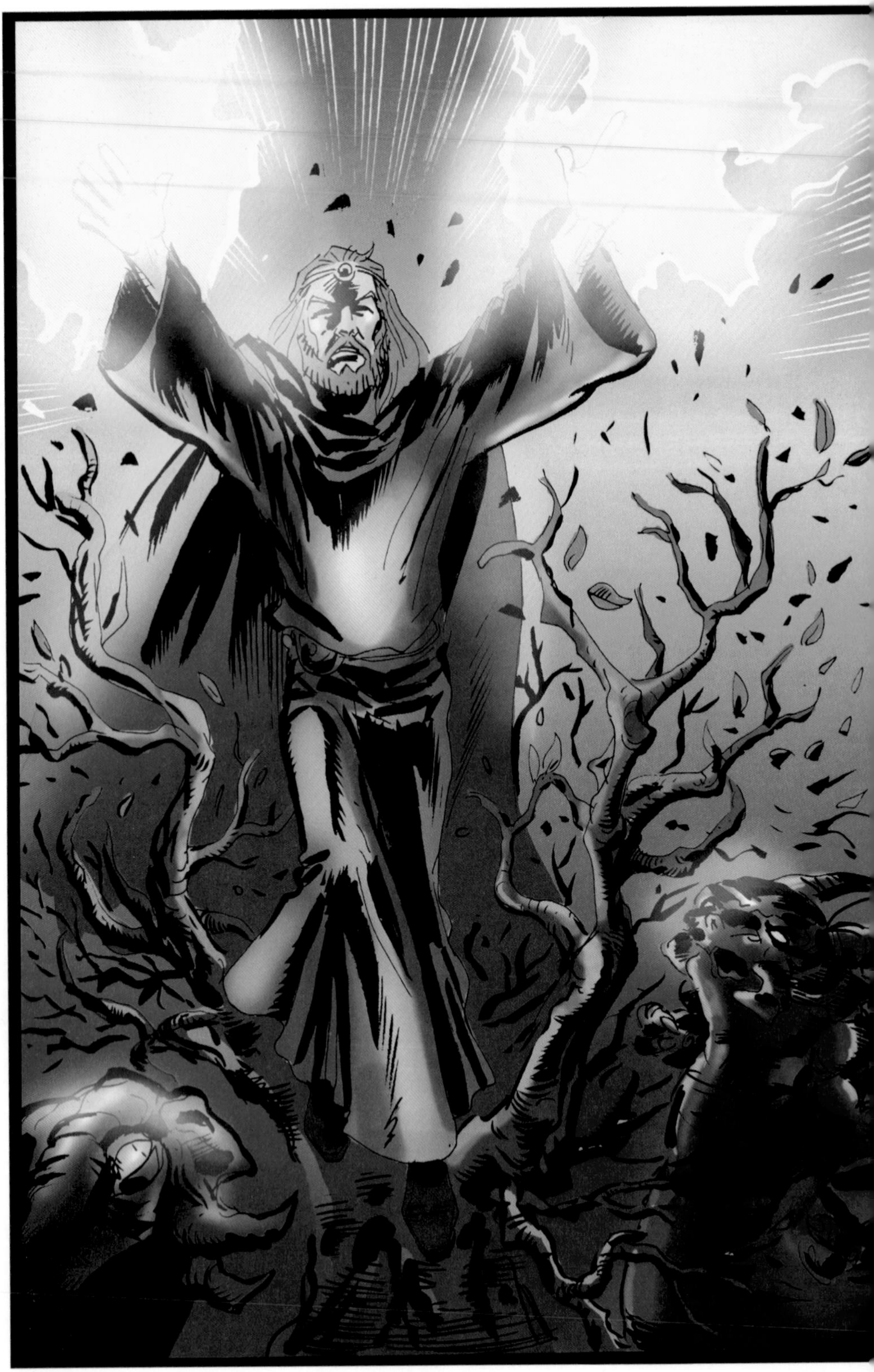

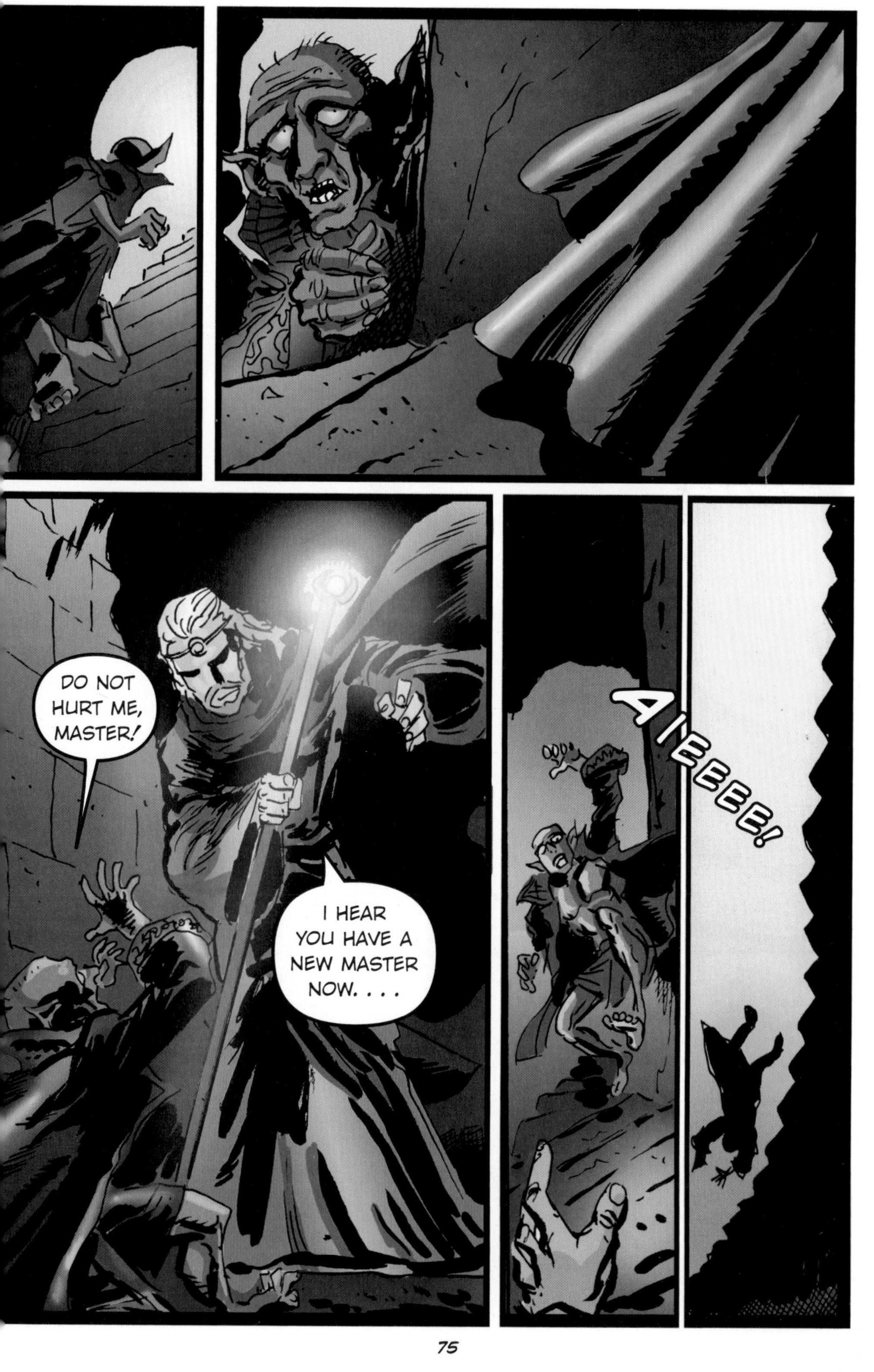
DO NOT HURT ME, MASTER!
I HEAR YOU HAVE A NEW MASTER NOW. . . .
AIEEEE!

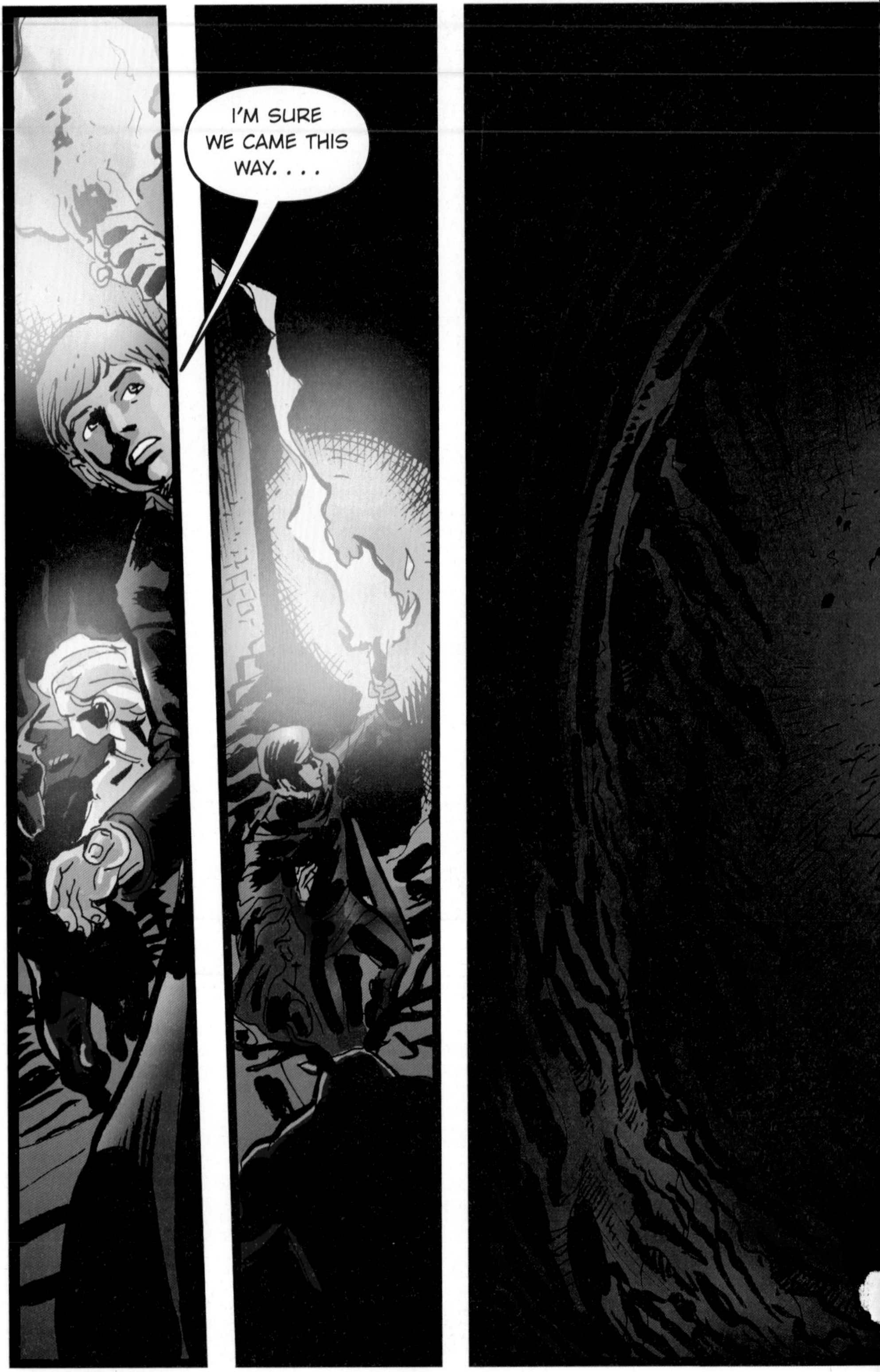
I'M SURE WE CAME THIS WAY. . . .

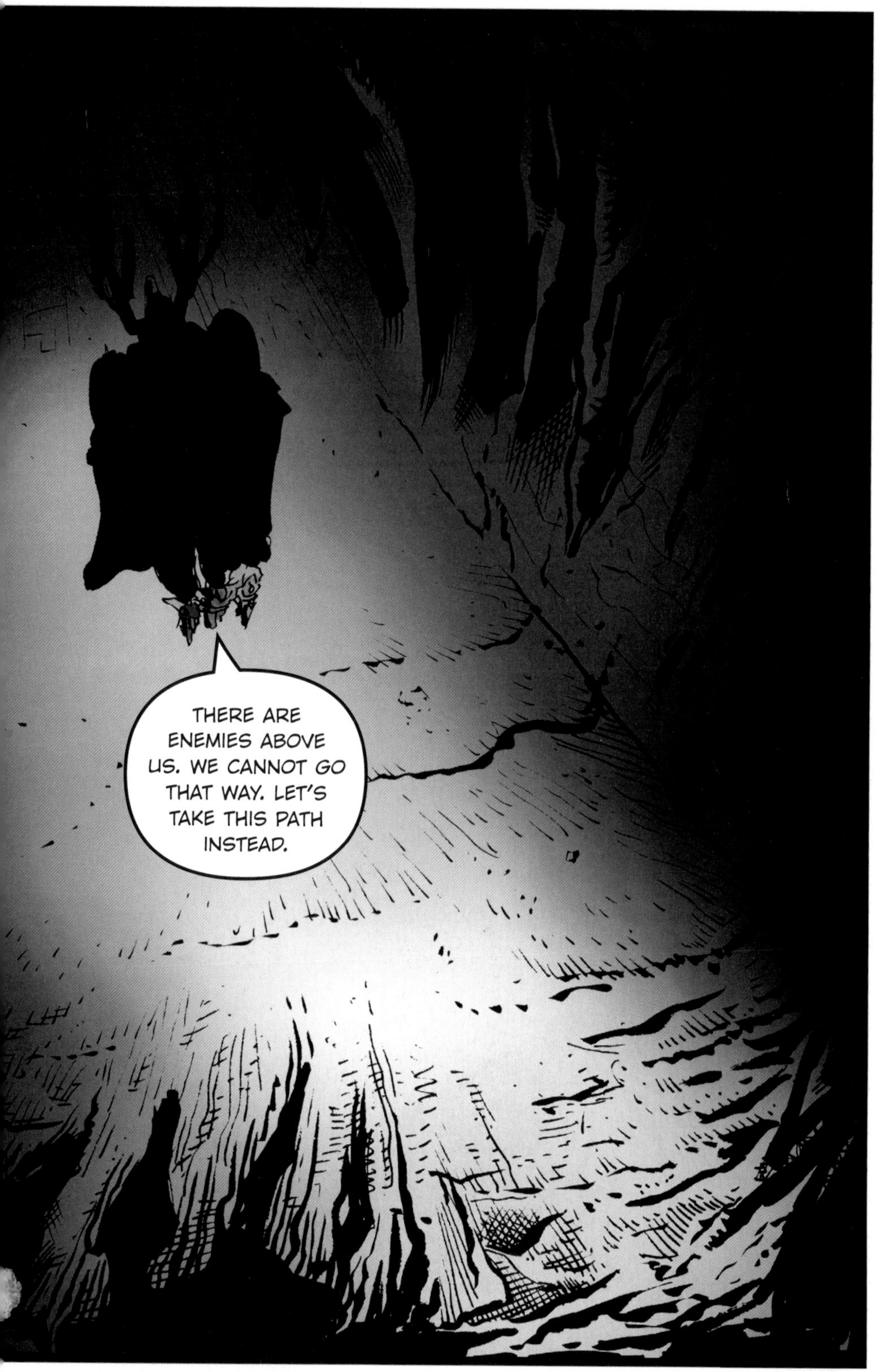
THERE ARE ENEMIES ABOVE US. WE CANNOT GO THAT WAY. LET'S TAKE THIS PATH INSTEAD.

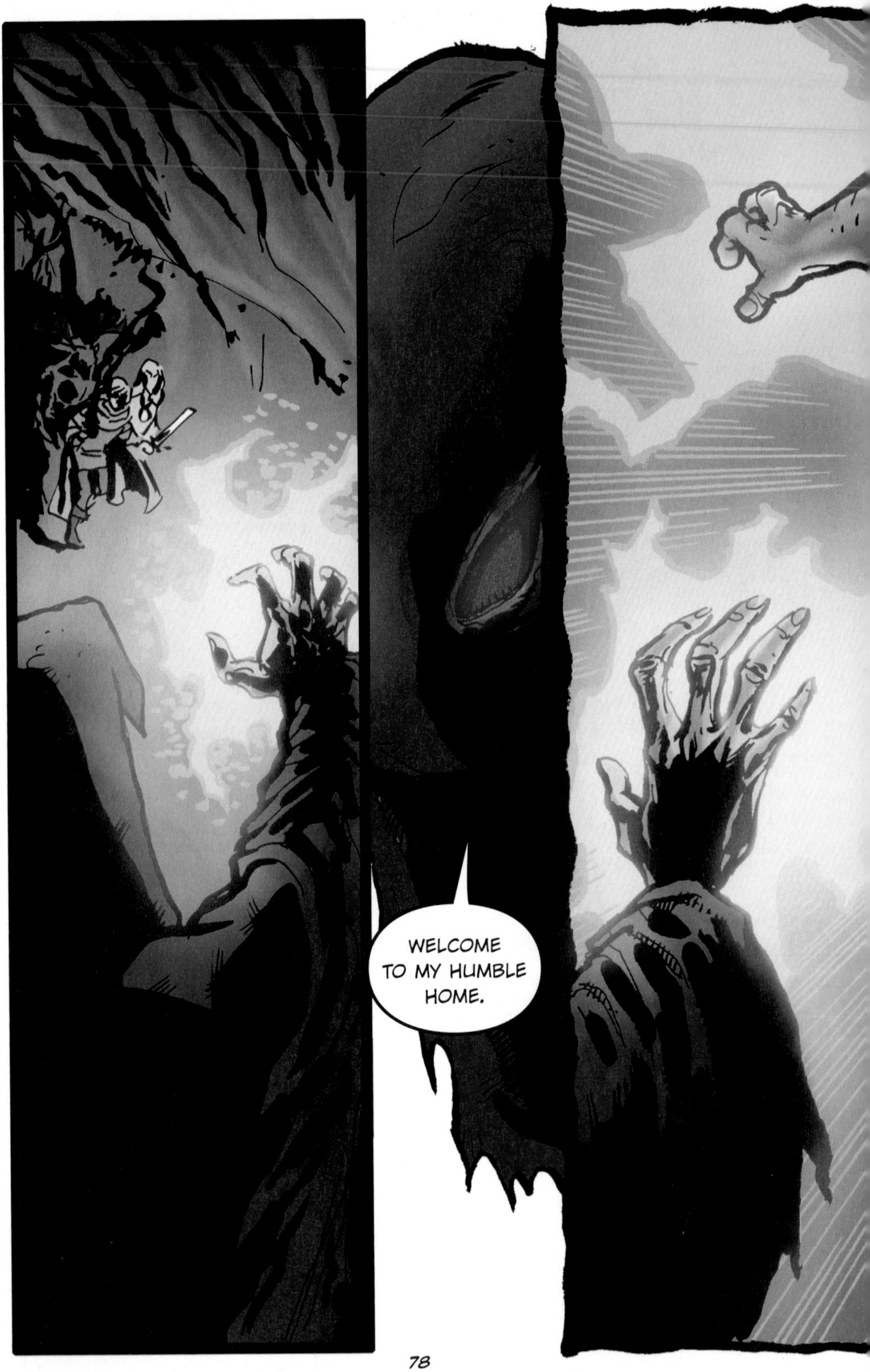
WELCOME TO MY HUMBLE HOME.

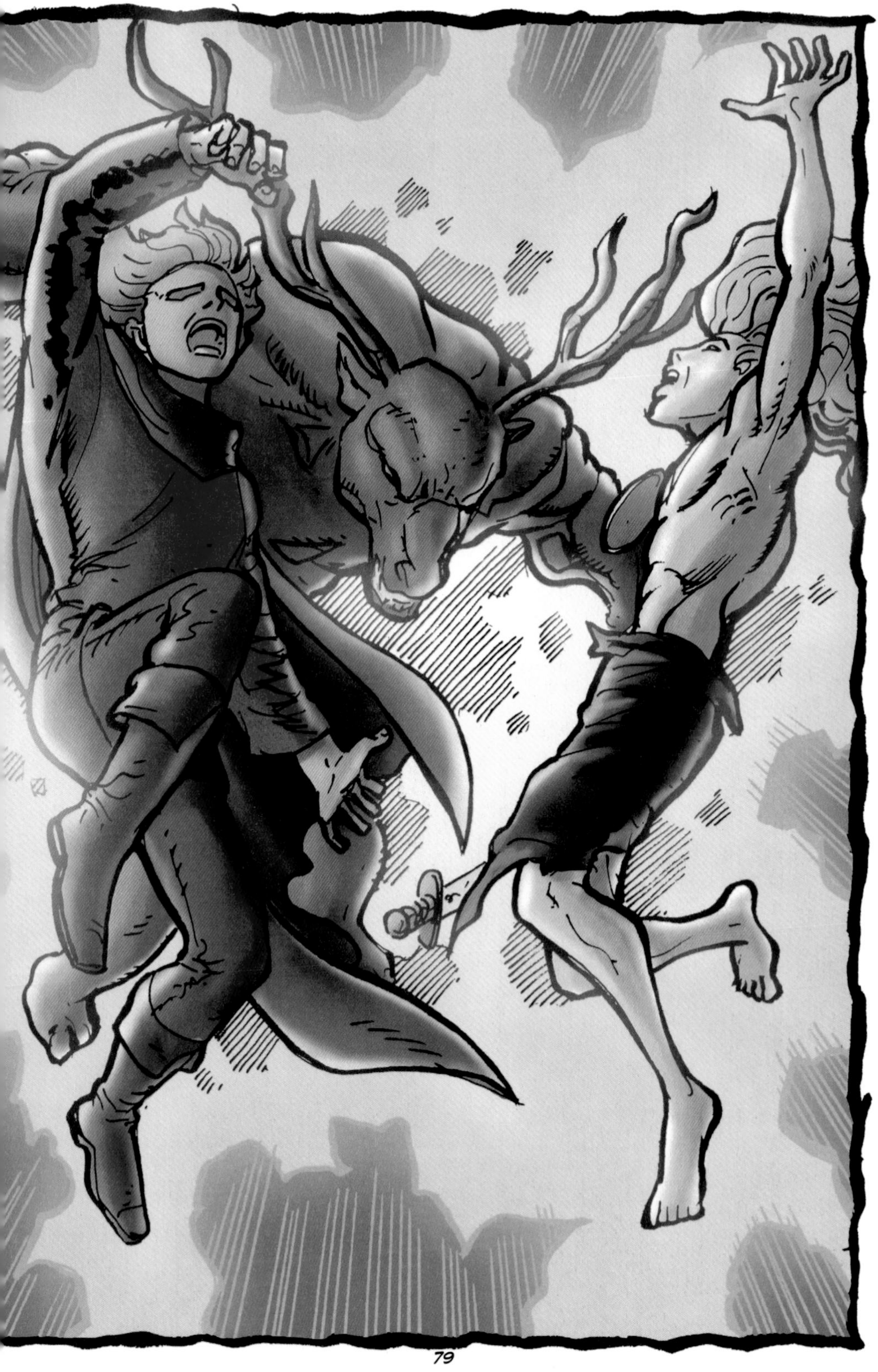

MERLIN. . . .

HE CANNOT HELP YOU NOW.

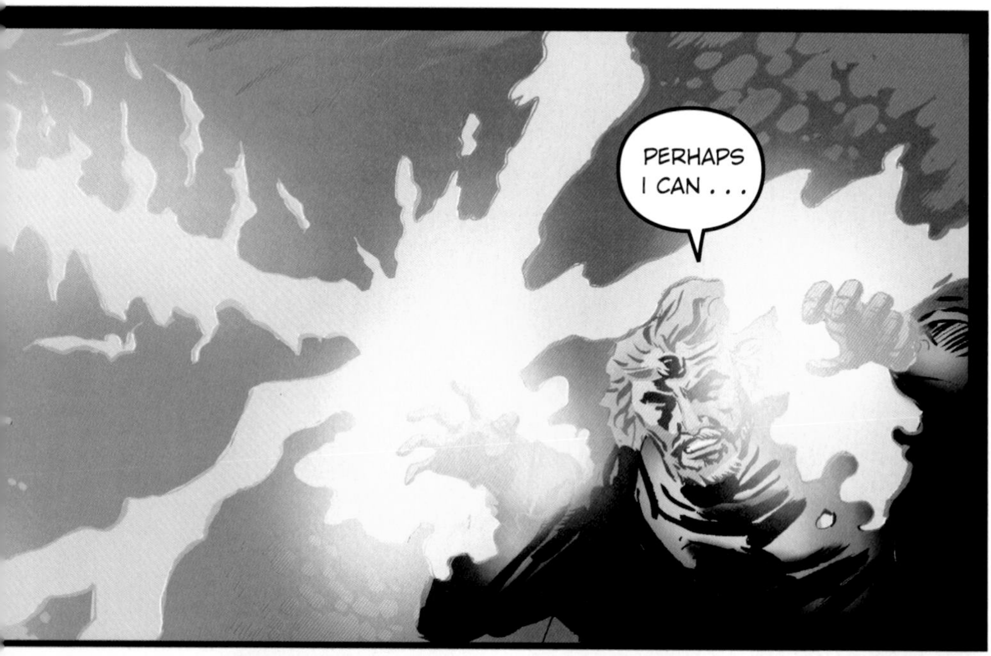
PERHAPS I CAN . . .

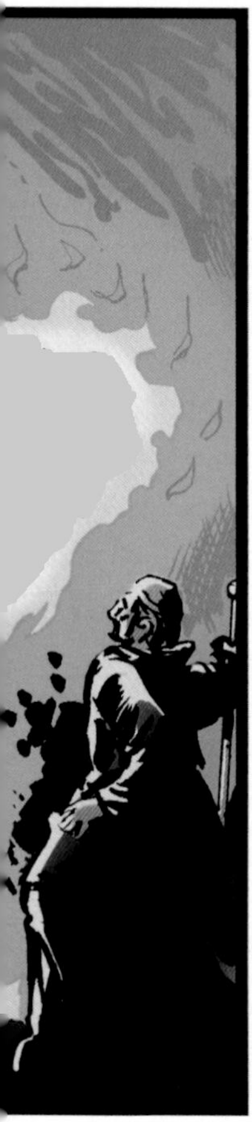

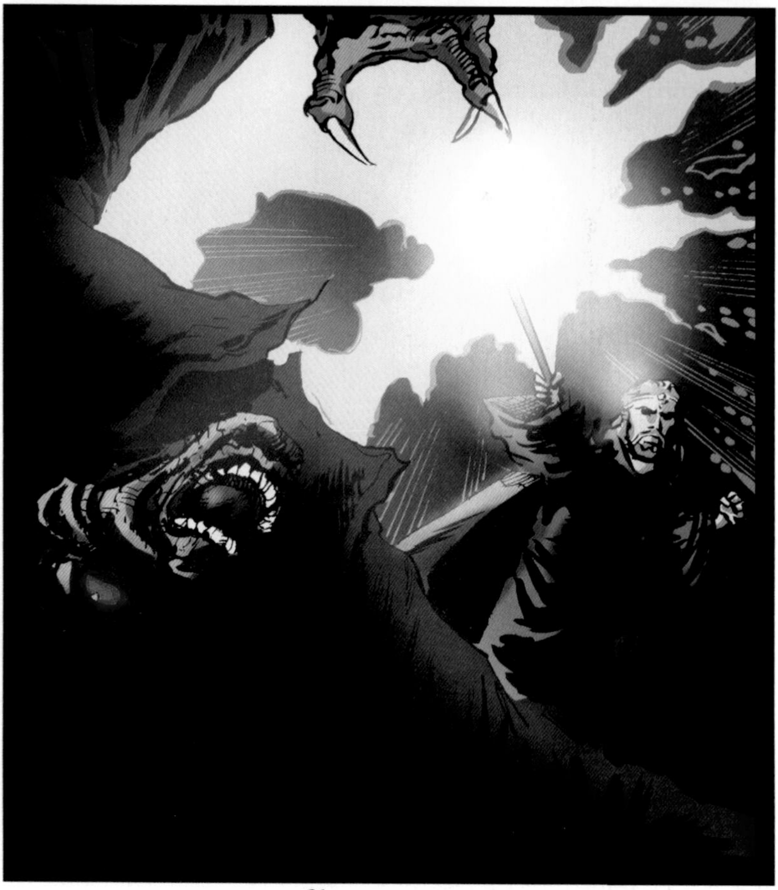

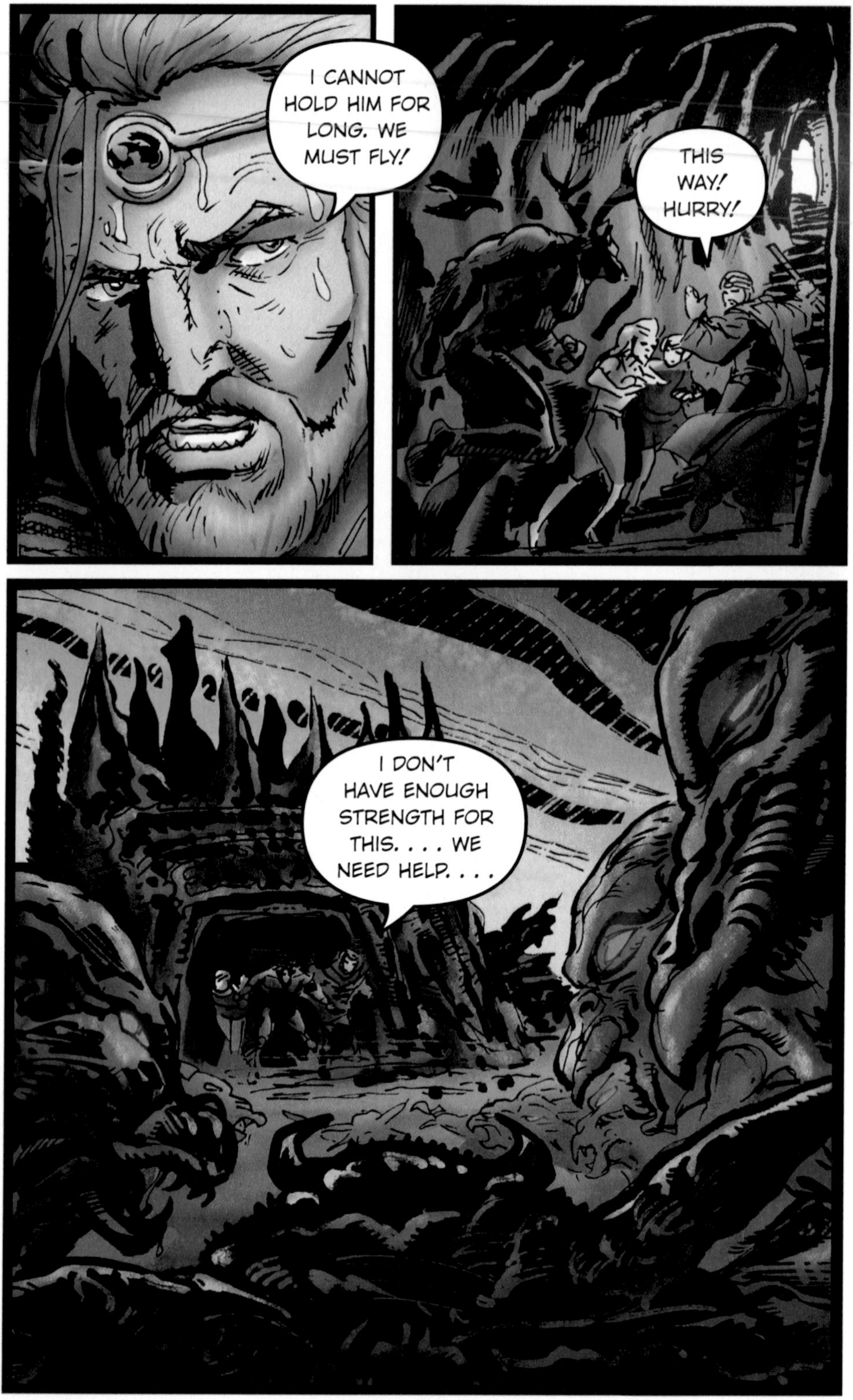
I CANNOT HOLD HIM FOR LONG. WE MUST FLY!
THIS WAY! HURRY!
I DON'T HAVE ENOUGH STRENGTH FOR THIS. . . . WE NEED HELP. . . .

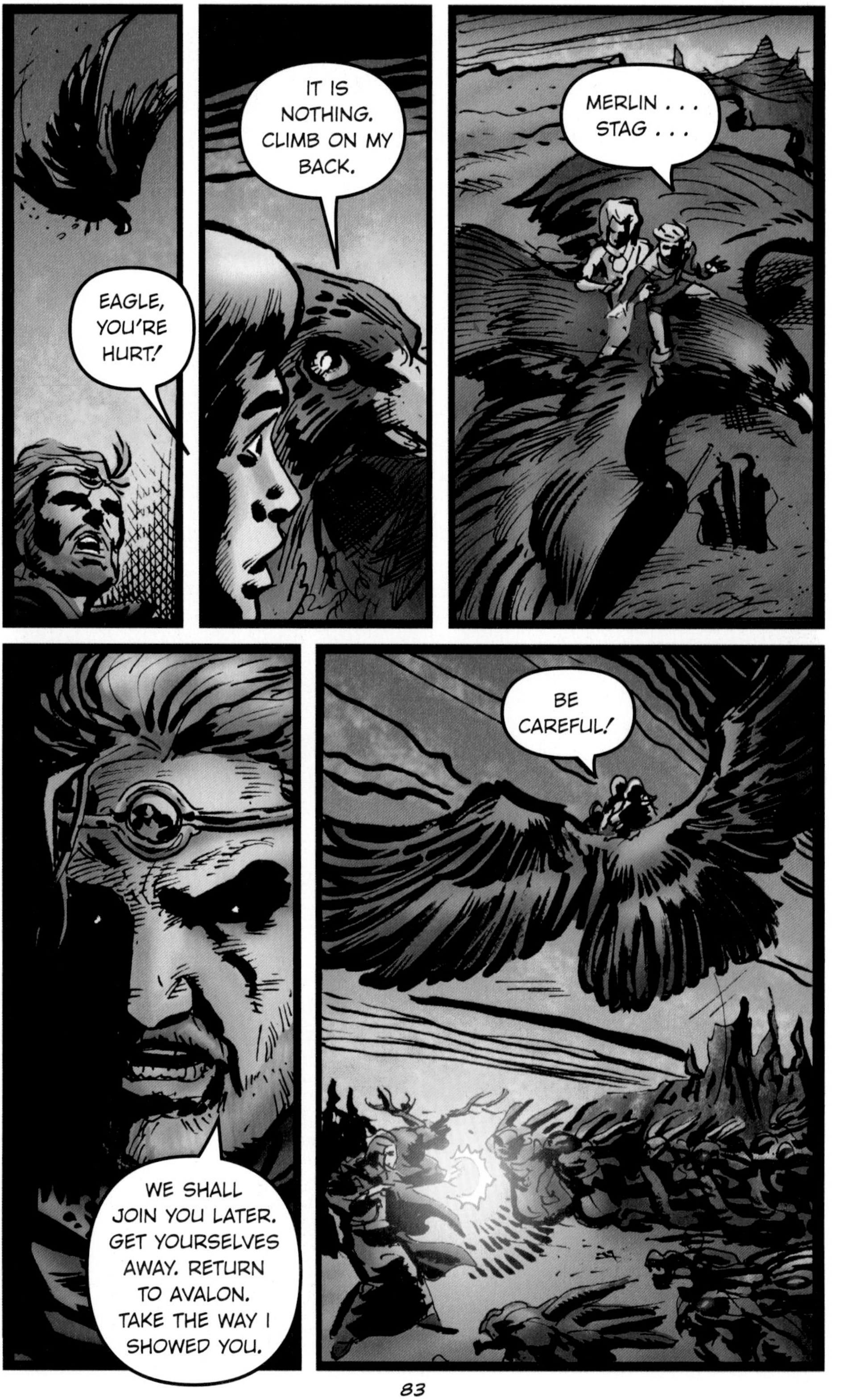
EAGLE, YOU'RE HURT!
IT IS NOTHING. CLIMB ON MY BACK.
MERLIN . . . STAG . . .
WE SHALL JOIN YOU LATER. GET YOURSELVES AWAY. RETURN TO AVALON. TAKE THE WAY I SHOWED YOU.
BE CAREFUL!

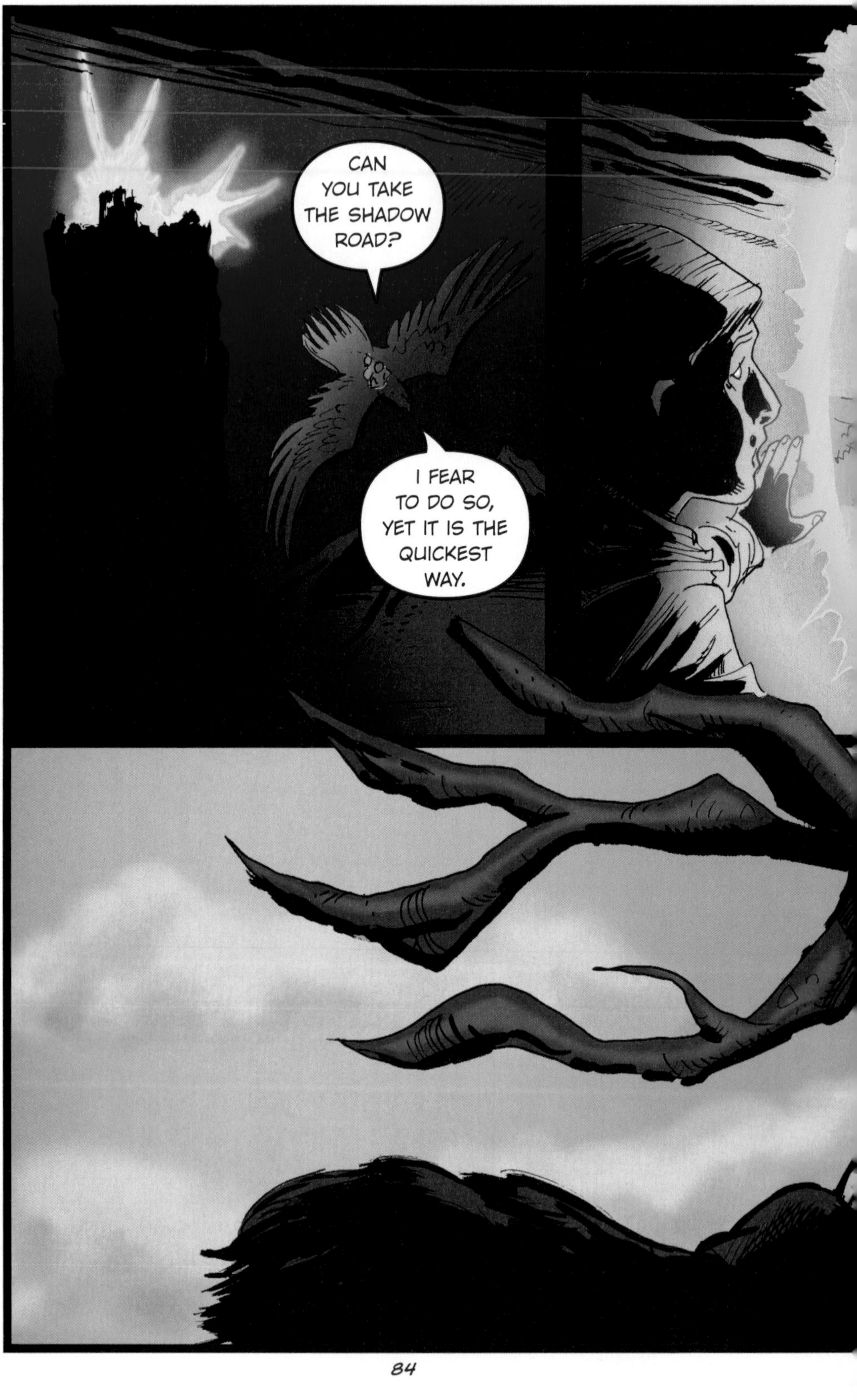
CAN YOU TAKE THE SHADOW ROAD?
I FEAR TO DO SO, YET IT IS THE QUICKEST WAY.

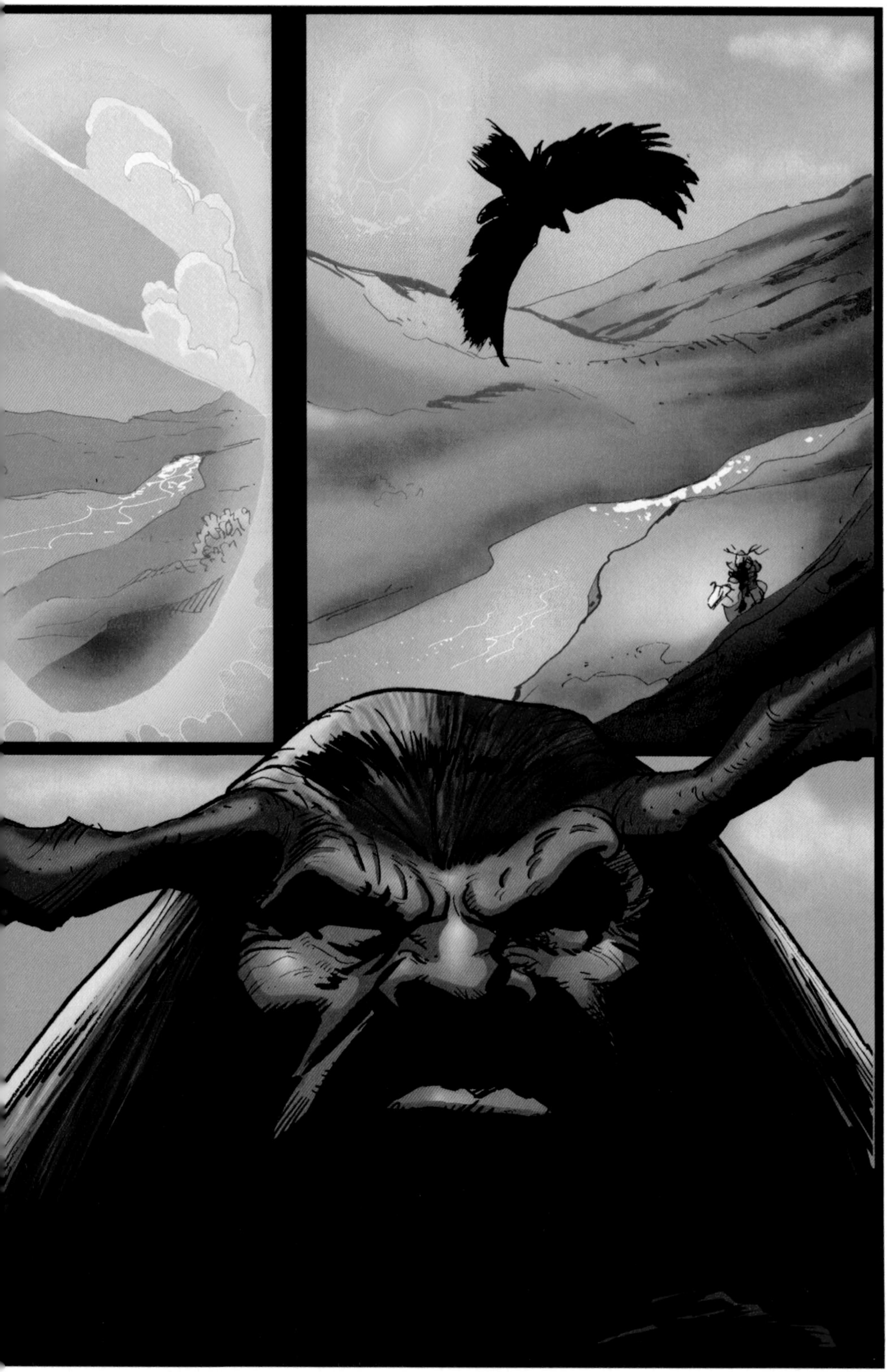

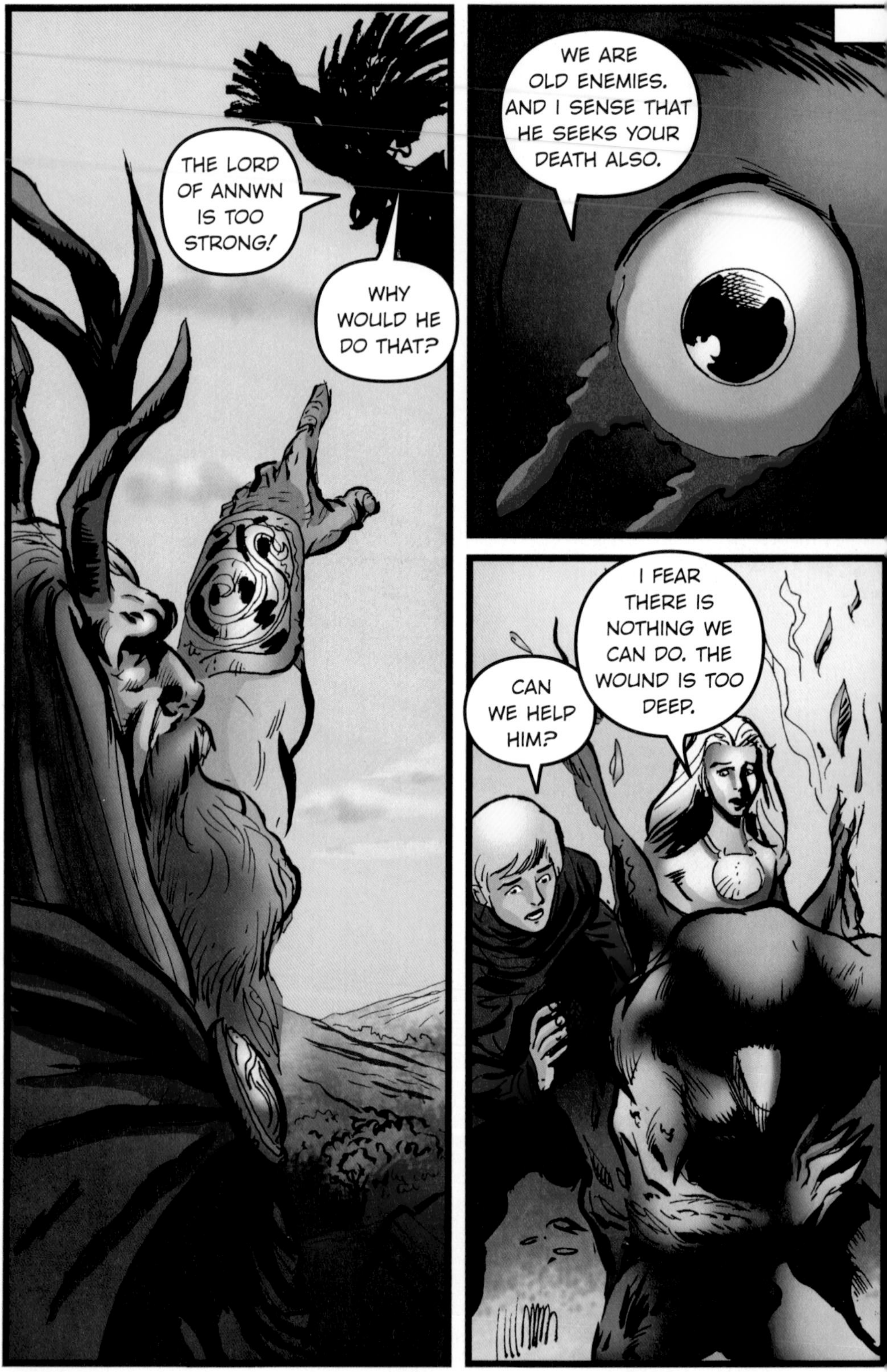
THE LORD OF ANNWN IS TOO STRONG!
WHY WOULD HE DO THAT?
WE ARE OLD ENEMIES. AND I SENSE THAT HE SEEKS YOUR DEATH ALSO.
CAN WE HELP HIM?
I FEAR THERE IS NOTHING WE CAN DO. THE WOUND IS TOO DEEP.

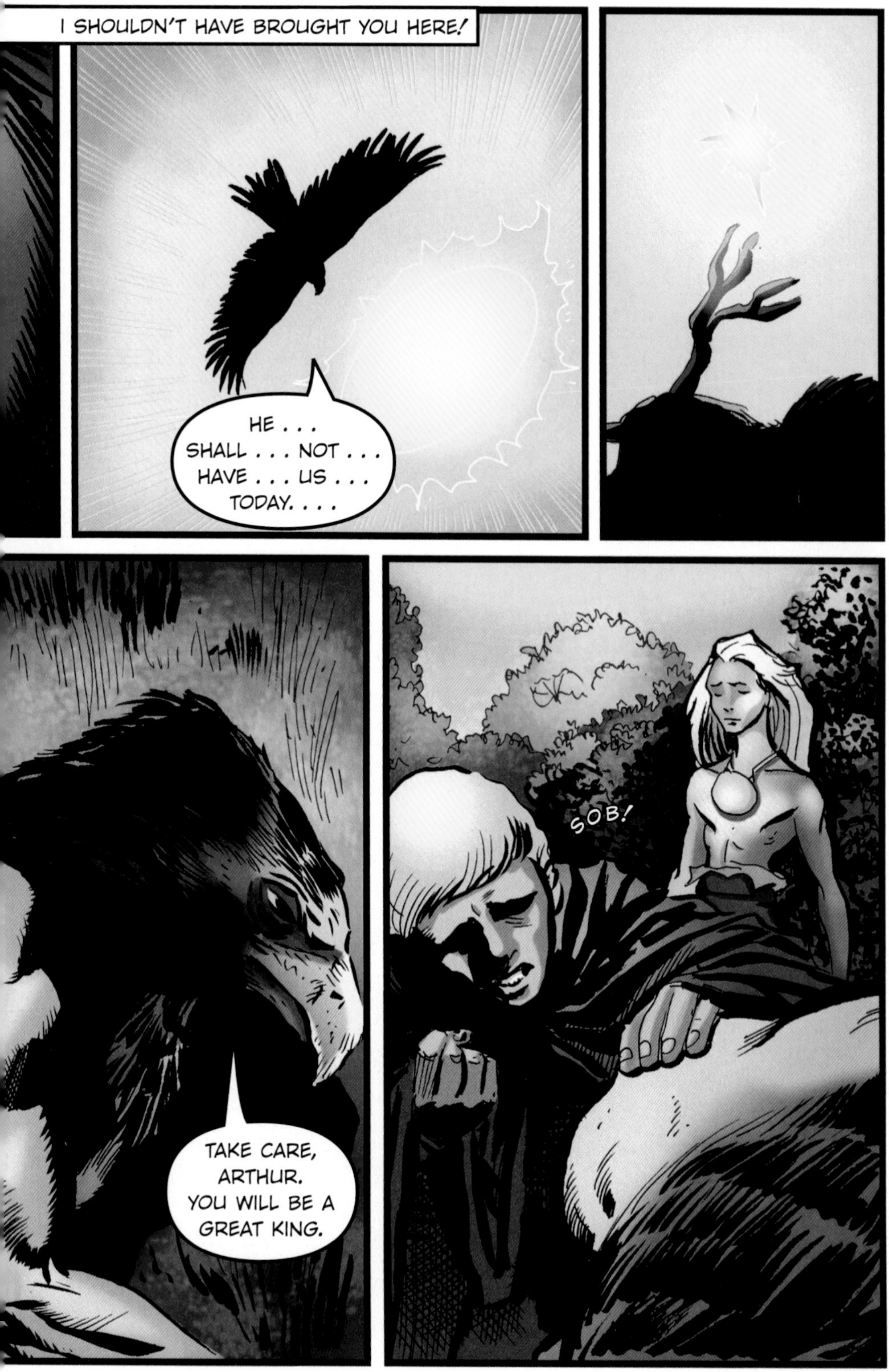
I SHOULDN'T HAVE BROUGHT YOU HERE!
HE . . . SHALL . . . NOT . . . HAVE . . . US . . . TODAY. . . .
SOB!
TAKE CARE, ARTHUR. YOU WILL BE A GREAT KING.

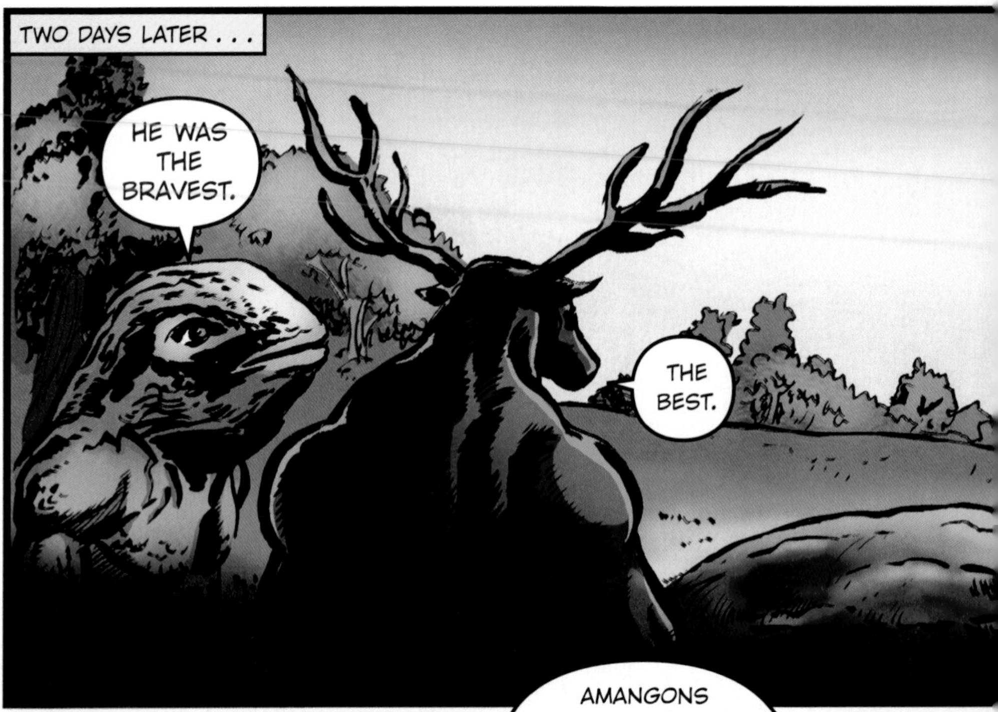
TWO DAYS LATER . . .
HE WAS THE BRAVEST.
THE BEST.

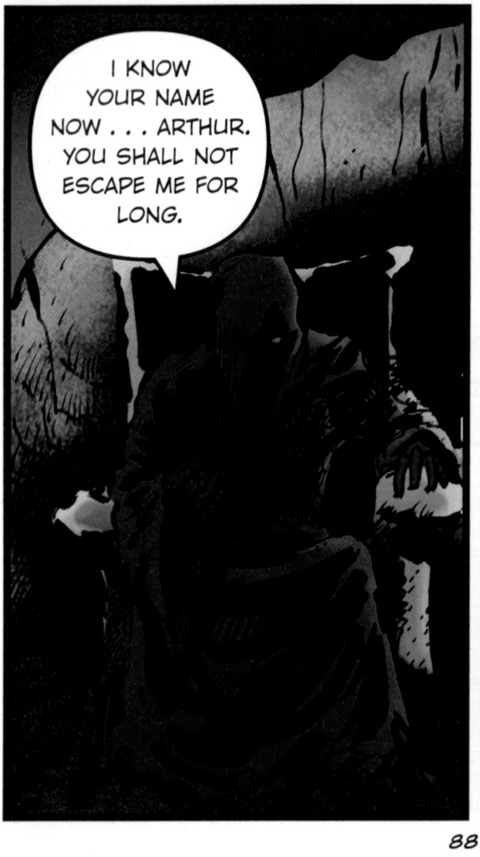
I KNOW YOUR NAME NOW . . . ARTHUR. YOU SHALL NOT ESCAPE ME FOR LONG.

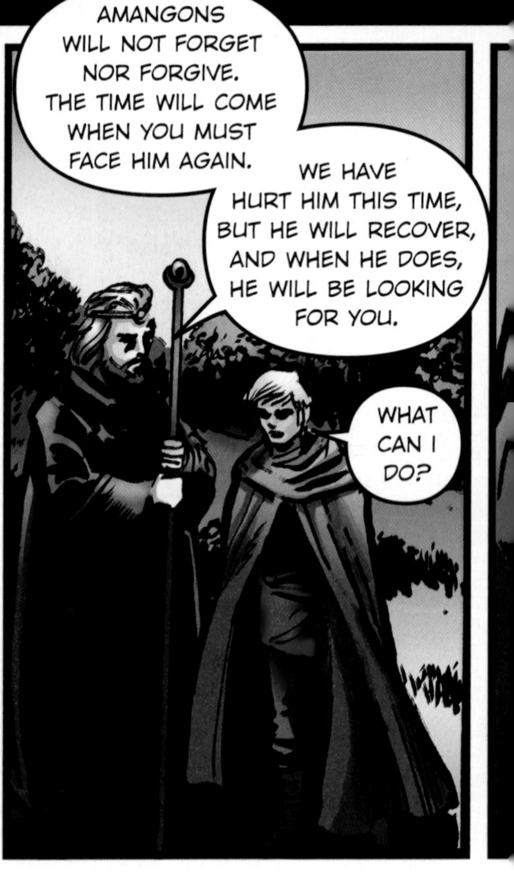
AMANGONS WILL NOT FORGET NOR FORGIVE. THE TIME WILL COME WHEN YOU MUST FACE HIM AGAIN.
WE HAVE HURT HIM THIS TIME, BUT HE WILL RECOVER, AND WHEN HE DOES, HE WILL BE LOOKING FOR YOU.
WHAT CAN I DO?

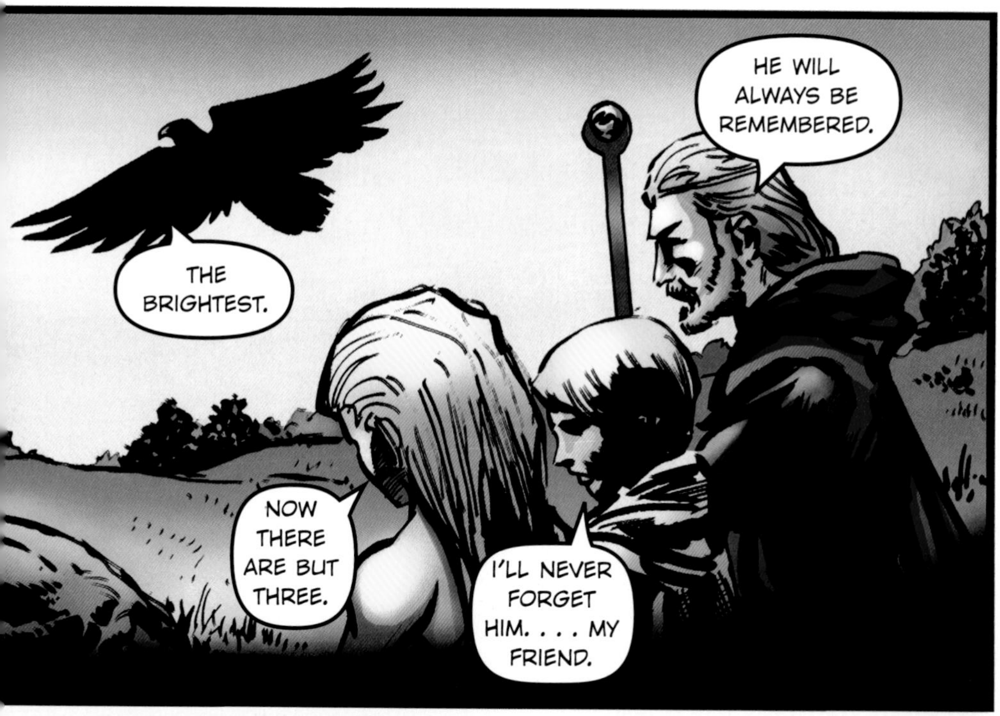
HE WILL ALWAYS BE REMEMBERED.
THE BRIGHTEST.
NOW THERE ARE BUT THREE.
I'LL NEVER FORGET HIM. . . . MY FRIEND.

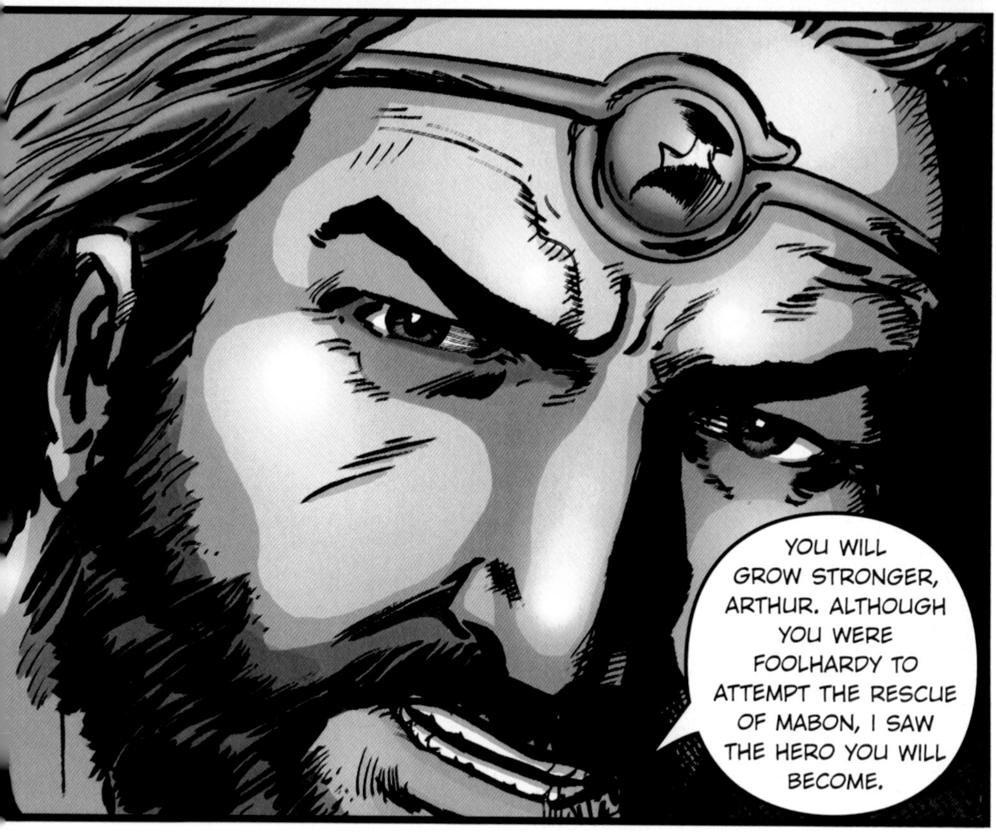
YOU WILL GROW STRONGER, ARTHUR. ALTHOUGH YOU WERE FOOLHARDY TO ATTEMPT THE RESCUE OF MABON, I SAW THE HERO YOU WILL BECOME.

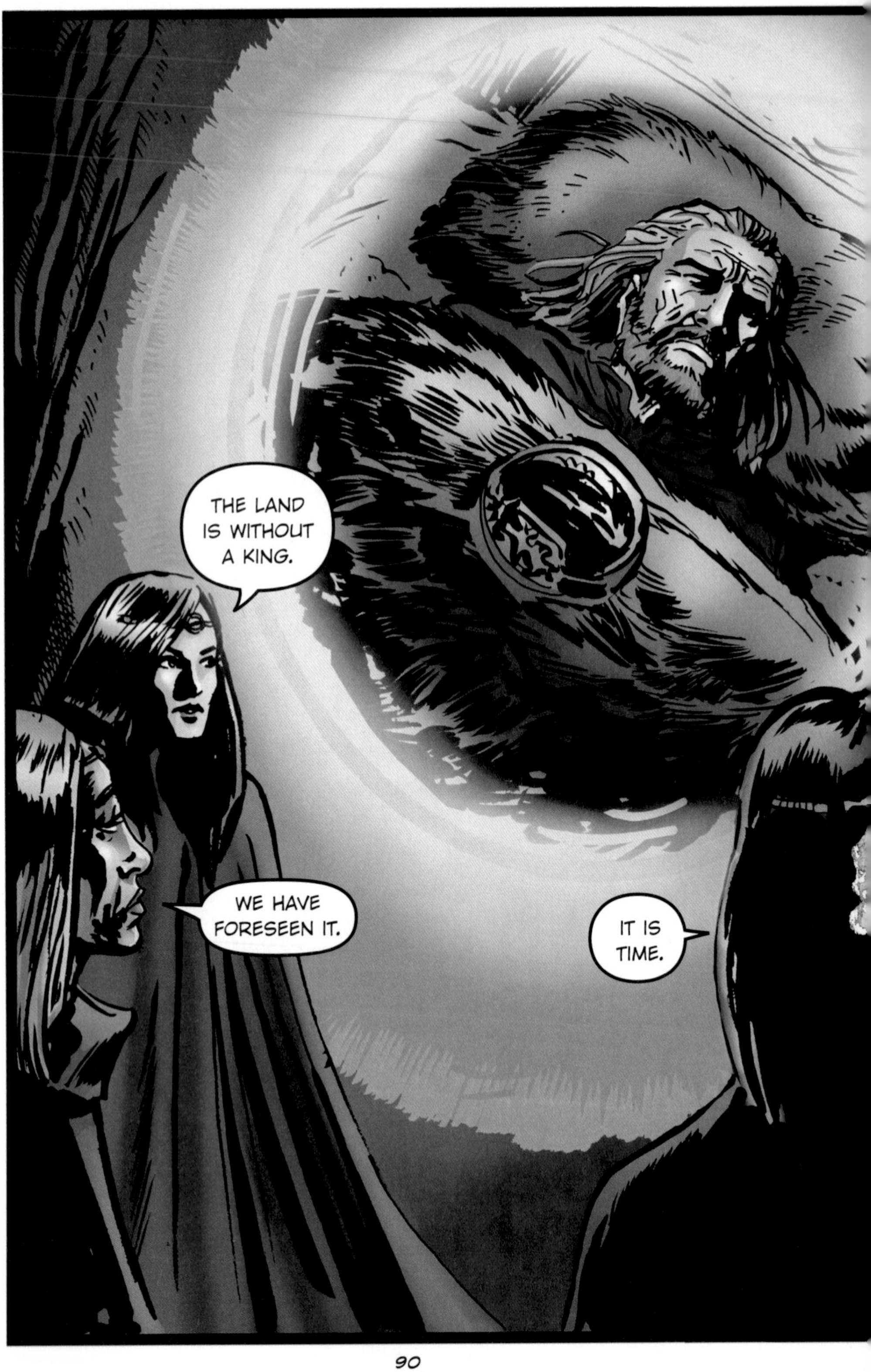
THE LAND IS WITHOUT A KING.
WE HAVE FORESEEN IT.
IT IS TIME.

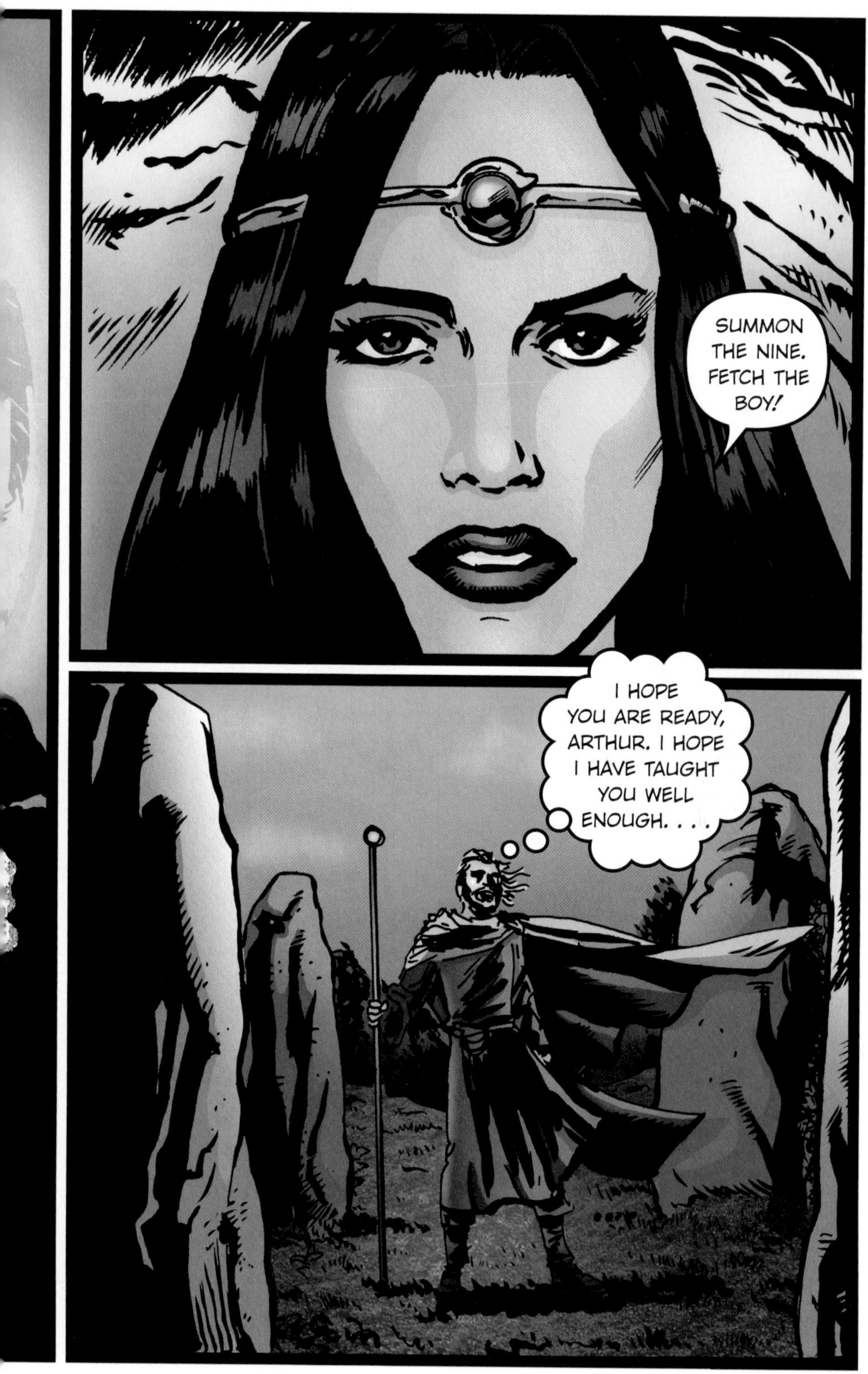
SUMMON THE NINE. FETCH THE BOY!
I HOPE YOU ARE READY, ARTHUR. I HOPE I HAVE TAUGHT YOU WELL ENOUGH. . . .

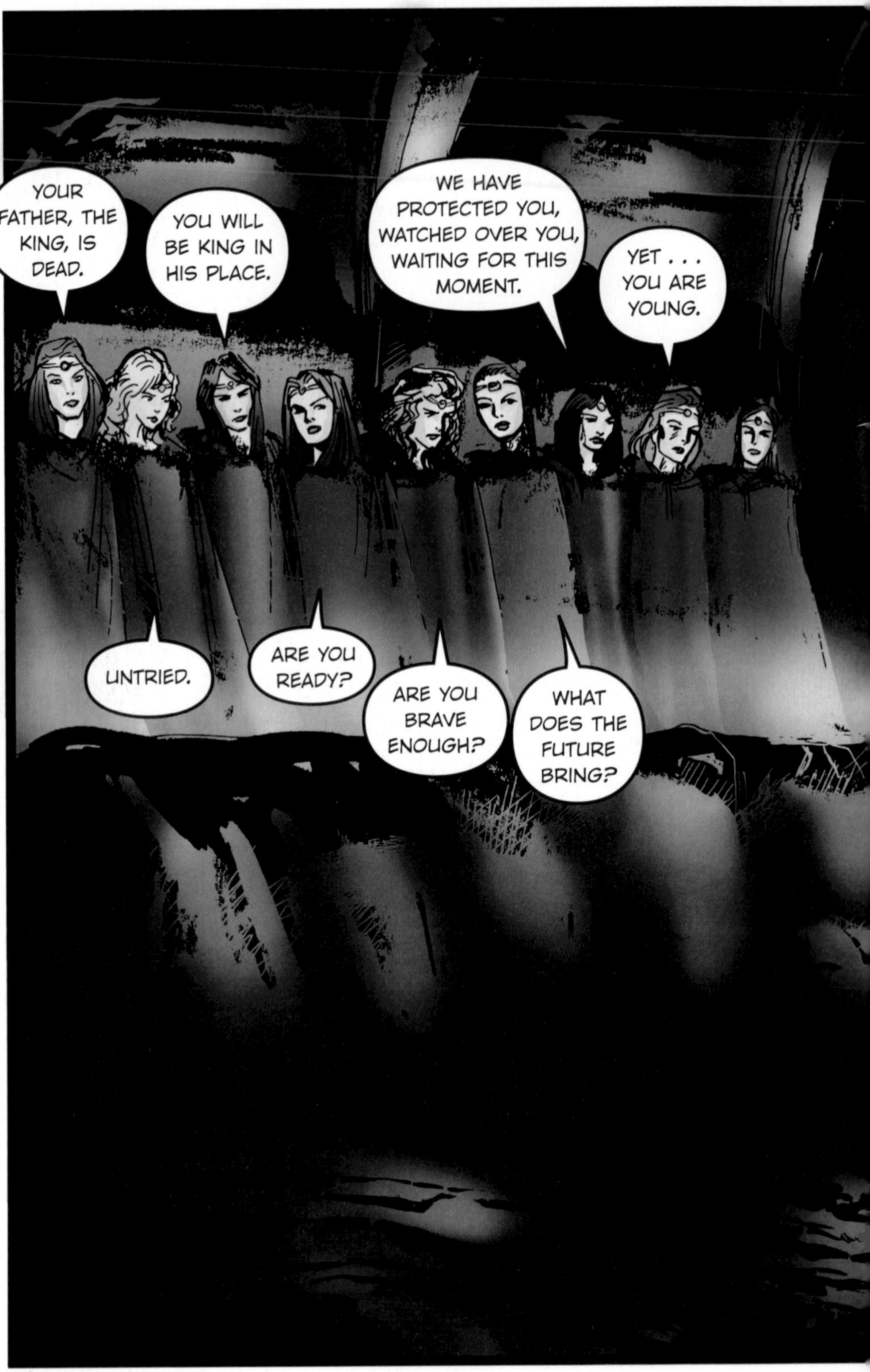
YOUR FATHER, THE KING, IS DEAD.
YOU WILL BE KING IN HIS PLACE.
WE HAVE PROTECTED YOU, WATCHED OVER YOU, WAITING FOR THIS MOMENT.
YET . . . YOU ARE YOUNG.
UNTRIED.
ARE YOU READY?
ARE YOU BRAVE ENOUGH?
WHAT DOES THE FUTURE BRING?

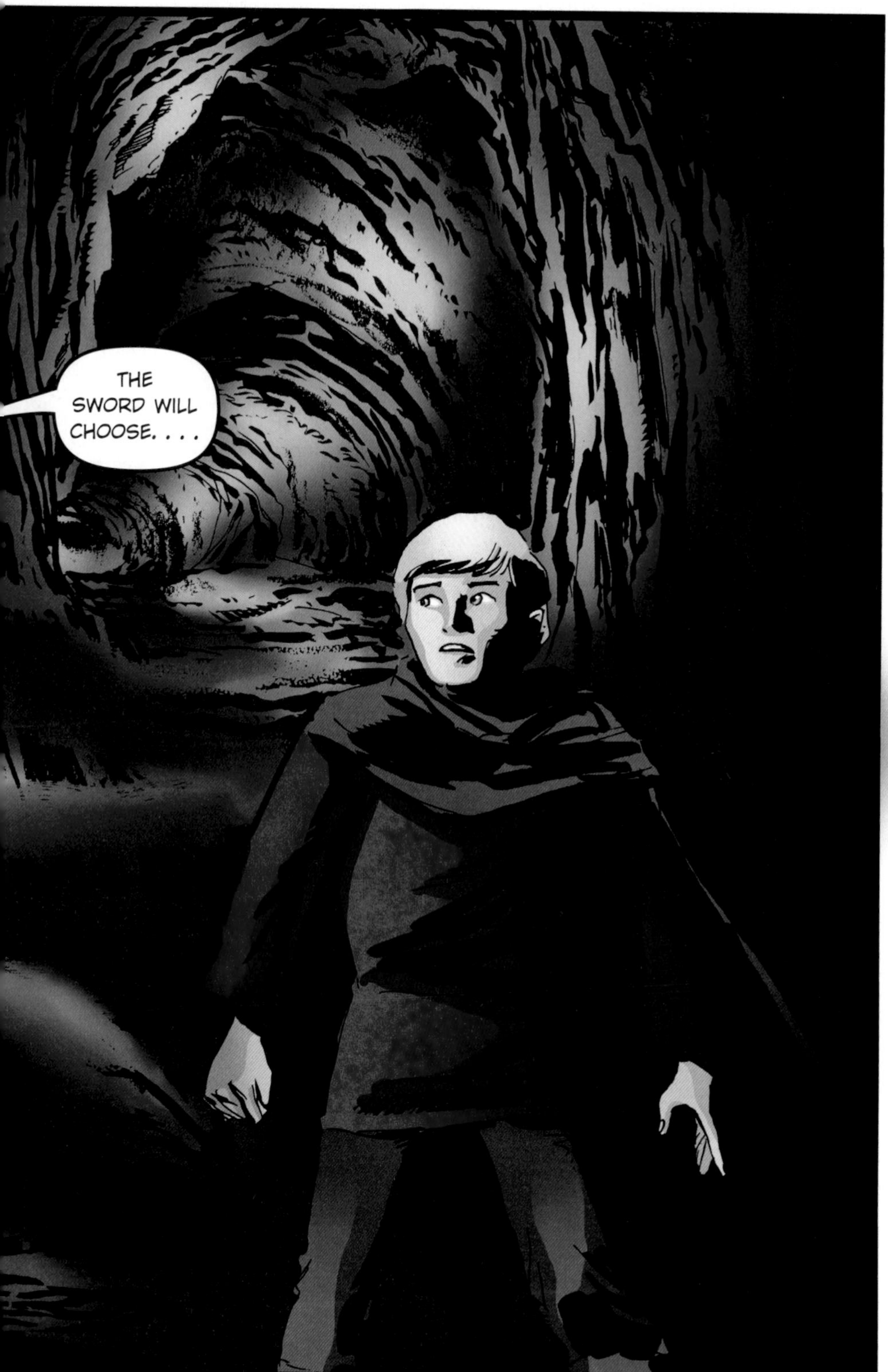
THE SWORD WILL CHOOSE. . . .

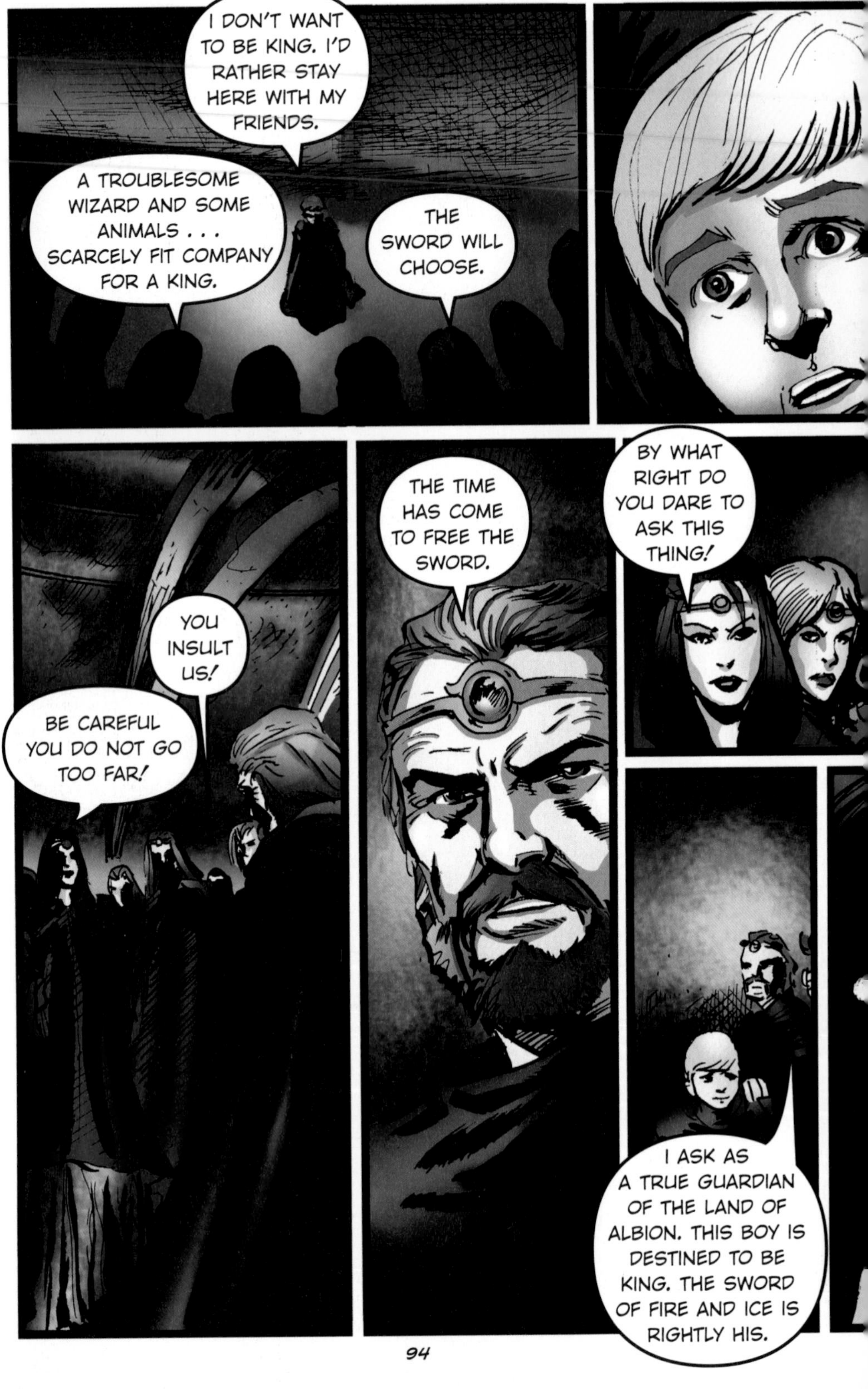
I DON'T WANT TO BE KING. I'D RATHER STAY HERE WITH MY FRIENDS.
A TROUBLESOME WIZARD AND SOME ANIMALS . . . SCARCELY FIT COMPANY FOR A KING.
THE SWORD WILL CHOOSE.
YOU INSULT US!
BE CAREFUL YOU DO NOT GO TOO FAR!
THE TIME HAS COME TO FREE THE SWORD.
BY WHAT RIGHT DO YOU DARE TO ASK THIS THING!
I ASK AS A TRUE GUARDIAN OF THE LAND OF ALBION. THIS BOY IS DESTINED TO BE KING. THE SWORD OF FIRE AND ICE IS RIGHTLY HIS.

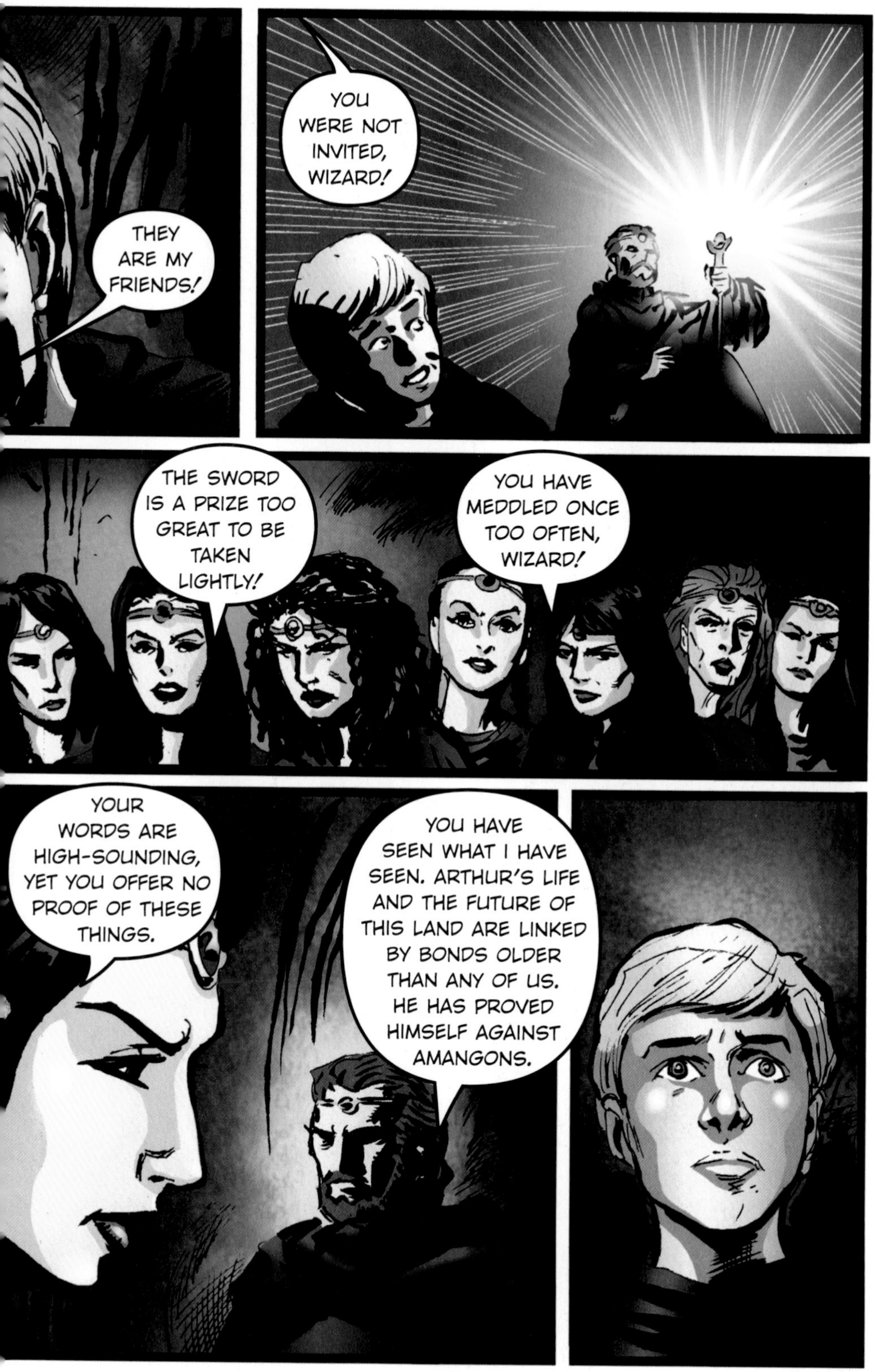
THEY ARE MY FRIENDS!
YOU WERE NOT INVITED, WIZARD!
THE SWORD IS A PRIZE TOO GREAT TO BE TAKEN LIGHTLY!
YOU HAVE MEDDLED ONCE TOO OFTEN, WIZARD!
YOUR WORDS ARE HIGH-SOUNDING, YET YOU OFFER NO PROOF OF THESE THINGS.
YOU HAVE SEEN WHAT I HAVE SEEN. ARTHUR'S LIFE AND THE FUTURE OF THIS LAND ARE LINKED BY BONDS OLDER THAN ANY OF US. HE HAS PROVED HIMSELF AGAINST AMANGONS.

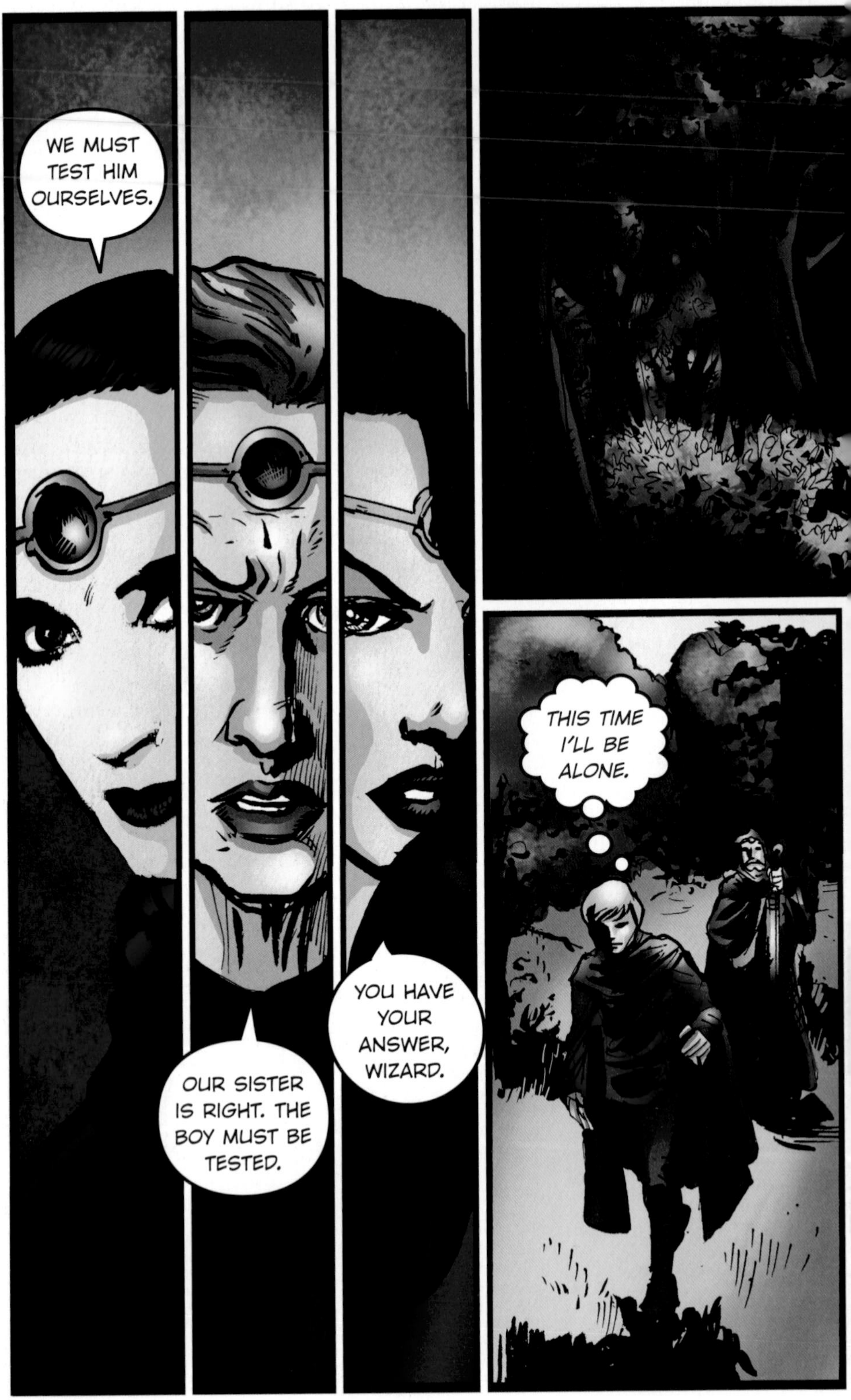
WE MUST TEST HIM OURSELVES.
OUR SISTER IS RIGHT. THE BOY MUST BE TESTED.
YOU HAVE YOUR ANSWER, WIZARD.
THIS TIME I'LL BE ALONE.

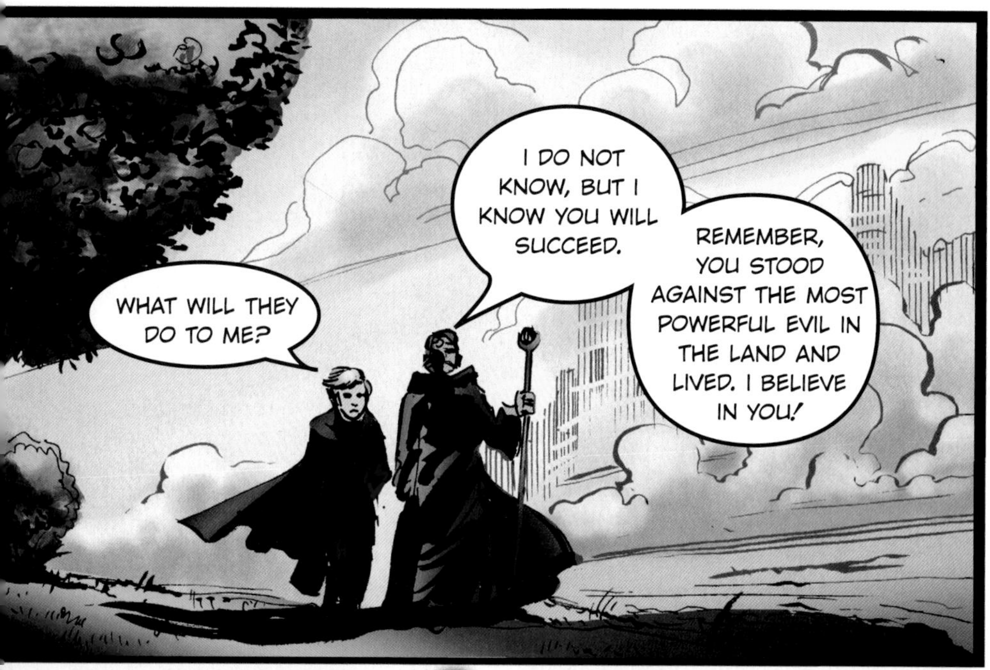
WHAT WILL THEY DO TO ME?
I DO NOT KNOW, BUT I KNOW YOU WILL SUCCEED.
REMEMBER, YOU STOOD AGAINST THE MOST POWERFUL EVIL IN THE LAND AND LIVED. I BELIEVE IN YOU!

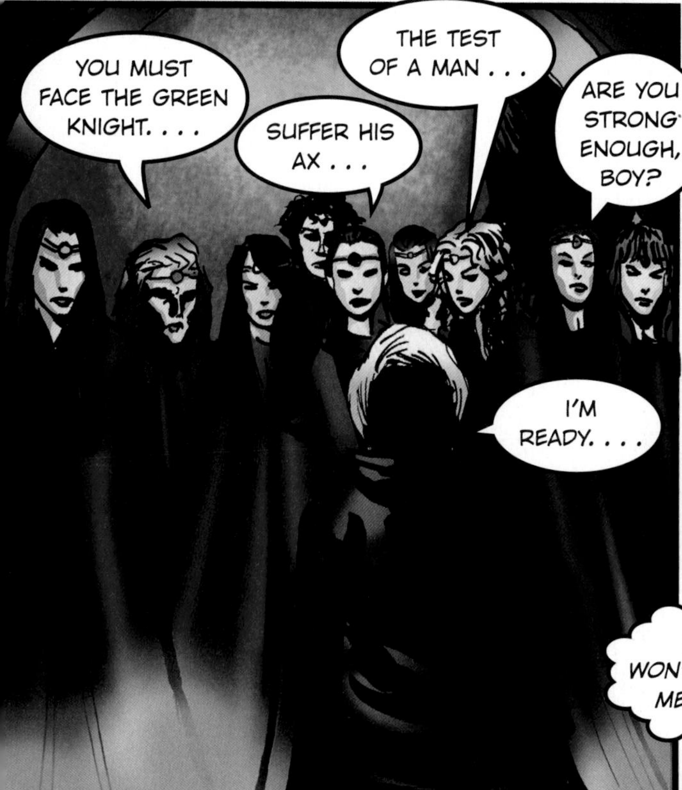
YOU MUST FACE THE GREEN KNIGHT. . . .
SUFFER HIS AX . . .
THE TEST OF A MAN . . .
ARE YOU STRONG ENOUGH, BOY?
I'M READY. . . .

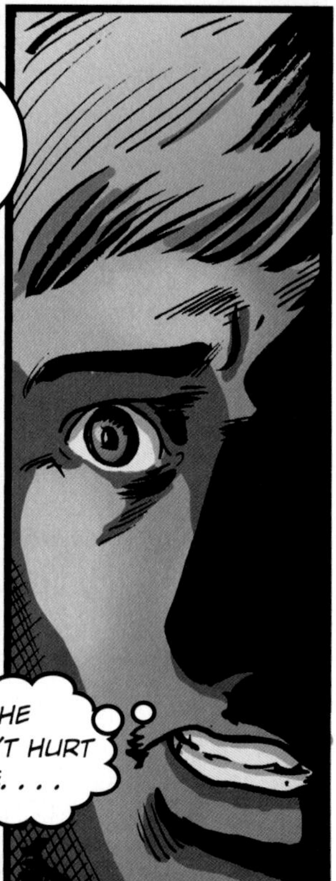
HE WON'T HURT ME. . . .

SKREE! SKREE!

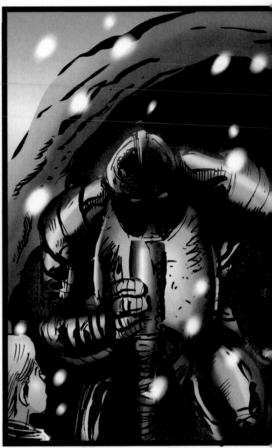

BOW BEFORE ME!

IT'S ME . . . ARTHUR . . .

BEND YOUR NECK!

I THOUGHT WE WERE FRIENDS. . . .

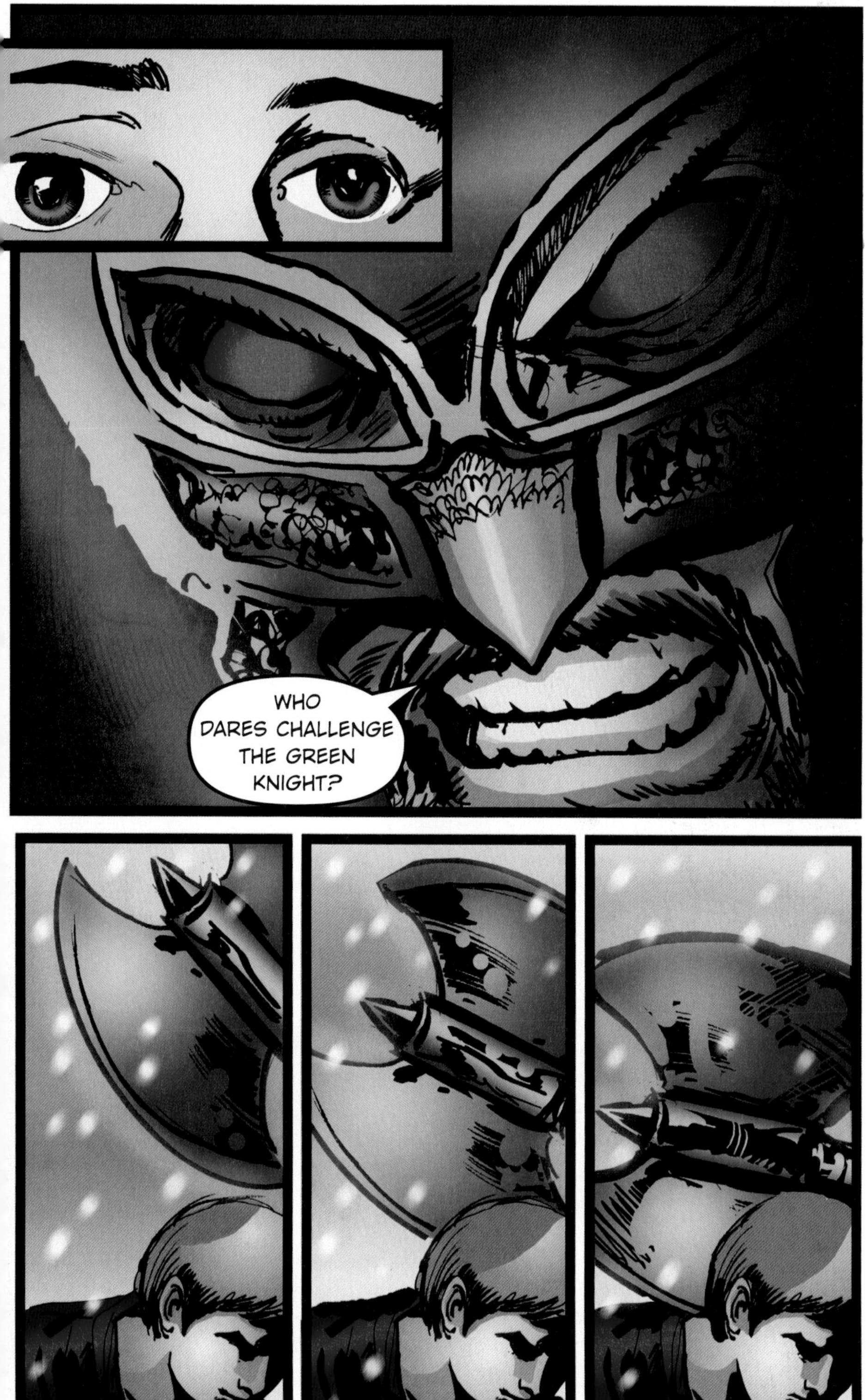
WHO DARES CHALLENGE THE GREEN KNIGHT?

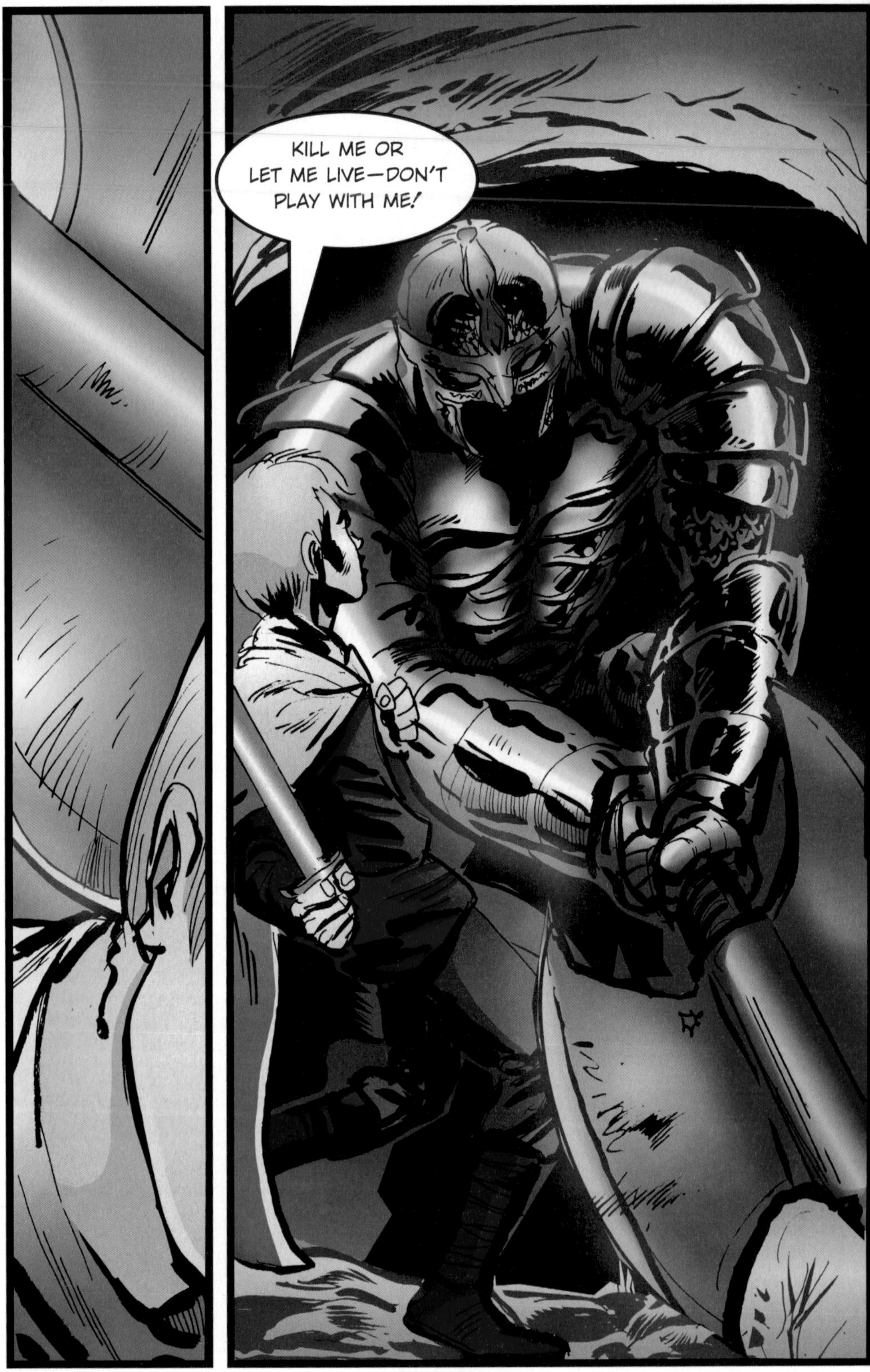
KILL ME OR LET ME LIVE—DON'T PLAY WITH ME!

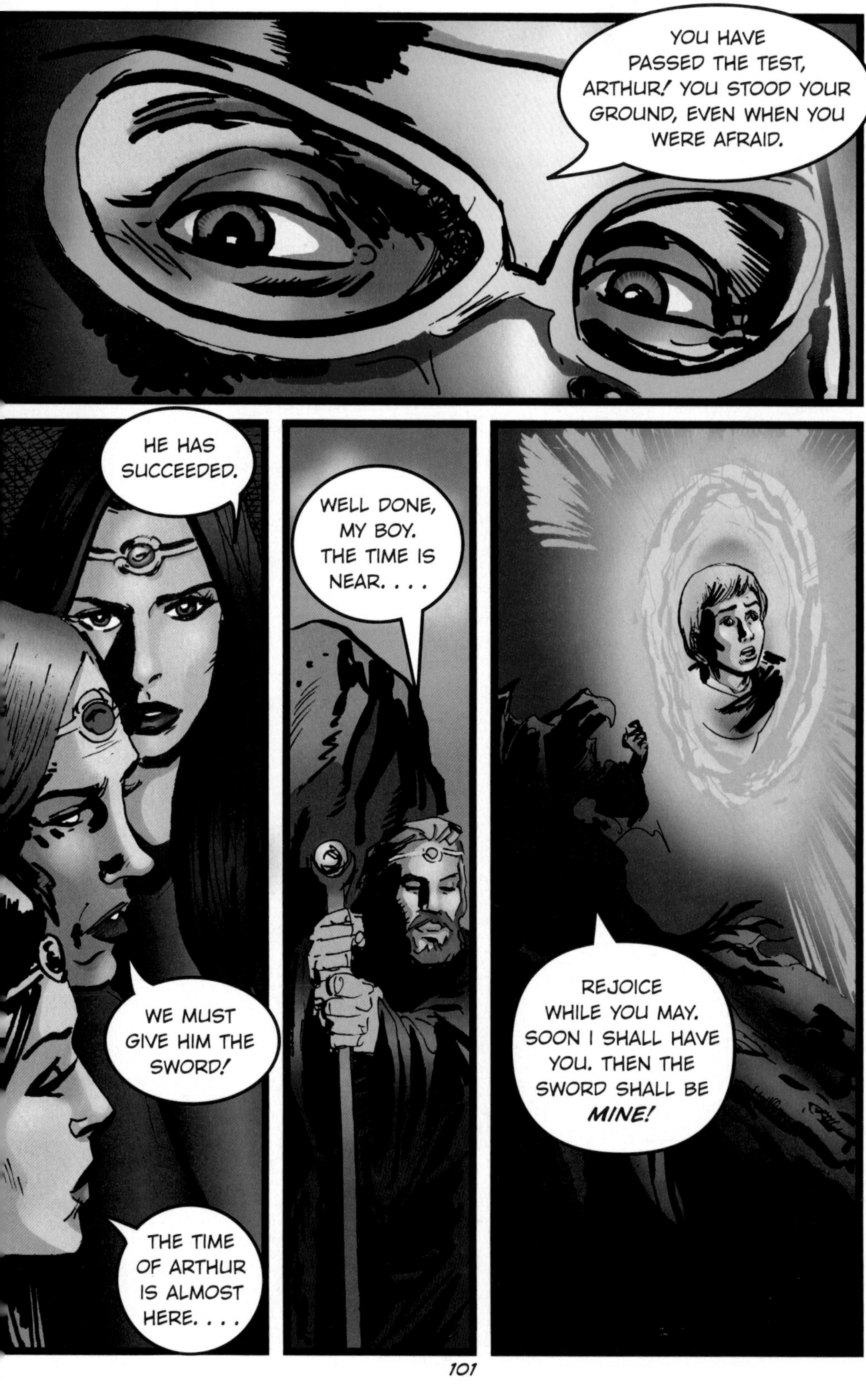
YOU HAVE PASSED THE TEST, ARTHUR! YOU STOOD YOUR GROUND, EVEN WHEN YOU WERE AFRAID.
HE HAS SUCCEEDED.
WE MUST GIVE HIM THE SWORD!
THE TIME OF ARTHUR IS ALMOST HERE. . . .
WELL DONE, MY BOY. THE TIME IS NEAR. . . .
REJOICE WHILE YOU MAY. SOON I SHALL HAVE YOU. THEN THE SWORD SHALL BE *MINE!*

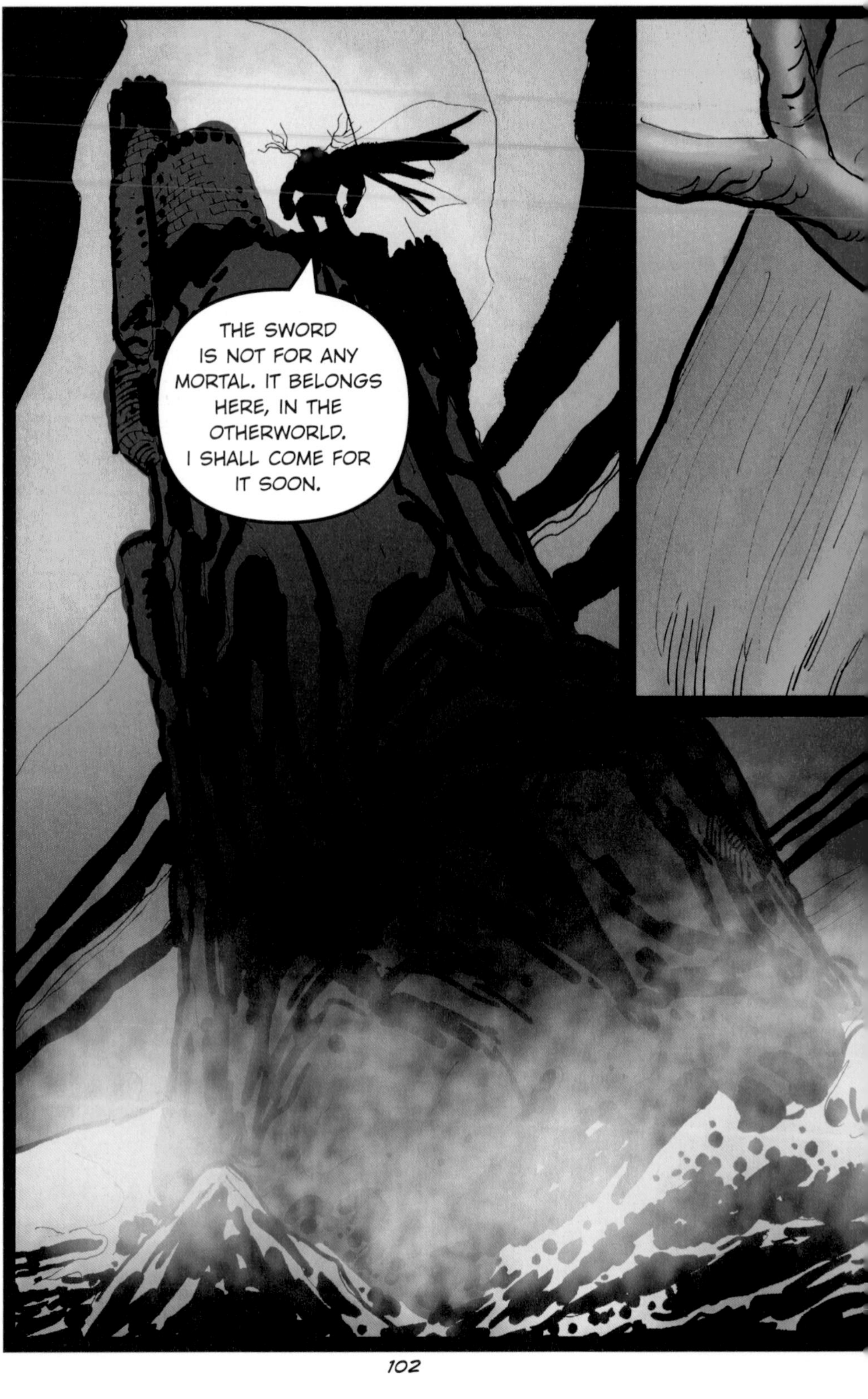
THE SWORD IS NOT FOR ANY MORTAL. IT BELONGS HERE, IN THE OTHERWORLD. I SHALL COME FOR IT SOON.

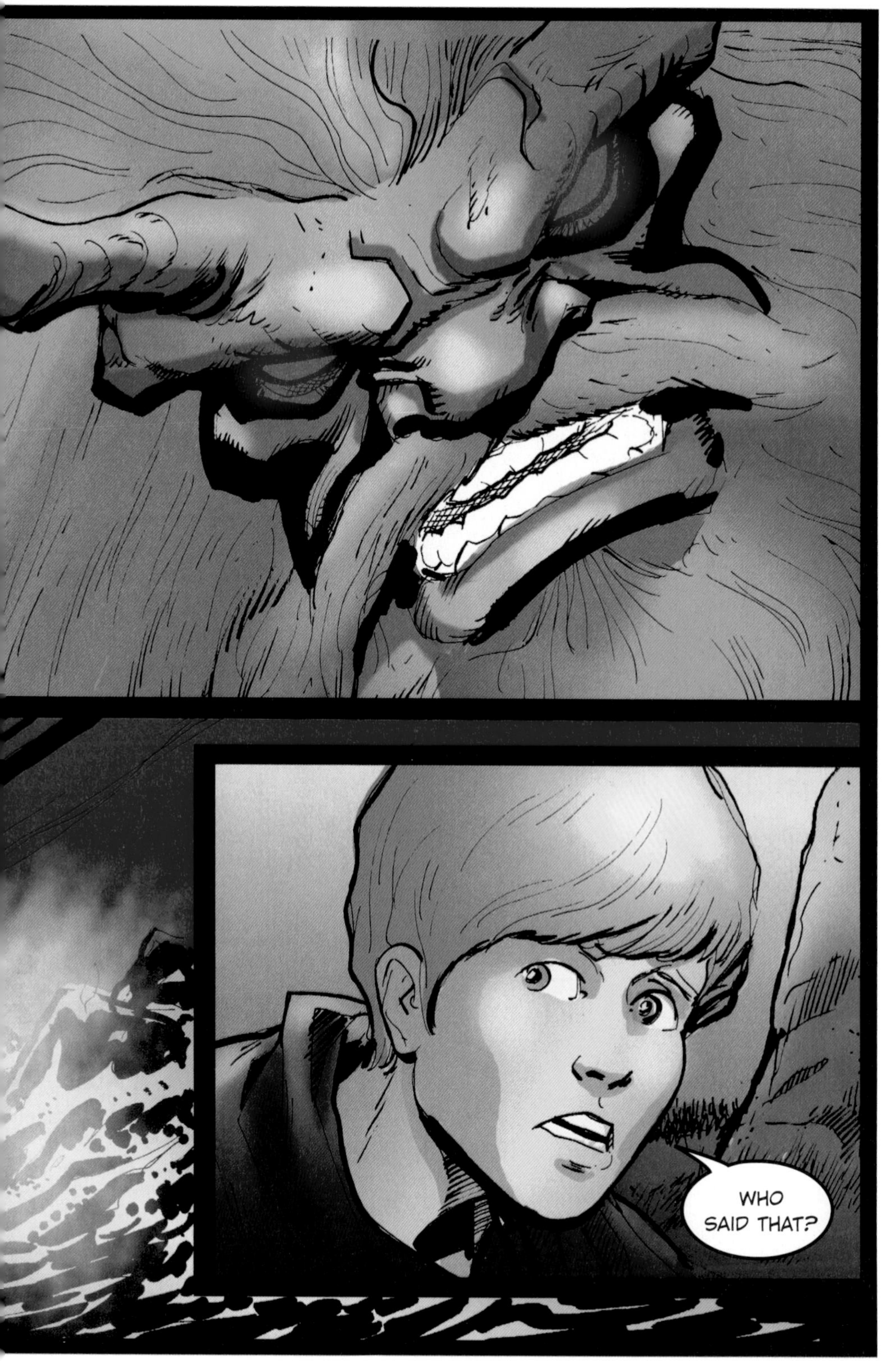
WHO SAID THAT?

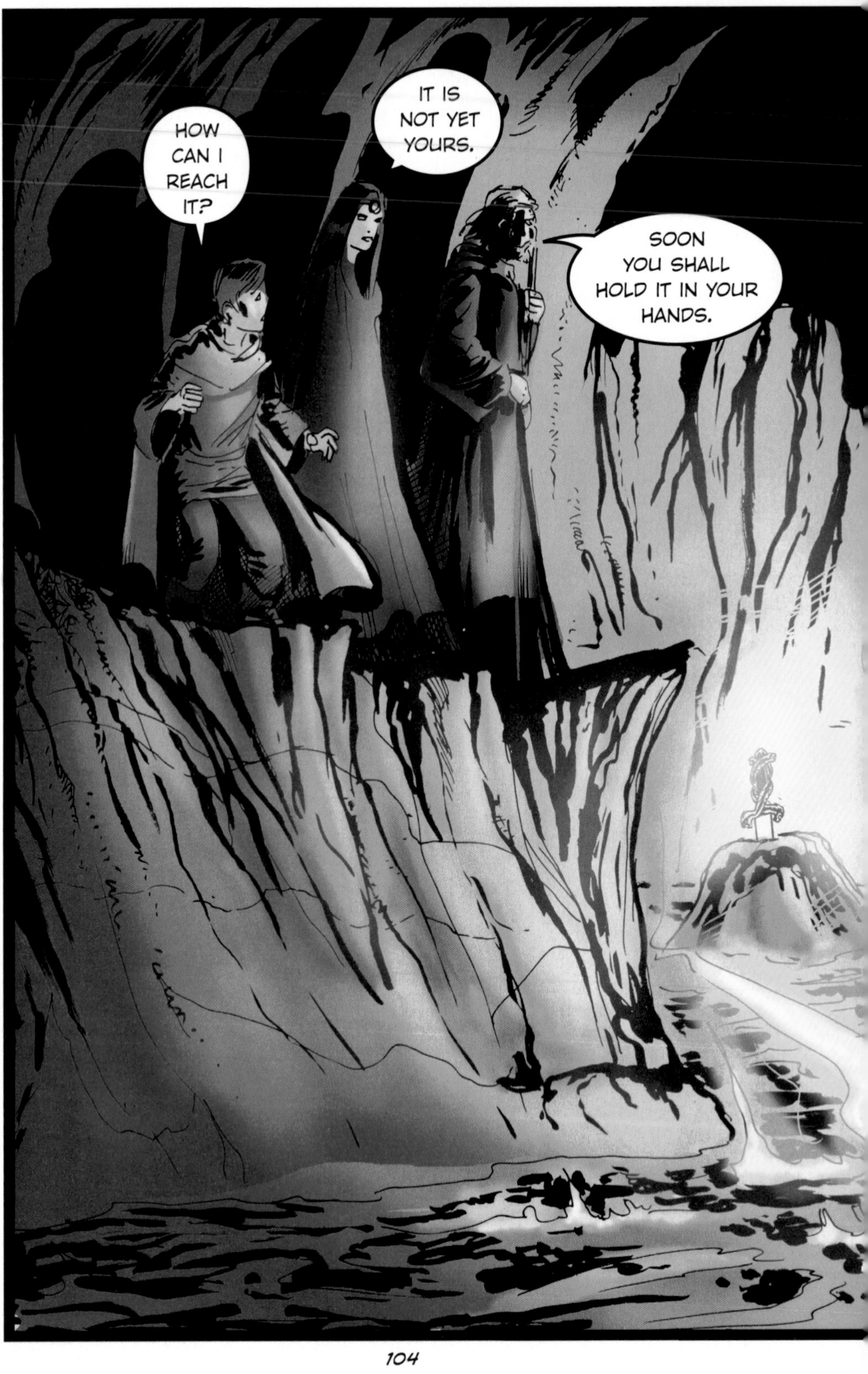
HOW CAN I REACH IT?
IT IS NOT YET YOURS.
SOON YOU SHALL HOLD IT IN YOUR HANDS.

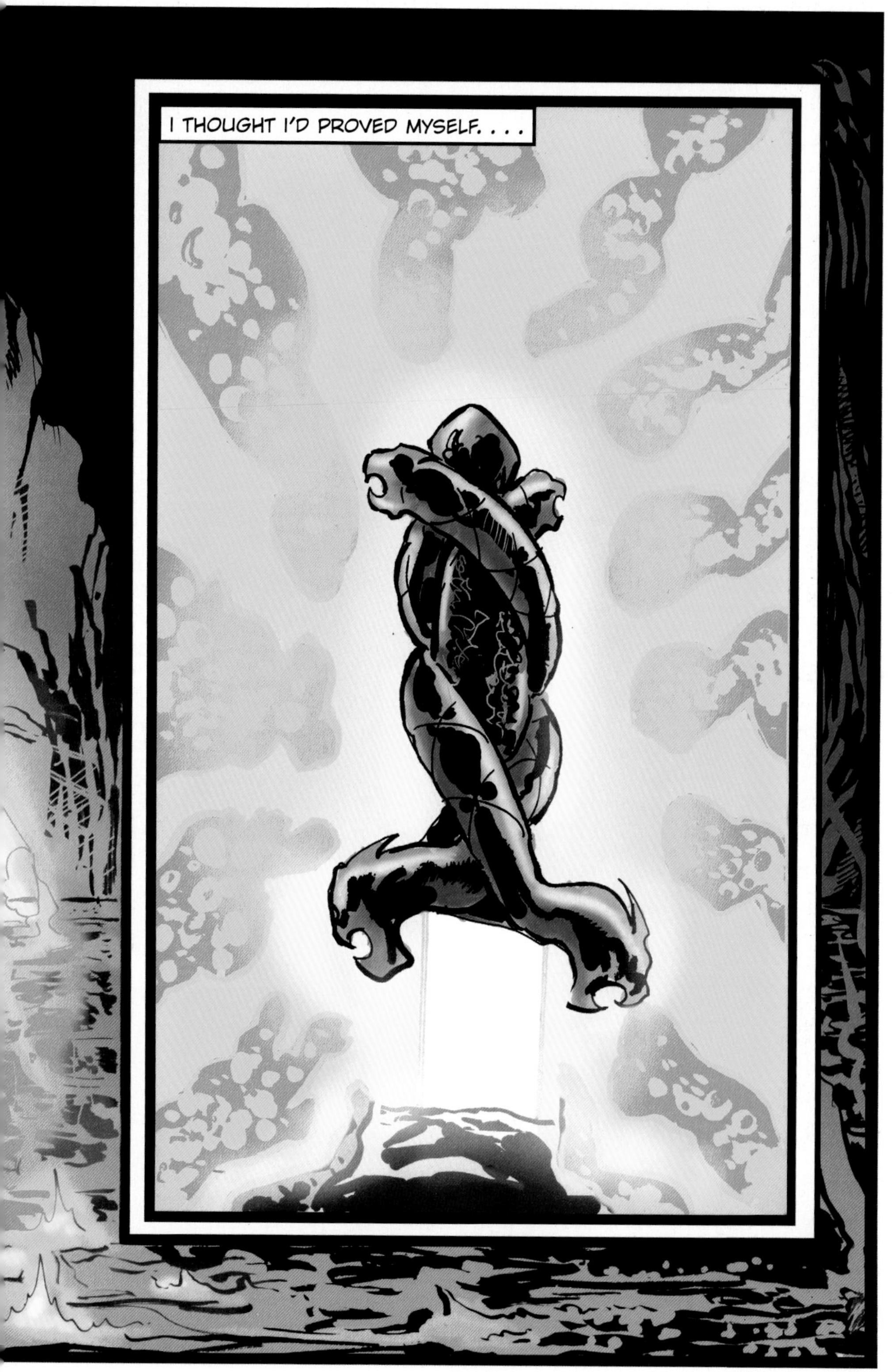
I THOUGHT I'D PROVED MYSELF. . . .

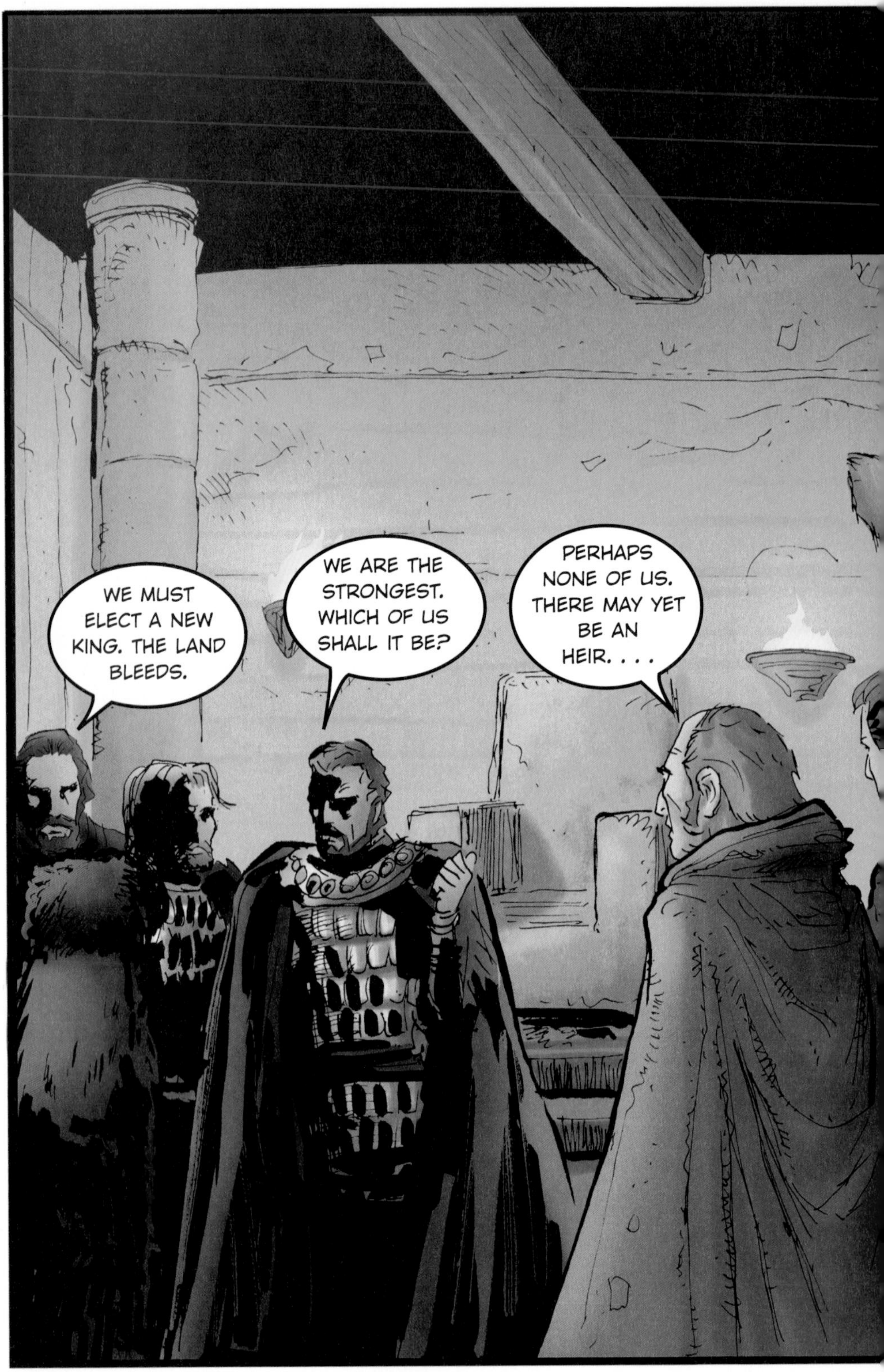
WE MUST ELECT A NEW KING. THE LAND BLEEDS.
WE ARE THE STRONGEST. WHICH OF US SHALL IT BE?
PERHAPS NONE OF US. THERE MAY YET BE AN HEIR. . . .

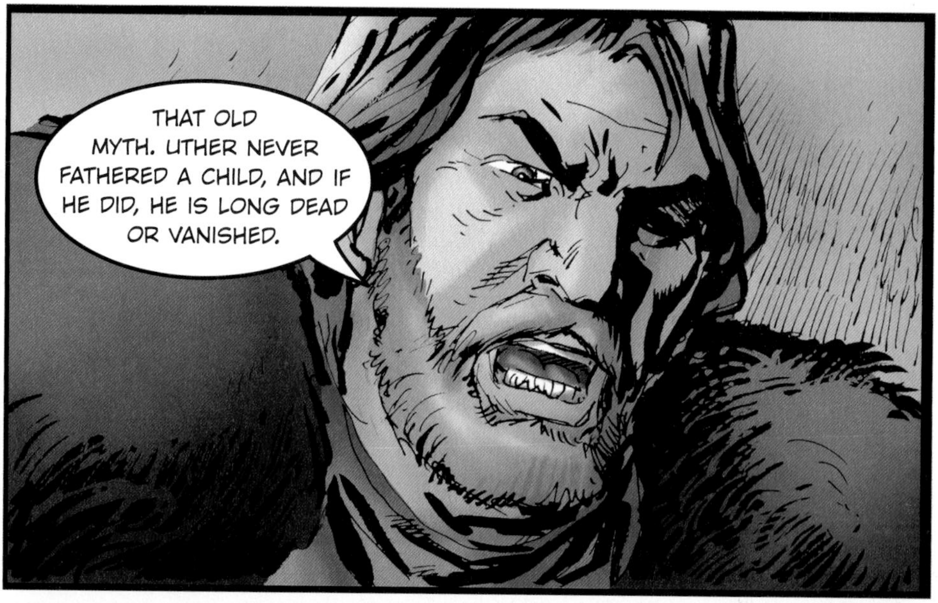
THAT OLD MYTH. UTHER NEVER FATHERED A CHILD, AND IF HE DID, HE IS LONG DEAD OR VANISHED.

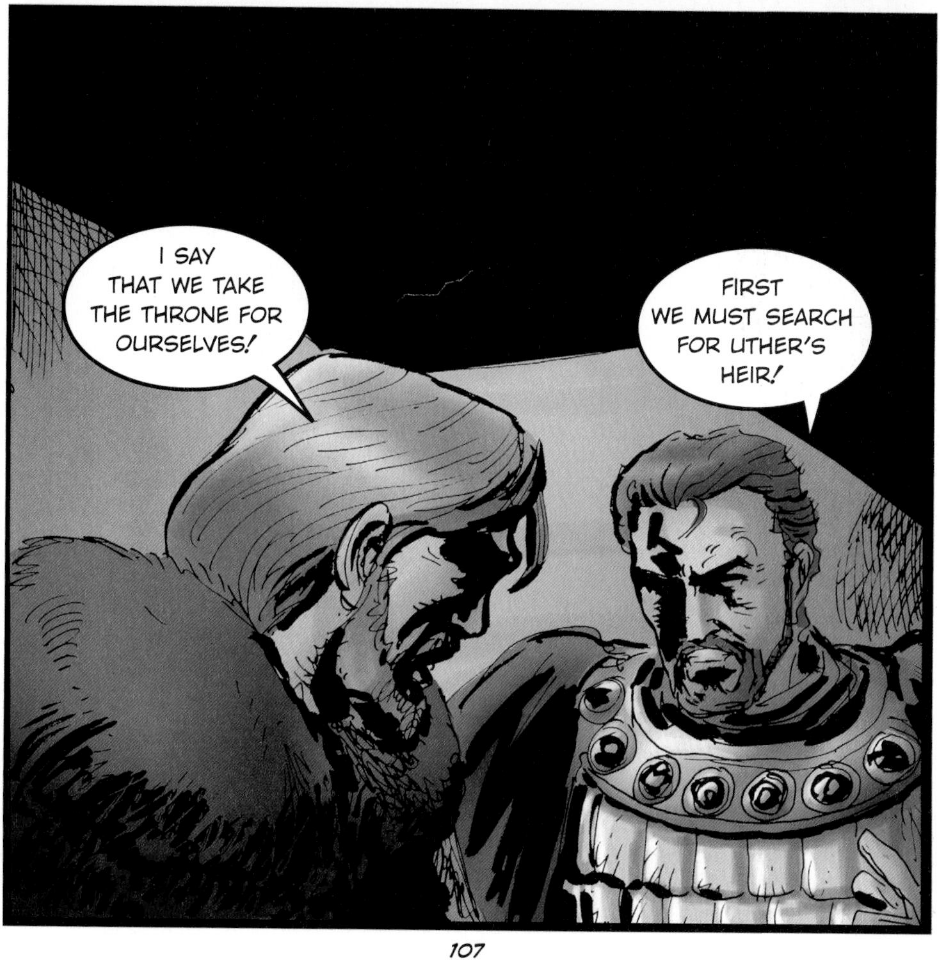
I SAY THAT WE TAKE THE THRONE FOR OURSELVES!
FIRST WE MUST SEARCH FOR UTHER'S HEIR!

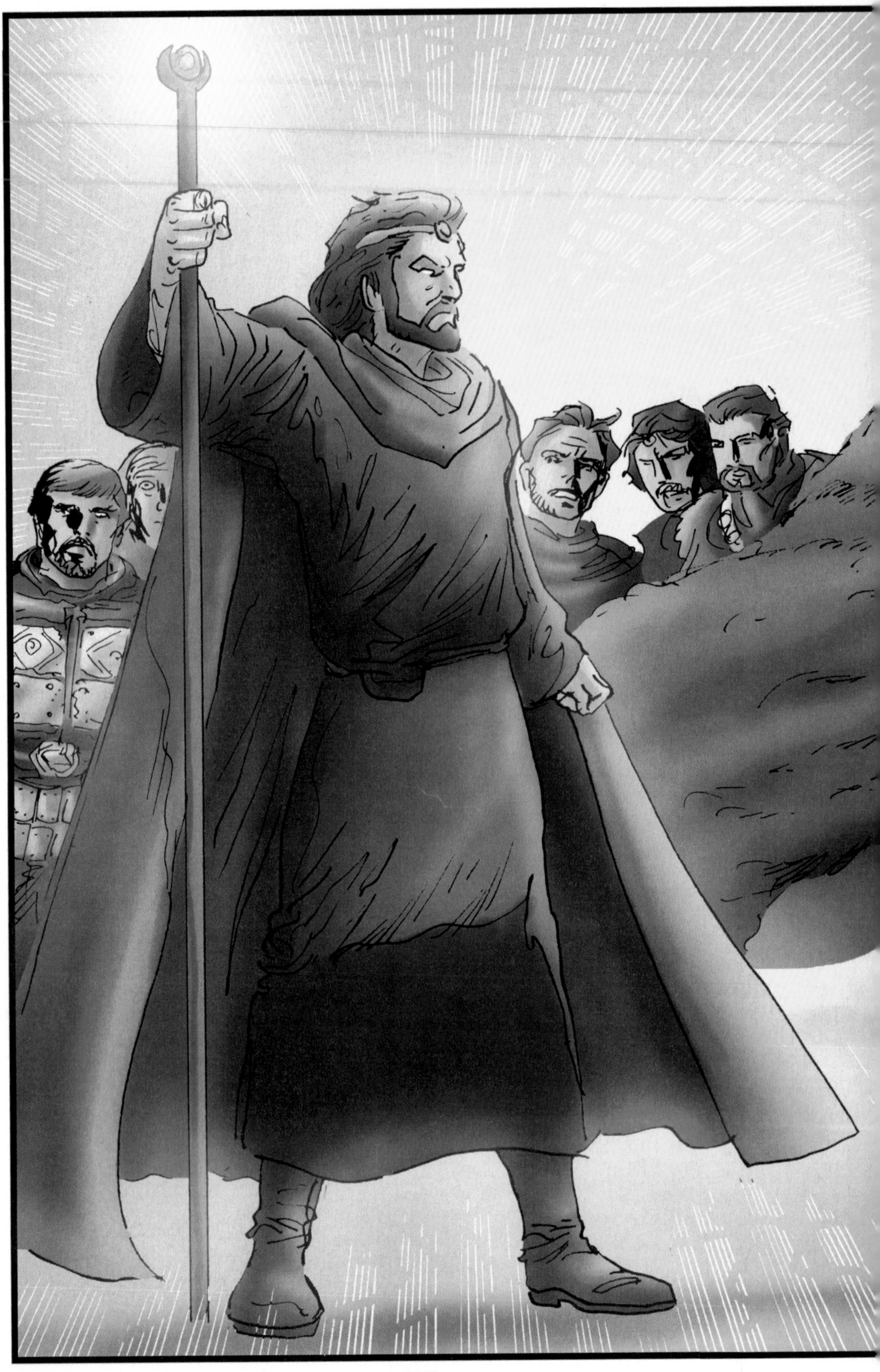

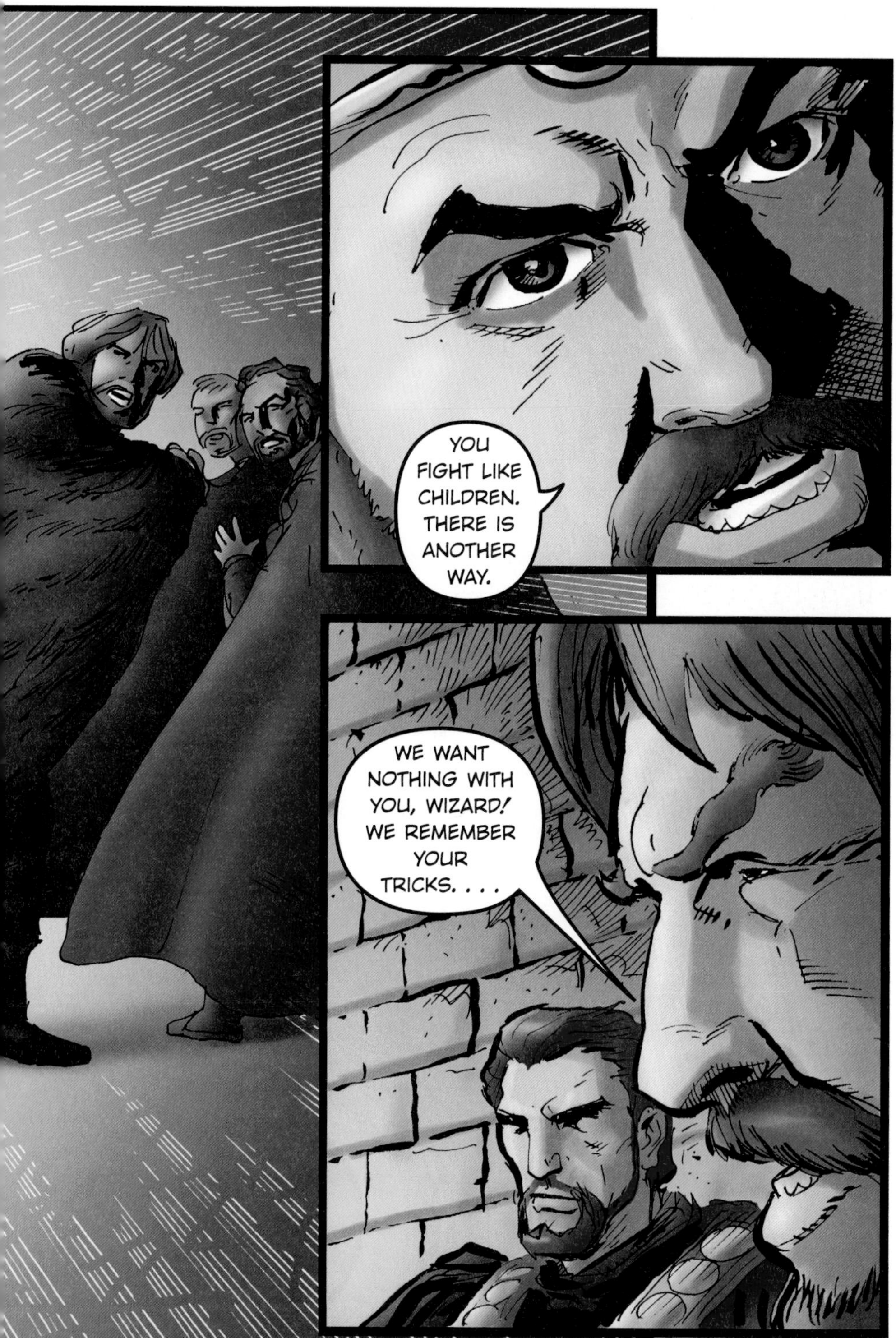
YOU FIGHT LIKE CHILDREN. THERE IS ANOTHER WAY.
WE WANT NOTHING WITH YOU, WIZARD! WE REMEMBER YOUR TRICKS. . . .

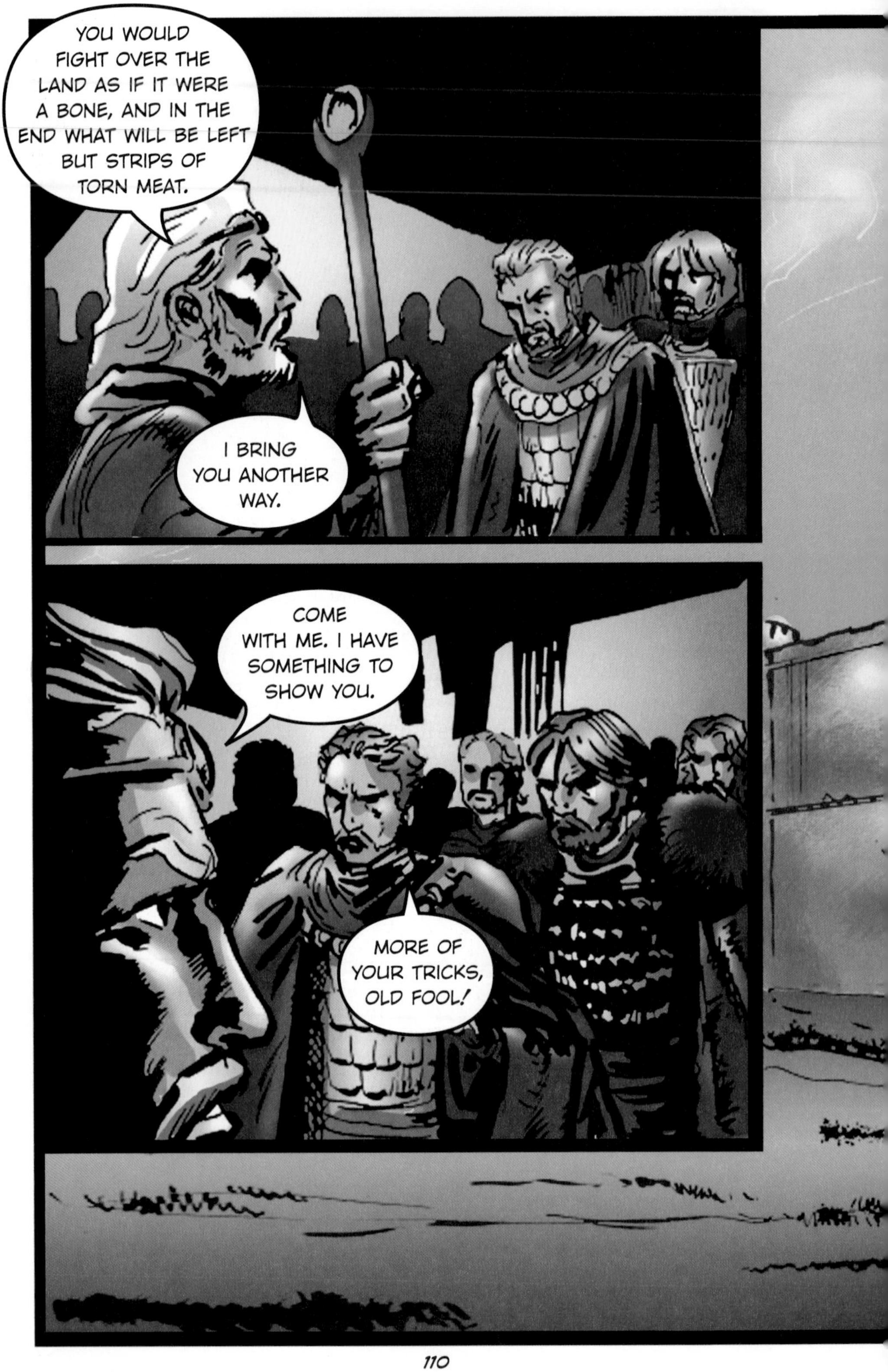
YOU WOULD FIGHT OVER THE LAND AS IF IT WERE A BONE, AND IN THE END WHAT WILL BE LEFT BUT STRIPS OF TORN MEAT.
I BRING YOU ANOTHER WAY.
COME WITH ME. I HAVE SOMETHING TO SHOW YOU.
MORE OF YOUR TRICKS, OLD FOOL!

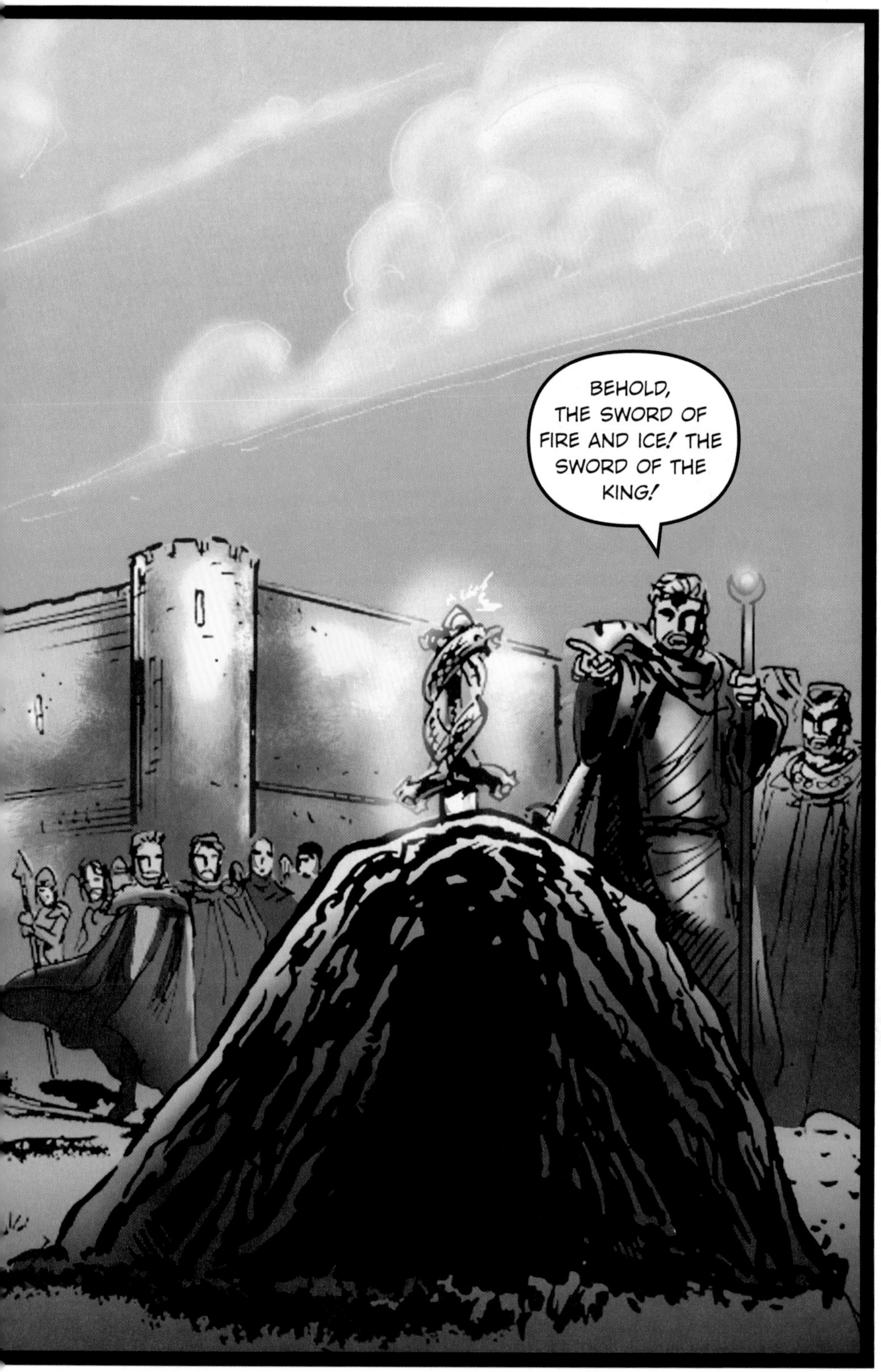
BEHOLD, THE SWORD OF FIRE AND ICE! THE SWORD OF THE KING!

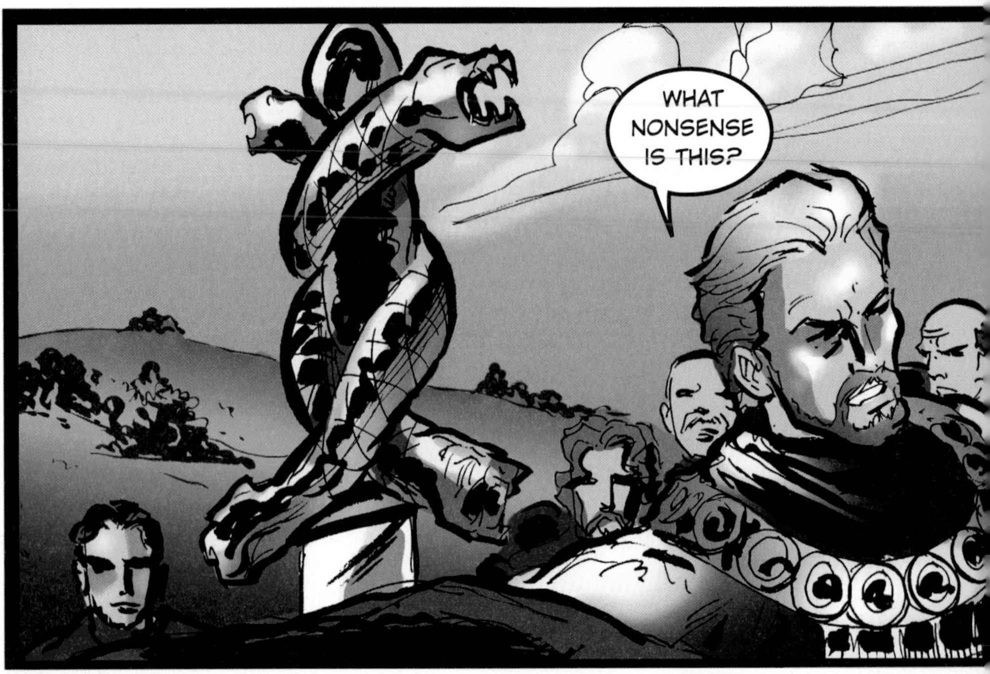
WHAT NONSENSE IS THIS?

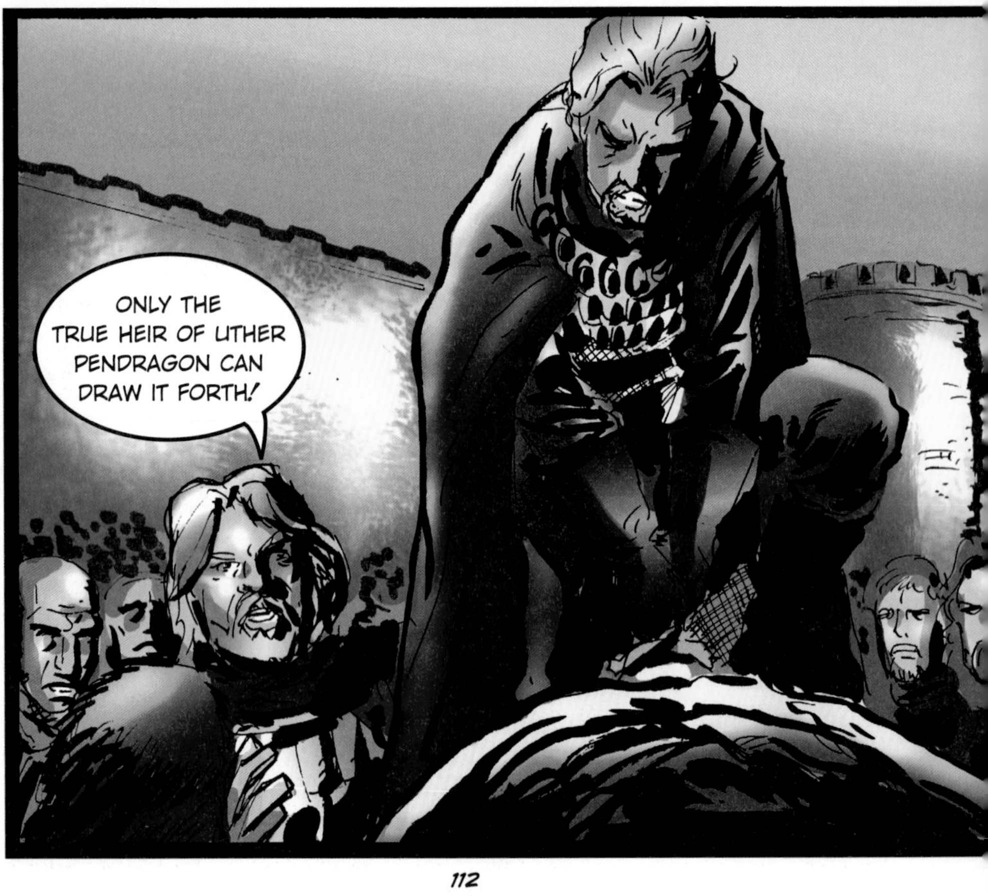
ONLY THE TRUE HEIR OF UTHER PENDRAGON CAN DRAW IT FORTH!

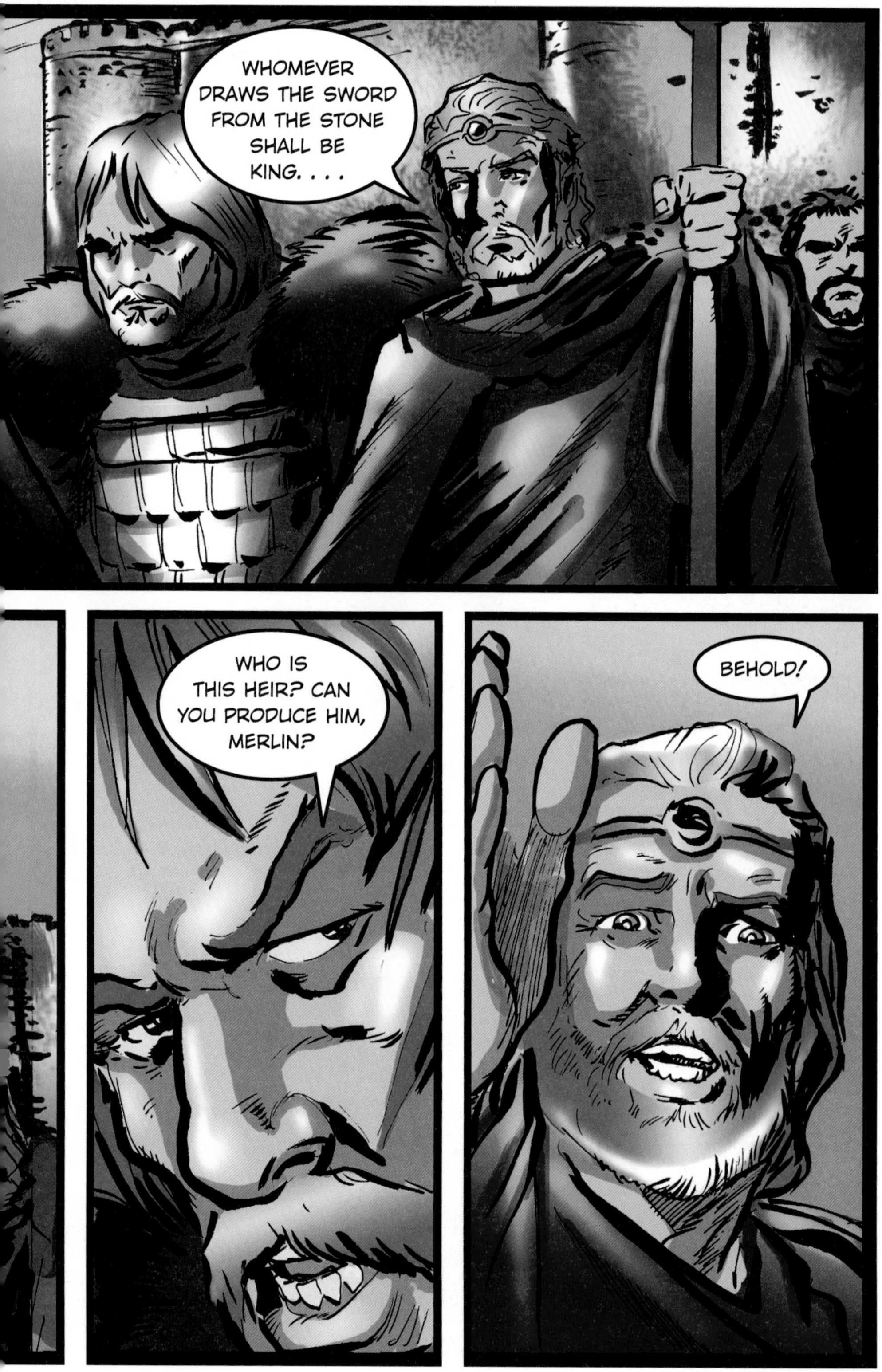
WHOMEVER DRAWS THE SWORD FROM THE STONE SHALL BE KING. . . .
WHO IS THIS HEIR? CAN YOU PRODUCE HIM, MERLIN?
BEHOLD!

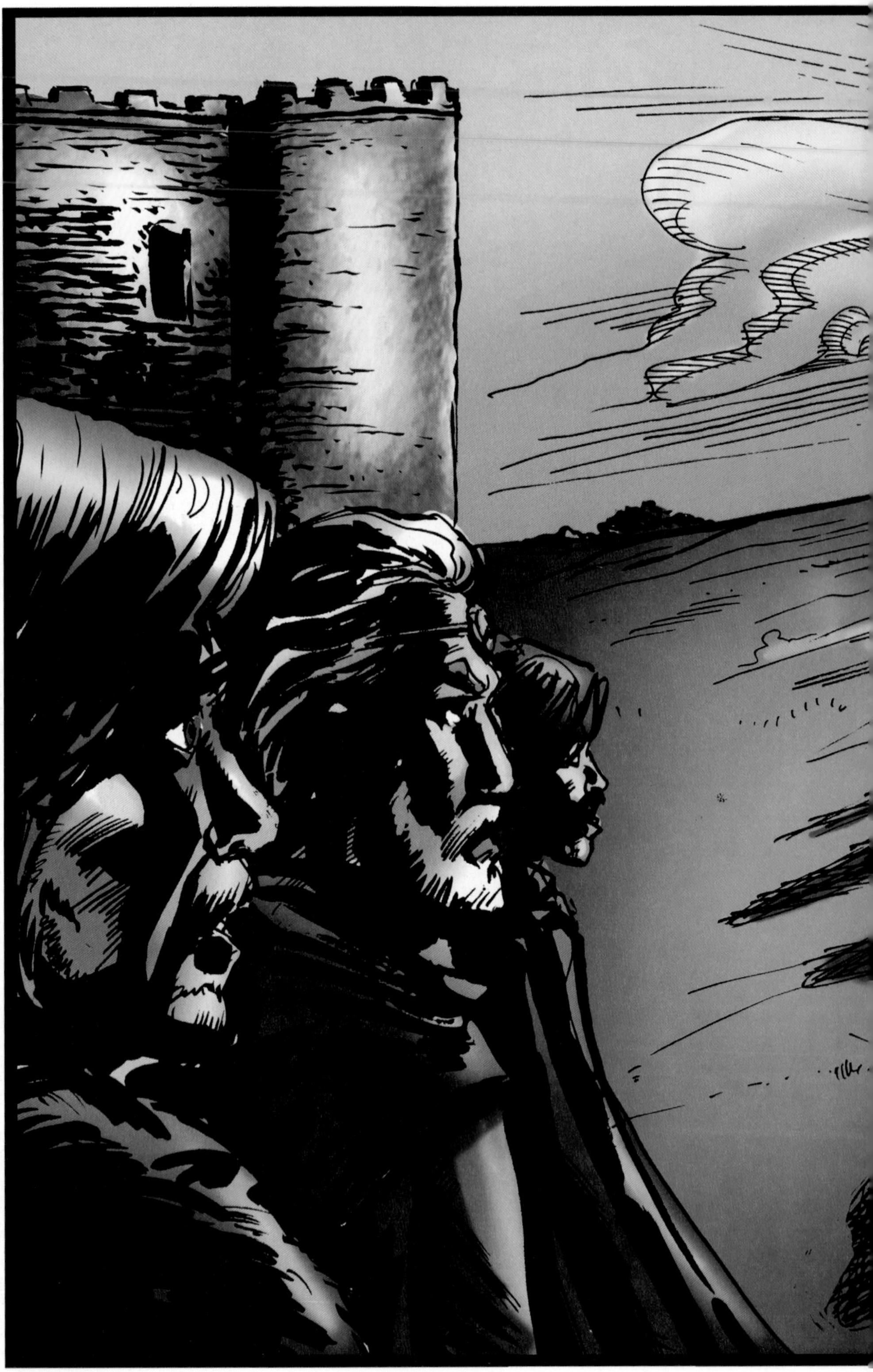

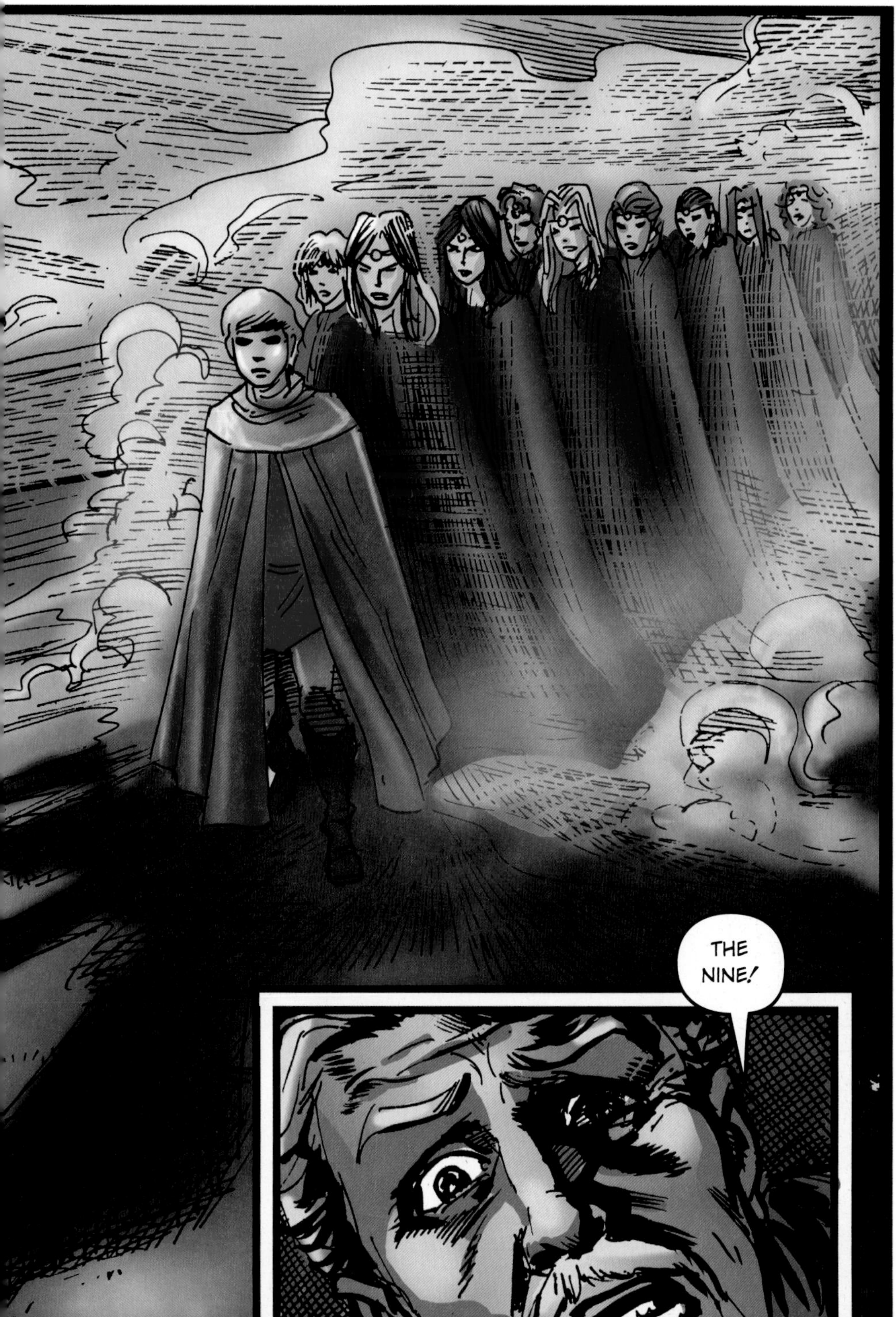
THE NINE!

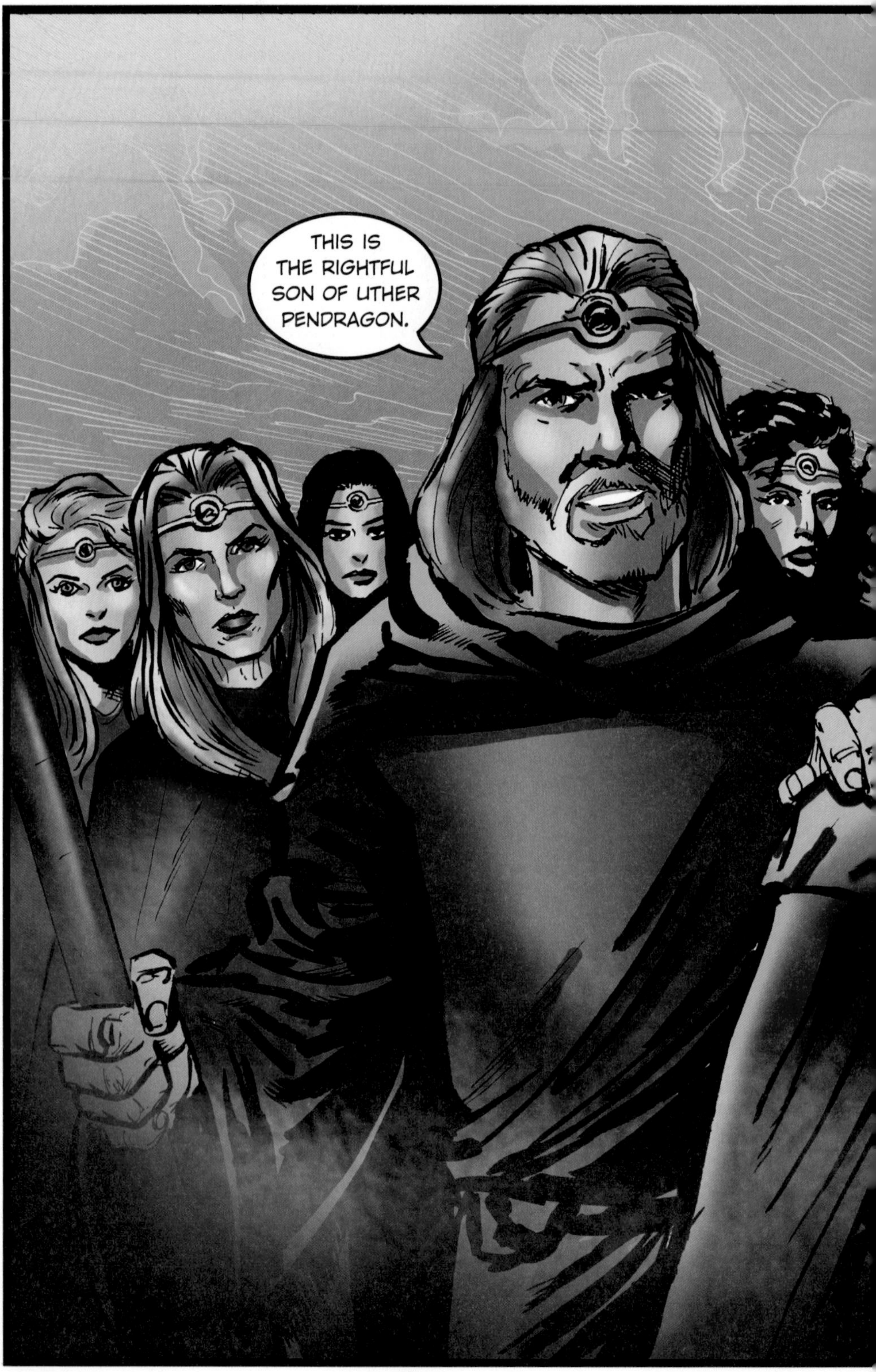
THIS IS THE RIGHTFUL SON OF UTHER PENDRAGON.

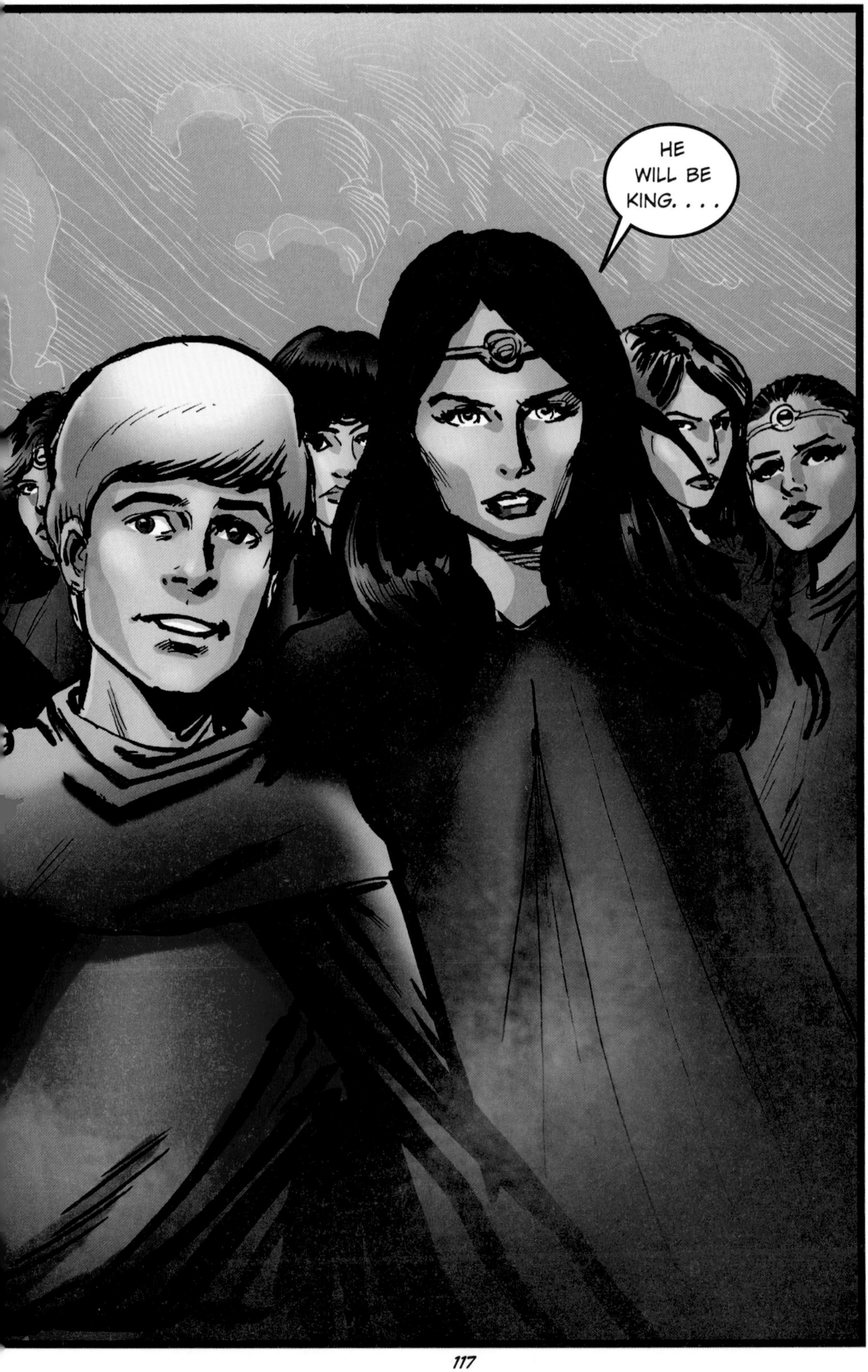
HE WILL BE KING. . . .

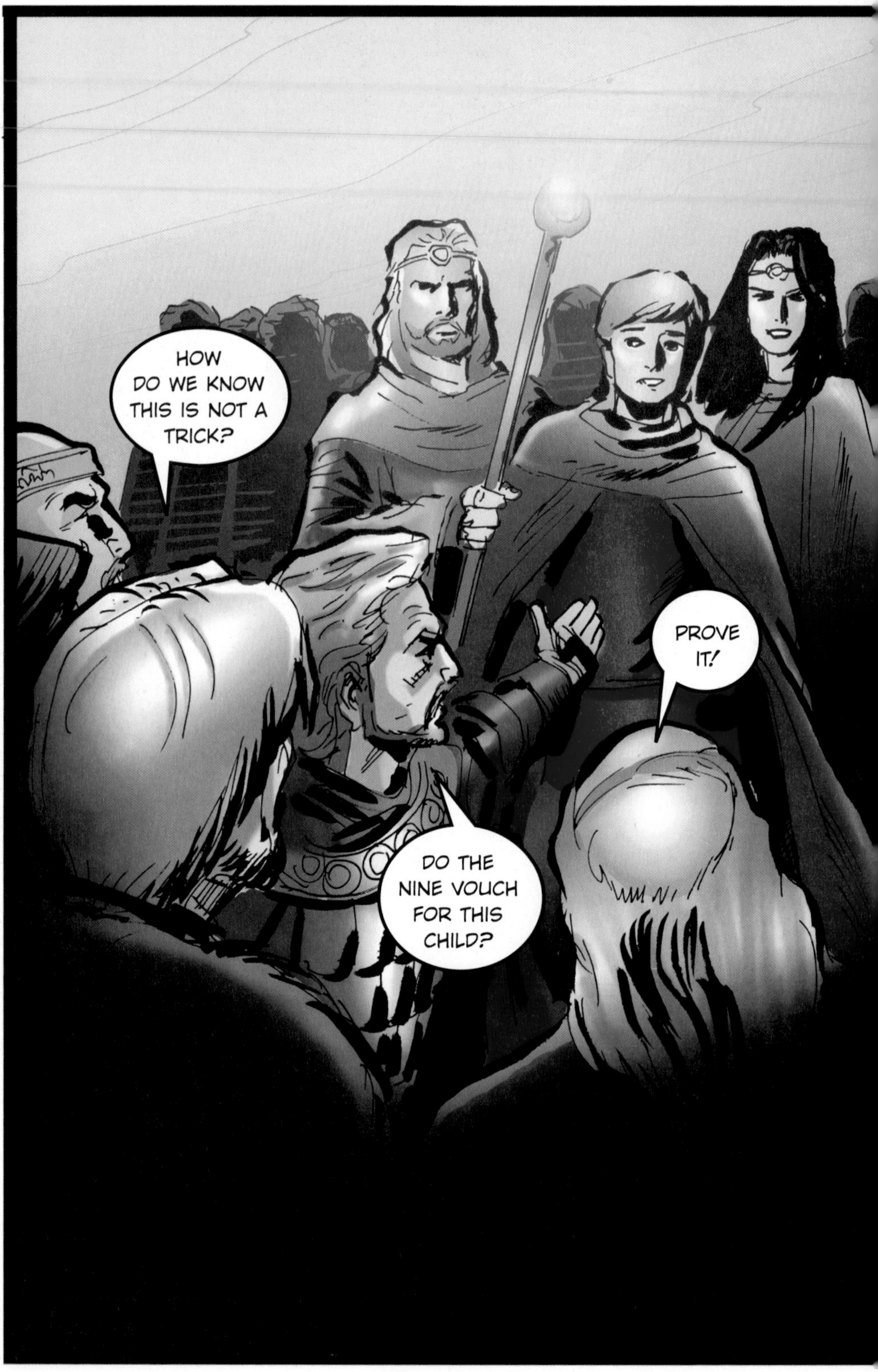
HOW DO WE KNOW THIS IS NOT A TRICK?
PROVE IT!
DO THE NINE VOUCH FOR THIS CHILD?

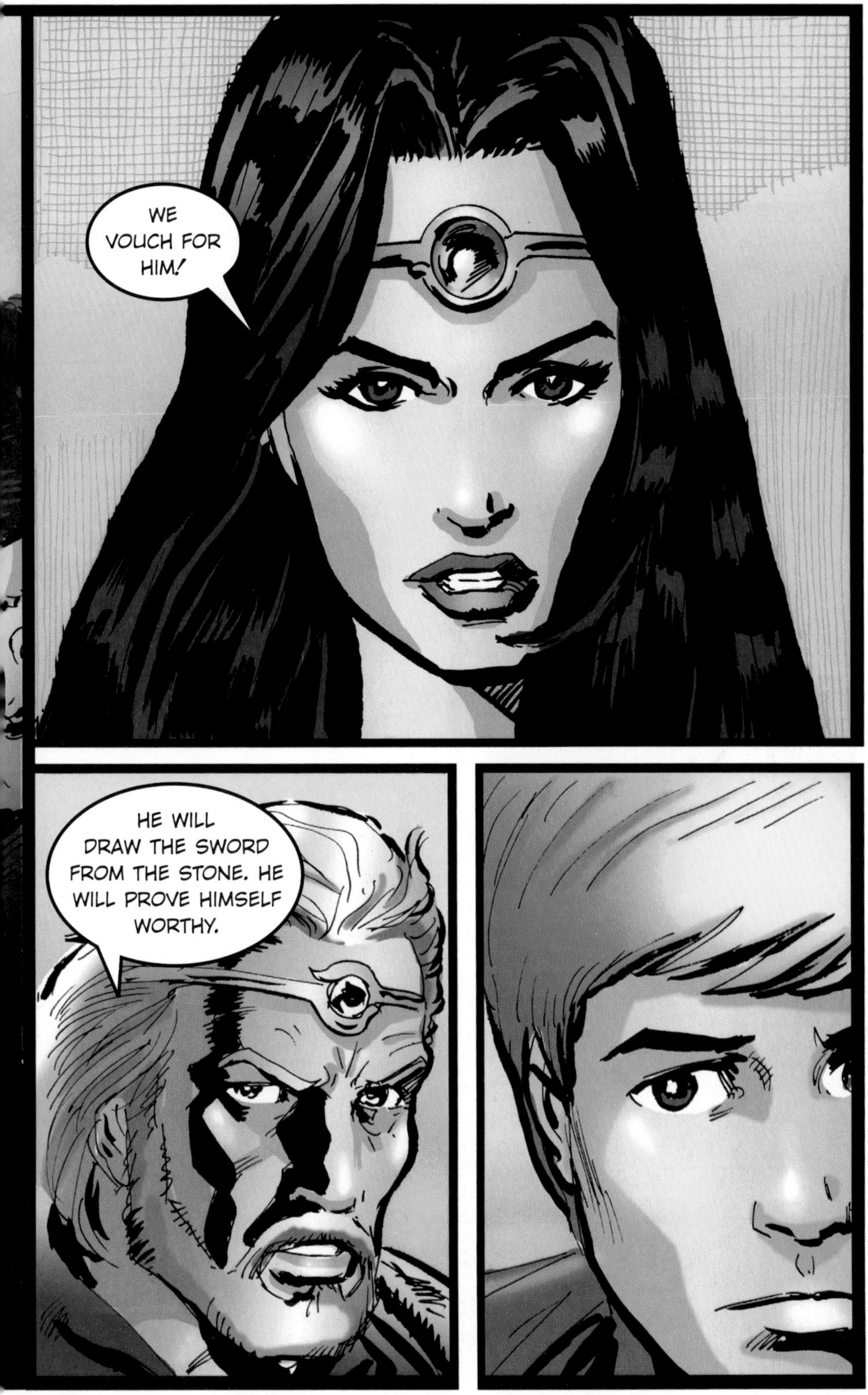
WE VOUCH FOR HIM!
HE WILL DRAW THE SWORD FROM THE STONE. HE WILL PROVE HIMSELF WORTHY.

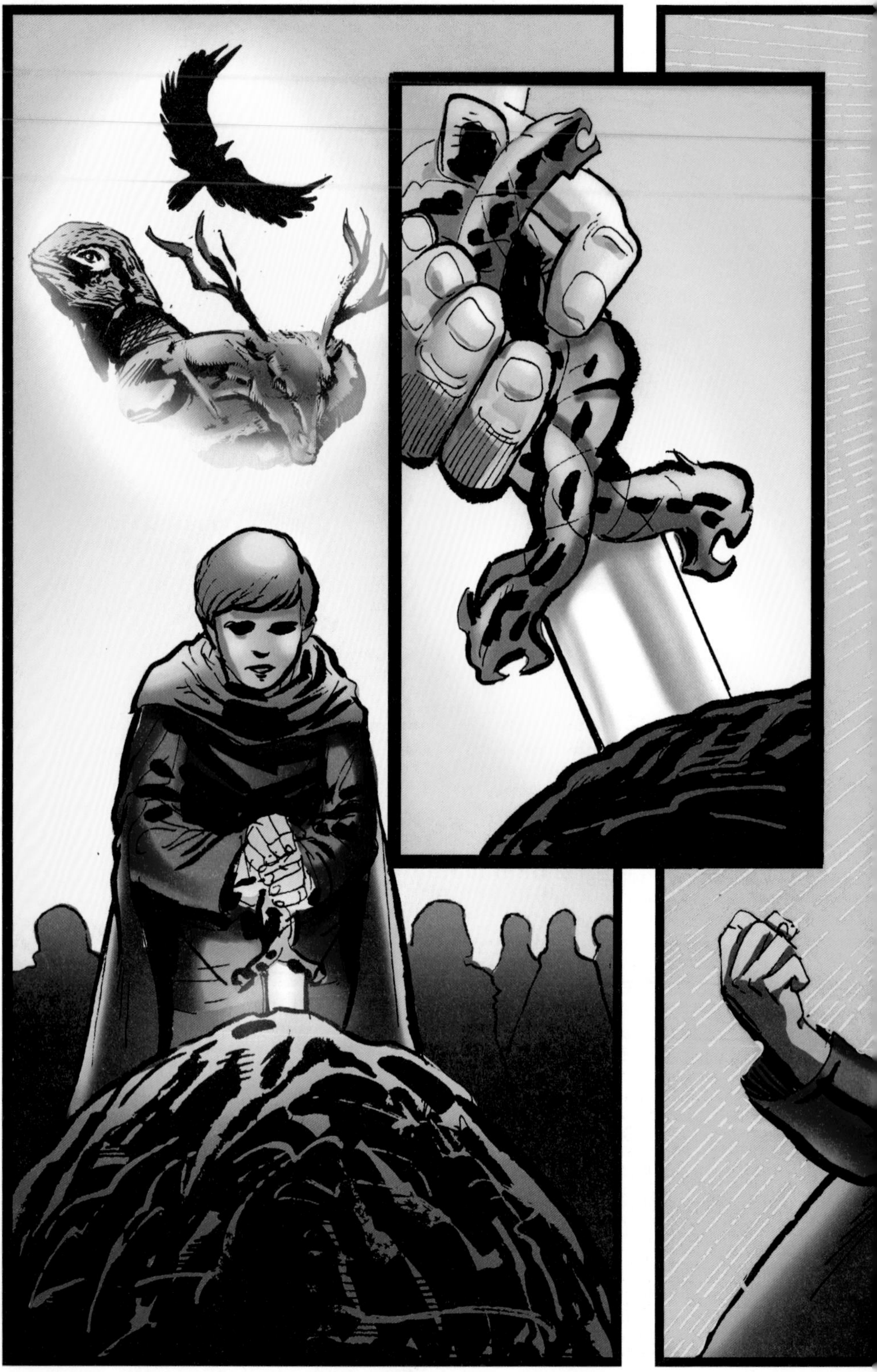

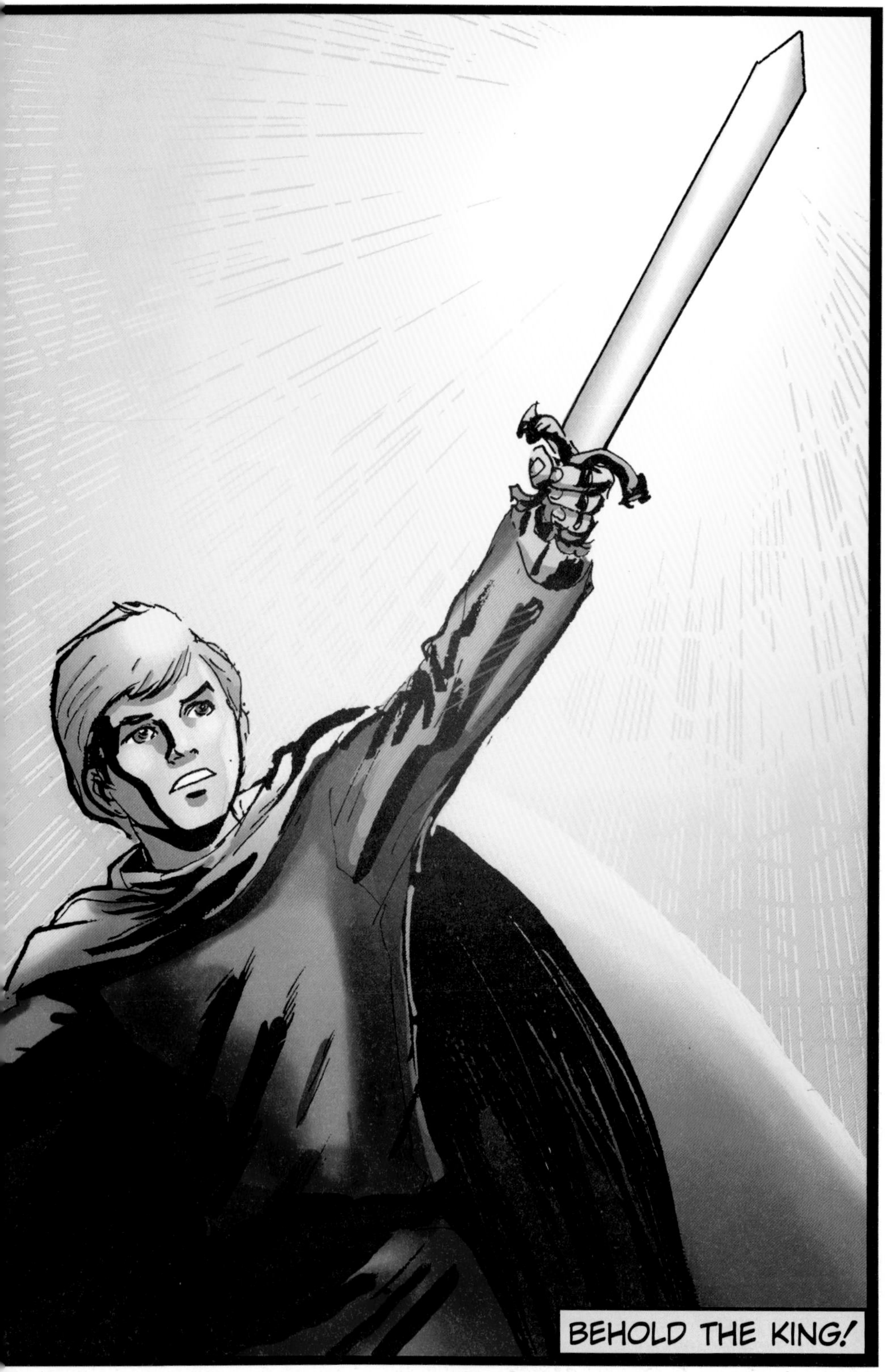
BEHOLD THE KING!

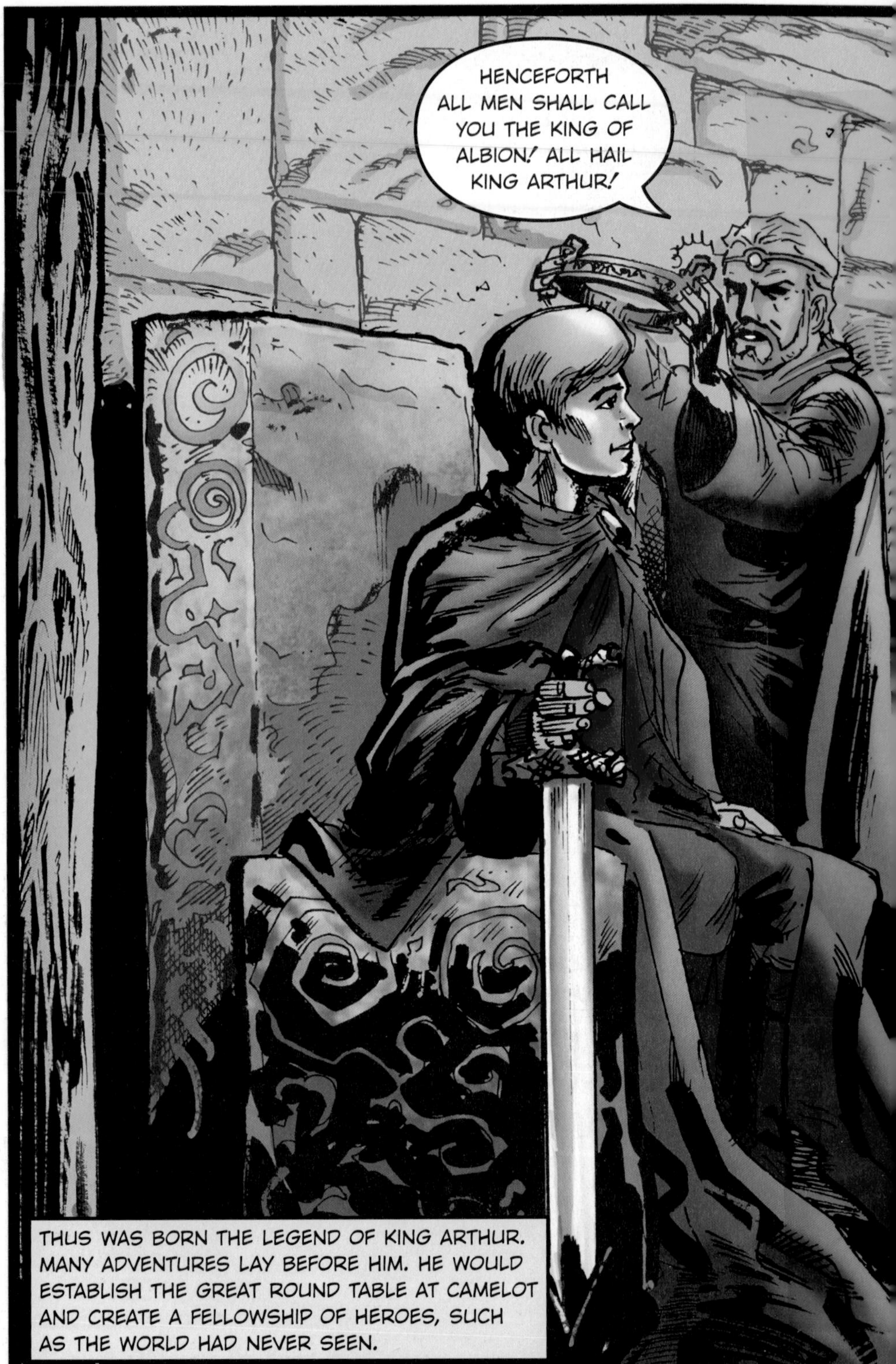
HENCEFORTH ALL MEN SHALL CALL YOU THE KING OF ALBION! ALL HAIL KING ARTHUR!
THUS WAS BORN THE LEGEND OF KING ARTHUR. MANY ADVENTURES LAY BEFORE HIM. HE WOULD ESTABLISH THE GREAT ROUND TABLE AT CAMELOT AND CREATE A FELLOWSHIP OF HEROES, SUCH AS THE WORLD HAD NEVER SEEN.